not quite
mainstream
Canadian Jewish Short Stories

not quite
mainstream
Canadian Jewish Short Stories

Edited by Norman Ravvin

Red Deer Press

Chaire de l'Université Concordia
en études juives canadiennes
The Concordia University Chair
in Canadian Jewish Studies

The Publishers
Red Deer Press
813, MacKimmie Library Tower
2500 University Drive N.W.
Calgary Alberta Canada T2N 1N4

Credits
Cover design by Duncan Campbell
Text design by Dennis Johnson
Cover photograph courtesy of Edward Hillel
Printed and bound in Canada by Friesens for Red Deer Press

Acknowledgments
Financial support provided by the Canada Council, the Department of Canadian Heritage, the Alberta Foundation for the Arts, a beneficiary of the Lot-
tery Fund of the Government of Alberta, the University of Calgary and Concordia University.

THE CANADA COUNCIL | LE CONSEIL DES ARTS
FOR THE ARTS | DU CANADA
SINCE 1957 | DEPUIS 1957

ALBERTA Lotteries | The Alberta Foundation for the Arts | Alberta COMMUNITY DEVELOPMENT
COMMITTED TO THE DEVELOPMENT OF CULTURE AND THE ARTS

Canada

Chaire de l'Université Concordia
en études juives canadiennes
The Concordia University Chair
in Canadian Jewish Studies

National Library of Canada Cataloguing in Publication Data
Not quite mainstream
ISBN 0-88995-246-9
1. Short stories, Canadian (English)* 2. Canadian fiction (English)–Jewish
authors.* I. Ravvin, Norman, 1963–
PS8321.N67 2001   C813'.01088924   C2001-910964-4
PR9197.33.J49N67 2001

5 4 3 2 1

ACKNOWLEDGEMENTS

Cohen, Matt. "Lives of the Mind Slaves." From *Living on Water*. Viking, 1988. Copyright © Matt Cohen. Used by permission of Anne McDermid & Associates.

Eisler, Irena. "Chestnuts for Kafka." Copyright © Irena Murray. Used by permission.

Fagan, Cary. "Nora by the Sea." From *The Doctor's House and Other Fiction* by Cary Fagan. Copyright © 2000 by Cary Fagan. Reprinted by permission of Stoddart Publishing Co. Limited.

Gelblum-Bross, Roma. "The Black Valises." From *To Samarkand and Back* by Roma Gelblum-Bross. Cormorant Books, 1988. Story first published in *Viewpoint*, Montreal, December 1984. Copyright © Roma Gelblum-Bross. Used by permission.

Korn, Rochl. "Bluma Zelinger." Translated by Abraham Boyarsky. Copyright © Rochl Korn. Used by permission.

Layton, Irving. "Piety." From *The Swinging Flesh* by Irving Layton. McClelland & Stewart, 1961. Copyright © The Estate of Irving Layton. Used by permission.

Levine, Norman. "Thin Ice." From *Champagne Barn* by Norman Levine. Copyright © 1984 by Norman Levine. Reprinted by permission of Penguin Canada Limited.

Naves, Elaine Kalman. "Hair." Copyright © Elaine Kalman Naves. Used by permission.

Ravvin, Norman. "A Story with Sex, Skyscrapers, and Standard Yiddish." From *Sex, Skyscrapers, and Standard Yiddish* by Norm Ravvin. paperplates books, 1997. Copyright © Norman Ravvin. Used by permission.

Contents

The editor thanks Shelley Butler, Ode Garfinkle, and Esther Frank for the Imperial typewriter, and Marla Becking for editorial assistance in assembling this collection.

not quite
mainstream
Canadian Jewish Short Stories

To acknowledge the significance of the writing styles reproduced in this collection, all originally published spellings, punctuation and grammar have been preserved.

Introduction

Norman Ravvin

F or a recent birthday I was given a strange and wonderful gift: a
shiny black portable Yiddish typewriter manufactured in England
by the Imperial company, its brand name transliterated into Yiddish characters on the machine's face. This particular typewriter made its
way to me from the family of Yaacov Zipper, whose story "The First
Morning" is included in this anthology.

Beautifully maintained, its ribbon fresh, the typewriter represents the
technology with which the earliest Canadian Jewish literature was created. For contemporary writers like me to recover what it meant to work on
an Imperial, a feat of great learning would be required. Writers like Zipper typed right to left. The first letter of their alphabet—the aleph—sits
high and centre on the Yiddish keyboard, unlike our own "a"; and most
importantly, the imaginative world of Canadian Yiddish writers was
fuelled, in part, by an ocean voyage and the memory of places far from
Canadian ports, such as Odessa, Lodz, and Warsaw. These were the literary capitals where some of the earliest Canadian Jewish writers found
their feet. Canada, truly a new-found-land was, to them, a place of
relearning.

For a time, leaders in the Canadian Jewish intellectual community,
particularly in Montreal, struggled to maintain a Yiddish literary life,
viewing such continuity as the best route to a viable New World Jewish
culture. One chronicler has called these cultural workers "lay Jewish rev-
olutionaries" and described their dreams for Yiddish in Canada as a utopian project.

Of course, the Jewish literary tradition that took shape in Canada has little to do with this utopian dream. The career of A.M. Klein, best known as a poet, represents a turning point between a Yiddish literature with roots in Europe and an English-language Canadian Jewish tradition. Though Klein translated his Yiddish forbears, he wrote for a contemporary English audience, making use of Jewish themes at a time when no popular readership could yet be said to exist for such a literature. As a poet, leftist political candidate, lawyer, and journalist, he followed the lead of his predecessors in striving to be both a writer and cultural worker, important in both his own community and on the broader Canadian scene.

Until his recent death, Mordecai Richler was the only working writer of fiction whose career addressed questions of politics and Jewish identity. Alongside his journalistic writings on Quebec, the breadth of his contribution is apparent in the impact of his best known character, Duddy Kravitz, who has gained the status of a Canadian Jewish stereotype. The responses to Richler's depictions of Canadian Jewish identity are telling. When he entered the public fray via his political journalism in *The New Yorker* and in his volume *Oh Canada! Oh Quebec!* he was cheered by all, except the more hardline separatists, for his willingness to present an engaged reading of the political problems shared by Jews, Anglophones, and Francophones.

Richler's novels, especially the early portraits of St. Urbain Street, received fewer accolades. Many believed Richler was revealing private stories, intimate narratives of Canadian Jewish life that did not require public airing. It's possible that his fictional voice proved more satiric and individual without the limits imposed by journalistic discourse. It may be that his fictional portraits of Canadian Jewish identity struck readers as distanced, even dismissive of the broader public debates in which the community was engaged (his novels represented, then, a kind of end run around conventional political discussions). Fiction, it seems, turned the debates inward and made them more threatening.

Richler is a distinctly instructive figure whose commitment to fictionalizing Jewish life in Canada, alongside a willingness to address the broader Canadian scene was matched only by Klein, whose active career was more or less over by the mid-1950s. As a kind of forefather and symbol of the mere possibility of becoming a Canadian Jewish writer, Klein is elegized by Richler, Irving Layton, Leonard Cohen, and Miriam Waddington, among others. The dramatic quality of his influence has left its mark on the Montreal landscape, as Cohen recalls his early meeting with an already reclusive Klein. Layton, in his memoir, *Waiting for the Messiah*, makes much of his scene of instruction:

> Klein and I met about once weekly in Fletcher's Field just across from the YMHA on Mt. Royal Avenue, and I vividly recall the first lesson: Virgil's *Aeneid, Book II*. I can almost hear again the sonorous hexameters falling from the poet's mouth.

Like Richler, Klein applied his talents to public political discussions, through his journalism in the *Canadian Jewish Chronicle*, legal work, and activism as a prospective Co-operative Commonwealth Federation (CCF) member of parliament; but he was, of course, committed to the more private literary discourse of his time. The motive behind much of Klein's work was to assert the possibility of a multilingual, polyvocal, heterodox Canadian culture. All this before the advent of multiculturalism as a national policy.

Notably, neither Klein nor Richler made his mark as a writer of the short story. Richler is represented here by the title piece from his book *The Street*, a collection of memoirs and stories unlike anything else he published; a look by readers at Klein's collected stories will find them to be below the quality of his other work. The focus by many Canadian Jewish writers on poetry and the novel puts the short story tradition in a particularly interesting context. When Canadian Jewish writers do turn to the short story, what are they doing there? And what does their accomplishment in the story genre tell us about the tradition more broadly?

In some countries the short story market is a place for novices to break into the public eye, while for writers who apply themselves most diligently to story writing (forgoing the novel), this market provides an environment to support themselves financially. Canadian writers whose careers have been devoted to the short story—Mavis Gallant and Alice Munro are the best known—have relied on American magazines to publish much of their work before it appears in collections. Canada's little magazines have provided the steadiest and most varied outlet for story writing, but the limitations of their audiences necessitate that they remain a kind of proving ground, a site of quiet dialogue between writers, uncommonly attentive readers, and critics.

Norman Levine, who may be the Canadian Jewish writer who has proved the steadiest and most profoundly committed to the story form, writes of a Canadian living in England in "We All Begin in a Little Magazine":

> I remember best the cold damp winter days with the fog thick—
> you could just see the traffic lights—and then going inside and
> having some hot wine by the open fire and talking about writing,
> what we were writing, and where we had things out. We used to
> send our stories, optimistically to the *name magazines*. But that
> was like taking a ticket in a lottery. It was the little magazines who
> published us, who gave encouragement and kept us going.

"Thin Ice," the Levine story included here, is a portrait of another look at the tenuous literary lives in Canada—the writer-in-residence stint.

A number of the writers included in this anthology fit Levine's portrait of patient practitioners and purveyors of the short story genre: they've experienced the market as a repeated crap shoot; they know the mail as the centrepiece of a writer's day. Claire Rothman, Robyn Sarah, Matt Cohen, and Levine himself have all followed the ups and downs of the short story market, at least in one phase of their writing career (Cohen was also a product of the small press ferment in 1970s Toronto; and Sarah is foremost a poet). But a number of the other writers collected here found their way to the short story by more indirect routes. Irving Layton's "Piety" appeared in the unusual 1961 collection *The Swinging Flesh*, which set poetry alongside a number of stories. In the book's characteristically aggressive foreword, Layton tells us that the stories "cover a period from 1943 until 1960." "Piety" is an intriguing specimen that we don't have an example of from Leonard Cohen: an effort by the poet to address his chosen themes in the uncharacteristic genre of the short story. Several poets choose prose in a number of the pieces in this collection, including those by Kenneth Sherman, Tom Wayman, Rochl Korn, and Joe Rosenblatt. In these cases, however, the ability to shift from poetry to prose, from fiction to nonfiction, is a feature of the writer's mature career. Rosenblatt's "Tommy Fry and the Ant Colony," a fractured children's story for adults, tries out the author's familiar poetic motifs, drawn from the animal and insect world, in fiction.

But what is the impact of Jewish writers on the broader Canadian tradition? What, specifically, can you find in the work of Canada's Jewish writers that you would not find elsewhere? Not necessarily Jewish content. Unlike other collections of stories by Jewish writers, I've not chosen pieces for inclusion strictly because of their explicit treatment of Jewish themes. Many of the stories collected here do address such themes, but in the case of some writers—Rothman and Fagan for instance—you will have to read further afield to discover how Jewishness has affected their career and outlook. In the case of Tom Wayman's Toronto story, "The Murder," the explicit Jewish theme is a departure from the writer's usual material.

A careful reader of this collection will note a distinct falling off, a downplaying of explicit Jewish themes as one moves from the early pieces translated from Yiddish to the more contemporary stories by Canadian-born writers. Yaacov Zipper, Rochl Korn, and Chava Rosenfarb transported to Canada a European Jewish world that informed their work in Canada, yet the literary landscape of that world did not ultimately become a part of mainstream Canadian Jewish culture (much less Canadian culture). A good deal of effort has been spent in recovering this early Canadian Yiddish tradition, and it may be that with time, its full wealth will become better known to English readers. For now, writers such as Cary Fagan and I make use of earlier Jewish literary traditions—whether Yiddish, European, or American—to imagine a different kind of Canadian tradition. Though Fagan's "Nora by the Sea," collected here, does not make use of this strategy, his novels *The Animals' Waltz* and *Felix Roth* focus on European-born writers in order to uncover a Canadian's search for identity. This movement outside a tradition may signal a dissatisfaction among writers with the local culture as raw material, and it may represent an effort to search for literary forefathers and foremothers who don't exist in Canadian literary history. It may also represent the pursuit of a larger audience—a market, to put things more practically—attuned to Jewish literary themes. When I first posed the idea of an anthology of Canadian Jewish short stories to one of the writers included here, he responded that he thought such a book would make "some sort of necessary statement. The Canadian literary establishment is so dominated by anglo-protestant values and aesthetics that something of a counterweight would be more than welcome."

I hope that the stories collected in *Not Quite Mainstream* will suggest to you the variety, the unpredictability, and the ongoing transformation of the Canadian Jewish short story. You will gain a view of a genre in the midst of constant change: it has no real kingpin, no geographical capital, no fashionable and repeated themes. Rather, it seems to be a place of true experiment and freedom from the conventional demands of the novel and poetry.

One further provocative turn in all this bears noting. It is worth arguing that two of the best early stories in English about Canadian Jewish experience are the excellent mid-forties pieces by Mavis Gallant, entitled "Good Morning and Goodbye" and "Three Brick Walls." These are stylistically spare, emotionally charged portraits of a young Jewish newcomer to Canada. Since they are not included in this collection, here is part of the former story:

> He lay there and looked at the leaves and the crooked pieces of
> blue between them, and thought "I, Paul, am going away again."
> He had changed his name to Paul because the other sounded too
> German, and every morning for a long time he had said "I, Paul,
> today will do thus and so." In this way he had become one with
> the name. It had finally divided him into two separate people;
> one here, and one almost lost, on the other side of an ocean.

Gallant's early stories are "Jewish stories," in that they are strange, diffident, oblique tellings of the complications that arise as a transplanted Jewish imagination addresses the blue of a Canadian morning. The stories collected here offer similar moments of comprehension and change, which make them worth reading.

That First Morning

Yaacov Zipper

"There is no need to carry it about with you here," said Uncle Chaim smiling, and with discernible pride in his voice he plucked away the passport which Shternberg was about to place in his breast pocket, just as he had always done in earlier years, before he left his house.

"No one will ask to see it here and no one cares who you are or where you are going. You only need to remember your address so you can find your way home. Leave the passport with your papers, together with your landing card; it will be required only when you want to become a citizen. Until then, as long as you have a house to live in you're a resident, and no one has the right to stop you and ask you questions. Here—that's the kind of country it is—as long as you don't bother anyone it is no one's business who you are," said the slim blond uncle in an almost celebratory manner as he stretched out his hand and with warm-hearted affection accompanied him from the house.

"May the occasion of your first walk be blessed. I would like to go along with you this first time, especially since it is a rare sun-filled day. Soon it will begin to grow so wild with snow storms that you won't be able to stick your nose outdoors. But I have to rush back to the store; the little chicks can't chirp without their boss. Your aunt thinks you're still a small-towner who is frightened of tall buildings and long streets, but I know my customers and I'm sure you can take care of yourself. Still, don't tell her that I let you go out alone; by the time she gets back in the late afternoon you will have returned. It's hard to get lost here. The streets are straight in all directions. For the first time don't go too far, and take care to look about before you cross the street, they drive like the devils here—everyone in a great hurry. You'll soon see for yourself; even while walking on the sidewalk, pay attention to the traffic on the street."

Of all his uncle's words, what stayed in Shternberg's mind was, "No one here cares who you are." Somehow this gladdened him yet at the same time left an empty feeling tinged with loneliness.

Amidst the bustling tumult of the main street that feeling intensified. Even when he stood at the entrance to a shop no one looked at him or asked if he wanted anything. Whenever he saw a policeman he would from long habit touch his breast pocket and a helpless fear twinged his heart when he felt its emptiness. A well-groomed, clean-shaven policeman passed him, quietly playing with his brown billy-stick as if silently counting the steps. Only after he had passed did the lump in Shternberg's throat dissolve. A warm feeling of security seemed to grow out of the unfamiliar street noises, the half-opened doors of the shops, and the steep grey stairs in the side alleys which, at the top, leaned against the high brown and red brick walls as if protruding from the windows while clinging with their last strength to the cracked sidewalks beneath.

Suddenly he was stunned—tears actually came to his eyes—when at the corner of the street he saw a policeman encircled by children who gaily chattered to him, and then, before he knew it, one was perched on the policeman's shoulder, a second under his arm, while the smallest was tucked against his heart as he carried them across the street. The sight of children waving joyfully at the smiling policeman so moved him that all the frightful stories of his childhood and his own experience of terror with gendarmes on the other side of the ocean melted into a sense of well-being. Unthinkingly, he began to chatter along with the children, repeating their few comprehensible words, "Thank you, Tom!" Within him there welled up his uncle's proud tone: "That's the kind of country it is!" He had the sensation that each step he took caressed the black asphalt with a refrain: "How good, how good and pleasing it is in this country."

Added to this, the openings in the middle of the row houses, which gave the appearance of one long wall divided by the sloping stairs, began to remind him of familiar alleys. The narrow back-yards to which they led were stacked with scrap iron or lumber; within them trudged men with wind-carved faces clad in heavy fur-lined winter coats. They called to one another in an odd dialect, a mixture of words which seemed like guttural Yiddish combined with a slurred Ukrainian, spiced with incomprehensible swallowed sounds in a language he thought he had heard on the boat but which he failed to understand at all. The whole scene transmitted a deep familiarity, permeated with old-country odours. It seemed that he had been here once before, but he could not recall the time. If only he could knock at a door and enter, he was sure he would remember.

An elderly woman hurried by, hidden in heavy winter wrappings with a black shawl covering her head and shoulders. He has already seen her somewhere, shabby-looking, carrying a basket full of giblets, several loaves of bread and other foodstuffs which diminished as she hobbled from house to house in her ungainly manner. In these alleys where poverty dwelt he could almost call her by name and if the curved steep wooden steps were swept away he would even know who lived in these houses and who awaited her arrival. Today is Thursday and in her basket she brings the preparations for Shabbos.

An angry voice from the highest window suddenly broke the spell of the dancing bounce of her basket, "You fool, you shlimazl, what will you do with it, where will you keep it and for what? All he does is drag together junk from who knows where!" A wrinkled face framed by a thin red kerchief shouted at a short man in a ragged grey jacket belted with a rope. Into the yard he rolled a wooden barrel and a rubber tire which repeatedly collided against the stairs. Triply bent over, he stumbled, breathing heavily, "Stop already! It's worth a whole dollar!"

A compelling curiosity to enter one of the houses and make himself at home drew Shternberg to every door. But he was deterred by the boisterous playing of a group of children right under the stairs. Vapours rose from their overheated bodies as they gripped bent sticks in their outstretched red and blue hands, chasing a flat, round disc which was always getting caught under the stairs or being arrested by the cracks of the broken sidewalk. Sweat poured down their reddened foreheads leaving white rivulets on their soiled faces. The players seemed indifferent to this, so engrossed were they in anticipating the exact moment when the disc would come within range, unobstructed by the stairs or the cracks. In the middle of the street, tired birds searching for crumbs of food in the horse manure, hopped back and with a flutter rescued themselves by flying up to the high snowy ledges near the roof tops of the identical row-houses,

דער ערשטער פרימאָרגן

ב

זאָ דאַרפסטו עס נישט אַרומטראָגן מיט זיך, — האָט דער פעטער
חיים אַ שמייכלענדיקער און מיט אַ היפש שטאָלצער מינע און
טאָן צוגענומען ביי אים דעם פאַספּאָרט וועלכן שטערנבערג האָט
געהאַלטן ביים אַרייַנלייגן אין בוזעם־קעשענע, ווי ער איז געוואוינט געוועזן צו
טאָן אלע יאָרן פאַרן אַרויסגיין פון הויז.

— קיינער וועט דיך דאָ נישט פרעגן אויף דעם, און קיינעם גייט נישט
אָן ווער דו ביסט און וואוהין דו גייסט. דאַרפסט בלויז געדאַנקען דעם אַדרעס
וואו דו וואוינסט כדי צו קענען טרעפן דעם וועג אהיים. באהאלטן אים צווישן
דיינע פּאַפּירן צוזאַמען מיט דער לאָדונגסקאַרטע. וועסט עס באַדאַרפן ערשט
ווען וועסט וועלן ווערן אַ בירגער. ביז דאַן, אַבי דו האָסט אַ הויז וואו צו
וואוינען, ביסטו אַ היימישער דאָ און קיינער האָט נישט קיין רעכט דיך
אָפצושטעלן און פרעגן ווער דו ביסט. דאָ, אַזאַ לאַנד איז עס דאָ, כל זמן דו
פאַרטשעפּעפּסט קיינעם נישט, איז עס נישט קיינעמס דאגה ווער דו ביסט,
— האָט דער בלאַנדער שלאַנקער פעטער כמעט פייערלעך אויסגעשטרעקט אים
אַ האַנט און אַרויסבאַגלייט אים פון הויז מיט אַ גוטמוטיקער היימישקייט
אין אַ גוטער שעה, מיטן רעכטן פוס אויפן ערשטן שפּאַציר! כ׳וואָלט אודאי
געוואָלט מיטגיין מיט דיר צום ערשטן מאָל. בפרט נאָך ווען ס׳איז היינט
איינער פון געשענקטע זון־טאָג. אָט אָט וועט עס נעמען ווילדעווע-ן מיט שניי,
אז מ׳וועט די נאָז נישט קענען אַרויסוויזן, מוז איך אַבער שוין לויפן אין
סטאָר אַריין. די קורטשיקלעך (הענדלער) קענען נישט קרייען אָן דעם
באַלעבאָס. די מומע דיינע, מיינט אַז דו ביסט עפּעס אַ קליינשטעטלדיקער
דאַרט, וואָס דערשרעקט זיך פאַר די היכע מויערן און לאַנגע גאַסן. איך זע
אבער מיט וועמען איך האָב צו טאָן, וועסט זיך שוין אַן עצה געבן. פון
דעסטוועגן זאָלסטו איר נישט איבערחזרן, אַז כ׳האָב דיך געלאָזט גיין אַליין.
ביז זי וועט צוריקקומען שפּעט נאָכמיטאָג, וועסטו דאָך שוין זיין צוריק. ס׳איז
שווער צו פאַרבלאָנדזשען דאָ. די גאָסן זיינען גלייכע אין דער לענג און אין
דער ברייט. אינעם ערשטן מאָל, גיי נישט צו ווייט. קוק זיך אַרום ווען דו

First page of the Yiddish original by Yaacov Zipper

locked into one another as if shaped by the same mold. Only then did he notice that as far as the eye could see not a single tree could be found on the whole street.

"Where do the birds have their nests?" it suddenly dawned on him to ask a boy racing by.

"What?" The small boy opened a pair of questioning eyes and called out, "Greenhorn!"

That this term was intended as an insult, Shternberg had already learned from a passenger on board ship who was on his way to Canada for the second time. Now, as the epithet suddenly struck him and quickly slid by along with the impatient mocking grimace of the excited boy, it sounded more like pity for someone, ostensibly an adult who doesn't even know the rules of the game in which a bystander should not presume to interfere.

The scurrying of the game abruptly ended in the midst of its urgency when a protracted sad niggun resounded from the corner of the street. The gravelly, monotonal melody rose from a run-down horse and wagon which rolled toward him step by step, stopping whenever the niggun was obscured by the noise of a window opened and shut again, then rolled on for another few paces until a coarse voice rang out from the wagon: "I pay cash! I buy junk! Gold for rags!" When no door or window opened, the tuneful cry rolled on in the same monotone, to the rhythmic squeaking of the wagon: "I-pa-a-y ca-a-sh!"

The excited youngsters rushed toward the wagon in one throng, their bent sticks held high, their shouts filling the street with sound, mimicking the pedlar's niggun with cheerful cries, "Gold for ra-a-a-gs!" The horse stopped and uttered an odd, peculiar neigh as if in recognition, answering them by twisting its head from side to side and flicking its tail back and forth. The wagon rolled a little further and, with a loud squeak, came to a stop. Even the heap of rumpled mattresses with extruding rusty springs shook, it seemed, with knowing familiarity toward the cluster of children. They surrounded the wagon yet kept their distance beyond the range of the whip in the hands of the thin, wiry pedlar. He sat on the hard wagon-seat in a crumpled stiff fedora, as if he were part of the greasy stovepipe extending from the black oven-heater on which he leaned.

"High, high,
Smoke reach the sky,

Grab an alley-cat
By the thigh."

The children mocked his drawn-out niggun and poked their sticks into the pile of junk—"I buy everything, hip, hip!"—then dashed away in all directions when the whip's crack awakened the sleepy street.

"Get away you ruffians! Don't touch the goods!" the pedlar shouted, jumping from the wagon. "Isn't it enough that the other boys don't let me ride through in peace." His outburst sounded more like a plea than a cry of anger. "May you never come to my bitter fate. Go find yourselves better playthings." He didn't make the slightest effort to pursue the children, just leaned against the wagon, threw his head back expertly and cast a squinted glance at the windows on both sides of the street. From a few open windows angry mothers called down to their children in dismay, "What do you want from the poor man? I'll tell your father and you'll get it!"

Taking advantage of the open windows the pedlar sang out, "Gold for rags!" in the highest register, which silenced both children and mothers. In a moment he rushed to one of the curved staircases and, in a short while, slipped down with another sack of rags for his loaded wagon.

Satisfied with himself, the ragman made the street resound once more to the crack of his whip. The horse began to trot along, turning its head back toward the children who were immersed again in chasing the round disc, no longer attentive to the horse and wagon from which only a stiff fedora could be seen and a half-drowsy tremulous monotone heard, fading further and further down the empty street.

Translated from the Yiddish by Ode Garfinkle and Mervin Butovsky

Yaacov Zipper *(1900–83) was born in Poland and came to Canada in 1925. He was principal of the Yiddish secularist Jewish Peretz Schools of Montreal. He played a leadership role in the Montreal Jewish Public Library, the labour Zionist movement, the Jewish Writers' Association, and Canadian Jewish Congress. His publications, appearing in Yiddish and Hebrew, included novels, stories, autobiographical fiction, and literary essays and criticism.*

Piety

IRVING LAYTON

A high fence divided our back yards and we can still remember—my brother and I—the odour of the slit bags drying on our neighbour's roof. They lay from Sunday to Friday like flat, brown shingles except when the wind disarranged them or cockled up their ends. And when that happened they looked like midsummer rabbits and our kitchen filled with a thin, sweet, warmish smell of decayed potatoes.

A maple tree, the only one in the district, grew in our neighbour's yard. It was considered joint property and sheltered the two houses during the tropic months of July and August. My brothers freely straddled its boughs, occasionally abetted by Maxie Karpal. Sometimes the three of them made for the topmost branches. When Mrs Karpal saw them, she flung away her sewing and screeched up at them her terrified, unavailing cries. Hearing her, my mother left the customer she was serving, and rushing to the nearest window, joined her forceful shouts to those of her neighbour's.

They were immigrants, the Karpal family, recently come from Galicia. The house which they tenanted was the shabbiest and most rickety in that street of shabby and rickety houses. It had a doleful, thrown-together appearance and when it rained the floors and ceilings wetted simultaneously. Damp and cold in the winter, in the summer their dwelling became a dangerous, suffocating furnace. And ours, a red-bricked, stunted building, was not much better. The first wave of immigrants from Eastern Europe had broken against Ontario Street and as it receded it dug narrow channels; mean, dusty, refuse-littered streets like St Dominique,

Sanguinet and St Elizabeth. Running parallel to them, Cadieux Street had had its name for delicate reasons changed to De Bullion; nevertheless the whorehouses were left untouched.

The immigrants lived together peacefully, swarming into new neighbourhoods, pullulating, learning the strange ways of America. Russians, Poles, Bulgars, Jews, Roumanians. Day labourers, factory hands, tailors, pedlars, bricklayers, basters. All having the same dream, to grow rich and move away to a better neighbourhood. Their children grew up together, fought and played in the streets, and went to the school on Sanguinet Street. No one envied his neighbour. Occasionally a drunk called someone a "Jew" and a misplaced French Canadian said "Juif." But the only really discordant element were the Italians, distributed along Demontigny Street. We dreaded the summer months. Stirred by memories of olive groves and warm skies, their youth descended upon St Elizabeth where the largest number of Jews lived. Brandishing stones and beer bottles they insisted, without regard for historical accuracy, that we had lately murdered their Christ. Only a blow to the face or a club landed sharply upon the obstinate head could convince them they were mistaken. Then the fight was on. It lasted until both factions had run out of stones or one faction, having a greater supply, had chased the other into their homes. Winter alone brought peace — with the approach of cold weather, an indifference superficially passing for harmony.

I remember Mrs Karpal more vividly than I do her husband, who was as unidiomatic as the refuse he collected in the city's lanes and alleys. There was a washed-out quality to him as though he had just escaped from his wife's corrugated washing board, a humility that was both irritating and attractive. His body was thin and slightly bent, his face always wore an air of troubled abstraction: as if wearied of announcing his salvaging mission through the unresponsive streets he had sunk himself, by an act of will, into an insulating silence that left him emasculated and alone. But Mrs Karpal was different. She was a stout, swarthy woman with bulging, Negro eyes and the nervous, energetic vigilance of a hungry cat. Her hair, prematurely greying, was coiled at the nape of her neck, and wavy, robbed the lined, bony face of some of its harshness. Her competent fingers were always busy, poking among her husband's multicoloured rags, washing and sewing them up into salable articles.

The older children, two daughters and a son, Phillip, worked in sweatshops for pitifully small wages. And since they were Jewish children their religion forbade them to work on Saturday. They had to search about for a pious, coreligionist manufacturer and when they found him likely as not he paid them less than the current rates—God, he reasoned, wished to reward him for keeping the Sabbath hallow. My sisters worked in the same shop with Chaneh and Bessie. Misery picked up its long needles and knitted a neighbourly friendship; although, to speak the truth, my family considered itself superior because we ran a small grocery while Mr Karpal earned his bread as a ragpicker.

That winter was an exceptionally severe one. The snow lay in a chain of inert hills upon the streets and sidewalks. It swirled down to cover the roofs and faded balconies and muffled everything in a silence that would last for months. The children watched the horses pulling their loads, the harness tight against their bellies, the vapour pouring from mouth and nostrils. The wind whistled and howled, and probed for loose boards and broken windows. About the first week in January Mr Karpal took sick. It's the flu, the young doctor said, he'll have to stay in bed. The same thing had happened a year ago, also the year before that. A trouble that comes regularly, my mother said, is no trouble at all. Mrs Karpal didn't contradict her, but the grocery bill grew bigger each week. Then the worst, the unexpected happened. The coldest day of the year, their dilapidated stove broke down completely. As if through accumulated spite it had become a piece of junk and resisted the frantic efforts to repair it. When the neighbours learned their misfortune, they got together enough money to instal a secondhand stove. Mrs Karpal was grateful but neither abashed nor truckling. She expected hard-pressed folk to understand. Today *we're* unlucky, tomorrow. . . .

Thirteen-year-old Maxie waited until his mother had done sweeping the floor. He took off his threadbare cap to scratch his head, closecropped as an insurance against lice. He fidgeted with it before putting it on again. Jewish boys never went bareheaded except in school where orthodoxy wasn't reckoned with.

"Ma," he said nervously, "I want to tell you something." He watched Mrs Karpal stoop to sweep the loose dirt onto a stiff piece of cardboard that did for a dustpan. She rose from her crouched position, supported herself by means of the broomstick.

"Well, Maxie, what is it?" she said crossly. "Can't you see I'm not idle?"

He hesitated a moment. Then taking a long breath he said hurriedly, "Ma, I'm quittin' school."

If the Messiah had suddenly appeared in the doorway, Mrs Karpal wouldn't have been more astonished.

"What was that I heard you say, Maxie!" she exclaimed, advancing towards him, her hand tightening on the broomstick. "You're what, Maxie?"

Maxie stepped back, but he met his mother's angry look unfalteringly. "It's like I say, Ma, I'm quittin' school."

Mrs Karpal caught her son's arm and her fingers sank into the soft flesh, and although they hurt him he made no effort to free himself. His imagination had rehearsed the scene for him weeks ago. To be accurate, when the doctor had ordered his father to bed.

"It's no use beatin' me, Ma," he said gently. "My mind's made up."

The quietness in her son's voice made Mrs Karpal release her grip. She sensed this was no disobedient child she was dealing with. She walked past him towards the corner of the room where she deposited the broom as if the weight had suddenly grown too much for her. From there she turned and faced him.

"Why do you want to leave school, Maxie?"

"School's a waste of time, Ma. Where'll it get us? I mean—Pa's sick in bed, there ain't hardly any food in the house. I wanna get a job."

"I thought you liked school. You've always been the head from your class. What will your Pa say? Don't you want to be a somebody, a doctor, a—"

"All I want is a job."

"Let's not do things in a hurry. I'll talk it over with Mrs Miller. Sometimes she knows from what she's saying."

My mother brushed the snowflakes from her shawl and undid the neat knot under her chin. Methodically she folded the shawl and laid it on the chair beside her. During the winter Mrs Karpal's kitchen was also the parlour and bedroom for the smaller children. The grey pipes radiating out from the squat, ugly stove made the room look like a boiler factory. They covered the ceiling and finally lost themselves in the streaked walls.

Mr Karpal lay in bed, sheltered by coats and rags which he himself had collected during the autumn months. He turned his face towards my mother and his vague, little eyes seemed to flicker in amusement. It was as if in that way he were making a commentary on human existence. This need not surprise anyone for ragpickers are thoughtful people. Since they deal with the castoff detritus of a city, they are as familiar with the final end of life as others are with its joyous beginnings. Theirs is the ripe wisdom of Ecclesiastes and with every cry of "rags . . . bottles" they pronounce the ancient judgement of "Vanity, all is vanity."

My mother regarded him compassionately and when she asked him how he felt:

"A little better, Mrs Miller. So little that why should we talk about it?" And drawing his hairy, white hands from under the covers he indicated the rags strewn over him. "God, as you see, provides for everything. I ask you, neighbour, could Rothschild be any warmer?" Mr Karpal made a noise with his gums and laughed into his pillow.

My mother turned to Mrs Karpal who was sitting at the foot of the bed. "Your Chaneh said you wanted to see me." Then she added as an afterthought, "Your Chaneh is such a pretty girl. With her, you don't have to worry already. The men will fight for her without a dowry."

Mrs Karpal made a quick, deprecating gesture with her hand. "With girls . . . who can tell? It's my Maxie I wanted to talk to you about."

"Yeh, Chaneh told me. He wants to leave school in the middle . . . is it true?"

"I almost broke a broomstick over his back. Only the devil has got into him. He says he wants to go to work." Mrs Karpal leaned forward and covering her mouth with a hand, snickered, "He thinks he can make a better provider for me than his father can."

"You have to give me needles yet?" her husband said mournfully.

"Who meant anything?" protested Mrs Karpal.

My mother interposed good-humouredly, "He's sensitive . . . like a poet. . . . Maybe Maxie could work at Chaneh's place."

"Then you think—"

"Well, maybe it's for the best. You know Mrs Simon's boy, Avram. He also stopped in the middle and as they say in America, he's certainly bringing home the brisket."

There was a silence, broken only by the coals settling in the stove and the long withdrawing roar in the chimney.

"Finestone is a pig!" said Mr Karpal with sudden anger. "Maxie shouldn't work for him. It's enough my two daughters work for such a one." And then as if startled by his own exhibition of spirit, he finished lamely, "What I mean—"

"Mr Finestone is no diamond," my mother completed the thought for him. "I know because my Sammy worked for him. But he's a *frummer mensch*. He keeps his shop closed on Saturday."

"Sure, sure," said Mrs Karpal. "Maxie can't take a job where he has to work Saturday. And if not Mr Finestone, who?"

My mother considered a moment. She played with the fringe of her shawl, allowing the tassels to fall across the back of her fingers. They waited for her to speak.

"Do you know Mr Grosnick?" she asked suddenly.

Mrs Karpal shook her head. "From where should I know him?"

"How foolish of me. I forget you don't run a grocery. You know how it is . . . in business you have a chance to meet people. Mr Grosnick sells me grocery bags, twine—"

"Then you think he has an opening job for Maxie?" said Mr Karpal.

"For me he would do the favour," my mother replied.

"And Saturday?" enquired Mrs Karpal, wishing to be reassured.

"How can you ask? . . . Would I . . . ? Mr Grosnick even has his business next to the synagogue. I'll speak to him tomorrow. Monday morning you can send Maxie to work."

Mr Grosnick was a middle-aged, stocky man, of medium height. He wore horn-rimmed spectacles with very thick lenses. When he removed them they left a broad scarlet line across the bridge of his nose. He spoke English fluently but like one who had learned it from a conversational reader. When he spoke he threw his head to one side with a jerky movement and mopped his face with a coloured handkerchief.

"You'll wrap the parcels this way," he explained, and before Maxie had a chance to begin he had taken the parcel out of his hands and was wrapping it himself. "My slogan is a very simple one—a place for everything and everything in its place. In case you need anything hurriedly, you know where it is."

Mr Grosnick patted his cheeks with his handkerchief. "Now again, what did you say your name was?"

"Maxie Karpal."

"Good. Now Maxie I want you to consider yourself like the superintendent of the stockroom. You're in charge here. There's nobody here but you, so you'll be fully responsible to me. Look around you. Is everything in tidiness, clean? Now do you think you can keep it that way?"

"I'll try, Mr Grosnick," said Maxie.

"Very well. Now come with me." He led the boy to where some cartons were lined up against the wall reaching as far as the back entrance. They were packed tightly with the brown paper and containers that Mr Grosnick sold to his customers.

"These boxes, I don't want you to touch, Maxie. 'Why?' you'll ask. Well, because they're too heavy for you. Do you understand, Maxie? If anything is to be done with them I'll do it myself. If I ever catch you touching them there'll be trouble. I don't want you to go straining yourself." Mr Grosnick smiled, showing his strong, discoloured teeth. "If you got a rupture, who would your parents blame? Not you . . . me, of course! You won't move them, eh Maxie?"

"No, Mr Grosnick, I won't."

"Swear it."

"I swear—by God."

"H'm." With that, Mr Grosnick turned on his heel and walked noisily out of the stockroom into the office.

"Miss Applebaum," Maxie heard him say, "how many times must I tell you to do your toilette at home? This is no place to leave hairpins. I don't use them, nor do my customers order them from me." There was a silence as he threw the hairpin upon her desk. "You've been my stenographer for so many years, I can't impress upon you I'm not running a beauty parlour."

Miss Applebaum raised her hands guiltily to her head. "My heavens, did I drop those things again?"

But Mr Grosnick had already forgotten her. He had seated himself on the edge of a chair and was reading the death notices in his newspaper. Suddenly he sprang up. "How terrible, Miss Applebaum—Saul Garson is dead! I can't believe it. Why it seems like only yesterday that he used to sit here and discuss affairs. Look at this pen, Miss Applebaum, you remember he gave it to me. A ten-dollar pen! Too bad, too bad. He was a very nice man, a gentleman, 'a frummer,' and a wonderful friend. Oh, poor Mrs Garson—she must be heartbroken. Write a letter to Mrs Garson and tell her how sorry I am, Miss Applebaum."

"Yes, it is too bad," said Miss Applebaum. "But you know he looked terrible the last time he was here."

"Terrible! Why he looked awful, he looked even worse than my sister, the sick one."

Mr Grosnick sat down heavily and pulled out his handkerchief, but he didn't mop his face. He held it in his hand, opening and closing his fingers over it. When the stenographer had finished writing he snatched the letter from her and read it over quickly. Then he laid it on the desk corner and Miss Applebaum had to lean forward to retrieve it.

"Don't seal the envelope and you'll only need a two-cent stamp. What a loss, my day is ruined!"

"Yes," said Miss Applebaum ironically, "I'm sure it is."

Mr Grosnick jumped up from his chair and rushed into the stock-room to see what Maxie was doing. He was back in a minute.

"Miss Applebaum, take a letter to Mrs Garson. Her husband owed me a hundred and fifty dollars, you know. Now's the best time to remind her, when she's settling all his affairs."

"Mr Grosnick!" Miss Applebaum exploded. "Why don't you let the man get cold in his grave!"

"Don't be stupid. Is it my fault if Garson didn't have a bean to his behind?"

"Shall I put both letters in the same envelope?" said Miss Applebaum coldly.

Mr Grosnick stopped pacing the floor to ponder the question. "No-o, that wouldn't be very nice," he said finally.

When he had gone, Miss Applebaum turned to Maxie who had been within hearing distance. "That's your boss. One moment he moans about the loss of his friend and the next he sends lawyer letters to his widow."

Spooning out the thick, aromatic cabbage soup, Mrs Karpal asked: "Well, Maxie, how's my big provider? Do you like your job?"

"It's alright, I guess," her son replied, and between mouthfuls he relat-ed the day's experiences.

"There's a lot I don't understand, Ma."

"What, Maxie?"

"Oh . . . nothing. Mr Grosnick took me with him to the synagogue. Says he's goin' to take me every day. It's right next door, you know."

Mr Karpal stirred noisily in his bed and his family glanced up from the table to look at him. "That's all that's necessary," he muttered, furrowing his colourless lips.

"And did you hear, Yankel," said Mrs Karpal to her husband, "he wouldn't let Maxie strain himself? That's what I call a good man."

"Te . . . te . . ." came softly from the pile of rags, and it sounded like a cricket chirping in the walls.

Maxie finished his supper in silence. He felt restless, cut off by new, inexpressible sensations from the family. At that moment its sovereign interest as a unit didn't exist for him, he was too remote. Anyhow he had always found it difficult to talk to his brother and sisters. He was a high-strung, stubborn boy and full of moods. Anything might set him off, and so the family forebore to question him. He watched his sisters helping their mother put the supper things away. Phillip had drawn up his chair beside the stove. A world different from theirs, greatly different, was beginning to shape itself within him. He tried terribly hard to put his feelings into words but they wouldn't come. The failure left him bitter, desolate, excitable. Maybe a walk outside would do him good. He rose, put on his goloshes and overcoat and closed the door noiselessly behind him.

It was a fine night, strangely mild. The street seemed unusually bright and a few people were visible. A cat crouched in a doorway. Maxie walked towards Demontigny, turned left and crossed the snow-filled lanes that were only a little less narrow and dark than the street itself. The Chinese laundry was still open, its warm, chemical smell penetrated from the doorway. When he reached De Bullion he noticed a group of people gathered in front of a house. He went towards it. A "raid" was on. The policemen had already banged the door open, the crowd was waiting to see the inmates led out. The girls came out laughing and joking, but the men crouched dejectedly beside their escorts, pushing their crushed hats against their faces. The men in the crowd guffawed when they saw them, every one pushed forward a little. Then someone standing beside Maxie said loudly:

"Well, kid, how'ja like the fat one . . . that one over there?"

This set the crowd to laughing again. Maxie became frightened because he didn't know why they laughed. Instinctively he moved towards a woman, feeling she would protect him, women were kinder than men. And now it seemed to Maxie that every one was looking at him. He moved closer to the woman. He heard her neighbour mutter something to her in a foreign tongue and they both began to snicker. There was something dark and brutal about these people, something full of danger to him. He backed away. And then the van drove off and the crowd began to disperse. Maxie darted out of the dissolving circle and ran towards the lights and illuminated windows of St Catharine Street.

Who were these people? Why had they laughed at him? He could still hear them, he thought, and he turned his head around fearfully, quickening his steps. A light, powdery snow was beginning to fall, the flakes twirled past the street lamps like soft, white moths. They clung to the shop windows and the men's bowlers. It was growing late. Maxie hurried on, keeping close to the buildings. He was still shaken by his experience; the wind was like a mocking laughter. And then he remembered something that had happened to him during the summer. Returning from an errand one afternoon, he had "stolen" a ride on the rear of an ice wagon. And another wagon had drawn up alongside and the driver reining his horses to one side had slashed his whip across Maxie's face. And as the horses pulled away the man had laughed. It was not the pain, though that had been sharp enough, which made him cry out. Why had the man done it? It wasn't *his* wagon that he was riding on. And now the remembrance of the man's cruelty and his laughter afterwards made Maxie run his finger down the faint scar across his cheek. He returned home nervous and exhausted. That night he dreamt a woman had tied him to an ice wagon and was whipping him. She was shouting at him in a strange tongue and if only he could understand what she was saying she would stop whipping him. But he couldn't and the blows descended on his face harder and harder. . . .

The months passed and at last the snow began to melt. The long, swollen, cruel icicles crashed down upon the sidewalks and the noise their breaking made was the sweetest music. Real touch of spring, the children appeared with their gay marbles. The streets became dirty and colourful, began to breathe again. Here and there the storm windows disappeared and it was as if the houses were expelling a long held-in breath. Even the puddles were welcomed because they held bits of warm, blue sky in them.

And now sex awakening in Maxie, he gave his heart to Miss Applebaum. He thought himself in love with her. She troubled his sleep and when he was near her he was ill at ease. He approached her tremblingly, stupidly. For her part Miss Applebaum was too preoccupied and efficient to notice her young lover. Sometimes his discomfort made him pass his hand over her back and shoulders and when she was late coming from dinner he would sit in her chair and move his hands along the edge of the desk where he thought her bosom must have pressed. The curve of the blouse over her hard, round breasts made him restless, frustrated him. When he met his former classmates on the street he felt superior to them—possessed of a knowledge they didn't have.

He worked hard and Mr Grosnick was pleased with him. A tidy boy, he called him. Maybe you'll grow up to be my partner, he said. When it grew dark, Maxie brushed his clothes, and waited for Mr Grosnick to take him to the synagogue next door. It was a small, dingy place that had formerly been a private residence. There were no chairs, only long, wooden benches one behind the other and an aisle between them leading up to the Holy Ark. Maxie intoned his prayers with deep feeling, thinking Mr Grosnick would like him to do so. He noticed that Mr. Grosnick himself recited the prayers as if he were shouting commands to someone. Maxie was embarrassed when he heard them above the murmured, indistinct supplications of the other worshippers. Was that the way to speak to God? Not that Maxie had any very clear ideas about God. He thought of Him as somehow imprisoned Friday night between his mother's old silver candlesticks, escaping only when the blue flame in the wicks had expired. He thought that for the rest of the week God was imprisoned in the Ark, the cabinet containing the holy scrolls. But since God was all powerful, Maxie reasoned it was a self-imposed imprisonment, like he himself going to work when his friends were still at school.

Maxie was tidying himself for the evening service.

"We haven't missed a day yet," commented Mr Grosnick from the carton he was sitting on.

"No, Mr Grosnick, we haven't."

"And why should we? It's right next door, after all. Does it hurt us to go in for a few minutes? It doesn't. Does it make us any poorer?"

Maxie had observed his employer's habit of asking questions to which he didn't expect an answer. He said nothing. Mr Grosnick continued:

"Well, the way I figure is like this, who knows whether there's a God, a Supreme Being, or not. I'm a self-educated man, and some philosophers say there is and some there isn't. Though the greatest, mind you, Platon and Aristootle, say there is. But who knows, who knows?"

Mr Grosnick jerked his head to one side and screwed up his eyes. This weightiest of problems was not really beyond him, it suggested. Then he took out a toothpick and began chewing it.

"I don't understand," said Maxie slowly. "Do you think there mightn't be a God? Is—"

"Now who said that?" exclaimed Mr Grosnick, shaken from his reverie. "I'm only telling you what the philosophers, the greatest thinkers of the human race, have thought, have conceived. Why a man without God is like—is like this toothpick." He flung out his arm, holding the toothpick so that Maxie could see it. His hand shook a little. "Why, of course there must be a God. I haven't missed a day at the synagogue, and you see how my business prospers. . . . Ah, you're ready. Come."

That evening, seated between Mr Grosnick and another worshipper, Maxie gazed apprehensively at the Ark, the cabinet containing the holy scrolls. He wondered whether God hadn't escaped from there too and was never coming back. God was free. But if that were so what were all these people doing here? There was no one to hear their prayers and like a strict teacher mark them according to the merits of their recitation. What were Mr Grosnick and himself doing here? His thoughts ran on until they frightened him, he raised his voice in prayer with greater earnestness than before.

A few days later Mr Grosnick called him into the office. He handed him his pay envelope telling him at the same time excitedly to open it. Maxie pulled out three soiled one dollar bills and then felt at the bottom of the envelope something hard and round. He let it fall into his open waiting palm. It was a fifty-cent piece. Mr Grosnick laughed at his surprise.

"A raise, Maxie. You've been a good worker, a tidy boy. From now on I pay you three-and-a-half dollars a week. Satisfied?"

"Thank you, Mr Grosnick," said Maxie and because he couldn't think of anything else to say, he added quickly, "Won't Miss Applebaum be glad when I tell her Sunday morning!"

"Oh, she!" Mr Grosnick's voice was disapproving. "She takes no interest in the business. She can be here another ten years and she won't get a raise."

Maxie's face fell. He busied himself with putting the money back into the envelope.

"It isn't six yet, and where is she? She's already gone home."

"Yes, Mr Grosnick."

"Well, I'm going out for a few minutes. If anyone comes, tell them they can wait for me."

Maxie walked back to the stockroom to give a last check up. Fridays he went straight home after work. From there, after washing himself and putting on his good suit, he went to the synagogue with his family. Satisfied that everything was in order, he took out the fifty-cent piece and pressed it between his fingers. He liked the hard feel of it. His mother would be happy and proud of him. He pictured himself telling the family at the supper table. He knew just how he would begin. Slowly at first, telling how Mr Grosnick had called him into the office, what he had said to him, and finally he would take out the money and show it to them. He pictured their astonishment and delight. And Miss Applebaum, maybe she would notice him now. He would buy some books, and read those philosophers Mr Grosnick had mentioned. He would be learned and wise and know what happened to God after he left the candlesticks and the cabinet.

He flipped the coin, once, twice, catching it each time in his cupped hands. He flipped it again. This time it came down on his wrist and, falling on the floor, began rolling towards the cartons. Maxie started after it but he was too late. It had disappeared through the narrow crack and he heard it scrape against the wall. Maxie stared for a moment in perplexity at the square, heavily filled cartons. Would he have time to move them before Mr Grosnick got back? He put his hands on one and with his back pressing against the other he managed to separate them sufficiently to slide through his head and shoulders. He felt with his fingers for the coin. As they curved over it, they came in contact with a strip of wire. He tried to pull it out but it was fastened to the wall. He squirmed between the cartons, pushing them apart to enable him to bring his head in further. What he saw filled him with horror. He tugged at the wire again to convince himself he was not mistaken. It refused to give way. He peered into the narrow space between the cartons and the wall and saw the wire extended towards the back door where it flowed into a socket-like arrangement to the right of it. At the other end the wire lost itself into a tiny hole that had been bored specially for the purpose. It could lead to only one place — the synagogue next door. Mr Grosnick was stealing electricity from the synagogue! Maxie quickly crawled out and began frantically to push the cartons back into place. When Mr Grosnick returned, he tried to look indifferent but his knees were trembling.

That evening when the family was ready to leave for the synagogue, Maxie said quietly:

"I'm not going."

"What's the matter, Maxie, don't you feel well?" Mrs Karpal asked, looking at her son anxiously, while the other children gathered around.

"It isn't that. I don't want to go to the synagogue any more. I'm never going."

He was trying, by licking his lip, to keep it from trembling and instinctively looked towards his father who was sitting up, an old coat thrown over his thin shoulders.

They all stared at him. "Have you gone crazy?" demanded his brother, Phillip. "Have you gone out of your mind? Get your coat on!" But Mr Karpal, closing his eyes and nodding his head, said mildly, "Don't be a *naar,* my son. It may not do you any good but it can't do you any harm either. Believe me, I wish I could get off this cursed bed and go with you."

"Pa, I can't go! What I saw—"

"Never mind what you saw," Phillip shouted hoarsely. "Get your coat on, I say."

"I won't. Why don't you—"

"Are you coming?" Phillip again shouted.

"No."

Mrs Karpal stared at Maxie as if he had taken leave of his senses. "Put your coat on and come," she said, her voice rising angrily with each word, so that at the end she too was shouting.

"I'm not coming, I tell you," Maxie persisted.

It was then Mrs Karpal rushed up to her son and with a lunge knocked him to the floor. Maxie fell on his face, his hands hitting against the bedpost. Mrs Karpal fell upon him with her knees, pressing them against the small of his back so that he felt he couldn't breathe, and with her elbows working like furious pistons she began to beat him about the neck and shoulders.

"You won't go to the synagogue! You won't go—you tramp, you atheist, you *mishimit!* I'll—show—you, you tramp!"

Mrs Karpal dug her fingers into his cheeks and tore at the flesh. The blows came faster and faster and Maxie, pinned under his mother's powerful knees, thrashed about with his hands and legs to defend himself. But he didn't cry out. The children watched silently, no one daring to interfere. Mr Karpal turned his face away towards the window. The bun at the back of Mrs Karpal's neck had come apart and a braid fell across her cheek. She was breathing heavily. Finally she rose and staggered towards the table for support. She looked fiercely at the quivering body of her son and said bitterly:

"You should have run out of my belly before you were born."

Phillip kicked his ankle and Maxie felt the crazy pain shoot through his body, exploding into numbness.

Mrs Karpal took a deep breath, smoothed her dress, coiled the braid into its place, and adjusting the shawl about her shoulders, glanced into the stove mirror to see if she was proper for the synagogue.

"Come, I don't think Maxie feels strong enough to go with us," she said.

As they closed the door behind them they could still hear Maxie sobbing to the floor.

Irving Layton was born in 1912 in Romania. His work has had a tremendous impact on successive generations of Canadian writers. He has published many collections, including A Red Carpet for the Sun, *which won the Governor General's Award. He was professor of English at York University from 1969–78.*

The Street

Mordecai Richler

In 1953, on the first Sunday after my return to Montreal from a two year stay in Europe, I went to my grandmother's house on Jeanne Mance street.

A Yiddish newspaper fluttering on her massive lap, black bootlaces unravelled, my grandmother was ensconced in a kitchen chair on the balcony, seemingly rooted there, attended by sons and daughters, fortified by grandchildren. "How is it for the Jews in Europe?" she asked me.

A direct question from an old lady with a wart turned like a screw in her cheek and in an instant I was shorn of all my desperately acquired sophistication; my *New Statesman* outlook, my shaky knowledge of wines and European capitals; the life I had made for myself beyond the ghetto.

"I don't know," I said, my shame mixed with resentment at being reclaimed so quickly. "I didn't meet many."

Leaning against their shiny new cars, yawning on the balcony steps with hands thrust into their trouser pockets or munching watermelon, pinging seeds into saucers, my uncles reproached me for not having been to Israel. But their questions about Europe were less poignant than my grandmother's. Had I seen the Folies Bergères? The changing of the guards? My uncles had become Canadians.

Canada, from the beginning, was second-best. It made us nearly Americans.

My grandfather, like so many others, ventured to Canada by steerage from a Gallician *shtetl*, in 1904, following hard on the outbreak of the Russo-Japanese War and the singularly vile pogrom in Kishinev, which was instigated by the militant anti-semite P. A. Krushevan, editor of *Znamya* (*The Banner*), who four months later was the first to publish in Russia the *Minutes of the Meeting of the World Union of Freemasons and Elders of Zion*, which he called *Programme for World Conquest by the Jews.*

My grandfather, I was astonished to discover many years later, had actually had a train ticket to Chicago in his pocket. Canada was not a choice, but an accident. On board ship my grandfather encountered a follower of the same hasidic rabbi; the man had a train ticket to Montreal, but relatives in Chicago. My grandfather knew somebody's cousin in Toronto, also in Canada, he was informed. So the two men swapped train tickets on deck one morning.

On arrival in Montreal my grandfather acquired a peddler's licence and a small loan from the Baron de Hirsch Institute and dug in not far from the Main Street in what was to become a ghetto. Here, as in the real America, the immigrants worked under appalling conditions in sweatshops. They rented halls over poolrooms and grocery stores to meet and form burial societies and create *shuls*. They sent to the old country for younger brothers and cousins left behind, for rabbis and brides. Slowly, unfalteringly, the immigrants began to struggle up a ladder of streets, from one where you had to leave your garbage outside your front door to another where you actually had a rear lane as well as a back yard where corn and tomatoes were usually grown; from the three rooms over the fruit store or tailor shop to your own cold-water flat. A street with trees.

Our street was called St. Urbain. French for Urban. Actually there have been eight popes named Urban, but ours was the first. Urban 1. He was also the only one to have been canonized.

St. Urbain ultimately led to routes 11 and 18, and all day and night big refrigeration trucks and peddlers in rattling chevvies and sometimes tourists used to pass, hurtling to and from northern Quebec, Ontario, and New York State. Occasionally the truckers and peddlers would pull up at Tansky's for a bite.

"Montreal's a fine town," they'd say. "Wide open."

Unfailingly, one of the truckers would reply, "It's the Gay Paree of North America."

But if the trucker or peddler was from Toronto, he would add, ingratiatingly, "The only good thing about Toronto is the road to Montreal. Isn't that so?"

The regulars at Tansky's felt it was a good omen that the truckers and peddlers sometimes stopped there. "They know the best places," Segal said.

Some of the truckers had tattoos on their arms, others chewed tobacco or rolled their own cigarettes with Old Chum. The regulars would whisper about them in Yiddish.

"I wonder how long *that* one's been out of prison?"

"The one with all the holes in his face smells like he hasn't changed his underwear since God knows when."

The truckers struck matches against the seat of their shiny trousers or by flicking them with a thumbnail. They could spit on the floor with such a splash of assurance that it was the regulars who ended up feeling like intruders in Tansky's Cigar & Soda.

"I'll bet you the one with the ears can't count to twenty without taking his shoes off."

"But you don't understand," Takifman, nodding, sucking mournfully on an inverted pipe, would reassure them. "Statistics prove they're happier than we are. They care their kids should go to the McGill? They have one every nine months regular as clock-work. Why? For the family allowance cheque."

When the regulars carried on like that, belittling the bigger, more masculine men, Tansky would regard them reproachfully. He would put out delicate little feelers to the truckers. His brothers, the French Canadians. Vanquished, oppressed.

Peering over the rim of his glasses, Tansky would say, "Isn't it a shame about the strikers in Granby?" Or looking up from his newspaper, pausing to wet a thumb, he'd try, "And what about our brothers, the blacks?"

Then he would settle back and wait.

If one of the truckers replied, "It's shit, everything's shit," and the other sneered, "I try to mind my own business, buster," Tansky's shaggy grey head would drop and he would have to be reminded to add mustard and relish to the hamburgers. But if the truckers were responsive or, more likely, shrewd, if one said, "It's the system," and the other, "Maybe after the war things will be different," they would earn heaping plates of french fried potatoes and complimentary refills of coffee.

"It's one hell of a life," one of the truckers might say and Tansky would reply fervently, "We can change it. It's up to the people."

Even in winter the regulars used to risk the wind and the ice to slip outside and stamp up and down around the enormous trailer trucks, reminding each other that they too could have been millionaires today, fabled philanthropists, sought-after community leaders, if only, during prohibition, they too had been willing to bootleg, running booze over the border in trucks like these.

Another opportunity missed.

Looking in here, landing a little slap there, the regulars always stopped to give the tires a melancholy kick.

"You should have what one of these babies burns in gas in one night."

"Ach. It's no life for a family man."

It was different with the peddlers. Most of them were, as Miller put it, members of the tribe. Even if a man was so stupid, such a *putz*, that he couldn't tell from their faces or if—like Tansky, perhaps—he indignantly held that there was no such thing as a Jewish face, he still knew because before the peddlers even sat down for a coffee they generally phoned home and looked to see if Tansky sold pennants or toys to take back as a memento for the kids. They didn't waste time, either. They zipped through their order book as they ate, biting their pencils, adding, subtracting, muttering to themselves, and if they were carrying an item that Tansky might feasibly use they tried to push a sale right there. If not, they would offer the regulars cut-rates on suits or kitchen ware. Some of the peddlers were kidders and carried come-ons with them to entice the French Canadian hicks in Ste Jerome and Trois-Rivières, Tadoussac and Restigouche. Hold a key chain socket to your eye and see a naked cutie wiggle. Pour seltzer into a tumbler with a print of a girl on the side and watch her panties peel off.

Segal told all the peddlers the same joke, ruining it, as he did all his stories, by revealing the punch-line first. "Do you know the one," he'd say, "that goes Bloomberg's dead?"

"No. Well, I don't think so."

So Segal, quaking with laughter, would plunge into the story about this traveller, one of ours, a man called Bloomberg, who had a cock bigger than a Coorsh's salami. Built stronger than Farber the iceman's horse, let me tell you. He went from town to town, selling bolts of cloth, seconds, and banging *shiksas* (nuns included) on the cot in the back of his van, until the day he died. Another salesman, Motka Frish, was also in this godforsaken mining town in Labrador when he died. Motka hurried to the mortuary where the legendary Bloomberg lay on a slab and sliced off his cock, his unbelievably large member, to bring home and show to his wife, because otherwise, he thought, she would never believe a man could be so well hung. He returns home, unwraps the cock, and before he can get a word out, his wife has a peek and begins to pull her hair and wail. "Bloomberg's dead," she howls. "Bloomberg's dead."

Afterwards, still spilling with laughter, Segal would ask, "Heard any hot ones yourself lately?"

Takifman was another one who always had a word with the peddlers. "How is it," he would ask, already tearful, "for the Jews in Valleyfield?"

Or if the peddler had just come from Albany it was, "I hear the mayor there is an anti-semite."

"Aren't they all?"

"Not LaGuardia. LaGuardia of New York is A-1."

The peddlers would usually ask for a couple of dollars in silver and retreat to the phone booth for a while before they left.

Tansky's beat-up brown phone booth was an institution in our neighbourhood. Many who didn't have phones of their own used it to summon the doctor. "I'd rather pay a nickel here than be indebted to that cockroach downstairs for the rest of my life." Others needed the booth if they had a surreptitious little deal to transact or if it was the sabbath and they couldn't use their own phones because they had a father from the stone ages. If you had a party line you didn't dare use the phone in your own house to call the free loan society or the exterminator. Boys who wanted privacy used the phone to call their girl friends, though the regulars were particularly hard on them.

Between two and four in the afternoon the horse players held a monopoly on the phone. One of them, Sonny Markowitz, got an incoming call daily at three. Nat always took it for him. "Good afternoon," he'd say "Morrow Real Estate. Mr. Morrow. One moment, please."

Markowitz would grab the receiver, his manner breathless. "Glad you called, honey. But I've got an important client with me right now. Yes, doll. You bet. Soon as I can. *Hasta la vista.*"

Anxious callers had long ago picked the paint off one wall of the booth. Others had scratched obscenities into the exposed zinc. Somebody who had been unable to get a date with Molly had used a key to cut MOLLY BANGS into the wall.

Underneath, Manny had written ME TOO, adding his phone number. Doodles tended toward the expansively pornographic, they were boastful too, and most of the graffiti was obvious. KILROY WAS HERE. OPEN UP A SECOND FRONT. PERLMAN'S A SHVANTZ.

After each fight with Joey, Sadie swept in sobbing, hysterical, her housecoat fluttering. She never bothered to lower her voice. "It's happened again, Maw. No, he wasn't wearing anything. He wouldn't. Sure I told him what the doctor said. *I told him.* He said what are you, the B'nai Jacob Synagogue, I can't come in without wearing a hat? How do I know? I'm telling you, Maw, he's a beast, I want to come home to you. *That's not true.* I couldn't stop him if I wanted to. Yes, I washed before Seymour. A lot of good it does. All right, Maw. I'll tell him."

Sugarman never shuffled into Tansky's without first trying the slot in the booth to see if anyone had left a nickel behind. The regulars seldom paid for a call. They would dial their homes or businesses, ring twice, hang up, and wait for the return call.

Tansky's was not the only store of its sort on St. Urbain. Immediately across the street was Myerson's.

Myerson had put in cushions for the card players, he sold some items cheaper than Tansky, but he was considered to be a sour type, a regular snake, and so he did not do too well. He had his regulars, it's true, and there was some drifting to and fro between the stores out of pique, but if a trucker or a peddler stopped at Myerson's it was an accident.

Myerson had a tendency to stand outside, sweeping up with vicious strokes, and hollering at the men as they filed into Tansky's. "Hey, why don't you come over here for once? I won't bite you. Blood poisoning I don't need."

Myerson's rage fed on the refugees who began to settle on St. Urbain during the war years. "If they come in it's for a street direction," he'd say, "or if it's for a coke they want a dozen glasses with." He wasn't kind to kids. "You know what you are," he was fond of saying, "your father's mistake."

If we came in to collect on empty bottles, he'd say, "We don't deal in stolen goods here. Try Tansky's."

We enjoyed the excitement of the passing peddlers and truckers on St. Urbain—it was, as Sugarman said, an education—but we also had our traffic accidents. Once a boy was killed. An only son. Another time an old man. But complain, complain, we could not get them to install traffic lights on our corner.

"When one of ours is killed by a car they care? It saves them some dirty work."

But Tansky insisted it wasn't anti-semitism. Ours was a working-class area. That's why we didn't count.

St. Urbain was one of five working-class ghetto streets between the Main and Park Avenue.

To a middle-class stranger, it's true, the five streets would have seemed interchangeable. On each corner a cigar store, a grocery, and a fruit man. Outside staircases everywhere. Winding ones, wooden ones, rusty and risky ones. An endless repetition of precious peeling balconies and waste lots making the occasional gap here and there. But, as we boys knew, each street between the Main and Park Avenue represented subtle differences in income. No two cold-water flats were alike and no two stores were the same either. Best Fruit gypped on weight but Smiley's didn't give credit.

Of the five streets, St. Urbain was the best. Those on the streets below, the out-of-breath ones, the borrowers, the *yentas*, flea-carriers and rent-skippers, *goniffs* from Galicia, couldn't afford a day in the country or tinned fruit for dessert on the High Holidays. They accepted parcels from charity matrons (Outremont bitches) on Passover, and went uninvited to bar-mitzvahs and weddings to carry off cakes, bottles, and chicken legs. Their English was not as good as ours. In fact, they were not yet Canadians. *Greeners*, that's what they were. On the streets above, you got the ambitious ones. The schemers and the hat-tippers. The *pusherkes*.

Among the wonders of St. Urbain, our St. Urbain, there was a man who ran for alderman on a one-plank platform—provincial speed cops were anti-semites. There was a semipro whore, Cross-Eyed Yetta, and a gifted cripple, Pomerantz, who had had a poem published in *transition* before he shrivelled and died at the age of twenty-seven. There were two men who had served with the Mackenzie-Paps in the Spanish Civil War and a girl who had met Danny Kaye in the Catskills. A boy nobody remembered who went on to become a professor at M.I.T. Dicky Rubin who married a *shiksa* in the Unitarian Church. A Boxer who once made the *Ring* magazine ratings. Lazar of Best Grade Fruit who raked in twenty-five hundred dollars for being knocked down by a No. 43 streetcar. Herscovitch's nephew Larry who went to prison for yielding military secrets to Russia. A woman who actually called herself a divorcée. A man, A.D.'s father, who was bad luck to have in your house. And more, many more.

St. Urbain was, I suppose, somewhat similar to ghetto streets in New York and Chicago. There were a number of crucial differences, however. We were Canadians, therefore we had a King. We also had "pea-soups", that is to say, French Canadians, in the neighbourhood. While the King never actually stopped on St. Urbain, he did pass a few streets above on his visit to Canada just before the war. We were turned out of school to wave at him on our first unscheduled holiday, as I recall it, since Buster Crabbe, the Tarzan of his day, had spoken to us on Canada Youth Day.

"He looks to me *eppes*, a little pasty," Mrs. Takifman said.

My friends and I used to set pennies down on the tracks to be flattened by passing freight trains. Later, we would con the rich kids in Outremont, telling them that the Royal Train had gone over the pennies. We got a nickel each for them.

Earlier, the Prince of Wales came to Canada. He appeared at a Mizrachi meeting and my mother became one of thousands upon thousands who actually shook hands with him. When he abdicated the throne, she revealed, "Even then you could tell he was a romantic man. You could see it in his eyes."

"He has two," my father said, "just like me."

"Sure. That's right. You sacrifice a throne for a lady's love. It kills you to even give up a seat on the streetcar."

A St. Urbain street lady, Mrs. Miller of Miller's Home Bakery, made an enormous *chaleh*, the biggest loaf we had ever seen, and sent it to Buckingham Palace in time for Princess Elizabeth's birthday. A thank you note came from the Palace and Mrs. Miller's picture was in all the newspapers. "For local distribution," she told reporters, "we also bake knishes and cater for quality weddings."

Our attitude toward the Royal Family was characterized by an amused benevolence. They didn't affect the price of potatoes. Neither could they help or hinder the establishment of the State of Israel. Like Churchill, for instance. King George VI, we were assured, was just a figurehead. We could afford to be patronizing for among our kings we could count Solomon and David. True, we had enjoyed Bette Davis in *Elizabeth and Essex*. We were flattered when Manny became a King's

Scout. Why, we even wished the Royal Family a long life every Saturday in the synagogue, but this wasn't servility. It was generosity. Badly misplaced generosity when I recall that we also included John Buchan, 1st Lord Tweedsmuir of Elsfield, Governor-General of Canada, in our prayers.

As a boy I was enjoined by my school masters to revere John Buchan. Before he came to speak at Junior Red Cross Prize Day, we were told that he stood for the ultimate British virtues. Fair play, clean living, gentlemanly conduct. We were not forewarned that he was also a virulent anti-semite. I discovered this for myself, reading *The Thirty-Nine Steps*. I was scarcely into the novel, when I was introduced to Scudder, the brave and good spy, whom Richard Hannay takes to be "a sharp, restless fellow, who always wanted to get down to the root of things." Scudder tells Hannay that behind all governments and the armies there was a big subterranean movement going on, engineered by a very dangerous people. Most of them were the sort of educated anarchists that make revolutions, but beside them there were financiers who were playing for money. It suited the books of both classes of conspirators to set Europe by the ears:

When I asked Why, he said that the anarchist lot thought it would give them their chance . . . they looked to see a new world emerge. The capitalists would . . . make fortunes by buying up the wreckage. Capital, he said, had no conscience and no fatherland. Besides, the Jew was behind it, and the Jew hated Russia worse than hell.

'Do you wonder?' he cried. 'For three hundred years they have been persecuted, and this is the return match for the *pogroms*. The Jew is everywhere, but you have to go far down the backstairs to meet him. Take any big Teutonic business concern. If you have dealings with it the first man you meet is Prince *von und zu* Something, an elegant young man who talks Eton-and-Harrow English. But he cuts no ice. If your business is big, you get behind him and find a prognathous Westphalian with retreating brow and the manners of a hog . . . But if you're on the biggest kind of job and are bound to get to the real boss, ten to one you are brought up against a little white-faced Jew in a bathchair with an eye like a rattle snake. Yes, sir, he is the man who is ruling the world just now, and he has his knife in the Empire of the Tzar, because his aunt was outraged and his father flogged in some one-horse location on the Volga.'

As badly as I wanted to identify with Hannay, two-fisted soldier of for-tunte, I couldn't without betraying myself. My grandfather, *pace* Buchan, had gone in fear of being flogged in some one-horse location on the Volga, which was why we were in Canada. However, I owe to Buchan the image of my grandfather as a little white-faced Jew with an eye like a rat-tlesnake. It is an image I briefly responded to, alas, if only because Han-nay, so obviously on the side of the good and the clean, accepted it with-out question.

In those days British and American influences still vied for our atten-tion. We suffered split loyalties. I would have liked, for instance, to have seen Tommy Farr pulverize Joe Louis. We were enormously grateful when Donald Wolfit came to town with a shambles of a Shakespearian company and we applauded and stamped our feet for George Formby at the Forum. Our best-known writers, Leacock, Hugh MacLennan and Robertson Davies, were clearly within a British tradition. Our dentist took the *Illustrated London News* and we all read Beverly Baxter's syrupy reports in *Macleans* about lords and ladies he had taken strawberries and champagne with.

Pea-soups were for turning the lights on and off on the sabbath and running elevators and cleaning out chimneys and furnaces. They were, it was rumoured, ridden with T.B. rickets, and the syph. Their older women were for washing windows and waxing floors and the younger ones were for maids in the higher reaches of Outremont, working in factories, and making time with, if and when you had the chance. The French Cana-dians were our *schwartzes*.

Zabitsky, a feared man, said, "It's not very well known, but there's a tunnel that runs from the nunnery to the priesthouse. It isn't there in case of an air-raid, either."

Zabitsky also told us how an altar boy could make himself a bishop's favourite, that a nun's habit concealed pregnancy, and that there was a special orphanage for the priests' bastards in Ste. Jerome.

To all this Shapiro said, "Well, snatch-erly," my father agreed, and Segal, warming to the idea, suggested a new definition for bishopric.

But when I recall St. Urbain I do not think so much of the men as of my old companions there. The boys. Mostly, we just used to sit around on the outside staircases shooting the breeze.

"Knock, knock."

"Who's there?"

"Freda."

"Freda who?"

"Fre-da you. Five dollars for anyone else."

Our hero was Ziggy "The Fireball" Freed, who was signed on by a Dodger scout at the age of eighteen, and was shipped out for seasoning with a Class 'D' team in Texas. Ziggy lasted only a season. "You think they'd give a Hebe a chance to pitch out there?"he asked. "Sure, in the ninth inning, with the bases loaded and none out, and their home-run slugger coming up to the plate, the manager would shout, "Okay, Ziggy, it's your ball game now."

Our world was rigidly circumscribed. Outside, where they ate wormy pork, beat the wives for openers, didn't care a little finger if the children grew up to be doctors, we seldom ventured, and then only fearfully. Our world, its prizes and punishments, was entirely Jewish. Inside, God would get us if we didn't say our prayers. You ate the last scrap of meat on your plate because the children in Europe were starving. If you got it right on your bar-mitzvah who knows but the rich uncle might buy you a Parker 51 set.

In our world what we knew of the outside was it wasn't a life-saver if it didn't have a hole in it. If you ate plenty of carrots you would see better in the dark, like R.A.F. nightfighters. Every Thursday night on Station CBM Fibber McGee would open his marvelous closet. Joe was always gone for a Dow. Never before had so many owed so much to so few. V stood for Victory. Paul Lukas was watching out for us on the Rhine. The sure road to success was to buy cheap and sell dear. In real life Superman was only mild Clark Kent. A Roosevelt only comes along once in a life-time. Scratch the best goy and you find the worst anti-semite.

After school we sat on the steps and talked about everything from A to Z.

. "Why is it Tarzan never shits?"

"What about Wonder Woman?"

"She's a dame, you jerk. But there's Tarzan in the jungle, week in and week out, and never once does he go to the toilet. It's not true to life, that's all."

In summer we bought old car tubes from the garage for a nickel and took them to the beaches with us. We made scooters out of waste wood and roller skates stolen or picked up at a junk yard. Used horseshoes nicked from the French Canadian blacksmith served us for games of pitch-toss. A sock stuffed with sawdust was good enough for touch football. During the worst of the winter we built a chain of snow fortresses on St. Urbain and battled, one side against another, shouting, "Guadacanal! *Schweinhund!* Take that, you yellow devil!" With regular hockey sticks and pieces of coal and copies of Macleans for shin-pads we played right out on the streets, breaking up whenever a car wanted to pass.

When we grew a little older, however, our big thrill was to watch Molly go by.

Almost everything came to a stop on St. Urbain when Molly turned the corner at six-oh-five on her way home from Susy's Smart Wear, where she typed letters and invoices and occasionally modelled garments for out-of-town buyers. The boys in the Laurier Billiard Academy would be drawn to the window, still holding their cues.

"Here she comes. Right on the dot."

"Hey, Molly. Molly, my darling. How would you like to try this for supper?"

High stiletto heels, long slender legs, and a swinging of hips. Lefty groans. "You shoulda been here yesterday."

"Wha'?"

"There was a breeze. She wears a black slip with itsy-bitsy frills."

Eyes crossed, tongue protruding, pool cue squeezed between his thighs, Jerry pretends to pull himself off.

"Hey," Morty says, "I'll bet you guys have no idea why they put salt-petre in your cigs in the army."

Down the street she drifts, trailing Lily of the Valley.

"You ever heard of this stuff called Spanish Fly? I'm not saying I believe it but Lou swears—"

"Aw, go home and squeeze your pimples out. It's the bull."

Across the street, toward Myerson's.

"Yeow! Take care, doll. Don't take chances with it."

Cars gearing down, windows rolling open.

"Here, pussy. Nice pussy."

"You dirty bastard," Myerson says, "take your hands out of your pocket."

"*All right.*"

Past Best Grade Fruit.

"You see this pineapple?"

"I dare you."

Molly stops—considers—stoops. A stocking seam is straightened.

"You know, Bernie, I'd give a year of my life—well maybe not a year, but—"

"The line forms at the right."

Tickety-tap, tickety-tap, she goes, bottom swaying.

Myrna raises an eyebrow. "If I was willing to wear a skirt as tight as that—"

"It's asking? It's *begging* for it," Gitel says.

"—I could have all the boys I wanted to."

At the Triangle Taxi Stand, Max Kravitz twists his cap around. "Up periscope," he says, raising his arms to adjust the imaginary instrument.

"Longitude zero," Korber says, "latitude 38-29-38. She carries twin stacks."

"Ach, so. A destroyer. Ready torpedoes."

"Ready torpedoes, men."

"Ready torpedoes," is shouted down the queue of waiting drivers. Cooper, the last man, calls back, "If you ask me all periscopes are already up and all torpedoes—"

"FIRE!"

A pause.

"*Nu?*"

"She's going down."

"Heil Hitler!"

Into Tansky's for a package of Sen-Sen, ten filter-tips, the latest issue of *Silver Screen*. Takifman adjusts his tie and Segal drops a mottled hand to make sure he's buttoned.

"If I was her father," Takifman says, "I'd turn her over for a good spanking before I let her go out on the streets like that."

"Me too," Segal agrees with appetite.

St. Urbain, we felt, was inviolable. Among us we numbered the rank-one scholars in the province, gifted artists, medical students, and everywhere you looked decent, God-fearing people. It was a little embarrassing admittedly, when Mrs. Boxer, the *meshugena*, wandered the streets in her nightgown singing Jesus Loves Me. Our landlords, by and large, were rotten types. Polacks, Bulgarians, and other trash were beginning to move in here and there. When that sweet young man from CHFD's "Vox Pop" asked Ginsburg, didn't he think Canada ought to have a flag of her own, he shouldn't have come back with, you do what you like, *we* already have a flag. Not on the radio, anyway. Sugarman's boy, Stanley, it's true, had had to do six months at Ste. Vincent de Paul for buying stolen goods, but all the time he was there he refused to eat non-kosher food. We had our faults on St. Urbain, but nobody could find anything truly important to criticise.

Then one black, thundering day there was an article about our street in *Time* magazine. For several years we had been electing communists to represent us at Ottawa and in the provincial legislature. Our M.P. was arrested. An atomic spy. *Time*, investigating the man's background in depth, described St. Urbain, our St. Urbain, as the Hell's Kitchen of Montreal. It brought up old election scandals and strikes and went into the housing question and concluded that this was the climate in which communism flourished.

The offending magazine was passed from hand to hand.

"What's 'squalor'?"

"*Shmutz.*"

"We're dirty? In my house you could eat off the floor."

"We're not poor. I can walk into any delicatessen in town, you name it, and order whatever my little heart desires."

"In our house there's always plenty for *shubbus*. I should show you my butcher's bills you'd die."

"This write-up's crazy. An insult."

"Slander, you mean. We ought to get Lubin to take the case."

"Ignoramous. You don't bring in ambulance-chasers to fight a case like this. You need one of theirs, a big-shot."

"What about Rosenberg? He's a K.C."

"Yeah, and everybody knows exactly how he got it. We would need a goy."

Takifman brooded over the magazine, pinching his lips. Finally, he said: "A Jew is never poor."

"Oh, here he comes. Takifman, the fanatic. Okay, we've got the Torah. You try it for collateral at the Bank of Canada."

"For shame," Takifman said, appalled.

"Listen here, *Time* is a magazine of current affairs. The Torah is an old story. They are discussing here economics."

"The Torah is nothing to laugh."

"But you are, Takifman."

"A Jew is never poor," Takifman insisted. "Broke? Sometimes. Going through hard times? Maybe. In a strange country? Always. But poor, never."

Tansky threw his dishrag on the counter. "We are the same as everybody else," he shouted.

"What the hell!"

"Now listen, you listen here, with Chief Rabbi Takifman I don't agree, but the same—"

"You know what, Tansky. You can stuff that where the monkey put his fingers."

Sugarman finished reading the article. "What are you all so excited about?" he asked. "Can't you see this magazine is full of advertisements?"

Everybody turned to look at him.

"According to my son, and he ought to know, these magazines are all under the heel of the big advertisers. They say whatever the advertisers want."

"So you mean it's the advertisers who say we're poor and dirty?"

"You win the sixty-four dollars."

"*Why*, smart-guy?"

"Why? Did I say I know everything? All I said was that according to my son it is the advertisers who—"

"Jews and artists are never poor," Takifman persisted. "How could they be?"

"We are the same as everybody else," Tansky shouted. "Idiots!"

"A Jew is never poor. It would be impossible."

Mordecai Richler's novels include The Apprenticeship of Duddy Kravitz, Joshua Then and Now, *and* Solomon Gursky Was Here.

Bluma Zelinger

ROCHL KORN

The wheels of the train clattered with relentless monotony as if to dispel the gloom of the dilapidated limestone huts which lay scattered along the empty late autumn fields. At night the cold wind blew through the broken windows, carrying with it from time to time smoke from the panting engine. The biting wind swept across the steppes, heralding another Russian winter, the third winter for those who had survived the exile in the labor camps of Siberia.

They had been traveling for five weeks and still no one knew where and when the train would stop. There was relief in every face to be heading further and further away from the cursed camps where so many corpses had been left. More than one of those who now thirstily gulped the air from the surrounding fields, and with childish joy read the signs of the unfamiliar train stations, bore the symptoms of disease which would soon consume them.

They only knew that each passing station marked their progress south where the sun would melt away the memories of the long Siberian winters. And perhaps, in the confusion of war, one would be lucky enough to escape to the free world across the border which was so close here.

Bluma wasn't bothered by the long journey. She considered herself to be the most fortunate passenger on the train: not one member of her family was missing. She held her four smaller children in her arms and continually checked their foreheads to see if they had caught a chill from the broken windows. Her gaze wandered from them to her older daughter Gitelle, to Chaim, the Yeshiva student, and to her husband Hersh-Leib, who had once been the ritual slaughterer of Christinapol. For the first time since they had been torn from their home, Bluma experienced a sense of calm and security.

Hersh-Leib was oblivious to everything around him; he was either absorbed in a holy book or reciting psalms, almost as if he were still in his little eastern Galician town. Meanwhile the train moved on through the dusty wasteland. A full day might pass before one saw a hut. Here and there rust-colored splotches lay on the broken ground, and beyond them ran white lines, tracing an ancient sea.

The children gathered around the broken windows and gazed somberly out at the desolate plain. There was no real vegetation, only the low prickly bushes that appeared from time to time. The children, who had grown accustomed to the Siberian climate and the howling of hungry wolves in the night, absorbed it all with a sense of discovery and fear. When for the first time they saw camels munching the hard desert brambles their eyes widened with astonishment.

"Mummy, Mummy, what are those?" they shouted, tugging at her dress. Bluma didn't know the name herself, so she tapped her brow as though it were a box from which the word would spring out magically.

"It's a kind of work horse with a hump. It had to pull heavy loads for such a long time that two mausoleums grew out on its back."

Chaiml, who tried to emulate his pious father, was perusing a holy book the entire time, but now and then he couldn't contain himself and threw a glance at the window. This time his glance lingered on the strange creature, which he had only seen in pictures.

"Dummies!" he called to his sisters and brothers. "That's a camel!"

"A camel! A camel!" the children's voices rang out. "We'll tell everyone at home that we saw a camel!"

"Don't shout so loud—you're not alone here." The word home touched her. She murmured to herself: "Let it be God's will to return us safely to our home."

On the train was a certain Itzik Radamer, who had escaped from the Germans to Lemberg. From there the Russians had sent him away with other Polish citizens to a labor camp in Siberia. Itzik used to wander through the cars entertaining the passengers with gossip.

"It's rumored that they're going to let us all out through Persia," he said one day to a group huddled around him. "We're being sent to a gathering point so that we'll be in one place when General Sikorski gives the command. You all probably know that the headquarters of the Polish Army is in Buzolok, which is not far from here."

"What does Sikorski need Jews for?" Bluma asked, a worried expression on her face.

"Go play with Sikorski! My dear auntie, you'll see what kind of soldiers he'll make out of us. Even the Russian Army needs Sikorski; when he grew stubborn and demanded that his army be transferred to England, they gave in to him."

"How do you know all this?"

"Such questions are better not asked," retorted Itzik, offended that his credibility was being questioned. "If one lives, one sees!" He terminated the discussion abruptly.

Itzik was very friendly with the conductor and knew in advance where and for how long the train would stop. He was the first to jump down from the high cars when the train drew in at a station and the first in the queue for boiling water, clutching his big patched kettle which everyone admired and coveted. He enjoyed trading with the peasants who lined up along the tracks with baskets and pots. At one station he bought a box of coarse salt and poured it into the knotted sleeve of his jacket. Further on, where salt was more expensive, he exchanged it for rice, tomatoes and eggs. The profits were shared with the Uzbek conductor. They spoke in broken Russian, but when it came to commerce they both understood at a glance.

Itzik used to roam through the cars holding his kettle and distributing candy to the children. Now and again he would force a tomato or a dried fish into someone's hand and hurry away. He was fond of boasting about his finely furnished home in Radam, where he had a big business, but he never mentioned his wife or children who had remained there. In the evenings, when his memories festered like a badly healed wound, he walked around more talkative than ever, as if trying to convince himself and others that nothing affected him.

"Now we're heading for Tashkent and from there to Fergana," Itzik informed the passengers one evening.

"Where is Fergana?" Bluma asked.

"You mean you never heard about the Fergana Canal which the Russians had built through the wilderness? I even read about it in the Polish newspapers. The snow that lies in the Pamir Mountains melts in the summer and is passed through the canal to irrigate the desert. It was a great idea. What I didn't know though was that it had been built by exiles like us, like you and me."

Itzik didn't make it to Fergana. While the train was stopped in Tashkent, he slipped through the lines of security officers and disappeared.

—II—

All night Bluma sat on the hard seat thinking about the strange name Fergana. She had never heard of it before. If in her little town someone had told her that one day she and her family would be on their way there, she would have spat three times to the left and three times to the right, as her grandmother—long live her memory—used to do.

In Christinapol Bluma had virtually forgotten that she had a name. The children called her mummy; the village housewives, who had great respect for her piety, used to refer to her as the ritual slaughterer's wife, and Hersh-Leib addressed her as a stranger, indirectly. He used to say: "Maybe the food should be served first?" or "Tomorrow morning it shouldn't be forgotten that I need a clean shirt and underwear because I'm going to Beltz for the Sabbath."

In Christinapol, Hersh-Leib was renowned as a scholar and a man of great piety. He was a ritual slaughterer who enforced the laws of kashruth far more rigorously than the other slaughterers. As a result, the butchers disliked him. "He's going to make paupers out of us," they whispered among themselves, because they knew that Hersh-Leib was capable of finding a blemish even in the most flawless cattle. They therefore drove their cattle stealthily, at night, to the neighboring villages where the ritual slaughterers understood that a Jewish butcher also had a right to earn a living.

Hersh-Leib was never a big breadwinner. To make ends meet Bluma was compelled to open a kiosk where she sold soda water and candy to the Gentiles. During the summer she used to chase away the Polish youths who enjoyed stealing from right under her nose, and in the winter her hands were always blistered from the cold. On the Sabbath and holidays she walked to the synagogue in her beautiful dowry dress, her head high, in her bearing generations of pride and dignity. One of her children carried the thick, worn prayer book. In the synagogue, mothers sat their daughters down beside her and asked her to keep an eye on them, so that they wouldn't lose their place during the services.

All that was until the third day after the New Year in 1939 when the Russian Army occupied Christinapol. The Jews breathed a sigh of relief during the first few weeks: as bad as it was with the Bolsheviks, it was certainly better than living under the Germans. At least one was assured of one's life. At first, little changed in the town. Only the shelves of the shops became emptier with each passing day—the soldiers and officers of the Russian Army took the liberty of sending home huge bundles of clothing and food. Before long, bread, sugar and other staples became scarce.

Since it was prohibited to slaughter cattle privately, Hersh-Leib spent the whole day in the synagogue. Besides, most of the cattle and fowl were requisitioned by the Army. The horses were sent to the collective farms in Russia.

Around Chanukah time, a rumor spread through the shtetl that former Polish officers, priests, wealthy industrialists and even ordinary law-abiding citizens were being transported out of Lemberg, a city not far from Christinapol. Nobody knew where the Russians were sending them. A few weeks later, the cobbled streets of Christinapol rumbled under the heavy wheels of army trucks. People ran to their windows and cleaned the frosty panes to see what was happening.

The crash of a rifle butt resounded through Hersh-Leib's house and the pungent odor of leather boots burst through the front door as the officers of the NKVD, the Russian Secret Police, entered and searched every corner and every crack in the house. The family stood gaping in shock. Bluma was the first one to shake off the numbing paralysis.

"It must be a mistake," she mumbled in her broken Ukrainian. "There are no rich people here—we're only poor workers."

"We have your name on this paper. Your husband is not a useful member of society; he serves the reactionary forces by feeding the poison of religious fanaticism to the naive masses. Get your things and let's go!"

They traveled for weeks in closed cars to the middle of a forest somewhere in Siberia. Each morning Hersh-Leib and Chaim went out with axe and saw to work. The guards howled with laughter when they saw

Hersh-Leib's axe dance in his weak arms and instead of striking the tree spring into the air. Having laughed their fill, they warned him:

"If you don't produce the required quota, you won't get your portion of bread!"

Hersh-Leib was never able to fill his quota. As a result, Bluma was obliged to go into the surrounding villages to exchange a shirt or some other piece of clothing for a little porridge and a few potatoes. Then she would go to the common kitchen and transfer to one of her own pots the doled-out cabbage soup. She mixed porridge and potatoes into the soup so Hersh-Leib wouldn't suspect that it wasn't kosher—she knew that he'd sooner starve than bring non-kosher food to his lips. Bluma took the sin upon herself. "Let God punish me," she whispered to herself in the heavy darkness of night. "But let them not get sick or waste away from hunger."

—III—

The sharp screech of iron cut through the train. The wagons shook and sighed to a stop.

"Where are we?"

"Can't you see? It's written there: Gor-Tsakava."

"How long will we be here?"

"The conductor said not less than three hours. A military transport has to pass."

The passengers who headed for the doors in the hope of getting hot water or doing a little shopping were stopped by the conductor. The Army commander had ordered that no one leave the train. Outside, the station militia didn't allow anyone near the train. Uzbek peasants stood about with pots of milk on their heads and baskets over their arms, ready to exchange their foodstuffs for a shirt or a pair of pants.

Bluma approached the conductor and pleaded with him to allow her to buy milk for her small children.

"I won't run away. Can't you see, my family is staying on the train," she pleaded, but the conductor looked at her angrily and walked away.

"Give me the bottle, Mummy," said eight-year-old Rivelle. "I'll get some milk for us. Don't worry, nobody will see me."

Bluma couldn't make up her mind.

"You can rely on Rivelle," said Gitelle. "She won't get lost —she speaks Russian as if she had been born here."

Just then little Joseph began to cry:

"Mummy, Mummy, I want a drink! I want a drink!"

Bluma pressed ten rubles into Rivelle's hand.

"But don't go far," she cautioned her. "Buy from the first one you see and don't haggle with him, do you hear?" Rivelle was already out of earshot, and in a moment she was on the far side of the fence separating the train from the station. Bluma watched her hold out her bottle while a veiled Uzbek measured off the milk with a glass.

Suddenly a shudder rippled through the cars; they swayed forward then backward, as if resisting the force that was pulling them away from their brief respite.

"What's happening?" came the sounds of frightened people.

"We're moving! We're moving!"

"It can't be!" Bluma screamed, falling against a window. "We're supposed to be here for two hours. In a moment, the cars yielded to the inexorable tug of the engine and the wheels turned faster and faster. The station was already out of sight, the stands and the peasants, everything. Bluma covered her eyes with both hands. "But my Rivelle is still there!" she moaned in shock.

A tumult rose in the car. Each person had a different suggestion for Bluma. Someone said that Rivelle had certainly jumped onto the last car and would soon make her way back through the packed cars.

"What are we going to do?" Bluma turned to her husband, complaint in her voice for the first time in her life.

"We must have faith," he answered quietly, avoiding her eyes.

Meanwhile Gitelle and Chaim had searched all the cars. When they returned, sweating, faces lowered and smudged, Bluma understood poignantly that the child was not on the train. She ran to the door to jump off; she'd make her way back to Gor-Tsakava on foot. But the door was bolted from the outside. When the conductor arrived she implored him to let her off.

"Do you want me to lose my job for you?" he shouted at her. "Go to the commander if you want!" She went back to her family in despair.

In the evening the train stopped at a small station. Bluma jumped up and ran to the front cars to find the commander.

"Don't you have other children?" the commander asked. "Be happy with that. The world doesn't come to an end because of one child. It's war time. Families are being torn apart everywhere. But it's not as bad as all that—remember you're in the Soviet Union, not Poland. We have homes for children here. Your child will be found and sent to such a home. You have nothing to cry about." Bluma continued crying, inconsolable. At length, the commander agreed to let her off at the station.

"Where is the train going?" she asked him, wiping her eyes. "I want to find my family afterwards."

"I can't tell you that, citizen. It's a military secret—there are spies milling about everywhere."

Bluma remained standing, helpless, her arms lowered as if no longer needed, her eyes gazing up at the commander's raw, suntanned face with its short broad nose and narrow watery eyes, shaded by the visor of his military cap. The face seemed so familiar to her. Then she recalled that that was how the peasants looked when they came to Christinapol on market day. A flurry of old memories erased her fear of the commander's uniform.

"Don't you have a wife and children waiting for you at home?" she said quietly, staring straight into his eyes. The twilight was deepening around them.

"Citizen, I warn you not to repeat a word of this to anyone. It's war time. This train is heading for Namongan. From there the passengers will be sent to the surrounding collective farms."

Bluma ran back to her car. Without waiting a moment she packed a few things and parted with her family.

"Gitelle, take care of everyone," she said to her eldest daughter. "Most of all, look after Yoselle and your father. With God's help, we'll all be together again soon."

—IV—

Three days and three nights Bluma waited for a train heading back to Gor-Tsakava. She spent the day on a bench, and at night she stretched herself out on the floor with the others who were waiting for the train. There were Uzbeks with tanned chests and faces, a few Russian women with children, and a Polish Jew who had become ill on the way and had been left here by the commander to avoid contaminating the passengers. He lay in a corner, moaning quietly. No one dared approach him.

Bluma stepped up to the shrunken body.

"What do you want?" she asked.

"I'm dying," he whispered tremulously, "and my bones, my bones won't be brought to Israel."

"Can't you see he's dying?" Bluma shouted at the people around her. "Why isn't he taken to a hospital?"

The Uzbeks sat silently, munching their bread-cakes. One of the Russian women called out bitterly:

"Let him die, who's stopping him? We have our own troubles. We can't be bothered with every stranger who turns up here. We don't know where our own men are and we have to feed our hungry children! What do you want from us?"

Bluma wiped her eyes. She was full of pity for the dying Jew and the people around her whom suffering and hunger had so debased. She wondered if she would become like them, and shuddered at the thought. She poured water into the small pot she had taken with her and brought the rim to the parched, parted lips of the Jew. He sipped the water with great pain. He stopped moaning, but now a hoarse grumble seeped out from between his clenched teeth.

In the middle of the night, a cleaning woman entered with a pail of water and a mop. She forced everyone out of the station, then waddled up to the Jew and poked him with the broom.

"Can't you see I'm cleaning here?" she shouted. "It's filthy as a barn and the Polack pretends not to see!" A militiamen passed near the window. "Hey, comrade!" she called to him. "Come help me get rid of this tramp." The militiamen came in and pulled the Jew by the foot.

"Get up!" he ordered, dragging the lifeless mass. He let the leg drop and took a closer look at the colorless face. "You old witch!'" he turned on the cleaning woman. "Why did you call me? Can't you see he's dead?"

"Dead?" she whispered, moving away from the body. "The devil take them, these damned strangers—you never know if they're faking or if they've really dropped dead."

Two days later a cart drawn by a donkey pulled up at the station. A militiamen and an Uzbek dragged the corpse outside and flung it into the cart.

The following day a tall, pockmarked Russian peasant arrived at the station with an open jacket and a sack over his back. A skinny boy limped after him, dragging a wooden leg. The peasant sat down on the floor, threw off his sack, and lit a cigarette wrapped in newspaper. The boy sat down near the door, his wooden leg stretched out across the doorway.

"Where from?" one of the women asked him.

"From far, very far, auntie." He paused for a moment, then went on: "The hail destroyed the wheat on our collective farm. My woman and the two young children came down with typhoid, and left me with him, that cripple over there." He waved his hand at the boy, who didn't remove his gaze from his father for an instant. "We drag ourselves from place to place in search of food and work."

"Bread!" interjected another woman. "We've been waiting here three days for the train and the children are faint with hunger."

"What a terrible punishment for the Russian people," said the peasant, glancing around to make sure that no one overheard him. "We have no choice but to bite into a plank. It's too much for the Russian people to endure. If it weren't for that cripple I could find a place for a while, but he drags after me everywhere. So many young women have been left alone, their men at the fronts. Don't you think one of them would want to take a healthy man under her blanket?" he asked through his blackened teeth, and laughed gratingly. "But who wants to feed a useless body, a cripple?"

"So that's what you're like? Searching for easy bread, eh?" one of the women exclaimed while another smiled and still another straightened her kerchief and buttoned her blouse.

"The train still isn't coming, eh?" said the peasant to change the subject.

Suddenly one of the women who was standing near the window cried out:

"There's an Uzbek coming with a full wagon! Maybe we can buy some bread from him." She ran outside, leaving behind her crying children. Through the window she shouted: "Zaya! Zaya! Take care of the children!"

The tall peasant strode to the door. His son jumped up as though he had been bitten by a snake.

"And you, where do you think you're going?" snapped his father, looking at him with bitter, narrowed eyes.

"I'm going with you, Father."

The peasant's face twisted into a strange smile.

"It's a pity you're so stupid. Can't you see I'm going to buy something to eat—I haven't eaten since yesterday. If you don't believe me, take my sack. You know I won't run away without it. But make sure no one steals it."

The boy gazed with strained eyes through the window as the women returned to the station with their aprons full of dried wheat-pancakes. Before long the Uzbek whipped the small donkey and the cart rolled away on its two huge wooden wheels, leaving behind deep tracks in the thick gray dust. The spot where they had stood outside was suddenly deserted. The boy gave a start and yelled: "My father's not there!" He ran out, as if possessed, to the spot where the cart had stood. He found the tracks of his father's boots in the dust and darted off in one direction, then in another, but soon returned to the same spot. An idea occurred to him: he ran into the station and began searching through his father's sack, sniffing it like a dog. A few old leggings and a torn shirt fell out on the floor. The smell of sweat filled the station. The boy shoved the clothes aside with his wooden leg and sobbed: "He left me, he left me."

Bluma took a few dry biscuits from her sack and forced them into the boy's clenched fist.

"Here, take it and eat, you're hungry. Don't cry, your father will be back soon."

The boy looked at her, his eyes filled with animal fear, then pushed her hand away and hobbled out toward the empty fields. The quickly thickening twilight gathered him into itself.

The boy's desperate call was heard in the distance: "Father, Father, don't leave me."

All at once there was a commotion in the station. Bundles were quickly tied and children swept up from the floor, which rumbled beneath their feet. Running outside, the waiting people saw the red flames of the approaching train.

—V—

Eventually Bluma arrived at Gor-Tsakava. She asked everyone she saw about her daughter, but no one knew anything. The stationmaster explained:

"Refugees from all over come here. It's not like it used to be when we had to wait for weeks to see a new face. If someone had found the child, the militia would have been informed. If the child is alive, you'll find her."

Bluma made her way to all the surrounding Uzbek settlements and collective farms. The Uzbeks eyed her suspiciously as she stopped near the playing children and spoke to them in sign language, showing with her hands the height of one of the little girls. Before long, the dogs came barking at Bluma's feet, and she returned to the station. Her little bag of biscuits was empty and she had only thirty rubles left. But she was determined to stay on. Bluma sensed the child's breath in the air, and she believed with all her heart that any day now her daughter's curly red hair would appear before her eyes.

Each passing day fell like a rock into a deep well, never to return, not even to her memory. Bluma remained at the station, waiting for each day to separate itself from the white mist over the endless plains. Perhaps this day would be the carrier of good news, a guarded hope flickered at dawn. But each day rolled to the western horizon and became a traitor in Bluma's eyes, a deceiver which had to be erased from her memory.

One evening a man wearing a military cap walked up to Bluma and tore her away from her contemplations with a tug on the sleeve.

"Come with me," he said gruffly. She followed him to the hut near the station which housed the local NKVD office.

"Let's see your documents," said the commanding officer. She handed him a document which declared that the Zelinger family was freed from duty in labor camps. The small room grew silent; now and then the piece of paper rustled in the officer's hand.

"Where's your family?"

"They're all in Namongan," Bluma said, and was immediately interrupted by the officer.

"We don't want to hear your stories," he said. "You'll have to leave Gor-Tsakava. You can't stay here any longer." He called to one of the adjutants: "Fyodor Stepanovitch, put her on the first train to Namongan."

In Namongan, Bluma ran from one official to another, inquiring about her family. But neither the city office nor the regional office, where the list of all the workers in the local collective farms was kept, had any information about the Zelinger family. She continued going to the offices day after day, and grew progressively more dejected and desperate.

One afternoon she stopped in the middle of a street and leaned forlornly against a wall. She saw people walking with quick sure steps, children with mothers, and children chasing others. But Bluma didn't belong to anyone and no one belonged to her. Should she fall from hunger and exhaustion no one would stop to help her. And might it not in fact be better if she never moved from this spot? There was nowhere to go. Again she'd have to spend the night outside, huddled up under a bench like an animal, and in the morning she'd have to drag herself from one place to another in search of a piece of stale bread. She slumped to the ground and, covering her head with her shawl, whispered to herself: "God of the Universe, why do I deserve this? Have I really sinned as much as all that?" Then she wept, and her whole body shook with deep sobs.

She felt drained; her head fell to her raised knees like a fruit on a stalk that is too thin to support it. Suddenly she felt her chin pressing something hard into her breast. She touched the object with her fingertips; she had completely forgotten about the tiny linen sack that contained the diamond earring. A warm wave of memory rippled through her, but she was afraid to follow it because she knew that sooner or later she'd have to wake up. Nevertheless she was too weary to fend off the old scenes, and in a moment she was slinking up to her old home like a thief. The Sabbath had settled on the little town, and Bluma was walking to the synagogue in her holiday attire, the diamond earrings—her grandmother's wedding gift to her—dangling almost to her shoulders. The streets were serenely quiet and all the stores closed, the hustle and bustle of the week locked away behind the doors. Suddenly Bluma stopped. One of her earrings had opened—she had felt it at once. She closed the loop and recalled her grandmother's words: "Wear them in good health, Blumelle. I received them from my grandmother, may she rest in peace. Wear them when you accompany your children and grandchildren to the wedding canopy."

Circumstances had forced Bluma to sell one of the earrings; with the money she bought bread and potatoes for her hungry children. She resolved never to part with the second earring.

"Forgive me for not having guarded your precious gift, Granny. I'm not worthy enough to see my children married."

Suddenly Bluma heard her grandmother's voice speaking the words she had spoken to Bluma's mother when her husband, the old woman's only son, had died: "Stop weeping and grieving. It's a terrible sin to lose faith in God. He gives in order to judge us, and He takes away in order to test us." Bluma's mother wrung her hands: "Mother-in-law, what will I do with my little children?" The old woman embraced the children with her eyes as they clung to their mother's knees: "A Jewish daughter has faith. He who sustains the lowliest worm will not abandon you and your children."

Bluma used her hands to raise herself—her limbs felt as if they had grown into the ground. Her knees shook with the first steps. She gazed at some distant, indistinct point. Creases appeared around the corners of her mouth, but in her eyes lingered the glow of her grandmother's words.

—VI—

Bluma sold her shawl in the market to help defray the expense of the trip back to Gor-Tsakava. When she arrived there, she slipped quickly out of the station to avoid being noticed by the NKVD, and took the road leading to the city. It was more than eight miles to Fergana.

In the city she met many Jews who had been released from prisons and labor camps. Half-starved, haggard, they ran from office to office begging for work. They spent their nights on benches in public squares and under the steps of buildings. The days were still hot in late October, but at night a bitter cold numbed their thin, poorly clad bodies. Those who still possessed a whole garment sold it and rented a room for a few nights.

Then, early in November, after eight months of drought, the rains came. The walls of the houses were still warm when the sun fell into the purple fog, as into an open bag. The trees in the field lowered their languid branches to the earth in deference to the black clouds that were forming overhead. Then lightning streaked the air and a whistling wind burst into the city. Heavy drops of rain burrowed into the parched sand, followed by the long-feared outburst from the angry sky.

Wearing her only clothes, a summer dress and a thin blouse, Bluma stood huddled against a veranda trying in vain to cover her head with a bag. Suddenly the door of a nearby house opened. A woman with a man's coat thrown over her head pulled Bluma by the arm.

"Why are you standing in the rain? Come in."

Bluma remained in that house for two weeks. It was shared by two women, Maria Zilberzweig and Lola Gilbert. The housing authority had given them this house because their husbands, former Communist Party members in Poland, had been mobilized by the Russian Army and sent to the front. Sacks and bags belonging to the many people who spent their nights in the house were strewn all over. Often one had to crawl between bodies to find a sweater or a coat. Maria's two-year-old daughter loved to crawl on the cluttered floor; inevitably, she would get tangled up, then would cry and scream as if lost in a forest. The two women had no idea how many people they were giving shelter to. When there was no room in the house, some of the guests moved onto the veranda.

In the evening, as she sat on a knapsack, Bluma was overcome by memories. When, at last, roused from them she gave a sigh and wondered: "Is it really possible that I'll ever see my home again?"

The only ones who never spoke about returning home were Maria and Lola. When the Germans approached their city, they ran away to the country they had dreamt about for so long. They were good-hearted women, but nevertheless the guests rarely spoke in their presence.

Bluma left the house early in the morning to avoid getting in anyone's way. Half the day she spent in a queue waiting for her four hundred grams of bread. Then she wandered through the streets until nightfall in the hope of running into someone who might have somehow met her family.

One evening she returned earlier than usual. She stood for a moment in front of the door, then entered the house. Her feet were ice cold. The sticky mud which had seeped in through the holes in her shoes squelched with each step. During the previous night a blizzard had struck the city, leaving behind wet snow, knee-deep. But by midday the sun had left no trace of the snow; only mud remained, covering the unpaved streets. Bluma felt a pulling in the loins and sharp pains under her left shoulder blade. "I must not get sick!" she murmured through clenched teeth. "I must live to see my children and Hersh-Leib again."

Sitting around a small rickety table, Maria and Lola raised their eyes in surprise, interrupting their discussion with a Russian woman.

"How come so early today?" Lola asked. "Any good news?"

"No, no news at all," Bluma answered, shaking her head. "My legs are numb from the cold."

While Bluma was removing her torn shoes, she overheard the Russian woman say:

"I don't lack anything. I even have more money than when my husband used to work as a civil servant. I can afford to take someone in to do the heavy housework, but I can't find anyone suitable. Sonia has her mother with her; the old woman plays with the children, cooks and cleans, while Sonia sits around with folded arms or goes dancing in the cultural park." She stood up to leave.

"Come again, Sonia Grigorievna," Lola said.

"Keep well," said Maria, accompanying her to the door. Bluma sat thoughtfully for a while, then asked Maria:

"What do you think, would she hire me?"

"You would do such work?"

"Why not? Am I better off doing nothing?" she asked, pointing to her cold, dirty legs.

"Speak to her," suggested Lola. "She lives close by, on Kalinina Avenue."

The next day Bluma began to work for Sonia Grigorievna, a generally amiable but nervous woman who tried hard to forget her peasant background and now wanted to show her neighbors that she too could afford to hire a person for the heavy housework.

A week later Bluma moved into a house in the Uzbek quarter of the city. With her earnings she bought a half-broken iron bed at the market. A sack of leaves served as a mattress. There was one shelf on the grimy wall; she placed her bowl on it and a patched-up pot which she had purchased with the hope of cooking the first meal for her family in it.

— VII —

Rumors began to spread that the Provisional Polish Government, which now made its home in London, was about to open offices in Central Asia for the purpose of registering its citizens and assisting them with food and clothing. About two weeks later, crowds of barefoot Poles and Jews in tattered clothes were encamped in front of a house on one of the side streets of Fergana to which trucks were hauling closed boxes and huge bales. Cans of condensed milk and old clothing were distributed, and for the Jews there was a special present: Matzoh for Passover from the Jewish communities of America.

Bluma received a velvet coat with baggy sleeves, adorned with spangles, which some American socialite had probably worn to the theater years ago. She went to work in the homes of the Russian commanders wearing this coat. People were accustomed to shabby clothes, torn shoes and bare feet, but the sight of this velvet theater-coat evoked smiles and laughter on the streets of Fergana. It didn't bother her; the more they gaped at her and laughed the prouder she became of the gift from America, whose smell of worn-out velvet reminded her of her home and imbued her with faith. She reasoned that her children and her husband would appear before her eyes as unexpectedly as the coat had come into her possession.

Day after day she continued going to the Regional Office to inquire about her family. One morning, out of desperation, she tried to hand some money to the clerk who worked at the main desk, in the hope that he would inform her at once if he heard anything. The clerk, a short man with short arms and a greenish-pale face like an unripe fruit, shoved her money aside and grumbled nastily. He gazed sternly at her; his eyes were unnaturally large behind the thick lenses of his glasses and seemed poised to swallow up his surroundings.

From the day she heard that some people had received news of the location of their families, an unremitting restlessness beset Bluma. It was particularly bad in the evenings when she was alone in her room and listened intently to every rustle from outside. The sudden arrival of spring, as though it wanted in those few short days of blossoming to dupe the world, upset her even more. The fragrant scent of almond trees burst through her small window, taunting her in her misery. It was two weeks before Purim and the air was already very stuffy. The Uzbeks brought their beds outside for the summer, and the small famished cows quickly began plucking away at the fresh grass while the wistful protracted cries of camels wafted over roofs and fences, like the sobs of abandoned children.

— VIII —

Bluma had been working all day cleaning Sonia Grigorievna's house in preparation for the First of May holiday. She finished work much later than usual. By the time she arrived at the regional office, it was closed. The next day, because of May First, it would also be closed. Two wasted days, she thought. There was nothing to do now but to drag herself home. On the way she felt a deep weariness in her limbs and an emptiness inside. Her strength suddenly gave way, abandoning her in the noisy holiday street. People were standing in long queues in front of shops where ration cards could get a half-pound of sugar and two dried fish. Men, holding cups and glasses, were streaming towards a booth at the end of

Lenin Avenue, where beer was being sold in honor of the holiday. The general mood of excitement and joyous expectation bore down on Bluma like an enormous weight.

The following morning she was roused by the voices of Uzbek children calling to each other over the clay walls. She felt nauseous and anxious. The nightmarish dream she had experienced sickened her, notably the image of its male protagonist, an Uzbek with a short gray beard and a tanned, ploughed-up face. Bluma was sitting next to him, atop a donkey-drawn cart. She felt as though she were in a cage; the hard planks pressed into her flesh as the cart rattled and shook over the desert sands hour after hour without pause. Bluma had no idea where she was being taken. Suddenly the donkey began to falter and sway from side to side. Bluma pulled the Uzbek's sleeve and alerted him to the situation with gestures. But he ignored her and continued to drive the animal, that was now crying with a human voice. The Uzbek lashed the animal across the back and the donkey lurched forward, pulling the cart to a ridge where the desert ended. A rocky slope descended into a dark abyss. On the other side hung a blazing sun; it came closer and closer to the gaping mouth, flames sprouting in all directions, a massive wall of fire. The donkey vanished into the blazing wall, dragging the wagon behind it. A moment later, Bluma felt the heat on her eyebrows and smelled the odor of singed hair. The Uzbek turned his head, with its slanting eyes, to her and brandished the whip at the flaming curtain. At that point Bluma awoke with a scream; she touched her head and face and the bed—only then did she realize that it was a dream.

She sat with folded arms on the bed and stared blankly across the room at the crannied wall. There was a knock at the door. Her knees were trembling as she went to open it.

"Who is it?" she asked.

"Good morning, Mrs. Zelinger. You didn't expect a guest so early, did you?"

Bluma didn't remove her gaze from the man who stood on the doorstep, his hat in his hands; she studied his blue, slightly protruding eyes and the firm lips between the two sharp vertical creases. She had seen him a number of times at the Polish government office. No one knew whether or not he was an employee there, because he seemed to come and go as he pleased, but one thing was certain: Leon Wasserberg had a great deal of influence. If someone was mistreated in the distribution of food and clothing, he immediately went to Leon's home to complain. Without a moment's hesitation, Leon Wasserberg took his walking stick and went to find out if the complaints were justified. He did not care about himself; he walked around with torn shoes and a worn-out jacket patched at the elbows. When the clerks, who were the first to snatch the American suits, suggested that he too take a suit because it simply wasn't proper for such an important official as he to go about in ragged clothes, he flatly refused. There were people who didn't even have ragged clothes, he answered them. Those who had known Leon Wasserberg before the war in Poland said that he was an outstanding lawyer as well as a city councillor and an indefatigable worker for the Socialist Labour Party. He was exiled by the Russians for his opposition to the Communist Party, and sent with his family to a labor camp near Archangelsk. There, under the most severe conditions, he comforted and encouraged everyone he came in contact with. All this Bluma had overheard during the long hours on the benches of the Polish government office. And now he was standing in her room while she rubbed her hands on her apron, lacking the courage to ask him what had brought him here. At length, she blurted out something quite irrelevant:

"How did you find out where I live?"

"Your address can be found at the office. Yesterday while I was going through the mail I came upon a letter which will interest you. It's a reply to our inquiries concerning your family."

Bluma's mouth fell open. Leon Wasserberg stepped up to her and smilingly put his hand on her shoulder. "There's no longer anything to worry about. Here is your family's address."

Bluma held the paper in her hands for a long time after Leon Wasserberg had left, drinking in with her eyes each letter, examining each stroke separately.

—IX—

And so began the vigil for news from Hersh-Leib and the children. Bluma awaited restlessly the day when they would arrive in Fergana. How she would pamper them. She took pleasure in opening the little sacks of flour, rice and beans which she had accumulated little by little from the Russian families where she worked. She couldn't pull herself away from her treasure. How happy she was that she hadn't used any of it for herself— her heart had told her all along that she would find them.

Now she began to worry about Rivelle. What would she tell Hersh-Leib and the children? It was because of her that she had left them, and now who knew if the child was still alive. Secure in the knowledge that her family was well, she concentrated all her thoughts on the lost child. In her sleep as in her waking hours she tried to imagine the places where she might be, how she looked and how she spoke.

Although it was only the end of May, it was so hot that one could have cooked an egg in the sand. The grass reddened, then darkened like the shabby skin of a diseased animal. Four weeks had passed since Bluma had sent off the first letter to her family and still there was no reply. In the Polish government office, which she still visited regularly for more information, fewer and fewer people were to be found. Some had died of typhoid, others of malaria, and still others from exhaustion and grief. The hope that they would soon be able to return to Poland darkened under the news reports from the fronts. No one stopped any longer near the radio speakers on Lenin Avenue. They were tired of hearing the names of cities and regions that had fallen to the mercilessly advancing German armies. The rumors that all Polish citizens would be evacuated to Iran were confirmed. But the Jews, even the ones who had been officers in the Polish Army, were refused permission to emigrate. A bitter certainty settled upon them: one way or another—on the earth or beneath it—they would have to remain in this miserable land.

One evening Bluma heard the barking of the neighbor's dogs and the screaming of Uzbek children.

"The Polish woman lives over there!" they shouted.

Before Bluma had time to walk down the steps, Gitelle, her eldest daughter, fell weeping into her arms.

"Mummy, Mummy!" she sobbed.

"Gitelle, it's you. Don't cry, my child, don't cry. We'll never part again, Gitelle—do you hear?—never!" Gitelle hugged her mother, burying her face in her shoulder. "Why did you come alone, Gitelle? Where's Father and the children?"

The child clung desperately to her, her emaciated body trembling, as if afraid of falling. Bluma led her slowly to the bed and covered her shaking body. She caressed the child's legs; how thin her body had become and how loose the skin. Under Gitelle's half-closed eyes lay reddish bags of swollen flesh.

"You'll have something to eat," said Bluma.

"Don't go, Mummy. I can't eat."

Bluma felt a stab in her heart at the sound of these words.

"Can you tell me how Father is and the children?"

Gitelle avoided her mother's eyes.

"Mummy, there's no one left," she murmured through lips which barely moved. "I alone survived. God punished me: he let me live so I'd have to bring you this terrible news." The room grew still.

—X—

Bluma didn't leave the room for days at a stretch. She stood like an animal over her child, muscles taut, ready to leap at anyone who threatened her. Her mind was clear, occupied with only one thought: she had to save Gitelle, at least her.

The Jewish doctor Izgur came every day. He took Gitelle's temperature and repeatedly advised Bluma to give her a lot of milk and cheese, and most importantly to let her rest. But the shrunken body could no longer digest the food which Bluma purchased in the market with her meager savings. The swelling in Gitelle's legs spread constantly upward. The child no longer had control over her body. A greenish fluid oozed from her skin.

One night Gitelle sat up in bed, leaned her head against Bluma's knee and began to speak very quickly as though she were being chased:

"I have to tell you everything, Mummy. They all died of hunger. Father refused to eat non-kosher food. Chaiml also. Nothing grew in the fields that we could eat. We got only a little bit of bread and had to work all day. The sun burned and there was no shade. Once I brought home a little soup from the kitchen, like you used to do. But Father didn't trust me; he looked into the pot and found out right away. He took the pot and poured out all the soup. Yossele died first, then Chaiml right after him. Father, Itta and Zelda died in one week. I had to bury them alone, Mummy. Alone."

Gitelle grew weaker with each passing day. The swelling had reached her heart and rashes broke out around her wrists and neck. Dr. Izgur could not do anything for her. Nevertheless, he continued coming, if only to calm Bluma.

A week later Bluma was mourning her eldest daughter. With glazed eyes she stared at the disordered bed, where only a day earlier her daughter had lain. Bluma was utterly alone in the world, and now she had to endure the greatest punishment of all—her own life.

—XI—

The letter was brought to her in the morning. Bluma didn't notice who had entered the open door and placed the brown envelope on the chair at her side. In the evening, when she accidentally pushed the chair, she noticed it. The white neatly folded sheet of paper opened before her with words that seared her heart. Rivelle's name leapt forth from the paper. Bluma read every line slowly, after a pause, afraid of the lines that followed. The letter stated that Rivelle had been located. A Russian couple had found the abandoned child and later turned her over to an orphanage, where she had remained until now. When the Polish citizens in that region were being registered, one of the registrars was told that a young Polish girl was living in the orphanage. The last sentence of the letter said that the child would be brought to Fergana as soon as possible.

Bluma sat all night with the letter in her hands. When she heard the first crowing of roosters, she went outside. In the distance, beyond the rows of huts and fields, the clouds slanted down to the earth like a veil. To the west, a granite sky reigned, interwoven with tired stars and a pale moon. All at once, the eastern horizon was ripped open and a red sun broke through the narrow fissure like a ripe fruit, the surrounding mists gradually becoming more transparent. In the distance the Pamir Mountains were unfolding, standing like guards in a semi-circle, surrounding the gray wasteland, their snow-covered peaks shimmering with a pinkish hue.

Beyond those mountains was a free world. She would take her child there, Bluma decided. No one would take this child from her. She would toil night and day for her. Rivelle would lack nothing. Bluma closed her eyes and saw herself tying her grandmother's ear-ring around Rivelle's neck—it would serve as an amulet against all that is cruel and evil in the world.

Translated from the Yiddish by Abraham Boyarsky

Rochl Korn *was born in Poland in 1898 and began her writing career as a poet. Her work was published in Polish and Yiddish, and her writing was awarded numerous prizes.*

The Greenhorn

Chava Rosenfarb

"Why do you stand there like a telegraph pole not saying a word? You want the job—okay; if not, get lost. There's plenty of others to take your place." This is how the foreman speaks to Barukh, all the while dialing a telephone number.

Barukh, a slender young man with a bent back, who wears a pair of glasses with cheap frames, blinks at the foreman as if he were straining to see him better. Finally, he answers: "Yes, I will take it."

The foreman does not hear. He is busy speaking into the phone. His English sounds like Polish Yiddish, but the words are incomprehensible. Finally, he finishes the conversation, hurriedly replaces the receiver, and turns his eyes again on Barukh. "*Nu? Ni? Well?*"

"Yes," Barukh answers again. He stares at the ring which the foreman wears on the little finger of his right hand. Mechanically, Barukh slides his hand into his left pocket and rubs his bare ring finger with his thumb, a habitual gesture whenever he feels lost. It was she who had once given him a ring. Their friends had mocked the gift as hopelessly bourgeois, but he had worn the ring with pride. Until that day. . .

"All right," the foreman exclaims. Barukh jumps as if jarred from sleep. "You punch in at ten o'clock." The foreman steps quickly behind a counter made of raw plywood, pulls a pencil from behind his ear, and prepares to write. "How do you spell your name?"

Barukh spells his name.

"How old are you?"

"Forty-one."

"Wife? Children?"

"Gone."

"All right. Go and punch in. There under the clock. You mean you never punched a card before?"

"Never."

The foreman accompanies him to the clock and punches the white card for Barukh. "Your number is sixty-one. Your card must always lie right here. You punch in four times a day. What did you do before?"

"I've only been here for three weeks."

"I mean there, over there."

"In Warsaw I was a typesetter for a Polish newspaper."

"Go hang yourself up over there," the foreman chuckles, motioning towards Barukh's coat. "I'll put you to work at the press. Do you know how the press works?"

"No."

"All right. François!" The foreman's voice booms over the noise of the machines. From somewhere deep within the shop, there is a flash of a striped red shirt. A scrawny blond fellow appears from between the racks hung with finished coats. He looks to be about sixteen years old. Two knots of curly hair cling moistly to his forehead. With both hands, he wipes the sweat from his boyish face.

Barukh hangs his coat on an empty coat rack. The solitary coat looks forlorn, and even more bedraggled than it actually is. It is no longer the season for wearing heavy winter coats, but Barukh cannot help himself. He cannot seem to get warm in this country, and he does not find the coat too warm for spring. He notices that the foreman and François wink at one other in amusement as they glance mockingly at the heavy coat.

"*Montrez garçon* pressing," the foreman says to François, indicating Barukh.

Barukh smiles shame-facedly at François, and follows him through the shop, negotiating his way first between the racks of coats and then between the rows of roaring machines. Here and there, workers look up as he passes. Some glance at him indifferently, then drop their eyes back to their work. Others stare at him with curiosity. The indifferent eyes belong to men, the curious ones to women. The men working at the machines are all middle-aged and almost all are bald. The women are almost all young and pretty. They are French. That little one over there, for instance, the one sewing buttons—what big warm eyes she has. And the ringlets around her head are thin and so light that the glow from the lamp shines through them.

François and Barukh come to a place in the shop where eight presses are arranged in a large rectangle. Next to each press stands a half-naked young man with unkempt hair. Steam rises from the ironing boards.

The heat hits Barukh in the face. "Speak English?" François asks him with a smile.

"No. French a little."

"*Vous êtes français?*"

"No. I just lived in Paris for a while."

"Ah, Paris!" Barukh can feel his stock rising in the young man's eyes.

The work, it seems, is not too difficult. One must lay out the pockets, the belts and other small items on a board, and then lower the press by hand. The first few pieces Barukh tries do not come out well, but François assures him that he will learn. Of course, he will learn. If only it weren't so hot here. He is covered in sweat, even though the window fans are constantly whirring. There should be some air, even a little breeze. Why is it so hard to breathe? He had better take off his tie, unbutton his collar and roll up his shirt-sleeves. It's airier that way. But in another minute, he again feels the sweat running down the back of his ears onto his neck. The shirt sticks to his back and rivulets of moisture tickle his spine. He will just have to get used to it. It's merely a question of becoming acclimatized, he tells himself. But his head aches, as if a thousand hammers were pounding inside, and his legs buckle beneath him—just as they did on that hot dark day that has not yet come to an end.

A bell. What is that ringing suddenly? As if by magic, all the machines stop. The shop catches its breath in the momentary silence. Of course: it is noon—lunchtime. At a loss, Barukh stands by his press and stares at the others rushing past him. No one looks at him.

Suddenly, he finds himself confronted by a pair of warm eyes. The girl who sews the buttons is standing next to him. "*Comment-ça va?*" she asks. For the first time, it strikes Barukh that French-Canadian French is full of charm. He attempts to smile, but immediately senses that his smile is foolish and without cheer. "*Vous êtes Parisien, n'est-ce pas?*" she asks.

How could she know this so quickly, Barukh wonders. "Yes . . . no," he stammers and explains that he only lived in Paris for a year.

"Oh, as a visitor."

"No, as a DP."

"Oh." She nods knowingly, but from the expression on her face, he realizes that she has no idea what this means. "Have you punched your card?" she asks. He shakes his head. "So come."

He lets her lead him to the clock and slides his card in upside-down. "No, not that way," she exclaims, taking the card out of his hand and sliding it in the proper way. She has a small hand. The pallor of her skin is even more evident against the bright-red of her polished nails. She smiles at him in a friendly way. "Aren't you going home for lunch?"

"I have no home."

Her smile displays two rows of tiny perfect white teeth. "So where do you sleep? On the street?"

"I have a room that I rent, but I have no home."

She finds this amusing, and bursts into laughter, giving him a friendly slap on the back. "Let's go eat. You can get some Coke outside at the counter. *Bon appetit.*"

He looks after her as she walks back down the length of the shop to her table. Her high-heeled shoes click against the floor with a light wooden tap. The white nylon blouse she is wearing trembles against her skin and the large flowers on her colourful skirt wrap themselves around her legs like a dancing bouquet. The girl possesses a carefree light-heartedness which makes Barukh feel more acutely the weight of the despair that he carries within himself.

He glances around the shop. Here and there workers sit by their machines absorbed in eating. Next to the window stands a group of Jews, chatting. The smoke from their cigarettes hangs in a cloud over their heads. Across the way, in the darker side of the hall are groups of young men and women, some of whom lie stretched out across mounds of raw fabric. Barukh can hear their whistles and their laughter. They are French Canadian. Why didn't a Jewish girl come over to me, he wonders. He looks about him. Where are all the young Jewish women? Better they should be anywhere rather than here in this damp sweaty shop. Better they should work in offices, or study, or be the mothers of small Jewish children.

Suddenly his thoughts focus on his own two children, who perished during the war. They are dressed in their holiday clothes and are seated on a high sofa. They peer into the camera and wait for the birdie to appear.

Barukh walks slowly over to the window. On the large table nearby lies an open *Forward*. A young man with an uneven bald spot, which he has attempted to cover with a thick strand of hair, lifts his dark unshaven face as Barukh approaches. Barukh asks if that is today's *Forward*. The young man shakes his head and once more lowers his bald head over the paper. Barukh's eyes skim the headlines. Nearby stands the group of Jews, discussing politics. A heavy-set Jew waves his index finger threateningly in the face of his listeners. He is wearing a green Bermuda shirt with a flowery design in loud colours and his collar is open.

"You have to be an American to appreciate who MacArthur was. Small thing, MacArthur! A folk hero!" he sputters. "What do you know about MacArthur? Listen . . ." He grabs the sleeve of one of his listeners, but the other, a flabby middle-aged Jew with a pointy nose and small merry eyes, laughs and interrupts him.

"Listen, shmisen." The flabby Jew pulls up his baggy pants. "Better ask us greenhorns who the folk heroes are. Believe me, mister, the biggest folk hero would be a lot bigger if you made him a head shorter. And you better cut out that song and dance about being an American."

"Did I knock the crown off your head when I said that you have to be an American?" asks the Jew in the Bermuda shirt, nervously winding the large gold watch on his wrist.

"Heaven forbid, my friend! You are too short to reach my crown! Do you really think that we greenhorns know nothing and understand nothing? Believe me, there are many things which you could learn from us."

"Like what, for instance?"

"A little bit of humanity, a little bit of friendliness."

"*Oh va!* No more no less!"

"You should know that," intercedes another greenhorn. "If you had come to us, after the kinds of troubles we've lived through, we would have welcomed you with open arms."

"Oh, when will there ever be peace between the old-timers and the newcomers?" one of the listeners sighs.

"When the Messiah comes," smiles the Jew with the merry eyes.

"Do you think that they will welcome the Messiah better than they did us? He will be a greenhorn, after all."

"Their Messiah has already come. They don't need anything more, those old-timers."

"Why are you talking nonsense?" explodes the Jew in the Bermuda shirt. "Do you think that my Messiah has come already? Of course, he has. I've blackened my life with forty years work at the sewing machine. Forty years, I tell you. And I'm still at the same level as you. What do you want from me anyway? What have I taken from you? What do I owe you? I like this country. What are you going to do about it? You don't approve, so go back where you came from."

An uncomfortable silence falls on the group, which disperses slowly and with seeming regret. For the first time, someone takes note of Barukh. "Are you new?"

Barukh nods.

"Where do you come from?"

"From Paris."

"A Parisian?"

"No. From Warsaw."

"Were you in Russia?"

"No. In the camps."

"Did you run into anyone from Ozorkov?"

"Only after the war."

"Did you ever hear of the family Zlotnik?"

"No."

A new circle has formed around Barukh and his questioner. Someone else eagerly addresses a question to Barukh: "Did you say you are from Warsaw? Where in the city did you live?"

"On Krochmalna Street."

"I'm from Otvotsk. My father had a cigarette stand next to the highway. You probably know . . ."

Otvotsk. Barukh sees himself with her on one of their first excursions together. He breathes in the air of Otvotsk, and inhales deeply. Cigarettes! He is suddenly overcome by a powerful urge to smoke. He deserts his companions and hurries away to the stand where his coat is hanging solitary and forsaken. He puts his hand into his pocket, extracts the pack of cigarettes and lights one. He inhales deeply. The air of Otvotsk burns and grates against his throat.

Suddenly the little French Canadian with the warm eyes is at his side again. The unease inside him grows. "Give me a cigarette," her red lips smile at him. He extends the pack of cigarettes towards her. She pulls one out and puts it in her mouth, waiting for a light. Her mouth is close to him, and there is a pleasant coolness emanating from her fingers. He feels drawn to this carefree girl, just as earlier he had been drawn to his cigarettes. "Did you enjoy it?" she asks, and seats herself on a nearby table.

He watches her. "What?"

"What do you mean what? The lunch." He smiles crookedly and shakes his head. She plays with the folds of her colourful skirt, and stares at him steadily with her laughing eyes. "Tell me something about Paris," she implores in an oddly childlike voice. "To have lived for a whole year in Paris! *Mon Dieu!* Some people have all the luck."

He looks at her legs dangling from the table. Small blond hairs peek through her nylon stockings. "Paris?"

"Yes, Paris."

Suddenly the girl vanishes, and Barukh sees himself in a dirty Paris hotel room. He remembers how he had to be constantly registering with the police and how he had to stand in line for days on end in front of the JOINT distribution offices. He remembers all the worries about having proper papers, about getting the proper tickets for the boat. "Yes, certainly, a beautiful city," he mutters.

"*N'est-ce pas?*" she exclaims. "Paris is my dream. What sorts of things did you see there? Tell me."

"Oh, the Eiffel tower . . ." He remembers a walk he took on a brilliant Saturday. The Trocadero was bathed in light. The fountains spat streams of crystalline water into the air. He did not have enough francs to buy a ticket to ride up the Eiffel tower.

"And I'm sure you went walking on the Champs Elysées," she remarks with enthusiasm.

"Of course." He sees the Champs Elysées as it was in the blue summer twilight. He spent many hours wandering about there, until, one day, he was accosted by a vision that froze his heart. He saw a woman standing by the exit to the metro. It was she! His wife. She had a suitcase in her hand, and was looking uncertainly about her. He knew that this could not be his wife, because he had seen his wife in the Umshlagplatz, the gathering place for those about to be deported to their deaths. Even so, with bated breath, he started to run towards the woman, only to be confronted by a pair of strange frightened eyes as he drew near her.

"And how are the Parisian women dressed? Very stylish and elegant, *n'est-ce pas?*" The girl looks into his face, as if she could find there the entire splendor of Paris. "Why are you silent? Tell me." Suddenly she giggles. "I guess you're not an expert on women's clothing. You certainly don't look like one. But you surely went to the opera and the theatre every night, didn't you?"

He remembers the few open-air concerts that he attended in Paris, and the gnawing despair that accompanied his return home after each one. His wife had played the violin. On their way to the ghetto, the violin had fallen from her hand and an oncoming wagon filled with furniture had run over it.

"They have some wonderful nightclubs there, don't they?" The girl's eyes are no longer laughing. They are large and eager. There is such a thirst in them! "They drink champagne there as if it were water, the music plays, and people dance in the half-darkness, while the voice of Edith Piaf comes over the loudspeaker, *'je vous aime . . .'*" She bends closer to him, and flutters her lashes seductively. But his desire for her has dissipated. "And tell me"—she is not yet tired of questioning him—"have you seen other countries as well?"

"I've seen them."

"And I've never been anywhere except Montréal and Trois-Rivières. That's where I was born. If you only knew how much I like to hear stories about other countries!" Once again, her face takes on a childish dreamy quality. He would gladly stroke her head, as if she were a little girl. "Where else have you been? Tell me," she implores.

"In Poland," he answers. "That's where I was born, in a city called Warsaw."

"Oh, Warsaw is really far! Did you like the city?"

"In the past I did."

"And today?"

"Today the city seems alien to me."

"Why? Well, of course, it's been a long time since you've been there."

"I am still there."

"What do you mean?"

"My childhood is there, and my youth is there, and my dearest possessions are all there. All that mattered to me is there, and it is all gone."

"I don't understand what you're saying."

"How can you understand? You were born in Trois-Rivières."

"Never mind that stuff. Tell me where else you've been. Go on. Tell me."

"I was in Czechoslovakia, in Austria, in Germany, in Italy . . ."

"Jésu Marie! You've seen the entire world! Were you so rich? You must have been one of the richest people in the world."

"No, one of the poorest."

"You were a businessman, weren't you?"

"No. A DP."

"I don't understand."

"In English it's called a 'displaced person'."

"Oh, you mean a displeased person. That's what I am too." She breaks into a full-throated laugh. Her voice is lusty and youthful. How long it has been since Barukh heard such laughter! But he cannot join in her mirth. He does not even smile. He feels suddenly claustrophobic and ill-at-ease. He leaves the girl sitting where she is and strides towards the door.

At the exit, behind the plywood counter, sits the foreman holding a bottle of Coke to his mouth. "Hey you! Come over here," he calls to Barukh.

Barukh's heart skips a beat. Someone else once called to him in just that tone of voice. The foreman takes Barukh's measure with a pair of cold eyes. Someone else once took his measure in just that way. Barukh has a feeling that this coming encounter is a replay of an encounter that happened some time in the past. Yes. He is in the concentration camp. There is about to be a selection. He hides behind the barrack. If he shows up at the selection, he is lost. He is too bloated. Suddenly, he hears a voice. "Hey, you, come over here!" Before him he sees the Jewish kapo. A raised fist lands on his back. Barukh falls into the mud. "Come. You are going to clean the latrines!" the kapo barks. At that moment, Barukh feels the stirrings of love for the fist that knocked him down. He is ready to kiss it in gratitude, because it has granted him his life.

"So, how do you like the job?" The foreman's voice sounds mocking.

All of Barukh's senses are awake. This is not the camp. This is freedom, this is the God-blessed country of Canada. The foreman's voice grates on him. "I told you already I like it," he snaps.

The foreman rises, and bangs the bottle of Coke against the plywood table. "So you told me already, eh? So now the question is, do I like you? He's told me already, the big shot with the manicured fingernails! That's some way to talk!" From under the counter, he abruptly pulls out the work which Barukh has done in the previous few hours, and lays it out with jerky fingers on the counter. Curious workers gather around, holding sandwiches in their hands and guzzling drinks. The foreman stares at them and shouts self-righteously. "Good work, eh? Ruined a few dozen pockets and belts."

"I told you that I'm not a presser," Barukh coldly replies.

"So, you told me again! You never stop telling me. Maybe you will tell me now how to run my business."

"I don't know what you want from me."

"He doesn't know what I want from him! You hear that? The guy ruins a few dozen pockets and belts and hasn't got a clue what the matter is. I ask you again, do you want this job?" Barukh careful nods yes. The foreman wags a finger at him. "So once and for all you should know, that I am the boss here and not you, greenhorn! You do as I say and as I please. And if you don't like it, you can go to hell." Having said his peace, the foreman reseats himself on the stool.

Barukh can feel his hands knotting into fists. One stride and he is standing in front of the plywood counter, his hot face breathing into the face of the foreman. "You can't talk to me like that!" he shouts.

But the foreman's eyes have lost their metallic edge. Unconcerned he pushes Barukh out of the way, unpacks his smoked meat sandwich and bites into it with large eager teeth.

Barukh is transported by his own rage. "Don't you talk to me like that! This is a free country. Understand?"

The foreman chews, shrugs, puts a finger to his temple and smiles at the others, motioning towards Barukh. "Crazy."

The others smile back meaningfully.

Barukh is beside himself: "You are not the boss of my life, do you hear? I am a human being, just like you. Just like you!" he shouts, his voice growing increasingly louder, the smaller he feels inside. "You will not curse me! No! I've heard enough curses in my life."

"So why don't you get lost!" the foreman laughs. "Did you ever hear such a thing?" he turns to the others. "I'm supposed to talk to him through a silken handkerchief. Who do you think you are, greenhorn?

And where do you think you are? In Bronfman's livingroom, maybe? This is a shop."

"Yes, a shop," Barukh retorts hotly. "But a modern shop, not from a hundred years ago. Those curses were fine then."

"Really? You would prefer some modern curses, then? Well, I'm an old-fashioned foreman. Go, do me something!"

"But we are modern workers. We won't stand to be insulted from such nothings like you. We have unions."

The workers, who have been listening to this exchange in silence, suddenly break into laughter. One of them, slaps Barukh on the back in a comradely way. "Here is not like back home, my friend."

Someone else waves his hand derisively. "This one is a real greenhorn from greenhorn land."

Barukh gives up the argument. He feels lost. He is alone, utterly alone in this strange place. All around him the workers are conversing in heated tones, discussing unions and wages. The foreman stares at Barukh with mock-innocent eyes. He unpacks another smoked meat sandwich and bites into it with relish. Barukh feels silly. He wipes the sweat from his forehead with a dirty piece of kleenex, and does not know what to do with himself. The bell rings. Still conversing, the workers go to the clock and, one after another, punch in their cards.

The little French Canadian appears next to Barukh. "Here. Have a chiclet." Her white hand pushes a piece of chewing gum between his lips. The tips of her fingers are wonderfully cool against his mouth.

Suddenly the foreman stands up and calls "François!" The thin boy with the large mop of hair appears by his side. "*Montrez garçon* pressing! Good pressing. Remember! And if you don't, may the holy plague take you, you goyish blockhead."

"Okay, boss," François nods smilingly, revealing two protruding front teeth. He pulls Barukh by the sleeve. "Come on."

Barukh would like to run away, but the foreman is smiling at him. "Why are you standing there like a telegraph pole with your eyes popping out? Go punch your card." The foreman's voice sounds paternal, forgiving.

Barukh punches his card. This time he does it correctly. Then he returns to the press machine. The heat beats against his face. Once again, the sweat runs in a stream down his back. The fans whirr, the machines

roar rhythmically. The little French Canadian is sewing buttons somewhere between the racks of finished clothing. Barukh chews on his gum.
A drop of sweetness melts in his mouth and soothes his temper.

Translated from the Yiddish by Goldie Morgentaler

Chava Rosenfarb *was born in Lodz, Poland. She is a survivor of
the Lodz Ghetto and of Auschwitz and Bergen-Belsen. She came
to Canada in 1950. Her Yiddish-language novels include the three-
volume* The Tree of Life, *which won Israel's prestigious Manger
Prize. Her own translation into English of the novels* Bociany *and*
Of Lodz and Love *won the John Glassco Prize for Literary Translation.*

Thin Ice

Norman Levine

In the Spring of 1965 a book of mine was published. And it got more notice and sold more copies than all my previous books combined. It was translated into several languages. The CBC and the BBC made half-hour films because of it. It went into paperback. Money began to come in from various places. Someone in Madrid wanted to use extracts in an English for foreigners textbook. Someone in Halifax wanted to make a recording of it for the blind. I was interviewed for British newspapers and magazines. Articles were written. I received a number of invitations: to open a new primary school in Cornwall, to give talks, to give readings. And one invitation came from the head of the English department of a university in the Maritimes offering three months as resident writer beginning in January. As I didn't know the Atlantic provinces and as I wanted to be back in Canada, I decided to go.

I arrived by plane on January 6th. I was met at the airport which consisted almost entirely of fields of snow piled high and long drifts. 'I can't remember when we've had so much snow and such cold weather,' the head of the English department said. 'We're blaming the Russians.'

His face reminded me of an Indian Chief but he smiled easily and was smartly dressed in a black winter coat, a white scarf, and a black Astrakhan hat that he wore tilted to the side. He drove, in a large low car with chains on the tires, to the best hotel in the city and led me to the top floor, to two comfortable rooms.

'Will this be all right?'

'Yes,' I said.

Suddenly the life of a near-recluse that I had lived before changed. I was in demand. I was interviewed for the student newspaper, the town's daily paper, the local radio and TV. I was invited to contribute a regular article to the local monthly magazine. The commercial radio station would phone up and ask what did I think of a particular current topic? And what I said on the phone was taped and then broadcast. There was a display of my books and manuscripts (in glass cases) in the university library. The main bookshop in the place filled a window with my books. I gave talks and readings to a variety of women's and men's clubs. The leading Jewish businessman, Pettigorsky (he owned the largest department store), gave a dinner in my honour at the Jewish community centre. After a filling meal (that included soup and mandlen, chicken, blintzes, and lockshen kugel) and I had made my speech and everyone was standing up and drinking and smoking, Mr Pettigorsky came over.

'It will take you a while to get used to living here,' he said apologetically. 'The first year you'll hate it. The second won't be so bad. After you have lived here three years you won't want to leave.'

But I liked it from the start.

I enjoyed going to the various teas, luncheons, and dinners. I liked being asked to meet visiting VIP's who were passing through. Besides professors and undergraduates, I was also meeting judges, politicians, engineers, surgeons, scientists, army officers, restauranteurs, businessmen.

And I had this warm office in the Arts Building that overlooked the snow-covered campus and the city. I would go to the office, twice a week, and there would be people outside the door waiting to see me. I was like a doctor. Undergraduates would come—possibly with their ailments, but they would express it differently. Girls would say: 'My boyfriend's too shy to come, but I've come,' and say that he was trying to write a novel.

I was the first resident writer the university or this town had. And, after the early hectic weeks, it was mainly people not to do with the university who came to see me.

The first were two Army Officers' wives from the large Army camp some miles outside the city. They told me that they were from Toronto and Vancouver and were only temporarily at the camp. They were going to put on a musical and wanted my approval. They intended to use the tunes of familiar songs—"Somewhere over the Rainbow", "You Made Me Love You", "It's All Right with Me"—but they would put their own words to the tunes. And these words were to be witty comments on local events, especially Army camp gossip.

'We thought of beginning,' said the lady from Toronto, 'by having a voice come over the loudspeaker. It would be a pilot on Air Canada speaking to his passengers. "You are now approaching the Maritimes—please put your clocks back fifty years."'

Most of the others wanted to tell me things.

When I was having a haircut the barber thought I should know the best ways to hunt duck and moose. A scientist, in charge of a unit to help the surrounding farmers improve their productivity, came over after a reading and said.

'This is a true story. I thought I would tell it to you. Perhaps you can use it. There was this priest. He lived in the country near here. He was middle-aged. And he liked women, especially girls. Whenever he went to visit people who were sick in hospital or at home—if they were girls—he put his hand underneath the covers. Things got so bad that the local mothers got together and wrote to the Bishop. Finally the priest was moved. And he was replaced by a much younger man. This young man didn't have the other's habits. But he began to ask for things. He said he needed a new car. The old one was too old. He wanted the house redecorated. Some special food he liked had to be flown in from Montreal. He wanted the best cigars. After a while the people again wrote to the Bishop this time complaining at the money this young priest was costing them.

'Being chaste is expensive, the Bishop wrote back.'

And Peter, the young owner of a Chinese restaurant where I sometimes went to eat, told me that before coming here he attended university in Red China. He thought I should know the best way to steal chickens off a chicken farm.

'You get this candle,' Peter said. 'It only comes from China. When you light it it gives off smoke. And you let the wind blow this smoke over to where the chickens are. You do it at night. One whiff and the dogs go to sleep for twenty minutes. So do all the chickens. They just lie down and go to sleep. You get a handkerchief and put it around your mouth and pick up these sleeping chickens and put them in your truck. Twenty minutes later, when they wake up, you are miles away—'

I listened to the strangest confessions, humiliations, suffering. And, as if to balance them, an amazing endurance.

By the beginning of February I was so well-known in the town that strangers in the street would smile and say hello. A tall blonde woman with glasses came up to me: 'I saw your picture in the paper — it looks like you.' Kids stopped throwing snowballs to call out. 'I know you Mister—you write books.' When I went into a restaurant heads would turn.

Meanwhile the invitations kept coming in.

One of the early ones was from the Professor of English at St Vincent's — a teacher's college which was affiliated to the university. But as it was a hundred and sixty miles away, I kept putting it off. Until the head of the English department told me that St Vincent's was after him to get me to come.

'It will be the usual thing,' he said. 'A small dinner before. Then you give your reading at the college hall. And there will be a party afterwards.'

I agreed to go next Friday.

Four days later in the faculty club he came over. 'I've just got back from St Vincent's. They're very excited about you coming. They've got posters stuck all over the place. There is a piece about you in their local paper. And they have put you up at the best hotel.'

He ordered coffee and doughnuts for both of us.

'The Board of Governors asked me to tell you that you can be resident writer with us for as long as you like.'

'That's very nice,' I said.

I was to fly to St Vincent's at noon. But fog came on Friday morning. The planes were grounded. The train no longer ran although the tracks were still there.

I took a small green bus from the bus station. Four other passengers were on the bus at the start, but they got off at the small towns on the way. For the first hour the roads were clear. Then it began to snow. The wind increased. It turned into a blizzard. Fewer cars and trucks were coming from the opposite direction and more were abandoned by the sides of the road. The driver kept stopping to wipe the windshield. The snow was coming down so fast and thick that the wipers were not clearing it. Then he stopped at a filling station to get a tow-truck.

'We'll never get to St Vincent's today,' he told me.

'But I'm supposed to give a reading—'

'It's impossible. I can't get through.'

I rang St Vincent's, told the Professor of English the position. He said he understood, that the weather was bad there as well, and it would be best to postpone it.

I went back to the bus and sat inside.

'How about going back?'

'Nothing is getting through *either* way,' the driver said.

The tow-truck towed us for about an hour and a half—where I don't know—as I couldn't see for the falling snow. Finally we arrived in a small town. The street lights were on but there was hardly anyone in the street—snow covered everything.

I asked the driver when he would go back.

'Soon as the roads are open. There will be an inspection tomorrow morning at nine.'

I said I would be there.

I went to look for a hotel but as soon as I stepped off the main road I sank to my knees in snow. I walked that way until I came to cross streets—the road was covered with freshly fallen snow but it was hard-packed underneath. I finally found a sign on a drab looking wooden building that said it was a hotel.

'Can I have a room for the night?' I asked the man.

'It's eight dollars a night,' he said.

'OK,' I replied. And waited for him to give me the room key.

'Is that all your luggage?'

'Yes,' I said holding on to my attache case.

'If that is all your luggage you will have to pay in advance.'

'I'm the resident writer at the university and I was on my way to St Vincent's to give a reading when the blizzard came—'

'Is your car outside?'

'No. I came by bus.'

'And that is all your luggage?'

'Yes.'

'You will have to pay in advance—eight dollars.'

I paid him the eight dollars. It seemed a long time since I was treated this way. I took the key and went up the creaky stairs to Room 2 on the first floor.

It was a small gloomy room—the kind I used to have in my early days when I was poor. A bare light hung from the ceiling. And I needed it on all the time. There was an iron bed, a rickety wooden dresser. No chair.

A cracked enamel sink with only one tap working. And every time I turned on the tap it made a wailing noise. The wallpaper was stained. I felt cold. I went over to the thin green-painted radiator. No heat. There were two grey blankets at the foot of the bed and a disinfectant smell when I pulled back the covers.

I felt hungry and tired. I looked in my attache case and took out the toothbrush, the toothpaste, the shaving lather and razor, and the copy of my book that I brought for the reading. But in my rush, or absentmindness, I had forgotten to take my cheque book. Not that I would have had any luck cashing a cheque here.

I took out all the money I had and counted it. It came to nineteen dollars and some change. If I'm stuck here another night that's another eight dollars. The ticket back is ten dollars. That left me a dollar and the change. I counted the change—thirty-seven cents. No need to worry, I said, I might be able to get away tomorrow. What I need now is food (I had been five hours on that bus) and a good night's sleep.

I went out to find a restaurant. It was still snowing. I went to the main street. The stores were on one side. The other side consisted of open fields covered in snow and some trees that were almost hidden. I went into a small supermarket and bought a loaf of bread, a tin of sardines, and two apples. That left me forty cents to spare.

I came back to the room. I ate the bread and the sardines sitting on the bed with my coat on. Then I dipped pieces of bread in the sardine oil. And washed it down with an apple.

I lay on the bed with the coat and the grey blankets over me. I thought that now that I was earning my living from writing and giving readings I was past things like this.

I went to sleep. And when I woke I was hungry. I ate the rest of the bread with the last apple. I remembered from my hard-up days that it was important to have something to keep up morale. I went out, found a small restaurant, had a cup of hot coffee and asked the woman if she sold any cigars singly.

'These,' she said, 'are twenty-five cents each.'

I looked at it wondering if I had enough.

'This one is fifteen cents.'

I took the fifteen cents cigar, smoked it slowly. The tobacco was kind of green. I took a long time over the coffee. Then went back to the room in the hotel to lie down. Instead I went to sleep.

Next morning when I woke up I was cold. I brushed my teeth and shaved in cold water and went out. The snow was still falling but it wasn't so thick. I walked to the bus station. The bus was in the garage. I found the driver—a different driver—in a stand-up eating place next to the bus depot. He was finishing his breakfast.

'No—no buses today,' he said. 'Next inspection tomorrow.'

'What time?'

'Around nine in the morning.'

'I know the ticket back costs ten dollars,' I said. 'Could you give me a ticket. And I'll pay when we get back?'

'We don't run the company on those lines,' he said.

I felt hungry and light-headed.

'I'll buy you a cup of coffee.'

'Thanks.'

He paid for his breakfast and handed me the saucer with the cup of coffee.

'I'll see you tomorrow,' I said.

When he had gone—in my nervousness—I spilled half of the coffee before I had my first sip.

I went back to the hotel.

'I'll stay another night,' I told the man.

'That will be eight dollars.'

I paid him.

All I had left was the ten dollar bill. I put it in my back buttoned-down pocket.

'How cold is it?' I asked the man.

'Thirteen below. But near here it's been thirty-five below.'

Saturday morning, I thought I'll go to *shul*. It will be warm. There might be a Bar-Mitzvah or some kind of Kaddish afterwards.

'Is there a synagogue here?'

'No,' he said looking suspiciously at me.

'Where's the nearest church?'

He gave me directions.

It was a wooden church painted grey in a snow-covered field. There was a narrow path freshly cleared to the door. A few cars and a few trucks were sunk in the snow by it.

As I opened the door a man in an ill-fitting blue suit said.

'Bride or groom?'

I must have looked puzzled. For he said.

'What side are you? Bride or groom?'

'Bride,' I said.

'—to your left.'

I went to the left side and sat down on the wooden bench at the back beside the Quebec stove that had large tin pipes going up and across near the ceiling. I don't know what kind of church it was but it was very plain, very austere. There weren't any religious figures or stained glass windows. About thirty people were separated by a wide aisle. Those on one side looked at those on the other. We all had our coats on. Up ahead, slightly ahead, slightly raised, were the bride and groom. And the preacher in a plain grey suit. There was a small wooden organ to the right where a woman was playing.

The wedding ceremony didn't last long.

Afterwards the guests walked in ones and twos along the snow-covered street, icicles hung from the boarded-up houses, down a turning to the main street and to a better hotel. And at the top of the stairs, in the centre of a large room, the bride and groom were sitting, side by side, on chairs against a wall. The guests came up to them, in ones and twos, with their presents.

I stayed near the door. There was food. A buffet. I guess that friends and relations of the bride thought I belonged to the other side. Just as the other side thought I belonged to the groom.

'Where are you from?' a man asked me.

'Out of town,' I said.

I didn't stay long. Long enough to have three ham sandwiches and two cups of coffee.

Then I went back into the street.

For some reason I couldn't find the hotel where I was staying. The town wasn't that large. If you walked five minutes in one direction on the main street that was it. There were several side-streets to the one main— but I kept getting into places that ended in dead ends.

I managed to get back to the main street. The place was now packed with people walking, people shopping. Outside a music store, over a loud-speaker, someone was singing, 'Everyone's Gone to the Moon'.

I felt like a vagrant.

I saw a bit of ice on the road and with a run I went down it. I was hungry and cold. But when I came back to the room my cheeks were rosy.

I lay down on the bed. Because of these last few years I had forgotten how it was to be poor. Now that I was back in it, I was hungry. All that had happened to me since the last book was published seemed some kind of fraud. I was a writer. In my world nothing is certain. I needed this reminder, I told myself.

Now, I must get myself out of it. I tried to remember what I used to do. I went though the pockets—of my suit, my overcoat. Not a cent. In my hard-up days I always left a coin or two in the pockets. What could I sell? There was the copy of my book from which I was going to read at St Vincent's.

I went out again. I couldn't find a bookstore. But I did find a secondhand place that had a lot of junk (mostly furniture) lying inside in heaps all over the place. There were some battered paperbacks on the floor.

A woman finally came.

'Yes.'

'I'd like to sell you this book,' I said.

She picked it up, turned a few pages. I hoped she wouldn't come across the parts I had marked with a pen that I usually read.

She closed the book. 'Fifty cents.'

'It sells for $5.95. And it is almost new.'

'Take it or leave it.'

I took it.

If I had to stay another night I could try and sell her my watch. But she would never give me eight dollars for it—of that I was certain.

With the fifty cents I went out and got myself a hot dog and a cup of coffee. And wondered what I would do tomorrow if I couldn't go back.

Outside it had stopped snowing. I went to the hotel room. I felt hungry and cold and went to sleep.

Sunday morning I slept in. I looked at my watch—ten to nine. I didn't have time to wash or shave. I walked as quickly as I could to the small bus depot. The bus was outside, its engine running. The door was closed. The driver was not inside.

Two men, also unshaven and unwashed, were standing by the door.

'Is it going?'

'Yes,' they said.

I went into the office and gave the driver the ten dollar bill. He gave me a ticket.

When I came out the two men asked me if I could buy them a cup of coffee as they hadn't had any breakfast and they were broke.

'Sorry,' I said.

I got back to the University town at noon. That evening I was a guest at a dinner party given in the Army Camp, in the Officer's Mess of The Black Watch. There were fourteen of us, some with wives in evening dress. The young officers wore their dress uniforms. We sat in tall straight-backed chairs around the table. The lighting was by candles. We were waited on by two waiters. There was fish and white wine. Roast beef and Yorkshire pudding with red wine. Then champagne with some exotic dessert.

I looked at the others. They were young, attractive, well-fed, well-dressed. How secure they all appeared. And how certain their world.

But outside I could see the snow, the cold, the acres of emptiness that lay frozen all around.

Norman Levine was born in Ottawa. He spent thirty-one years in England, mostly in St Ives, Cornwall, before returning to Canada in 1980. His books include From a Seaside Town, Thin Ice, *and* Canada Made Me.

Lives of the Mind Slaves

MATT COHEN

When sandstorms, freezing cold, or sudden bursts of rain caused Nellie to cough or hesitate, Norman would caress the steering-wheel and murmur encouragingly, "Come on, Nellie. You can make it, Nellie." Or in desperate circumstances, "Nelliebelle honey, I love you." Nellie was a 1962 Ford V8. In her youth she had been maroon, a dark lustrous red endowed with flowing curves and a motor that could snap your neck back when you pressed her pedal to the floor. Those had been Nellie's salad days, and days and nights of her first youth, the years of careful washes and hand-shining, valve-jobs and cylinder re-fittings, the days when her engine always hummed with clear creamy oil and when her evenings were spent at drive-in movies, her springs gently rocking.

Nellie's first owner had cried real tears when he sold her to Norman. The deal took place in downtown Vancouver, outside a liquor store. That was where Norman saw her first. Drawn by her glowing curvaceous body he stepped closer to look at the FOR SALE sign taped inside a window. He was still wondering whether to copy down the telephone number when a man appeared beside him, kicking the tires, stroking the fins, talking in a low steady mumble which ended, "You wouldn't believe the loving I had in this car. But now the wife wants a station-wagon for the kids." The lover was a wispy-haired pot-bellied man with a sad smile.

Norman was tanned and streaky blond from a summer planting trees on Vancouver Island. The year before he had been crowned by a Ph.D.— an accomplishment rewarded by a job teaching remedial English to immigrants in Halifax. This was followed by his months on the island.

There Norman met his first Nellie: a young woman who wore white running-shoes and wanted to make love to him every night all night. Then arrived a letter from the McGill-Queen's University press offering Norman a contract to turn his thesis on "The Roots of Symbolism in American Narrative" into a book. Norman was lying on a beach as he opened the envelope. Reading the letter he felt the sun burn brighter. So it was good-bye to Nellie the human and hello to his new driveable Nellie. Destination: three thousand miles across the continent to McGill, where he had earned his degree, for six months of post-doctoral research. He didn't finish the book, but another piece of luck came along—the offer of an actual appointment, one-year extendable at the University of Calgary. A proud event, his first full year teaching, but due to a sudden plunge in the departmental budget the appointment was not renewed. Fortunately the sympathetic department chairman helped him find a life-saving two-year term as a sessional lecturer at the University of Winnipeg—at a much lower salary than he had been receiving in Calgary. After Winnipeg it was back once more to McGill for another two-year appointment, this time on the understanding that he would finally finish his book and—if he did— take his place in the pantheon of the tenured.

Between cities, jobs, universities, was the desert. The desert was emptiness. The desert was life with no future. Also, like any desert, it was dry and thirsty. Although during the day the sun burned hot, the night was cold and scary. Likewise fine weather was followed by storms of obfuscation. Life would have been not life at all had the dry and stormy desert not been punctuated by oases in the form of congenial pubs where fellow mind slaves could always be found. And after the slaking of thirst—so many thousands of mugs of draft had been consumed that Norman had the permanent taste of foam at the corners of his mouth—followed manna. Manna was love. Manna was emotional relief. Manna was the security of flesh compared with the insecurity of jobs with no future, students with no talent, tenured professors with no compassion. Manna was the pressing of body to body, the rites of sex the point of which was not so much ecstasy—though ecstasy he would not have refused —but the complicity of imperfect nakedness and sex, the sequel of long talks in the darkness about whether life in the desert could ever give way to something better.

At McGill the first time, he had met Elisabeth.

Dark, slim, with a brittle pretty face and a sharp laugh, she was a Blake specialist who taught part-time and most evenings spent an hour in the pub sipping beer before going home to make dinner for her lawyer husband. Norman was twenty-six then, Elisabeth almost thirty.

The second year in Winnipeg, she showed up again. By this time Norman was himself pushing thirty; and that year he developed the uncomfortable habit of looking closely at himself as he shaved. Lines had started to grow out of the corners of his eyes, his mouth had begun to take a particular downward turn, his hair which had been dramatic during the tree-planting summer was now brown, except at the temples where dustings of grey had mysteriously settled. Worse, the nights at the oases followed by manna/mamma had begun to sour. The love of many gave way to the love of one. When a fourth-year student dazzled and pursued him, he fell in love. After that it was no longer mind over matter, but vice versa. Love and jealousy, storms of passion and lightning moments of pure happiness. Then she had gotten pregnant. The pregnancy was announced in the summer after graduation. The girl, whose name was Ruth, told Norman about it one day at breakfast. As she leaned over the coffee, blue eyes opened wide and trusting—or so Norman believed at the moment—Norman had a picture of himself with a beautiful blue-eyed daughter in the circle of his arms. "Let's get married," he said.

That afternoon Ruth broke the news to her parents, who were big givers to the alumni fund. Scenes ensued. The parents, who had envisioned a brilliant academic future for their precocious daughter, complained to their good friend the university president. Ruth decided on an abortion. Norman was informed that although—technically—he had broken no laws and therefore could not be sued, his appointment would be terminated at the end of the following year. By September Ruth, womb scraped virgin clean, was off to graduate school at Harvard while Norman was left to contemplate his disgrace and his future.

When Elisabeth walked into the pub Norman didn't recognize her right away. Her face was fuller, and demarcation lines of bitterness divided eyes and cheeks. As it turned out, she no longer had a husband, but there was a child. It was two years old and like a queen talked about herself in the third person: "Mona wants a cookie. Mona wants ice cream."

"Mona wants to talk. Mona wants to sit down. Mona wants television." Norman took up with Mona. Every Saturday afternoon he called for her; once or twice a week he collected her at the day-care centre, then brought her home and fed her dinner. He told Elisabeth about what had happened to him with Ruth; she told Norman about her marriage. Recounting past disasters, struggling through a difficult evening with Mona, looking at Elisabeth across the kitchen, Norman felt as though he and Elisabeth had constructed for themselves a sort of shelter for battered survivors, an emotional refuge in which they were the patients, slowly healing, and Mona, unbeknownst to herself, the physician. One night Norman—to help himself get through a particularly excruciating set of essays—brought over a bottle of scotch and his six favourite Miles Davis records. Near midnight he became aware that he was upstairs, in the bathroom, splashing water onto his face. He raised his eyes to the mirror; his cheeks looked yellow and numb, which was also how they felt. When he stepped into the hall something in his blood went to sleep. "Something in my blood has gone to sleep," he said. Elisabeth was downstairs, listening to Miles Davis. She had her own essays to worry about and, Norman realized, they made her far too busy to be concerned about dormant aspects of his blood. He turned. He looked into Elisabeth's bedroom. She had a large bed and it was empty. Soon he was lying on his back. Time passed. Then he was lying on his belly, on top of Elisabeth. The light from the hall made her eyes glow, and the face that had been growing so familiar now seemed to belong to a stranger.

At the beginning of November Ruth phoned. Just her voice was enough to set him seething, whether with love or despair he had no idea. "I'm dying without you," she said. Norman, sitting alone in his half-furnished apartment, looked at his cold wooden floor littered with unread books, indigestible essays, the remains of half-eaten meals. "I'm dying without you," she had said. Norman wondering what it was he was doing without her. "Well?" she asked. Any protective layer he might have formed was now shattered. "Will you come to see me?"

"Yes," Norman said, his voice choking. And then Ruth said some things about how she had missed him and what she was eager to do to him when he arrived.

"This will be my most embarrassing moment," Norman announced to Elisabeth, thinking even as he spoke how odd it was that people like Elisabeth and him, chattels to a system which despised them, were in fact so enslaved that a clever little phrase could grease the stickiest situation.

But Elisabeth agreed to take his classes so that Norman could have a long weekend in the Promised Land.

The bus left Winnipeg at dawn. By the time the stony grey light of morning had filled the sky, they were on the highway. Thirty-six hours later he arrived in Boston—palms sweating, clothes soaked in cigarette smoke, stomach knotted from tension and white-bread sandwiches. Ruth, all smiles, received the weary traveller in her scented arms, brought him back to her apartment for a night of passionate love. Just as his stomach began to unwind, the recriminations began. Before Norman could unpack the clothes he had so carefully folded, he was on his way back to the bus station.

The last year at McGill, everything went wrong. First, Norman turned thirty-two. Until then he had been able to believe that the sojourn in the desert was a necessary part of the larger story. And, too, he had discovered no lack of fellow wanderers. Fellow, yes; there was strange fellowship in this life after fellowships, fellowship in the expertise in subjects about which no one else would ever care, fellowship most of all in the curious roles they all played—knights errant of the mind, intellectual mercenaries with knowledge for sale at cut-rate prices.

But the week after his thirty-second birthday Norman discovered he had contracted a "social disease." The doctor assured him that it was harmless, relatively speaking, and that a bottle of pills plus a month of abstinence would make him a new man. But they couldn't. Norman had been going seriously with a girl for the first time since Ruth. When confronted with the medical evidence, she admitted she was about to decamp and move in with someone else. "The thing is," Norman wrote to Elisabeth, "this would have been funny a few years ago. The wronged lover comes home to discover that his girlfriend wants to play house with the musician who has just given her VD. But now I'm too old. I don't want my life to be a comedy any more. I want to settle down, be loved, have children, enjoy the fruits of my labours. Is this not the natural destiny of man?"

"No," Elisabeth wrote back, "it is not the natural destiny of man—not of man, mankind, men, or you. If nature has anything in mind for you, Norman Wadkins, it is that, like all matter in the universe, you shall be subject to the second law of thermodynamics, to wit: decline, decrepitude, death."

"Thanks a lot," returned Norman.

"You missed my whole meaning," Elisabeth protested. She wrote her letters to Norman on departmental stationery. Nor were her letters posted from Winnipeg, as they had been in previous years. Now they emanated from Vancouver and were complete with weather descriptions. "Brilliant light. Mountains rising out of mist. Another heart-rending sunset." Even when it rained, Elisabeth persisted in lauding the softness of the falling water. "City of mountains, city of dreams," she called it in one letter. Not just for the scenery, Norman supposed, but also because Elisabeth had arrived at middle age in style: she was in Vancouver as an Associate Professor as well as being Assistant Dean of Women.

"What I mean is that although destiny has nothing special in mind for you, you could do something for yourself. Awake O Blind and Passive One! Join the club of positive thinkers! Have you ever considered being Saved? How wonderful it would be to know that God Was On Your Side. Failing that, you could at least finish that book. Others would kill for a contract with a good university press —you're sitting on yours like a neurotic student afraid to hand in that really big paper. What are you waiting for, Physician?—heal thyself."

When spring came he was offered a one-year terminal extension of his sessional appointment. In other words, they would hire him as slave labour for a final year, if he would promise to go away when it was over. Norman telephoned Elisabeth.

"Is that what you want?"

"Of course not."

"What are you going to do?"

"Tell them to hire me properly or stuff it."

"Good."

The next three days Norman spent writing a letter outlining his experience and pointing out that he was doing, for half the price, the work of tenured professors whose qualifications did not exceed his own. Proclaiming his own virtues, Norman found, was a strange experience. At the pub he complained that it made him feel like a prostitute. In fact, writing about himself he discovered that, parallel to his dubious life of intermittent affairs and jobs grasped in desperation, he had enjoyed a scintillating career grooming illiterates across the giant breadth of the country. By the time he had signed his letter and put it in the mail he was convinced that the university would reward his years of diligence with dignity and affluence.

He was wrong. The day he received his letter of refusal from the university he sold his furniture, his stereo, most of his books, and traded the proceeds, along with a clunker grandmother Nellie that only started in dry weather, for a Nellie young enough to know the meaning of kilometres. This newish Nellie, Nellie LaBelle he named her because he bought her from a woman in the French department, was a Japanese sedan with a leather-wrapped steering wheel, a built-in cassette player, and—Norman discovered when he was already on the highway—a glove compartment full of yearning country-and-western tapes.

From the day he arrived in Vancouver, the sky was always blue. And from Elisabeth's house he could see the mountains, their snow-peaked tops jutting into the sky like jagged postcards.

The idea was that he would live in the basement apartment as a paying tenant. Even so, Norman felt guilty, and insisted that he help Elisabeth by taking Mona to daycare in the morning and picking her up in the afternoon. Then—the idea continued— while the house was empty he would work on the book. But in fact he preferred sitting in Nellie LaBelle and driving around the city. Sometimes he stopped to explore the parks, eat hamburgers if he was hungry or bored, walk along the beaches or through downtown streets. He took on the shopping so he would have an excuse to drive around the city reading notice boards.

Young girl, 18, seeks babysitting. References.

Three men need woman to share two bedroom apartment. Kitsilano.

Moving and other odd jobs. Phone Ray.

Middle-aged couple, will do anything legal.

Norman imagined himself placing his own advertisements:

Male, non-starter, seeks inspiration. Write Norman.

Easterner, reluctant immigrant, wants to be swept away by passionate young woman with private income. Phone Norman.

Notice-board reader, available 24 hours a day, wishes to be kidnapped by illiterate nymphomaniac for serious caring relationship. Find Norman.

The Farradays, Mark and Heloise, were middle-aged and legal. They did not, however, need to place advertisements. Mark was a one-time physicist who at the age of forty had discarded job, wife and vocation to become a playboy real-estate developer. Ten years later he controlled millions of dollars of half-used space in Vancouver's new downtown office towers, owned an expensive yacht moored in the company of other such yachts, and had re-married to a professor of women's studies with whom he had produced a perfect pair of twins. These five-year-old twins and Mona met at the university day-care centre and insisted on visiting each other. The parents trailed along. "I've explained that you're a friend and not a lover," Elisabeth told Norman. "But you don't have to see them if you don't want to."

Curious, Norman went. The Farradays had a cedar mansion on the water; while the children sequestered themselves inside to watch television, the adults sat on the lawn drinking martinis and exclaiming over the perfect weather and the terrific view of the mountains.

"It drives me crazy, too," Heloise said to Norman. "People here talk about the weather as though it were the most important thing in the world. Wait until you've been here a whole year. Summer is always long, winter late, spring early."

By the time dinner came, Norman was on his fifth martini. "I'm a beer drinker," he confided to Heloise in the kitchen. He was also thinking of confiding to her that he found her very attractive, extremely attractive, that in fact he could imagine them melting together. He realized, however, that were he to take his confidences so far, he would have also to add that it was not him speaking, but the martinis.

"Elisabeth tells me you're working on a book."

"Such is the current excuse for my existence," Norman said. Then added: "That was supposed to be clever."

"I know," Heloise said, and then raised her eyebrows as if perhaps she realized all sorts of things deep and misty. In theory Norman's excuse for his existence in the kitchen was that he was helping her prepare the salmon steaks. In fact he was standing by the window, waiting for something to happen.

Then Heloise suddenly smiled at Norman, and Norman found himself looking into the eyes of a woman who did not care he had drunk four more martinis than he should have, a woman disarmed, a woman who could love him for himself alone, a woman offering a whirlpool of possibilities.

"Am I drunk? Am I imagining things?"

"Yes and no," said Heloise.

Norman carried the platter of salmon into the backyard. Mark was standing over the barbecue. He had precise square-fingered hands—hands that were, like the rest of him, perfectly preserved, perfectly in tempo.

Norman placed the steaks on the red-hot grill. "The flesh sizzled," Norman said.

"What?" Mark asked.

"It's the sizzle," Norman said. "Did you ever wonder what it would be like to walk on coals?"

"I did it," Mark replied. "The man around the corner gives lessons. An amazing person, really."

One day after a morning of nothing and lunch at a health-food bar where he felt comfortable reading the paper while he ate, Norman went walking through a park near the beach. In the centre of the park some teenagers were playing basketball. Norman stopped to watch. "You want to play?" one of them called out.

Norman looked down at his feet. He was wearing sneakers. He stubbed out his cigarette. "Sure."

The first time he was passed the ball he dropped it. For a while after that, he just trotted up and down the court, trying to save his breath and remember who was on his team. Then the ball came to him again and suddenly he was running with it, free, his hand bouncing the ball up and down against the packed dirt as though twenty years had just fallen away. "Go, go!" someone shouted, and Norman found himself turning to avoid a check, twisting in towards the basket. Then he was high up in the air and the ball was sailing free—sailing past the backboard and into the grass. An explosion of laughter, a slap on the back. "Nice try, hey, we thought you might be too stoned to move!" And then he was running up and down the court again. As he ran, he was suddenly aware of the encumbrances of time; the layers of flesh that formed a girdle around his belly and hips—one which he wished could now be shrugged off like an unnecessary heavy sweater. Muscles in his legs, his back, his shoulders had softened and forgotten what to do. Dead zones had created themselves in the nerves that connected mind to body. When he leapt for rebounds, he found himself tied down by gravity, his hands batting awkwardly in the air. Nonetheless the ball began to follow him around. But instead of trying to shoot he passed it to his team-mates, slowing at centre court while they carried on to the other end. By the time half an hour had passed his lungs felt like wet shopping bags and the soles of his feet were burning. He crouched, gasping, at the edge of the court while the others, shirtless and muscled, played on. Norman looked at his watch. It was time to pick up Mona. He left without saying anything and drove to the day-care centre. When he arrived he was drumming on Nellie LaBelle's leather-wrapped wheel and singing loudly.

Two days later Norman showed up at the park again. This time he was wearing anti-blister bandages on his heels and an extra pair of socks. For a while he stood at the edge of the game—then the same boy who had welcomed him the first time waved him onto the court. The boy was tall and thin with an unlikely cloud of red hair that sprayed out as he leapt, flattened when he ran. Now Norman noticed how easily he moved, how he controlled the traffic around both baskets, how his team-mates passed to him when they were in trouble, looked to him for the ball when they were in the clear. Norman found himself getting the ball more frequently and twice, when he drove for the basket, he actually managed to hit the rim.

"It's coming back," the red-haired boy said encouragingly. As though he, eighteen, fluid as mercury, knew what it was to be blocky and awkward, what fifteen years of drinking beer and smoking two packs a day could do to your body.

"Stick" was what the others called him. In every high school in his town there'd been, Norman remembered, a boy called Stick, a tall athlete whose brains resided in the fluid motion of his body. For boys like Norman, non-athletes but willing players, there had been no nicknames; boys like Norman had been only the background against which the more gifted ones could display their talents.

Every day for two weeks Norman went to play basketball in the afternoon. It was something to do, an excuse to leave the house, something for him to dream about in the City of Dreams. That is, when he wasn't dreaming about Heloise. Not so much the charms of Heloise, but the prospect of Heloise. Once, as he'd expected her to, she had even telephoned. It was during the morning, and when he answered she asked for Elisabeth—as though she didn't know that Elisabeth would be at work.

"And you," she said, "how are you finding Vancouver?"

"It's still perfect," Norman replied, surprised at the cool formality in her voice.

"That's good," Heloise said. And with those words her voice was back to the way it had been that afternoon in the kitchen—breathy, open, waiting for Norman to take the plunge.

Why not? Norman thought, why not now? "Let's go to lunch sometime," he could say. Or, "Have you any sights to recommend?" Or even, "Will the sky stay blue forever?"

But instead he made his lame good-bye and went down the basement to make sure he had two pairs of dry socks for basketball that afternoon. Bending over his laundry he felt a twinge in his stomach, a twinge he thought was a pulled muscle at first, but then, when he straightened up, he recognized as a familiar pre-boiling, a bubbling tension that used to start a couple of months before the end of one job and continue until the beginning of the next. "Phone her now," Norman said aloud. In the kitchen again, making himself lunch, Norman realized that the tingling in his stomach had actually started weeks ago, the afternoon he had first met Heloise Farraday.

He was slicing cucumber on a cutting-board he had bought at the health-food store. The board was red cedar, its flaming grain brought to a dramatic peak by several coats of oil. He took the moist slices and arranged them in piles. Each pile was a chapter in a junior creative-writing assignment. First chapter: the illicit meeting—accompanied by increased tension and feelings of pleasure; second, the illicit sex — tension to be replaced by pure pleasure; third, the disastrous dénouement—pleasure replaced by tension that increases until Norman loads up Nellie and drives to another city. Grade: C-. Comments: An idea too often repeated. Norman looked down at the cutting-board. The entire cucumber had been sliced away and now his stomach burned so much that he couldn't eat.

On the last day of the second week Norman noticed there was another stranger watching the game. He was wearing only khaki shorts and running shoes. He had glossy black hair that fell straight to his shoulders, and his skin was darkly tanned. "Paki," one of the players said right away.

Norman, running past the stranger, was uncomfortably aware of his stare. "If *you* can play," the stranger seemed to be saying, "then why not I?"

An hour passed. The stranger stood waiting to be invited.

"He wants to play," Norman finally said to Stick.

"Sure," Stick said. He beckoned the man forward with a tiny motion of his hand. Soon the new player was running up and down the court. But unlike Norman, he was in excellent condition. Every time there was a loose ball he was there, pouncing on it, dribbling it in a mad frenzy until he got to the basket where he hurled himself upwards and scored.

"Whirling dervish," someone said.

But no one passed the ball to him, nor did he pass the ball back. Soon it began to seem as if the stranger were a team of his own. Then, during a scramble for a loose ball, Norman was knocked to the ground. When he got up he saw the stranger racing down the court, his frenzied dribble carrying him straight to the basket. Norman brushed off his shoulder. His T-shirt was ripped and the flesh of his shoulder was scraped.

After supper Norman proudly displayed his wound. "The gladiator returneth unto his home and showeth his blood to the women who weep."

"You're crazy. I thought you were supposed to be working on your book." But that night, as Norman was falling asleep, Elisabeth opened the door to his room and joined him in bed.

Later, smoking a cigarette, Norman looked at the ceiling and said, "I have an announcement to make."

"The gladiator speaks. All fall silent therefore."

"You have to promise not to take it personally."

"Let the sword cut where it may."

"I feel good."

"You feel good?"

"I feel good. I hereby declare myself a member of the human race."

"You need a visa."

"You told me Vancouver was the City of Dreams and I laughed. I admit it. I thought you were just another Eastern convert to West-Coast boosterism. I thought I knew it all."

"You did."

"No, I didn't. I didn't know anything. Now I am here. Now I am lying on my back and looking at your ceiling. Now my muscles are sore and my flesh has been torn by honest exercise. I have just had sexual intercourse for the first time in months and my body is covered in miscellaneous fluids. I feel good."

"You feel good."

"And I have had a vision. Yea, after fifteen years or more or less of wandering in the desert. Yea, after more than a decade of having sand kicked into my face, camel dung dropped on my curriculum vitae, cactus needles stuck into the most delicate of my theorems, I have had a vision."

"Tell me your vision, master."

"I have looked into the mirror of the oasis, woman, and I have seen what I am not to be. I am not to be a mind slave, an intellectual, a member of the employed class. I am to miraculously become six-foot-three, superbly co-ordinated, and the best basketball player at the playground. And when this comes to pass I am to be known as Stick."

"Stick?"

"What surpasseth understanding shall be the bearer of Peace."

"But in this wasteland there is neither peace nor understanding. Only you and I, my lord."

"If I were your lord, I would marry you and make you happy ever after."

"But you are not."

"I know."

Saturday the blue sky turned milky with heat and Norman suggested he take Mona swimming. Once he was in the car, habit led him to the park. From his window Norman could see the players moving up and down the court.

Norman looked down at his feet. He was wearing brown lace-up moccasins that Elisabeth had bought him when holes appeared in his running shoes. The moccasins were made from caribou skin and had a strange musky odour. Flexing his toes, listening to the irregular staccato of the basketball against cement, glancing suddenly over at Mona who was sitting quietly with her hands folded and her eyes half-closed, Norman had a sudden desire to try to explain the hopeless logic of his life to her—the Nellie she was sitting in, the Nellies past and future.

On earlier wanderings he had found a special place, a sheltered cove with public access that he preferred to the larger and more crowded beach. Carrying a bag with Mona's things he helped her over the bleached logs until they reached the edge of the water.

Mona took her bucket and shovel from the bag and began digging furiously at the sand. Norman, meanwhile, lit a cigarette and looked out at the gently rolling sea. In the blue light the waves heaved up and down like a serenely obese belly. He undid his shirt, let the sun soak into his skin. After a while he closed his eyes and began dozing to the sound of water slipping in and out of the sand.

The night before, after Elisabeth had padded back to her own room, he had wondered if this summer in Vancouver was in fact the long-awaited exit from the desert—the resignation to his fate that would finally lead to release from bondage. He wanted to settle down; Elisabeth was available and even had a ready-made child. He wanted security; Elisabeth knew about a job in the English Department that had conveniently become vacant—a job that needed to be filled so quickly that there was no time for one of those competitions that drew hundreds of over-qualified wanderers like himself. Easy? What could be easier? Of course he would owe her. On the other hand she would be getting a husband, a father for her child. She had said she wasn't for him—but surely she could be persuaded otherwise, if only he would try to persuade her.

Persuasion, yes—although it wasn't persuasion she was wanting: what she wanted, he knew, was dedication, a proposition emanating not from desperation but from his own free will, from the part of him she had written letters to, the part of him that needed self-help. "Physician, heal thyself," she had commanded; now was the moment for the garments of doubt to be cast off, revealing the real Norman Wadkins—lover, father and husband.

Then as night followed day the inner man would propose to the long-waiting, long-suffering Elisabeth James that they combine in a Pact Against All. Only in Pacts and Alliances could permanent escape from the desert be assured.

Norman imagined himself being masterly. He imagined himself telephoning one of the babysitters who advertised themselves at the Health Food Bar. "I read your notice," he would say. "Would you be free at seven this evening?" He imagined himself with Elisabeth at a restaurant with tablecloths. Over wine, in the light of candles moulded by Buddhist vegetarians, to the crackling of burning logs and the hiss of breaking waves, he would make his pitch. "Elisabeth, for heaven's sakes, I've loved you this whole time. Let's drop the pretences, darling, my heart is yours."

Just as he had fixed this perfect scene in his mind, the actors began to change: instead of Elisabeth, Norman saw in front of him Heloise: Ruth: the girl who had advertised her services in the health-food store. The music played louder. Norman felt his heart beat faster. These were women for whom he did not have to cast off the garments of doubt. These were women who tore them from his back. These were women who could bring him brief moments of joy followed by months or years of unhappiness. "Norman," Norman said to himself, "these are the women you have learned to avoid."

"I want an ice cream," Mona said. Over the years she had switched into the first person. Norman stood up. As he was dusting off his jeans he heard a noise behind him. The stranger from the basketball court was sliding down the path. He looked briefly at Norman, no recognition in his dark eyes, then walked quickly down the beach and around the corner. Norman followed slowly. Beyond the small sheltered cove was a more inaccessible stretch where huge trees arched out from the last edge of land and hung over the water. In the shelter of those trees were a few huts and lean-tos where people had set up camp for the summer. Feeling like a spy, Norman watched as the stranger went to the first one and ducked inside. A few seconds later he reemerged, an apple in his hand. Norman backed away before he was seen.

At the top of the path he met the other players. They were laughing, talking, smoking cigarettes. Stick clapped Norman on the back, the way he always did, then offered Mona a drag from his cigarette. She backed away, frightened. "Sorry," Stick said, "I didn't mean to scare her." Then he put his hand on Norman's shoulder. His hand was huge, the long fingers that held the ball so lightly now seemed almost inhuman. "See you Monday," Stick said. He had small even teeth, a smile that was like a blush.

When Norman and Mona got home, the Farradays were sitting in the living-room, a bottle of white wine had been opened, and the adults were laughing while the Farraday twins played with Mona's toys.

By the time the second bottle was empty, Norman had decided that if the bomb fell right that minute he might grab Heloise and take her downstairs to the safety of his basement bed. Then suddenly the Farradays and their twins had gone off taking Mona with them to spend the weekend at their cabin on the coast.

"I'll make some dinner," Norman said.

"Let's go out."

"My treat," said Norman. And then, unable to stop himself: "In fact, let's get dressed up and go to a restaurant with tablecloths."

Another couple of hours, another bottle of wine, and Norman found himself back in his dream of the afternoon. Only this time Elisabeth was with him and he was looking into her eyes, trying to feel love in the pit of his stomach. Or wherever. "The dream has come true," Norman considered trying. Instead he said, "You know, I finished the book revisions last week."

"You did? When?"

"Wednesday and Thursday nights. I stayed up late."

"That didn't take long."

"I guess basketball cleared my head."

"Are you going to apply for the job?"

"Un-hunh."

"Is that yes?"

Norman took a sip of water. "If I get a job, I'll have a salary."

"That would be one of the benefits."

"With a salary I could pay more rent."

"If it's not nepotism, it's bound to be corruption."

"Whatever happened to ordinary people, struggling to earn an honest dollar?"

"Us," Elisabeth said.

The waiter was standing above them. "More to drink?" Norman asked. "Coffee? Liqueurs?"

Elisabeth laughed. She had a smile, Norman suddenly noticed, like his friend Stick. Small and quiet, well-organized, the smile of generals who watch life fall into patterns around them. But no blush. "Do you want me to ask you to marry me?" Norman tried to imagine himself saying. But he couldn't say it. He couldn't even imagine it.

When they were in the car again, Norman put on "Your Cheatin' Heart" and with the music to encourage him drove towards the playground. He parked by the edge of the grass, turned off the motor. Through the open windows drifted the smells of late summer: water, grass, the city's exhaled heat. Nights like this he had parked other Nellies in random spots in other cities; cutting bonds, inspecting tires, running his hands over the steering-wheel and preparing once more to drive out blindly into nothingness. No, not nothingness, he corrected himself, but onto that long single highway on which the country's cities dangled, uncomfortably separated, uncomfortable at the prospect of each other.

Now he was gripping the wheel, stroking it. Elisabeth's hands covered his. He turned to her. *Now,* he thought, *now is the time to kiss her.* Then his thoughts sloughed away like old ice and he was bent over her, gratefully tasting on her lips the same wine that had passed through his own.

When they got out of the car they were still holding hands. It was a new experience, thought Norman, a sort of trial marriage. He led Elisabeth towards the little cove he had visited with Mona that afternoon. "I know a place where we could neck."

At first the moon lit their way, but when they got to the path the light was blocked by trees and they found themselves stumbling over stones and twisted roots. "The light at the end of the tunnel," Elisabeth said, just after a fallen log had brought them to their knees—but left them a view of an opening only a few steps away. Norman tried to imagine what Stick might reply if handed such a sentence. Perhaps, like an errant pass, he would simply redirect it to a more likely target.

The tide had gone out, the small beach of the afternoon was now a glistening expanse of wet sand. Still holding Elisabeth's hand Norman stepped towards the water. In front of the shelter he had seen that afternoon a huge fire was burning. The muffled sounds they had heard on the path now resolved themselves into excited talking and singing to the strumming of a guitar.

"Let's go over there," Elisabeth said. She tugged at Norman's hand and Norman reluctantly followed.

As they drew closer, Norman saw that all the basketball players from the afternoon were clustered around the fire, each accompanied by a case of beer. The stranger was the one playing the guitar; he had his eyes closed and he swayed back and forth as he sang.

"Look who's here."

"Just dropped by."

Soon a cold beer was pressed into his hand and Norman was talking to Stick and his girlfriend, a tiny voluptuous creature whose hair was an exact match for Stick's."

"Your boyfriend is a wonderful basketball player," Norman said.

"He was on the all-star team."

"Are you going to play at university?"

Stick shrugged his shoulders.

"He's working for my dad. He owns the semi-pro team. Then we're getting married in a few months."

"You are? That's wonderful." Norman leaned forward, smiling. He lifted his bottle to toast the event, and raising it to his mouth was aware suddenly of the absolute gravity of the bottle—its weight, its fullness, its cold perfection in containing the holy fermented liquid of communion. "Is this my second beer?" Norman asked.

"I wasn't counting," said the girl. She gave him a certain kind of look, a look filled with speculation and suspicion, a look which Norman had not seen for decades but now recognized from his high school years as the look residents give to tourists who are passing through. On their way to university and better jobs, Norman had then thought, but that was before he had gotten lost in the desert.

Norman stepped back from the girl. Beyond the crackling red light of the fire, beyond the slow moon-silvered waves sliding into the wet sand, he could see boats parked in the middle of the channel. Some of them were festooned and blazing, others had only a few identifying red and blue lights strategically placed. To be on a boat, Norman thought, to be riding the water surrounded by nothingness. Across the bay was a glittering stretch of apartment towers. And then, rising into the distance, the jagged silhouettes of the mountains.

His bottle was empty. He took another from a case that seemed to have appeared beside him. The years in the desert had turned him into a beer drinker but his body was unused to mixing beer and wine. As he swallowed he felt his stomach protesting. Another swallow, a more vigorous reaction. Stepping away from the firelight, Norman walked towards the bushes, looking for a place to be sick discreetly. He sat down on a rock, blearily drunk, and watched the channel boats rocking with the tide.

"With a salary I could pay more rent," he remembered saying. But Elisabeth had refused to rise to the bait: Norman staying, Norman leaving, Norman proposing, Norman failing to propose—she had cleverly contrived to leave it up to him. She had somehow become the sun that had simply to wait and shine while he, the planet, spun helplessly in her orbit.

Norman knew he was drunk. "I am drunk," he said to himself. Not because he had had too much to drink—although he had—but because he was trying to hide from the truth. From the truths. Truths that shone as bright as Elisabeth's sun. Other truths invisible and hidden black truths buried like hidden seams of coal. He was drunk, he was hiding and meanwhile meanings were waiting to be deciphered. Careful thought, textual analysis, semiotic deconstruction. These techniques—others too—were available and waiting for him.

As he had once explained to an indifferent class, the English professor is a surgeon who operates on the body of the text. Words were only on the surface—supporting them was a whole anatomy of structures, subtexts, themes, literary devices. And passion? Where did passion fit in? Passion was only a word, a concept, a single arrow in the large quiver. Or, on the other hand, perhaps it was a word that camouflaged other words—foolishness, youth, self-destruction. Unless on the third hand, the hand that wasn't, passion was all that mattered.

Norman let himself slide from the rock onto the more comfortable sand. The strumming of the guitar and the singing had grown louder. He closed his eyes and had a dim vision of the entire human race as overexcited water-bugs, each locked in its own shell, each in a frenzy over nothing. Then he thought of Mona. She was not a waterbug. She clung to his hand every Saturday and sometimes during the week. She laughed when he tickled her and cried when he wouldn't give her two ice creams in one afternoon.

There were the sounds of splashing, of gleeful shrieking as people dashed into the water. Norman stood up. He kicked off his shoes, stripped himself naked. Carefully he folded his clothes on a log then, still holding his bottle of beer, he advanced towards the sea. As he passed the fire he saw Stick's girlfriend look curiously at his naked body. Self-consciously he sucked in his stomach. He peered around for Elisabeth. Then he moved more quickly, first running along the wet sand, then straight into the water.

After a few steps the sand gave way beneath his feet and he was in over his head. Norman released his beer bottle and began to swim towards the boats.

It was years since he had gone swimming. But basketball had given him back his wind, and he felt powerful and strong as he sliced towards the centre of the channel. Then suddenly he was out of breath and gasping. He turned towards the shore. In front of the fire figures were waving—whether at him or at each other he couldn't tell. And then above the pounding of his heart he thought he could hear voices calling him. "I'm here," he shouted back. He was surprised at the loudness of his voice. He shouted again. He was treading water. The waves that had been so gentle when he entered the sea now seemed to be pushing harder, slapping against his neck and the side of his head. He decided to rest a moment, floating on his back. When he turned up to look at the sky, the water flowed over his eyes, into his mouth and nostrils. He began swimming again, towards the shore, but a current had gripped him and it seemed no matter how vigorously he swam, the fire was growing dimmer. Once more he rolled onto his back. Ripe clusters of stars hung above. "This is the way I want to die," he thought. He could hear music. His body would sink to the bottom of the channel, but his soul was flying into the white sky. He closed his eyes, surrendered himself to this final embrace.

When he woke up he knew right away he was in a hospital, knew right away that the face looking down at his belonged to Elisabeth, knew right away that the tears were coming from Mona. "I'll do a book on post-death experiences in modern literature" was his next thought. He pictured himself sitting at his tenured desk, smoking filtered cigarettes and drinking a small glass of beer.

"Don't worry, I'm all right," he said. He was holding tightly to Mona's hand, he was crying and couldn't stop. Tears slid down his cheeks and the wetness brought it all back; they had hauled him out of the water and up onto one of the yachts. Wrapped him in a thick towel and given him something to drink. For a few minutes he had stood on the deck in the towel, looking at the shore and chatting as if the whole thing had been a humorous escapade. Perhaps the yacht belonged to Mark and Heloise, perhaps his shivering would stop when the warm flesh of Heloise was finally wrapped around him.

But Heloise did not appear. Nor Mark. It was strangers who surrounded him. Strangers who were looking at him curiously as he realized that nothing on earth could enable him to dive back into the sea and swim home. And he wasn't laughing, he was shivering uncontrollably. He had a first drink, then a second. Someone took him inside and he slid into a hot bath. The water burned at his skin but inside his muscles and guts were still frozen, still shaking uncontrollably, and even a third drink and a fourth didn't make any difference.

"I'm a doctor," someone kept saying. Norman looked up to see a man bending over him, a young rich-looking man of his own age with a friendly face and thick moustaches. "I'm going to give you a shot," he said from under the moustaches. And then the needle had entered his arm, a painful biting sensation that finally softened, sweetened, sent its sweetness and sleep humming through his blood until finally he was only aware that he was lying in the bath, enclosed by warm watery lips, floating in water, on water, the sky ripe and waiting above him.

When he woke up again Mona and Elisabeth were gone. He had a throbbing headache. He was wearing his own flannel pyjamas and a thick terrycloth bathrobe that belonged to Elisabeth. He thought about the book on post-death experiences. He would have to say how good it was after dying to be warmed and wrapped by the clothes of others. It made one feel part of the tribe again. It made one feel as though forgiveness was being offered.

In the pocket of his bathrobe Elisabeth had placed a note: "We love you, Mona and Elisabeth." The folded corners of the paper dug sharply at his palms, then he realized that even the air was clawing at his skin. Another after-death observation: "Upon their return to the world of the living, certain individuals are rendered hypersensitive. This manifests itself in reactions ranging from pure sensual pleasure to exaggerated feelings of terror."

When Mona and Elisabeth returned the next morning Norman had prepared his proposal of marriage. "A Provisional Document Detailing Terms of Total Surrender" was the title but before he could deliver it he fell asleep.

His sleep was a transparent one. He saw himself lying on his back, hands stretched out to either side. Holding them were Mona and Elisabeth. They flanked him. They pressed their warm bodies against his so that he would be sustained. But Norman Wadkins was not dreaming. He was seeing, foreseeing.

He was foreseeing the future and in that brilliant future were man, wife and daughter.

In his mind the future was already the past. He had become a full professor, he had purchased new furniture for Elisabeth's living-room, he had converted the basement apartment into a combination study and sauna. In addition, he spent two evenings a week playing basketball for a semi-pro team. Not a front-line player, too old for that, rather a highly-strung specialist called into fill the breach, a pure shooter, a brief explosion of energy that might at any moment be seen skimming down the court, a blur among the slower, more awkward players. And then, when arms reached down for him, he was suddenly airborne, a soaring desert hawk: untouched, untouchable.

Matt Cohen won the Governor General's Award for his novel Elizabeth and After *shortly before his death in 1999. He published poetry, novels, books for children, and collections of stories, including* Living on Water.

Nora by the Sea

CARY FAGAN

From the window Nora watched the car, a mustard Citroën, jerking out of the hotel drive as if it were in one of those Mack Sennett comedies they had once laughed over. The Citroën paused where the drive met the road, beyond which rose a tangled wall of subtropical trees and, farther, the tiled roofs of private estates. Directly below, when Nora leaned against the window, she could see new guests tumbling out of a taxi and the hotel porter starting to unload their baggage.

When she looked again the Citroën had disappeared. And with it her husband, Michael, who only yesterday had learned how to drive a standard shift when Nora had endured the ninety minutes down to Cannes. Not again; Michael would have to go without her, and besides, she looked forward to being alone — if keeping an eye on four children and a seventy-two-year-old man could be called being alone. This morning for the first time she had put on the yellow dress purchased in Paris, sandals on her feet, and silver earrings like seashells made by one of her own craftspeople. She felt light and summery; perhaps for once she even fit her name, Nora, like one of those cheerful English girls in wartime films that Michael used to tease she'd been named after.

She turned from the window and walked — waddled, the children exaggerated when they wanted to be mean — through the bedroom and across the hallway to the facing room whose door was unlocked. Her children's room was, as expected, a disaster, the three beds and extra cot like separate war zones, yesterday's underwear strewn about, and the wrappers from the chocolates left each morning on the pillows heaped on top of the television set which had been left on to a bicycle race. Nora turned off the television and picked up the underwear, not because she had failed in resisting the inheritance of her own mother's fastidiousness (at home her kids could make as much mess as they cared to live in), but out of respect for the maid. Then she stepped onto the balcony.

How odd that this hotel, with its air of archaic charm, should actually be quite modern, having been built in the early seventies in the international style that, according to the better magazines, was now discredited. Perhaps it was the way the hotel nestled into the cliff, its series of levels connected by stairs and escalators. Nora stood against the aluminum rail and felt her dress flutter against her legs. The sea was turquoise and dotted with boats. She could hear gulls. All of it—the view, the softness of the air—gave her a feeling of both stillness and movement. Just as she had wanted; just as she had hoped.

This stretch of shore, far below the hotel, was all rock and cliff, too dangerous for swimming. To the children's disappointment there wasn't a decent beach for twenty miles but Nora was glad of the isolation and the touch of wildness. From here down to the water there was no path, just glinting rock and scrub and, on either side of the hotel property, more estates with flat rectangles behind them that were tennis courts. The hotel pool two levels below was, at this time of morning, deserted. Nora could also see the informal garden, canopied with palm leaves, the stone steps that ran down to the pool, and the hotel's outdoor café with its round tables and wicker chairs. She also saw, sitting at one of those tables, her elder son.

Ananda, she could see, was writing in the journal she had given him before the trip. Her purpose had been to focus his attention on a family holiday he had resisted joining and to improve his writing skills, for his grades were poor. But she never could have predicted that Ananda would hardly put the journal down since the trip's beginning and that he would be there now, scribbling away, with a demitasse cup and a croissant set before him.

She was, of course, pleased about the journal, if not with the sight of a fifteen-year-old drinking espresso. That was too much, even if the management was French. She couldn't forbid Ananda, that wasn't how the family operated, but she could open a little reasoned discussion on the effects of caffeine. Nora, about to turn away, paused: from inside the hotel the waitress had appeared. She wore the typical black dress complete with frilly apron that showed a lot of stockinged leg and Nora recognized her as the same young woman who, dressed in grey and with a kerchief holding back her hair, came in to make their beds. Apparently the staff, despite the hotel's size, did double duty, like a family-run pension. The waitress had a rather sweet round face and a good figure and Ananda, who had refused to look happy for days, smiled.

Nora was again about to turn away when a man appeared, sweeping the café floor with a twig broom. He was another who did double service, for she recognized the same young athletic fellow who acted as porter. This was becoming a little drama; the waitress said something to the athletic man and then disappeared into the hotel. The athletic man leaned on the broom, next to Ananda but without speaking as Ananda, to his mother's amazement, tore a page from his journal, folded it, and placed it in the athletic man's back pocket. The man, carrying the broom, disappeared by the same door as the waitress.

That her own chronically shy Ananda had the courage to send a note to the waitress deserved his mother's admiration, accompanied by a perceptible tightening of anxiety. Certainly he deserved a relief from the months of moody silence, the evenings alone in his bedroom engaged in what seemed hours of desperate masturbation. Nora would not interfere now except to watch and, if she could, prevent her son from being hurt. No, not even that; this was her son's experience, not hers. She felt her heart beating, as if a car had brushed her. Yet a moment later she was already pleased with her decision. What a good day it would finally be, she was sure of that now.

A blueprint of the hotel's complex series of levels, its multiple staircases and escalators, would have appeared as confusing as a labyrinth, but the orienting views of sea or road from the high windows allowed guests (Nora had gone in search of her other children) to know just where they were. The colours of the hotel's interior were desert—white, grey, beige, yellow—the windows like lush paintings on the walls. For a hotel this size the halls seemed quiet to Nora, perhaps the result of a lower occupancy than the developers had anticipated, owing to the distance from Cannes. But this morning she liked feeling that any moment might bring an unexpected meeting round a corner and, indeed, she had two on her way down to the first level. The first was with the widow from Switzerland who yesterday had confided to Nora that she had not taken a holiday since the death of her husband. The second was not really a surprise for she heard the party of Germans before she saw them yawning their way into the dining room. Nora took the next door outside—there seemed to be dozens leading to the paths around the grounds—and breathed in the fecund air that sent a run of shocks along her thin allergic nose.

Nora started and looked down; the hotel's sleek tom was rubbing against her legs. She believed that cats (not dogs, including their own Lhasa apso—they liked everybody) were innate judges of character and as she bent down to scratch this one's gingery ears she was happy to take its appearance as another omen for the day. And looking ahead she saw, just before the gravel path disappeared round a corner, the twins.

Nora never said "the twins" aloud and had always insisted on their being treated as individuals; but as even now, at the age of eleven, they spent all their time together, it seemed natural to think of them as a pair, not the same but complementary. "What's up?" she said coming towards them. Gordon gave his infamous grin. Eileen giggled.

"Look, Mom," Gordon said, getting up to drag her over by the hand. He still wore the cabbie's cap that he had insisted on buying from a street vendor in London, his hair tucked inside and the brim turned up. With his wide face, big eyes and tremendous smile he looked—goofy.

"I almost caught a lizard. We've been trying all morning. But he got away, see?"

On the ground a lizard's tail. Writhing.

"Do you think it hurt when the tail came off?" Eileen said, her face a frown of concern. She had a sprinkling of freckles across her nose that could be accounted for in the family even if the fragile blondish-red hair couldn't.

"No, he didn't even feel it, did he, Mom? The tail just grows back."

"I don't suppose he enjoyed it much. Gordon, why do you wear your hat like that?" she said, fixing it. But he pushed her away and tipped up the brim again. Gordon liked to look goofy.

"Did you two have breakfast?"

"Uh-huh," Eileen said and began a careful explanation of how the four languages on the cereal box required different amounts of space.

"Can we go swimming?" Gordon asked.

"A little later. Where's Rose?"

"Outside Grandpa's door, waiting for him to wake up. Boy, does he ever sleep late."

"Mom," Eileen said and as she hesitated Nora could tell she was working out her thoughts. One needed a good deal of patience to have a conversation with Eileen. "Why do different languages take different room? I mean, aren't they just different words for the same thing?"

"I don't think so," Nora said—had she made a mistake not enrolling Eileen in French immersion?—"Languages aren't like pairs of shoes all the same. They're—let's see, now—like shoes of different colours and when you put them on you dance in a whole different way."

"Oh," was all she said, but she was thinking.

"Can we go swimming?"

"I said later, Gordon. Right now I'm going to have some breakfast with Ananda. Where are you two going to be?"

Gordon squinted up at her.

"That's classified information."

Eileen giggled.

The path that Nora continued on wound past the kitchen window that opened on hinges like elbows and from which drifted the same Madonna tune the kids were listening to on their Walkman these days. The café was entered through a trellis of vines in blossom beneath which Nora stood for a moment, the sound of a bee near her ear, looking at her son. The half-eaten croissant forgotten, he was absorbed in writing, his left hand clutching the pen near its nib and his face inches from the page. He wore army shorts picked up at some secondhand shop back in Toronto and a T-shirt imprinted with a grainy portrait of some new-wave band, just bought in London. How Nora loathed that haircut of his, shorter than a marine's, his scalp visible in spots and a little tuft at the back. Why couldn't he see that the haircut violated his beautiful and gentle face? Besides, the vaguest sense of history ought to have told him what such a military look signified to her generation; his own father had come to Canada to avoid the war, a story he had heard for years. Why, he looked just like the students they had once called—she could hardly say it, even to herself—fascists.

But fascists didn't wear earrings, at least not in her day, two bronze studs in a single lobe. These Nora liked, almost.

"Ananda," she said, but too quietly for him to hear. She loved his name that was so like a poem and that she and Michael had carried back with them from India where they had lived for eight months after her graduation. Of course she had returned to Toronto and the competence of Mount Sinai Hospital for the birth, but the name—meaning "joy" and in India as common as "Frank"—still meant for her that state of grace in which she and Michael had lived. As for Ananda himself, its vague femininity and foreignness would have been embarrassments enough, but as he grew older his name became a reminder of the appalling fact of his own conception. When he came home at the start of every school year, complaining, she and Michael would give the same response: "It's nice to be a little different." "No it isn't," Ananda would grumble. He still hadn't forgiven them.

It was seeing Ananda so withdrawn into the privacy of his journal that caused the first uneasiness of the day, that it could be something other than lovely. But she refused to let his slapping shut of the journal or the suppressed little frown as he looked up wound her. "Good morning," she kissed his cheek while he slipped his pen into a pocket on his shorts, meant for a bayonet or something worse. The speech on caffeine could wait for another time. Besides, how could *she* talk, who with Michael and two of his college friends had once dropped acid while hiking up Mount Rainier in Washington?

"Don't you want to finish your breakfast?"

"I've had enough," he said. "Where's Dad?"

"Gone to Cannes. He won't be home until this evening. I've got an idea, Since you're so interested in films, why don't you go in with him tomorrow? You can see a film at the festival, maybe even attend one of the press conferences and see a director."

"I don't think so, I'd rather just stay here. We're leaving the day after tomorrow, aren't we?"

"That's right. We fly to Paris and then home."

"You aren't going to change the ticket and make us stay longer?"

"Has it been so horrible to be with us?"

"I didn't mean it that way."

"I know, that's not what I meant to say either. I think it's been our best holiday in a long time."

"Sure." He pushed his chair back and rose.

"Where are you going?" There was, against her will, the slightest note of panic in her voice. "Won't you keep me company?"

"I want to go for a walk."

"Where?"

"Just around."

He walked away with that springy gait of his, bouncing on the balls of his feet. Nora watched him cross the café and hesitate before the trellis, not because he was reconsidering, as Nora momentarily hoped, but because the waitress was coming through from the other side. She smiled at him—it seemed to Nora conspiratorial—as he let her pass.

But Nora would not let herself brood over Ananda, nor over the failures of the holiday, for the weather was too fine and she could not think of a prettier place to sit than at this café table. She had looked forward to a day alone but now she wished that Michael was here and that they could have the kind of talk that had once been so frequent and expected between them. When she and Michael had met she was the only Canadian student at the small Massachusetts college and he was a teaching assistant from New Jersey who made experimental films. One of his films had won an award at a state film festival and he was trying to raise money for a more ambitious project which already had the name *Quantum*. He wore his hair in a pony tail and was prepared to leave the country to avoid the draft.

They did leave after Nora graduated, using the money he had raised to take them to Europe, the Middle East, India. On returning to Toronto they had moved into a cooperative house and Nora, waiting for the birth of their child, began to make jewellery, imitating the designs she had studied in her fine arts courses and had sketched in India. Michael started hunting for more money to make *Quantum* and took a job as assistant manager of an art cinema. Eight months later he was working for the country's largest movie-house chain, soothing his conscience with calculations of the money he could save. The job meant cutting off his pony tail. He began wearing ties.

Michael got promoted and *Quantum* never got made. At present he was vice-president in charge of Ontario distribution, had developed an obsessive interest in espionage films, and wore his hair, if not in a pony tail, at least elegantly long. They had renovated their third house, in Moore Park. Nora, between bearing children, had gone from selling her own work to hiring other jewellery makers and opening miniature boutiques in department stores. She now had twenty-one craftspeople, eleven stores, and her designs had just been featured in *Toronto Life*.

The trip to Cannes had been something of a perk for Michael, who was only peripherally involved in choosing films for distribution. But he was spending a few days attending screenings and lunching with producers, getting, as he told Nora, a larger sense of the business. Yesterday she had accompanied him to Cannes only to endure frantic crowds, soundtracks blaring from speakers, traffic jams caused by Finnish and Israeli television crews. In a hotel lobby a young woman, hoping to be discovered by a Hollywood director, had dropped her robe for the newspaper photographers. Nora and Michael had entered the hushed ambience of the hotel restaurant whose prices had been doubled for the festival and where Michael received the supplications of an independent film maker from New York. She was surprised to see her husband, author of the never-made *Quantum*, play with him so ruthlessly.

Nora wanted some coffee but lacked the courage to attract the waitress's attention and merely pulled apart the end of Ananda's croissant, leaving a buttery gleam on her fingers. The waitress appeared just outside the trellis but turned her back as Nora waved; the gentleman at the next table raised a sympathetic eyebrow and returned to his Italian newspaper. Three weeks ago Nora had sat on the living room sofa, holding the small brass Krishna that usually stood on the mantle next to the menorah, and waited for Michael to come home. She had heard the sound of his Mazda pulling into the drive and watched him come through the door, briefcase and squash racquet under his arm as he juggled with his keys.

"Michael," she had said. "I'm not happy."

Michael had stood there, his smile frozen, looking so much like Gordon, a clumsy enthusiastic boy. He put the racquet on an armchair.

"What we need is a little vacation," he had said, still smiling. It's been years since we've gone to Europe. How about it?"

Nora had looked down at the Krishna, waving its arms and legs. "All right," she had said. And then as an afterthought, "If we can bring the kids. And my father."

Six days in London, six days in Paris, and now the Riviera. They had waited hours to get into the Tower and the Louvre, had been swindled by no fewer than three taxi drivers, while the children, spitefully she was sure, had pointed out every billboard for McDonald's and Coca-Cola. That was what children remembered, not the British Museum or Rodin's drawings; what they remembered was the Guinness spilled into Daddy's lap, the pigeon with a deformed foot, free chocolates on the pillow.

"Morning, daughter."

Her father, sauntering between tables, handsome in white slacks, blazer, cravat flowering at the neck. He moved a touch stiffly as always, his pencil moustache precisely trimmed and his white hair combed back. "God, what's all that sun for?" he rasped, sitting down and crossing his legs. He peered at the other breakfasters as if incredulous that anyone could be up at such an hour.

"I need coffee."

"Did you sleep well, Dad?"

Her father just narrowed his eyes, as if to keep out the light. He hadn't slept well since Nora's mother died, but perhaps it was simply age. The waitress arrived, allowed this handsome old man to flirt with her, and went for coffee. How did he look so right, so at ease here? "You ought to eat something," she said. "You're getting too thin."

"My dear, I'm simply in fashion," he chuckled, lips barely parted. "The only thing I can digest first thing in the morning—"

"Is the news, I know. Where's Rose? I thought she was waiting for you."

"Yes, I found her sitting in the hallway outside my room just like a little orphan, that's what I told her. She watched me shave."

"She never watches Michael shave."

"Michael, Rose informs me, uses an electric razor."

"But where is she now?"

"I sent her to the kiosk to buy me a *Herald Tribune* and a packet of cigarettes."

"I can't believe this, Dad. You know I don't want you smoking around the kids."

"She likes doing errands for me."

This time the waitress's appearance didn't even elicit a glance from him. He picked up the cup almost as she set it down and closed his eyes for a moment. Before the trip they had seen her father only two or three times a year since he had returned to Montreal and the old, unrecognizable neighbourhood. He only taught part-time now, to "gifted" students as he put it, and he liked to joke that the other teachers treated him politely out of deference to his Russian accent and impeccable manners. As for

Rose, Nora had never known a more serious child. Rose's first-grade teacher had even telephoned Nora to tell how her daughter shunned friendships with the other children. To Rose her grandfather should have been almost a stranger. But from the moment of their rendezvous at the Toronto airport Rose had taken to him and barely left his side. Nora's father, to her surprise, submitted to her presence. He slowed to her walking pace, talked in a reasonable tone, even occasionally held her hand. Nora discovered what could only be a previously hidden and ugly side to herself, for only that could explain her not being absolutely delighted.

"Rose doesn't like Hebrew school," her father said.

"But it's only her first year, and just Sunday mornings."

"I don't like to interfere but I'm afraid I couldn't help agreeing with her. What does she need it for?"

"That's pretty obvious, I should think. To learn about being Jewish."

"Ah," was all he said, and tipped back the cup of coffee. How he could make her furious. If her father wished to cling to whatever views he picked up in some dingy Moscow restaurant half a century ago that was his business, but to undermine what she and Michael taught their children was inexcusable. But what could she say—

"Hello, orphan."

Rose came running, through the trellis, past the other tables, and into her grandfather's arms. Chuckling, he patted her fraternally on the back. Rose wriggled around to sit between his white-trousered legs on the edge of the chair.

"Just think, making me wait all this time for my newspaper."

Rose was breathless. "The lady gave me a green package—menthol. But I know you won't smoke them, Grandpa, so I wouldn't take it. You should have heard her swear, in French but I could tell. She had to look on all the shelves."

For the first time Rose looked up at her mother, the corners of her mouth turned down, Nora leaned over to brush the hair from Rose's forehead, a reason to touch her. Of all the children Rose looked the most like her—the thin nose, high forehead, the dark crescents under her eyes.

"Rose, honey," Nora said, "you've got your shirt inside out."

"I don't care."

"Where's the waitress? I want to order you some breakfast."

"Grandpa doesn't eat breakfast."

"Grandpa is very stubborn. We love him but we don't agree with him. How about we order you some cereal and fruit?"

Rose didn't protest, her sign of acquiescence. Nora's father deftly tapped a cigarette from the package and drew a box of wooden matches from his blazer. "You'd better shift into the next seat, orphan," he said. "I don't want you to get my smoke."

"Smoking is bad," Rose said, pulling herself into the wicker chair.

"Yes, very bad."

"But won't it hurt you, Grandpa?"

"I'm ancient, it's too late for that. Just being alive hurts me."

"Please, Dad," said Nora.

"Your mother protests my small act of self-dramatization. She's right, of course. Ah, here's that pretty waitress."

Rose's breakfast was duly ordered and delivered and, once the strawberry halves had been arranged by her into a pattern whose meaning was necessary but obscure, she began to eat. Nora's father leaned back in his chair, cigarette held aloft, and scanned the newspaper's headlines. "I hope Michael is finding his excursions to town productive," he said.

"I think so. If you'd like to go in, I'm sure he'd love to take you tomorrow."

"Oh, I don't think so. It's rather pleasant here. No sights to see, no galleries to look serious in. Right, orphan?"

Rose looked up and smiled, her teeth red with strawberry.

"Not one bit of Canadian news," Nora's father said and rattled the paper. "We don't exist, we're still a few handfuls of snow. No, here's something, a profile of the West Edmonton Mall. Biggest in the world, apparently. That ought to boost our international image."

Rose inexplicably laughed and kept eating. She had wild hair that defied brushing and skin pale as wax. God, Nora loved her children, she loved Rose, but they made her—how, she hardly understood—afraid to show it, as if something fragile would fissure and crack. Rose looked up to make sure her grandfather was still there, and began to eat again, tipping the bowl to capture the last sweetened spoonful of milk. No, there really was nothing wrong, it was she who didn't appreciate all that she had.

"Nora, dear. Morning!"

Nora saw Malcolm Moriarty waving as he drew out a chair for his wife. Just when she did not want to move, but Malcolm Moriarty was the sort of man who treated bare acquaintances like the best of friends and meant it. Nora sighed. "Be right back," she said and got up smiling.

"How rude of us not to come over," Malcolm said. "We wanted to greet your father and your daughter, what is her name again . . ."

"It's Rose, dear." Dorothy Moriarty's apologetic tone was warm and polished from years of use. She had aged very handsomely, hair in white curls and a soft, highly coloured face. "What Malcolm is saying, or rather not saying, is that we would have come over if my silly knee hadn't been asserting itself all morning. He wanted me to sit down."

"Yes, that's it," Malcolm smiled broadly. The dip and rise of his vowels no doubt identified in just which English town he had been raised. "Dorothy suffers, you know, but not a peep out of her, she's not a complainer. You've got quite a father, Nora, he looks just the musician. I must have a chat with him about Ravel. I don't know a blessed thing about music but I do love Ravel."

"Nora, if you'd like sit down a moment. Your children have such interesting names and so diverse. There must be a story behind that."

There was a story, of sorts anyway, and the Moriartys, who really were sweet, listened with so much interest that as she spoke of her children Nora felt herself flush with emotion. Malcolm had introduced himself in the dining room last night after she and Michael had returned from Cannes. Malcolm's red hair had receded to the very back of his head and he had a scrubbed, shining scalp. They were such a nice couple, fussing over one another; childlessness seemed their one sadness.

"Dorothy must show you the things she bought in the market yesterday. Last year we went to the Costa del Sol, but talk about crowds. A rumour went along the beach—well it's true, Dotty—that someone had spotted human faeces floating in the water. The plumbing system can't take the numbers, you see. Now, in England . . ."

Nora listened, about cottage rentals in Penzance, the influx of hooligans to London, but in spite of her instinctive liking for Dorothy especially, she was conscious of her father and daughter at their own table and, as soon as she could, excused herself. The table had been cleared, although Nora had hoped for a last cup of coffee, and her father and Rose had pushed their chairs together to the point of touching. Rose, her bare legs pulled up beneath her, rocked slightly as her grandfather spoke, his cigarette held just before his lips. Nora's expectant smile of return, having gone unnoticed, seeped away, and she stood like an unwanted listener at a party while her father spoke in that calm and formal voice she had always known.

"Wait a minute and I'll tell you. Your mother used to wait on the front steps for me to come home. On our street there was always something interesting for a young girl to see. The houses had rails and stairways running up their fronts—that's how apartments were built in Montreal, because of fire. Our door was on the second storey and Nora used to look through the rails at the boys playing hockey below or the girls skipping rope. She could speak some French then, picked it up by listening. At the end of the street, three or four blocks away, there was a small church that no one outside the neighbourhood knew existed, and sometimes the nuns would walk past. Nora said they looked like angels. But when the street really looked its best was after the first snowfall. Nora would stand with her nose pressed to the window and watch the people come out of their doors with brooms and sweep the snow away. And she would ask, 'Why are they doing that, Daddy—'"

Nora fled; how else to describe the sight of a woman running flat-footed with her skirt flying, hands in the air as if someone were flinging stones at her? Down the path and into the garden, not the formal garden on the other side of the hotel with its immaculate bushes of cubes and spheres, but the "English" garden with its wildflower beds and dusty path, surrounded by an ivy-hugged wall. She stood against the wall to catch her breath, a hand stretched across her breast. Why had her father's talk been so distressing? She knew only that she could not breathe, as if they had somehow sucked away the air from around her. All she could examine rationally was that she and her father had in the last years been anything but close. Their arguments had started when she was a teenager, the break when she and Michael had flown to other worlds. If the arrival of the children had introduced a formal truce and even, eventually, cordial relations, not even after her mother's death had they settled their oldest resentments. What had made this separation hurt so much and for so long was the affection she had known from her father, and how she had adored and admired him. She had never felt that way again until Michael.

A bird, of a startling green, lighted on a branch and began to trill. Another appeared, duller, and the two chased one another about before skimming over the wall. A shame Eileen hadn't seen, she loved birds.

Rose was afraid of them, they fluttered in her dreams. Nora began to think her reaction exaggerated and even to feel as if she had made herself ridiculous. After all, a mother should be glad when a daughter shows an interest in the mother's childhood. Hearing about those years in Montreal that Nora had forbidden herself to dwell on might even bring Rose closer to her. If only Nora could have patience. She had let the day get away from her again, but if she could just be a little stronger she could rescue it.

She was sitting on an iron bench and lacing on her sandal when the hotel dog, a woolly hulk with a flat smiling face that must have been the descendent of some obscure European breed, came pounding down the path, followed by her hooting twins, Gordon with his cap pulled to the side and Eileen waving a paper flag on a stick. The dog ran over Nora's feet but the twins stopped and stood before her in a little mushroom of dust.

"We want to go swimming but Ananda won't watch us even though he's just sitting at the pool writing in that dumb book."

"I was just coming down. You find Grandpa and Rose while I change."

"Mom," Eileen said, tracing a line on a path with her shoe. "I don't like my bathing suit."

"Why not?"

"It's too thin. I mean up here."

She pointed to her chest which was flatter than chubby Gordon's. So self-conscious already, the daughter of a generation that had tossed away its bras. "You can wear a T-shirt overtop," Nora said.

"That's a good idea. Let's go, Gordon."

"I'm going to wear a T-shirt too."

And they were off, back the way they had come.

Light everywhere, on the surface of the pool, on the pink deck that was as porous as coral, on the glittering rail that overlooked the cliff and the sea. Nora, a bathing suit beneath a tie-dyed shirt, squinted from her lounge at a view as bleached out as a colour photograph left in a window. She saw Eileen hugging herself by the edge of the pool as Gordon, still wearing his cap, threw himself over the water and accomplished his object of making a big splash. The cap came up first and beneath it a grinning Gordon. Closer to Nora sat her father, his trousers rolled up and his feet dangling in the water. A breeze from the sea crossed Nora's ears, bringing Rose's voice, " . . . but if Mommy was afraid of these boys . . ."

Nora turned her head, not wanting to listen, and saw the young man who acted as porter and, apparently, pool attendant, scurrying down the stone stairs balancing a tray of drinks. He distributed them to the tables pulled together by the family of Germans who were judging two of their wives in a diving contest. When the young man had one drink left he brought it to the chair beneath the umbrella where Ananda sat. Her son's hairless chest looked narrow next to the athletic man in his tight tennis shirt with the crest of the hotel on the pocket. They spoke for a moment until Malcolm Moriarty, sitting with his wife under the awning, called the attendant who, after taking their order, bounded up the stairs again.

Nora shifted the lounge so the sun fell across her face. With her eyes closed she could smell the sea and, when the breeze picked up, something stronger, like gutted fish and diesel fumes. The sound of wet feet slapping, voices in German and French, the faint whine of music.

"Quick, Mom, you've got to come."

She opened her eyes to see a dripping Eileen. "What's wrong?" The image of a child, Gordon, Rose, at the bottom of the pool, drowned.

"Gordon wants to show you something. I'm not allowed to tell what."

Eileen pulled Nora along, past the tables of Germans who were counting, "*Ein . . . zwei . . . drei!*" and then an arc of spray, down to the end of the deck where Gordon stood on a stool to peer through a telescopic viewer meant for spotting ships.

"Look at this, Mom. Topless."

"What are you talking about?"

When Nora looked through the viewer she could see the hazy image of a sun deck and two women who had laid their tops aside.

"Pretty funny, eh Mom?" Gordon said. "Who else can we tell?"

"It isn't necessary to tell anyone," Nora said, her hand already swinging the viewer towards the sea. "We shouldn't spy on people."

"Come swimming with us," said Eileen, wishing to make amends.

"Yeah!" said Gordon. "I want to go back in the pool."

"A swim would be nice. Let me just take off my things."

"Mom?"

"Uh-huh?"

Gordon pointed to the party of Germans. "Are those people really

Nazis? Ananda says they have keys to our rooms and could come any time in the night and take us away."

"Ananda told you that? Jesus. You two go ahead and I'll meet you in the pool."

Back at her lounge Nora dumped her sandals and, pulling her shirt over her head, saw the world go pink and red. On her way to the pool she stopped by Ananda, who sat with the journal in his lap, sipping his drink from a straw. From above, Nora spoke to the bristly curve of his scalp. "I would appreciate you not telling your brother and sister nonsense about Nazis and God knows what else. Kids have a hard enough time understanding these things without being encouraged in stupid prejudices. If that's all you have to say then you better keep to your silent routine."

When Ananda looked up, Nora was shocked by how stricken he looked. "I'm sorry," he said.

"It's all right, you didn't mean it."

"But I did. Don't—don't—uh, I'm a shitty person, Mom."

"Ananda, how can I—"

But when she tried to put her arms around his shoulders he twisted away in his chair. "I'm going swimming," Nora said and headed for the pool. She walked to the deep end and slipped over the edge, the water passing over her legs, her breasts, her eyes.

She felt hands tugging at her and, opening her eyes, saw the bubbling grins of her two children, their hair wisps of seaweed. They all came up together.

"Let's play underwater charades," Gordon said, paddling furiously to keep afloat.

"Mom goes first," said Eileen.

"Yeah, and make it a hard one."

"You want hard?" Nora said. "You got it." And held her breath.

By the time Nora hooked her arms over the side of the pool and hung there she had little enough wind to spare for words. "That's it," she gasped as the twins bobbed beside her. "I'm waterlogged. You dolphins will have to cavort without me."

"Aw, Mom."

But Nora wasn't listening. She had seen Ananda, still under the umbrella, talking to the pretty waitress. Her tray was covered in empty glasses and she and Ananda were having a tug-of-war over his. Which meant, Nora realized, that even as she appeared to give him a lecture in French manners, their hands were touching.

"Everybody out," Nora said. "After we dry off it's time for lunch. A *family* lunch."

Rounding up the family, yanking dry shirts over their heads and herding them around a table on the café patio required the tenacity of a schoolmistress. And just when they had settled down, the hotel dog came lumbering across the café, to be pounced upon by the twins while Rose climbed shrieking into her grandfather's lap. Nora got the children seated again while the dog settled contentedly beneath the table so that she had to straddle it with her legs. "That isn't a dog," Nora's father said. "That's a rug in need of a beating." He looked, as usual, regal, hair wetted and combed back, cravat a perfect topsail. "Hmm," he mused, considering the menu. "On such a splendid day lobster seems appropriate."

Nora sighed; the children didn't eat shellfish. She kept a kosher house not from some religious superstition but to give the children what Michael called cultural definition. Her father, on the other hand, defied such signs of faith with the same glee he had felt as a sixteen-year-old music student newly arrived from the village. Rebellion made him nostalgic.

"What are you going to order, Ananda?" Nora asked.

"I'm not very hungry."

"But you didn't eat breakfast."

He shrugged.

"Ananda, please."

"All right, I'll have a hamburger."

"There's no hamburger on the menu. Can't you be a little adventuresome?"

"No."

"Look at this, Andy," his grandfather—who knew how he infuriated Nora by using that name—pointed to the menu. "I think this *steak frites* ought to be pretty good. Just like a hamburger only they forgot to grind it."

Ananda looked reluctant to give in. "Okay," he finally said.

"I want that too," said Gordon.

"And me," said Eileen.

"That was easy," said Nora. "What about you, Rose?"

"I want lobster," Rose said.

"Honey, lobster isn't kosher. Besides, you've never eaten it and you won't like it."

"I want it."

Nora pressed her fingers against her brow. It was at moments like this that theories of child-rearing proved less than adequate. "I don't think so. You'll have what the other kids are having."

Rose fixed her mouth shut, a bad sign. Her grandfather leaned over. "You can try mine, orphan."

"Don't interfere, Dad."

"I simply thought—well, you know best. Perhaps I'll indulge in a glass of wine."

From their side of the table the twins watched this drama in which they were not participants with their different proportions of fear and interest, but its finale was merely the waitress's arrival to take the order. Nora was not so preoccupied with Rose that she could not keep an eye on Ananda in the young woman's presence, but he did not even look up.

"Mom," Gordon said after lunch had arrived and he had stuck two fries under his lips to look like fangs, "Are we ever going to go to the beach?"

"Maybe Dad can take the afternoon off tomorrow and drive us. Does everyone want to go?"

"I do," said Eileen.

Ananda shrugged. "Sure, why not."

"How about you?" Nora said, running a hand over Rose's hair.

Rose shook her head.

"You don't?"

Rose tilted her head to look at her grandfather. He peered down at her through half-closed eyes.

Rose nodded. "Okay."

"Ah, the beach," said Nora's father. "Sand in your bathing suit" (the children giggled) "no bathroom for miles. That's my idea of paradise."

"Mom?" said Rose.

"Yes, love?"

"Do you think they have ice cream for dessert?"

"You know, I think I saw ice cream on the menu."

"Strawberry?"

"Sure," said Gordon. "And they also have cabbage flavour."

"Yech," said Eileen.

"And dog food favour and medicine flavour . . ."

Rose laughing, Eileen banging her fork, the dog barking under the table.

"Nora," her father said, wiping the edge of his mouth with his napkin, "I am not related to these hoodlums."

If only she could have kept them around that table forever, but it was enough, that hour, she wouldn't ask for more. The twins ran off together to investigate a rumour that the pond in the formal garden was inhabited by a turtle; Ananda bounded away, hands buried in the oversized pocket of his shorts and the ties of his sneakers dragging behind; and her father and Rose got up together in silence, as if speech weren't necessary, like an old couple.

With the others gone the waitress dropped her smile and, leaving the chit among the table's debris, turned her back. Nora signed a generous tip and retreated to her room where she undressed by the afternoon light diffused through the sheers. The lunch had gone off so well and here she was, sitting on the edge of the bed, a breath away from weeping. It happened with an increasing frequency that terrified her. She was breathing quickly, gasping almost, and felt a rising curl of nausea. Think of something good; think of Michael. Those conversations in the college dormitory, late at night, when the deep regularity of his voice had soothed her out of loneliness. From those first days she had been grateful for Michael's interest in her; she still was, when he showed it. Remembering the book she had once read to the children over many nights, she wondered if she were like Tinkerbell, who, if she were not believed in, would fade and fade.

The telephone sounded, two short and foreign trills. Nora lifted the oversized receiver and held it to her ear.

"Hello?"

"Hi, sweetheart."

"Michael. I didn't expect you to call. Oh, I'm glad."

"I've just got a few minutes between meetings. If you thought this place was crowded yesterday—today it's a madhouse. But Nora, you won't believe who I met not half an hour ago."

Michael's voice sounded far away, as if he were calling from the end of a tunnel. "Who did you meet?" she said.

"You'll never guess."

"Please, Michael."

"James Bond."

"Who?"

"Come on, Nora, you know—Sean Connery. The original. He's here promoting a new film. I couldn't believe it, he even signed an autograph for me. It was incredible. Nora?"

"I'm listening, Michael. When will you be back?"

"In time for dinner, so hold the kids until then. After we put them to bed we can have a little time to ourselves and straighten everything out. All right?"

"All right, Michael. Be careful driving."

"No problem, I'm getting to be a real pro with the shift. See you later."

After Nora hung up the receiver she lay down on the bed, head on the pillow, eyes closed, and whispered into the room, not a word but a sound. She was asleep. The light through the sheers grew dimmer; she did not move. When finally Nora stirred, the sensation was of pulling herself up from the bottom of a well. She groped for her watch on the dresser and stared, hardly believing that it could be almost seven. She must have been more tired than she knew; perhaps that had been the cause of her mood. Mechanically she sat on the toilet and then turned on the shower, first cool, and after the shock, hot. As her head cleared Nora even began to anticipate the evening if not with pleasure at least without dread; after all, the day so far really had been as fine as she had hoped. After the children had gone to bed she and Michael could sit in the bar and talk and she would order something nice, a glass of champagne. Nora brushed out her hair, put on stockings and slip, and shimmied into the evening dress that Michael had insisted she buy in Paris. And she who still preferred jeans and old sweatshirts stood in front of the mirror and had to admit that she looked ravishing. The dress was of heavy satin, large shoulders, a low neckline, belted at the waist and finished in a full skirt. Nora put on her heels, a silver necklace, and looked again. "My God," she said aloud, for she remembered the days when her father still gave concerts and Nora would watch her mother, who always accompanied him, standing before her own bedroom mirror, just like this.

Gordon and Eileen she found in their room, sprawled on the beds watching *Dallas* dubbed into French. "Where are Ananda and Rose?" she asked.

"I don't know," Gordon said without looking away from the television.

"Get dressed for dinner, you two. And we're eating in the dining room, so put on your good things."

"Aw, Mom."

"I want to see you moving."

She began a hunt for the others, through the hotel corridors, in the sitting rooms, even out to the café where the young athletic man was closing the umbrellas for the evening. It was while considering where to look next (and a gaggle of tennis players entering the lobby looked her satin figure up and down with, she was sure, amusement) that Nora looked through the revolving glass doors and saw Rose and her father, standing at the edge of the hotel drive, watching the cars coming back from the city.

Her father had always loved automobiles, and as Nora made her way down the drive, heels catching between bricks, she could see him, oblivious to the billows of exhaust, pointing at each arrival and describing its history and handling. "Well, hello there," Nora said, but a convertible gunning up the drive drowned out her voice and her father, who seemed not to have noticed her, kept talking to Rose.

"Now there's a nice Mercedes, you don't see that colour in North America. Reminds me of our first new car, '53 Dodge, a real beauty. We'd only bought used until then. Now those were real cars, the size of battleships. When I leaned on the horn all the neighbours came running and your grandmother brought Nora down the stairway. 'Is this your car, Daddy?' she said. 'Are you becoming a salesman now?' We laughed and laughed . . ."

Whatever Nora shouted, it made both her father and Rose turn and stare. After a moment her father said, "Yes, Nora?"

"Dinner. You have to get ready."

"Of course."

And Nora turned around, back to the hotel. She did not know where to go, or rather where to hide, and so she stood before the newspaper kiosk, so close that the words blurred before her eyes. She was now only this myth, a little girl on an iron stairway, and the Nora who stood before the papers was fading and fading, leaving only a satin shell —

"Without my glasses I can't see, only the big words."

The woman from Switzerland, the widow, appeared beside her, peering at the hanging newspapers to read the headlines. "Nothing so important, I think," she said.

"No," Nora said.

"Are you and your family having a good holiday?"

"Yes, thank you."

"They always treat me well. My husband, he was once printing the menus for the hotel, the bills, everything. He was demanding of perfection."

"You must miss him."

"This is natural."

"I don't know what I'm doing here," Nora said and raised her hand as if to stifle a laugh. "I'm looking for my son."

"The big one?"

"Yes, I have to go."

"I saw him just some time ago, on the upper level. I always take a room on the upper level. The stairway is good exercise."

"Are you sure it was my son? I don't know what he could be doing there."

"Perhaps he is making a friend."

Nora just looked at her and a moment later was tripping up the escalator, holding aloft her skirt. Why she was going after him, whether she would yank Ananda and the waitress apart if she found them—all she did know was that she wanted to slap them across their faces until her own hands became real again. The corridor of the upper level was more narrow than the others because of the angle of the cliff and as Nora looked down she realized that she had expected to know in which room Ananda would be. She started to walk, stopping to listen and try each door before passing on to the next; on one she pounded with the flat of her hand but received no answer. Before the second to last she paused and heard what might have been a moan or merely the scrape of a chair. She put her hand on the knob—the bolt was only half turned in the lock and with pressure slipped out—and opened the door.

When she had last seen her son naked she did not know. He was tense as a bow, kneeling before the stillmade bed, the window behind open to the darkening Mediterranean. The young athletic man had neatly folded his porter's uniform and left it on the chair and as he sat on the bed he turned his head—apparently only he had heard the door—and looked at Nora with what seemed to her the most inconsolable grief.

When she returned to her own room she pulled a chair from the desk and for the next hour watched through the window as evening turned to night. The curving drive of the hotel was traced by merging circles of lamplight and the awning had turned a luminous gold. After a time the athletic man appeared in his uniform to relieve the doorman and when a car pulled up he would stride forward to open the door. What Nora felt about him, or her son, did not matter now; they were silhouettes turning end to end against the sea.

An arc of headlights appeared on the road and, sliding into the drive, became the mustard Citroën. Nora rose, paused before the mirror to brush her hair, and left the room. The whisper of satin accompanied her to the main level of the hotel, past the dining room where white cloth and crystal glasses waited. Gordon and Eileen came skipping from the lobby, dressed decently, and ran into the sitting room, from which she could hear the unmistakable touch of her father's hands on a piano, precise and formal. He was playing Scriabin, as he always did when he wanted to show off, and when Nora entered she saw a dozen enraptured guests. Rose, in a white dress and with a ribbon in her hair, sat on the piano bench beside him, watching not his hands but his stern face. Nora listened and when Michael came in from the opposite doorway she did not move but waited for his eyes to find her. When they did he smiled and mouthed across the room, so that she could read the words, *you look beautiful.*

Cary Fagan is the author of five books of adult fiction including the novel Felix Roth *and* The Doctor's House and Other Stories. *His novel* The Animals' Waltz *will soon appear in Germany. He has won the Toronto Book Award and the Jewish Book Committee Prize for Fiction. He has also published three children's books. He lives in Toronto.*

A Minor Incident

Robyn Sarah

For a few years beginning around when I was twelve, my father worked for a Jewish organization, a branch of it devoted to fighting anti-Semitism. To his desk came samples of printed materials against which complaints had been lodged; he had to read these and decide what action, if any, need be taken—he was a sort of filter for hate literature. Sometimes he brought it home with him in the evenings. I remember a kind of pained face he'd have, like the face of someone who has been walking all day in shoes that are too tight, and whose feet have blistered; and he might call to me from his desk in the alcove, when I was doing my homework at the dining-room table: "Esther. Come here, I want you to see something. I want you to read this. Look, look what they say about us, terrible things . . . look . . ."

But I would not; instead I'd gather up my books without a word, and go to my room and shut the door, clenching and unclenching my hands; would he call me again? would he insist? If he did, my mother might protest to him, in a low voice, in Yiddish which I did not understand; and he would reply audibly, in English, "She's old enough. She should see it. She should know."

I do not remember being told about the Holocaust, not when, nor by whom, though it must have been one of them, my father or my mother, who told me, before it was called the Holocaust, before it had a name attached to it whereby it could be handled, contained, dismissed. I do know that only a few years elapsed between the time when, waking from nightmares, I was reassured that there were no wicked witches, that there weren't any monsters, that I didn't need to be afraid because there were no such things, they were just "made up"—and the time when I knew that men in uniforms, ordinary human beings, had dashed out the brains of babies against concrete walls before their mothers' eyes, and then shot the mothers dead; and that this was not a bad dream, not a made-up story, but was the truth and had really happened. Who could accept that and need to hear more? The one image contained the Holocaust for me; in it I felt my knowledge to be complete. The rest was numbers. Say it isn't true? Say it didn't happen *really?* No, it really happened. It happened over and over.

I know now, too, that the years when I lay awake in the dark, fearful of witches, were years when the full extent of the horror was still being uncovered; in our house, years of hushed conversations in Yiddish and rustling newspapers, radio babble, grownup talk behind closed doors. My grandmother was alive, then, and lived with us; I remember her room at the end of the hall, with a smell all of its own that permeated everything in it, the maroon plush chair, the chenille bedspread, the patterned Indian rug. She had her own radio, an enormous one with a wicker front, on a shelf above the bed; she had hatboxes in the closet in which were hats of crumpled felt garnished with glazed wooden cherries, curled black plumes, pearl-tipped hat pins; in her closet, too, there hung old nylons stuffed at the bottom with clove and dried orange peel; on her bureau was a glass bowl filled with rose petals. I remember that every once in a while, my mother would call her to the telephone in a tense, urgent tone, and with one hand to her heart she would go; the conversation that followed would be a trading of names, of people I did not know and of what I later realized were towns in Galicia; yes, she would say then, yes? No. No. No. And she would shake her head at my mother, who hovered listening. No. No. Her face would slacken, she would wish the caller good health in Yiddish, and good luck. "A different Charney," she would say, putting the phone down. "Not related." It was her brother she was hoping to hear from, or have news of. People with the same name, arriving in new cities, would do that then—look up the name in the telephone book, call each listing, seeking family connection, word of relatives. They would look up every spelling. Calls came to us from Charneys, Cherneys, Chierneys. To no avail.

Years passed before I understood the significance of those phone calls. That Gran hoped to hear from her brother, yes; but not why; not what might have become of him, what was more likely with each passing day to have become of him. Years, before I realized what had happened to Gran's sister, the one I knew I was named for. The sister Gran only ever described to me as the small girl whose hair she, Gran, had braided each day, as she now braided mine: Esthie, Gran's littlest sister, still a young girl when Gran came to Canada. Years, before I connected the Holocaust with my family, in a moment of shocked comprehension. That was a connection they never made for me, and why was that? A question I've never answered. There are many such questions from my childhood. The question about Mrs. Howick is one.

When I was twelve my best friend was Rhoda Kendal, quiet like me, studious and shy. We were friends more by circumstance than by our choosing, both of us having transferred from other schools (I in fourth grade, she in fifth) at the age by which girls have formed tight bonds and cliques and are not easily receptive to newcomers. I made no friends in my first year at Wilchester School, and I knew what that felt like, so when Rhoda showed up in my class the next year and I saw her standing alone and diffident in the schoolyard, I took her under my wing. She was a sweet-natured girl with a round smooth face, placid features, and dove-soft black hair that waved. She had an air about her, among the harder-edged, more socially conscious girls, of still being a child, somehow untouched by sophistication; she seemed defenceless to me in her pleated, regulation tunic—a style the other girls, myself included, had discarded in favour of the "A-line" pleatless tunic older girls at our school were permitted to wear.

My own defences were already in place. Close on the realization that I would not be invited into the circle, at Wilchester, came the realization that I did not want to be. I signified this by fastening my pleatless tunic with the old regulation two-button belt, declining to purchase from the office the long, shiny-threaded sash the other girls rushed, thrilled, to trade theirs for. I continued to clump around in navy-blue Oxfords even after the principal, badgered by mothers of unhappy girls, conceded to allow an alternative, more stylish shoe. In this I differed from the two or three other loners in my class: Donna, the only Gentile girl; Brina who had a mysterious illness that absented her for weeks at a time; Jana who was cross-eyed and came to school with egg on her blouse. They, like the rest, opted for sashes and loafers, hoping thus to avoid becoming targets for whispering.

I for my part might be ignored, but I was not whispered about because my marks were too good. I did not strain for this. It was my luck, I was so constituted, that term after term, effortlessly, I led the class; and it was also my luck that Wilchester was a place where that counted.

Rhoda studied much harder than I did and got "Very Goods" and "Goods" where I got "Excellents." It was indicative of her nature that she did not in the least resent me for this, but wholeheartedly admired me and exulted in my successes as if they were her own. "Gee, you make me sick!" she might say, looking at my report card, but she couldn't stop smiling. The other girls who rushed over to compare their marks with mine, subject by subject, said flattering things to me, but their voices betrayed them, barely masking bitter envy.

As my marks protected me from being targeted, so being my friend protected Rhoda. By seventh grade we were inseparable. We spent recesses together, griping about Home Economics, discussing which girls were "boy crazy." On Saturdays we exchanged our books at the library and rode the bus home to her house or mine, giggling too loudly, dropping potato chips in the aisle. At the end of the day, we would walk each other "half-way home," and the half-way might stretch to all the way, then, "I'll walk you half-way home," till it was dark out and we were giddy with the silliness of it. Looking back on it, I think that if Rhoda had not come late to Wilchester and had not met me first of all, she might have become one of the crowd—she had it in her to fit in—whereas I, even had I not come late, would have remained singular and apart. But Rhoda had a loyal heart, and though she ditched her pleated tunic and succumbed soon enough to the sash and loafers, she was staunchly my friend and stuck by me.

Rhoda's parents had been in the camps. I didn't know this at the time; I'm not sure how I know it now. Somebody must have told me, long afterwards—perhaps my mother, perhaps Rhoda herself when we ran across each other again, years later, in graduate school. There was little to show it. They had a home like other homes in that neighbourhood, a brand-new, fashionable split-level, white rugs, sunken living-room, sofas in plastic slipcovers. It was much fancier than my parents' house; the hall floor was parquet instead of vinyl tile; the bedrooms had wall-to-wall carpeting. In the bathroom a basket by the sink contained coloured, scented soap puffs for visitors; I had to ask what they were. Everything was always immaculately clean and tidy; Rhoda and her younger brother and sister, who were twins, were generally not allowed in the living-room. It was a sharp contrast to my house, where a comfortable level of clutter prevailed and everything—furniture, flooring, fixtures—had a well-used, time-worn look.

I preferred for Rhoda to come to my house because I never felt entirely comfortable in hers. Her parents (when they were around, for both worked) spoke Yiddish most of the time; their English was poor, formal, and thickly accented. About them I felt a foreignness, an apart-ness, that I could not read or gauge. Rhoda's mother was not friendly like mine. She would smile at me and say hello when she came in, but she never conversed with me or drew me out, as my mother did with the friends I brought home, and she never sat down to chat with us when we fixed ourselves snacks in the gleaming kitchen; instead she would retire to another room. Once, I confessed to Rhoda that I did not feel welcome in her house, that I thought her mother disliked me; but Rhoda, stunned, told me her mother liked me very much and was happy she, Rhoda, had me for a friend. "She's shy, Esther," she told me, "and she thinks her English is bad. Maybe she's afraid you'll laugh at her. I tell her all the time how brilliant you are—"

Of Rhoda's father I have only one clear memory, and it strikes me now as being an odd one. It is of a hot spring afternoon when I arrived at the house to call for Rhoda; we were going somewhere together, I don't remember where, and as I turned up the walk, Rhoda called to me from her bedroom window, "I'll be down in a sec, I'm just changing." To pass the time, I strolled around the side of the house to look at the lilacs, and came suddenly upon her father on a ladder in the driveway, shirtless, painting the garage door. He had a cap on, and for a moment I thought he was a hired worker; then he looked up from beneath the visor and smiled at me, an oddly warm, sad smile that crinkled the corners of his eyes. He was amused to see that I had not recognized him, and motioned me nearer. "Esther. So, Esther. You like my hat?"

I felt awkward and shy. It was the first time I had seen him alone, or exchanged more than a word or two with him. I can't remember the conversation we had there, in the sunny driveway, with faint breezes wafting the smells of lilac and wet paint; but I remember that the tone was kindly, gentle, sad, and oddly intimate. "It's hard, to be a Jew," I remember him saying to me in his European accent, slowly shaking his head (and my sudden, forlorn sense of discomfiture) — "You know what they say, Esther? It's hard to be a Jew."

What was the context? I cannot at all remember. And did this scene take place before, or after, the incident with Mrs. Howick? That, too, evades me.

Seventh Grade was at that time the final year of elementary school, a year in which teachers strove to prepare students for the comparative rigours to come. Our teacher, Mrs. Howick, was strict and uncompromising, but scrupulously fair. She was a short woman in her mid-forties — the bigger girls already had the edge on her — but she commanded respect in every fibre by the way in which she planted herself at the front of a classroom: square posture, legs placed slightly apart, chin erect, hands on hips. She wore pleated skirts, high-necked blouses, dark support hose, "sensible" shoes. No jewellery, no perfume — indulgences of the younger teachers on staff. Her hair, a nondescript light brown as yet unmixed with grey, was centre-parted and cut short, it stood out a little from her face, giving her a severe yet slightly dowdy appearance.

I liked her well enough. She had a brisk, animated classroom style, could be salty, was not boring, gave a reasonable amount of homework, and expected us to deliver, without coddling. Her digressions, when she digressed, were interesting. She quickly recognized my abilities and acknowledged me matter-of-factly, without effusions; she also gave me to understand that it was the thoughtfulness of my answers, rather than the correctness, that she valued. "Think, think, think," she used to exhort us, "don't let anybody else do your thinking for you." Or sometimes, if she asked for a show of hands on who agreed with a particular answer: "What are you looking around at your neighbour for? I'm asking what *you* think! *You!* Never mind the others! Else you're nothing but sheep." Her words were often accompanied by so vigorous a tapping of her pointer against the blackboard or floor that the wooden stick would snap in two, the broken end bouncing off somebody's desk to the accompaniment of stifled giggles.

The comparing of marks, whenever a test was given back, was something that evoked equal vehemence from her. "Keep your paper to yourself. What do you care what *she* got? "What did you get, what did you get?"" (she mimicked, in mincing tones). "Is that all that matters to you? Look at your *own* paper! *Read* the comments on it—do you think I write them to amuse myself? Look at your mistakes, *learn* something!" And shaking her head in exasperation: "It's marks, marks, marks, with you people—that's all you're interested in. Just like with your parents it's money, money, money. Who's got the most—isn't that true? Today it's marks, marks, marks, and when you grow up, it'll be money, money, money."

One afternoon in midwinter, as I was getting my books together to leave, she spoke to me from her desk in an uncharacteristically personal tone. "Esther, do you have a few minutes to spare? Please stay behind. I want to talk to you about something."

My heart lurched for a second, but my conscience was clear. Maybe she had plans for me for the school concert. Maybe she wanted me to help her with something. Wondering, I followed her out of the classroom—away from a group of girls who were staying for detention—and down the hall a distance. "Esther," she said then, in a confidential voice, putting a hand on my shoulder, "I don't know if you've heard that I've been accused of saying things against Jews." Her eyes looked straight into mine, transfixing me. I shook my head; I was tongue-tied.

"Esther," she repeated. "You're Jewish. You're my brightest student. Please tell me. Have you ever heard me say anything against Jews?"

Again I shook my head. My heart was pounding; I didn't know why. It flashed through my mind that I had never thought of Mrs. Howick as being non-Jewish, or as not being Jewish. I had never thought of the student body at Wilchester, a Protestant school, as being almost all Jewish, even though I knew that in our class, only Donna wasn't, and that on Jewish holidays the handful of students from all grades who showed up were pooled in one classroom and had Art all day; Donna had told us.

"Esther, you know what I say when people in the class start comparing their marks—that they want more marks just like their parents want more money? Tell me the truth. When I said that, did you ever think that I was speaking against Jews?"

No, I had not thought so, I said, completely taken aback.

"Good. I'm glad. Well, dear, some people have thought so. Your friend Rhoda mentioned it to her parents, and her parents complained. They brought it up at the P.T.A. meeting last week, and some parents were upset and called the principal." She tapped the squat heel of her shoe against the shining floor; I saw that the edges of her hair were quivering. "Esther, you know that it was *people* I was talking about, not just Jews, but the kind of person who is always wanting more than the next one; you know some people are like that, don't you?"

"Yes," I said. The tone of entreaty in her voice dismayed me.

"I wanted to ask *you*, because you're a very intelligent girl, and very mature, and because I know you and Rhoda are friends. Maybe you'll talk to her about it. Explain to her that I didn't mean it that way. Will you do that for me?"

I said, "I'll try," and she patted my shoulder, gratefully, and said, "Good girl," and then I left.

That was the end of it; there was no sequel. The episode blew over without further ado; presumably, apologies were made, and the matter was allowed to drop. I did talk to Rhoda, but I don't remember what we said — only that it was a little uncomfortable, a little strained. I think she felt pulled between respect for her parents and loyalty to me; that she neither challenged my opinion nor concurred; but I don't remember. I never mentioned the affair to my own parents, who had little use for the P.T.A. and doubtless had not attended the meeting in question. At the end of the year, Rhoda and I went off to separate high schools and gradually, as our lives diverged, lost touch with each other.

But I still sometimes think about Mrs. Howick. Though I shovelled it under at the time, I know that something opened up beneath me, that afternoon in the dim-lit school corridor, like a section of floor caving in. I see her plain, earnest, sometimes sardonic face; I remember that I liked her, and that she liked me. I hear her voice reiterating the offensive phrases and I wonder: Was it a slur, or wasn't it? And was it fair of her to ask me to decide? I could not argue with her observation as it applied to my school and neighbourhood: the kids were as a rule competitive and pushy for marks; the parents were typically brash, upwardly mobile suburbanites of the fifties. But what gave her the right to say it, and *for whom* was she saying it? "You people," she called us. And what was she asking me to uphold—the thoughtfulness of her statement, or the correctness of it? What unexamined premises of hers did my answer endorse? In retrospect I know that even as I gave her what she wanted, even as I said I had not taken her remark to be a slur, I began to wonder whether it had been; and over the years, off and on, I have gone on wondering.

At first what I wondered about was simple: if I liked her, how could she be an anti-Semite? But if she was an anti-Semite, how could I like her? Later, painfully, having allowed that both could be the case, I wondered which of us I had let down the most.

I remember coming late out of school, that winter dusk, and trudging across the empty schoolyard alone, over the bumpy, frozen crust of old footprints. Rhoda had not waited for me; there was no point, as we walked home in opposite directions. I remember how it began to snow lightly as I reached the gate, and how the snow fell thicker and thicker, in swift dizzying flakes, across my path home.

Robyn Sarah's poetry began appearing in Canadian small magazines in the 1970s. She is the author of seven books of poetry and two collections of short stories, including A Nice Gazebo.

Tommy Fry and the Ant Colony

JOE ROSENBLATT

> the body you think you own is not your own
> as in a rented tuxedo where a dweller shines
> in motions of a little ant in its livingroom
> editing a meal for some lumbering molecule,
> spreads an enormous crumb on a table cloth.
>
> *Tommy Fry*

Tommy Fry had the best pair of eyes a boy could ever own. He could see the ants yards and yards away: millions of black dots trecking frantically across the school yard. Tommy's friends always left him alone when he was concentrating on ants. He would think so deep and hard that his mind would slowly sink behind a gargantuan anthill. People would stop and stare at this strange youngster, his eyes fixed on the ground.

'What you doing, kid?' chirped Mr. Arachnede, the postman. He had no idea that Tommy was watching ants delivering essential twigs, pebbles, meat, assorted slaves, and tidbits of leaves to a central anthill.

Arachnede blew his dog-repellent whistle to get the boy's attention. It seemed to have absolutely no effect on Tommy.

The devoted civil servant proudly dashed off down the block to deliver the rest of the mail. Tommy Fry didn't mean to be rude but he was so absorbed with his tiny friends that everything else was naturally crowded out of his mind.

'Anything wrong, Tommy?' It was Ms. Aphido from down the street.

Line drawing by the author for "Tommy Fry and the Ant Colony"

She was always working in her garden, planting here and there, joining different parts of plants together, taking soil samples to see if the earth was properly fertilized with chemicals, watering the plants with artificial growth aids so they wouldn't wilt, even adding strange compounds to the flower beds so they'd grow much quicker. And to protect her 'creations' she'd mine her precious garden with round sweet poisonous ant traps thus earning the name, *Dirty Thumbs*, from her neighbours who discovered armies of ants surrendering to the sky—

'You're rude,' snapped Ms. Aphido, 'Don't you have any manners? I'm speaking to you!'

Tommy could see her greenish lips frothing soundlessly. Unaware of Tommy's telepathic communication with his little friends, Ms. Aphido marched away in a loud huff. Had she the required antennae to tune into Tommy's wave length, this is what she would have heard:

1st ant:
Tommy, are you still here? Why aren't you in school?

2nd ant:
Hey Charlie! It's the same kid that was here yesterday.

3rd ant:
Tommy, you haven't seen Dirty Thumbs around lately? I'm still sick from those chocolate delights. Some free meal! Why, my second stomach hasn't been the same for a month!

4th ant:
My third leg is growing back thanks to Tommy. He pulled me out of that sugar pail: it was loaded with glue.

5th ant:
Yeah, I lost a leg in that snapdragon. Some machine! If Tommy hadn't opened those jaws—

6th ant:
I hate Dirty Thumbs. I'm on a disability pension because of her—

7th ant:

Tommy, you should be in school today. I've got a little munchkin about your age and he's learning to count pebbles at his school. Education isn't such a terrible thing—smartens up a young fellow.

Tommy was about to tell the six-legged old geezer precisely why he didn't care for school when out stepped the largest ant that he had ever laid his eyes on. He had to be the big wheel.

'What's going on here?' roared the boss. 'Move on, you're holding up the work.' Tommy tried to apologize but before he could mumble *boo*, the boss stood up on his hind legs and growled, 'Listen kid, you've got to move out of the way, nothing personal you understand, I've got a lot of injured workers to get to the hospital.'

'But I can help,' pleaded Tommy, jumping free of two ants carrying an injured worker on a leaf. The boss tried to wave Tommy out of the way again but he was already helping a solitary ant who was labouring tediously in circles. A light breeze (which Tommy detected easily with a wet thumb) had wafted the scent trail away from the main highway. The grateful worker extended one of his antennae, and thanking Tommy, waved goodbye.

The youngster glowed: he had done his good deed in directing him back to a road gang who were clearing away pebbles.

The boss surveyed lines and lines of toiling ants moaning as they ached to lift their burdens over high ground. Their woes amounted to a symphony, and loving those sweet sounds he drove them piteously. But once in a while he rewarded their obedience: he allowed them the delectable refreshment of golden dew.

'Golden Time!' sang the boss. Ambling over to an airhole, be bellowed, 'Come forth, O Mighty and Generous Golden Dew! Your children are famished.'

A transparent golden bovinity (the width of several mature ants) with stubby legs surfaced. The boss kissed her between her wee horns.

'ONLY ONE DROP TO EACH CUSTOMER AND THAT MEANS NO SECOND HELPINGS—'

Tommy watched as each ant revitalized after drinking a drop of golden dew. A shine spread over her face like a deep sunburn. Her eyes sparkled—

'Could I have a drop,' Tommy perspired. *'Please.'*

'Do you think we'd waste our most precious resource on the likes of a silly pinch like you?" came the reply. 'Golden dew is served only to deserving help, not to puppies playing truant.'

Tommy was about to cry when one of the bolder ants said: 'No— wait—Tommy—I'll share my dew with you.'

The young worker ant lumbered above the crowd, his lean legs and headset trembling.

'You remember Tommy. He warned us about Dirty Thumbs' poisonous sweets—those chocolates in the tray—the ones that made us all very sick—remember?'

The boss jumped back as if the truth itself had stung him. He had the sweetest tooth and as a result had suffered the most acute abdominal pain. Greed shadowed the chocolates into his first, second and tertiary stomachs.

'So you're the one,' he squeaked, extending a friendly feeler. Millions of joyous workers cheered Tommy, infusing him with so much mental power (minute electrical blue particles—) that he felt like a giddy ant gorging on a ripened ham sandwich that had been abandoned in the sunny grass; a succulent happiness more brilliant in hue than Aphido's salient thumbs.

'HAIL HAIL TOMMY FRY! HAIL HAIL TOMMY FRY! HAIL HAIL TOMMY FRY!' the ants chanted. Tommy bowed according to ant custom.

He felt like a tank commander returned from the front. Although there were no large silver or gold medals pinned on his chest, his enthusiastic fans noticed a faint aura above Tommy's head. It was not as rich in hue as the Golden Dew, nor half as nutritious, but the keen infinitesimal eyes of ants could discern it. Tommy was *one of them.*

'In the name of the Control Committee,' announced the boss, 'I invite you to a second and *a third indulgence of golden dew.'*

The multitude pushed forward to obtain a better view of their hero. 'And who are you, little fellow?' said Tommy, with disdain for his former adversary who had publicly humiliated him only a few minutes before.

'You mean you don't know my name?' blurted the boss. 'My friends call me Balooza, but in your case—'

Suddenly, a sound like crackling egg-shells, filled the air. What strange music, thought Tommy, scratching his head. Blue and orange sparks collided with headgear. Instinctively obedient ants swiftly formed single lines of restless dots. Tommy snapped to attention. He felt like a mightly general at a reviewing stand.

Gee, they're kind of cute, he muttered.

'Follow me, young fellow,' said Balooza, pinching Tommy out of his reverie.

'Why should I?' asked Tommy.

Balooza pointed in the direction of the central anthill. 'Hip one two—hip one two—hip one two,' he chanted.

Tommy marched obediently at a pace that would have shamed Arachnede, the speedy postman. Balooza gestured to an opening in the central anthill. Tommy couldn't believe that he expected him to scramble through a hole half the size of a pea, a *shrunken pea*.

'You surely don't expect me to drop through there, do you?' blanched Tommy who now for some inexplicable reason could see every detail of Balooza's wee eyes: blood vessels so fine that they throbbed in the light.

Balooza assumed the kindly airs of a father trying to instill confidence in his son on the first day of school.

'Tommy, the Golden Dew needs you. And so for that matter does the rest of the colony. At our Control meeting we decided that you would be Supreme Commander-in-Chief of our Armed Forces. Congratulations, Tommy! I urge you to concentrate on that hole.'

Thoughts flew out of Tommy's ears, mouth, nostrils: useless thoughts, absolutely tasteless. Tommy squeezed his eyes, tweaked his nose, and as if to say, *here goes*, broke through sky. Much to his surprise, he landed on a mound of wet earth.

Gosh, that was great—boy, I'd like to try it again. Balooza, holding his lamp high, led Tommy through a labyrinth of tunnels. Deeper and deeper they descended. Tommy whiffed sweet vegetation and crowds of juicy mushrooms suffusing an aroma of fermented dark earth. Natural nutrients and minerals sang their health. Tommy reflected on how lonely the mushrooms were as they gleamed a deep embarrassed purple. They weren't crusty green like Aphido's thumbs.

Balooza pinched Tommy and dragged him forward toward a high barn. Tommy chanced to look above and, to his utter amazement, he saw stars flittering like moths.

Suddenly, a very lyrical MoooooooooooooooooooooooooooooOOOoooo greeted Tommy's ears.

'She needs you,' whispered Balooza. 'Please go to her! First, I must caution you. Our shift begins very early.' Balooza stared very hard at his luminescent watch.

'080000: 432 *Maboza time. At that hour, give or take a few molecular seconds, we launch our attack. This is war, Tommy, war—casualties will be very high—. Dirty Thumbs is tough, cruel as the poisons she issues—we must be tougher—tougher—We attack bright and early—victory or endless shadows!'*

Tommy nodded. Balooza, noting that he was listening very carefully, continued: 'You'll find your sleeping quarters in the barracks next to the Golden Dew. And now, my good fellow, I bid you good evening.'

Balooza extended a friendly head stem that Tommy shook. Dog-tired, the boy limped toward the barn.

Tommy hadn't pressed any enquiry into the nature of *Maboza time.* Balooza assured him that he would receive a bi-hourly watch. A hundred jewels, accurate to one ten thousandth of a micro second; instantly translatable into either Maboza or Aphido time.

I bet that watch is worth billions, he thought, licking his lips. *Yeah, billions.*

His bed of fresh leaves smelled of mint laced clover, refreshingly dry and clean for an honoured guest.

Tommy drifted into a dream the shape of a poem. Not a real rhyming poem, but one with lines drifting across his mind like nervous caterpillars.

Tommy smiled. An ant poem. The ODE had the flavour of long stemmed mushrooms.

OOOOOooooo moaned Tommy kicking his legs out.
What pretty colours!
oooooooooooooooooooh
ooooooooooh   ewwwwwwwwwwwwww
wow
euuuuuuuuuuuu

—II—*(to be read by two girls & a boy)*

TOMMY'S ANT POEM
An ant clears away grits of mind

dead tissues of thought
we shall all become storage bottles
munch up the leaves & deposit
that residue
it ll grow into MUSHROOMS
hellow   your secret MUSHROOM
& mine
in the dark   secret transplants
yours & mine
O an ant is a NATURAL chemist depositing
a prefungi residue
you & I in the dark
fungus farmers grow their food in beds of dead leaves
fungus farmers grow their food in beds
fungus farmers grow their thoughts in bed
weight lifter ants grow their thoughts
being reborn & reborn
solitary ants   dots of thought   strung together
fungus farmers grow their thoughts in dead beds
more ants than stars in the sky
each ant is a moment
each ant is a moment
ants are surrounding you & eating you
gangleon-on-leg   together eating you
a solitary moment follows you to a sandwich
in the field   a sandwich for a hungry ant
& you open open open   & it cries hello hello hello
have a bite of me
& six soft legs reach out   please be eated
for you're a honey sandwich   yes you are
suppose I woke up & found tongs reaching out—

suppose i woke up

The poem floated away like tired smoke. In its place appeared specks of green blood, braying dray-beetles, wounded elephant bugs, wings of crushed reconnaissance moths: Atlas, Tiger Swallowtails, Pygmyblue,

Spring Azure, Common Wood Nymph—Arctic Skipper—shards of battle plans, fatigued medics: brown ants with white and red armbands strung around their dangling limbs—secret communiques—makeshift emergency surgical tents—soiled flags flapping—dark tunnels—and one huge stone mushroom—

A *national monument*, gasped Tommy in his sleep.

The following morning Tommy was pleasantly wakened by the pressure of a lilypad against his cheeks. He opened his eyes and saw the Golden Dew. She began a more melodic Mooooooooooooooo. Tommy felt stabs of hunger. Golden Dew read his mind, and produced a few delicious drops. His hunger appeased, he patiently waited for Balooza to show him the way to the War Room. Finally, after what seemed like hours (distorted Maboza time), Tommy heard the patter of six approaching pads.

'Hello,' chirped Balooza. Tommy noticed a purple scarf wrapped neatly around his middle. This was a war sash of the colony—the *colours*.

'Time for the War Room,' said Balooza smartly. Marching quickly through endless corridors they arrived at the entrance to a brightly lit room. Seated around were the Elders: *the Control Committee*. The pair were greeted by a doddering senior who extended a tendril in Tommy's direction, and a leg toward Balooza, indicating that they may be seated. After a moment's silence, the patriarchal sextaped spoke in a tremulous rasp.

'General Tommy, and you, Sir, welcome to our circle. This morning I took the liberty to assemble the elders of the colony to hear your Master Plan regarding the horde of brown sugar in Dirty Thumbs' house. Gentlemen, I needn't eleborate to you and the Council the vileness of her weaponry—oh, the orphans, the cripples, the blind—'

Venemous drool glistened on the corners of his fissured mouth. 'Tommy, how do you intend to destroy her chemicals? Those deceitful poisonous cafes—buckets of lethal honey—not to mention unconscionable meat-munching orchids and the other sick extravagances! Heavens, I can't stand to witness so many casualties.'

'Tommy, we have heard of your incredible military exploits—therefore the Council in its wisdom has appointed you *Field Commander, general of generals*.'

Field Commander, Field Commander. A nice ring to it.

'Now young fellow, have you the Victory plan?' Tommy nodded. 'Well then, make your presentation.'

Tommy began his cool delivery.

'My friends, we're going to need a stronger attack force. More allies, energies. A battering ram if we are to succeed: and *succeed* we shall—'

Tommy halted, puzzled by the frozen expressions on those ancient faces. The spokesman explained the situation to him: 'Commander, last night while you slept near our Golden Dew, *(bless her)*— our scouts established communication with other colonies: *Harvesters, Carpenters, Bulldog Rippers*, a combined force of TWO HUNDRED AND FIFTY MILLION SOLDIERS ON FULL COMBAT ALERT. And now, dear Commander, your plan. Do speak up. You tend to mumble.'

'Yes, of course,' piped up Tommy. He began to outline his supreme military plan (in vivid chromaphotonic colour). This had been revealed in one of his many dreams.

'We must hit her chemical complexes, spill that blasphemous XZONO-B-2XC MORDANTO cleanser right down her drain. Gentlemen, in order to accomplish this and make off with the brown sugar, we must first create a DIVERSION. We need to distract Dirty Thumb's attention with a lightning Bulldog Ripper attack at the front. This will keep her busy with her obnoxious sprays. Those Bulldozers are tough. While she's busy with that frontal attack, my select Maboza commandos can sneak around the garden entering the cellar. Harvesters and Carpenter divisions will move directly to the treasury, removing the sugar.'

I *guarantee* that my elite corps shall secure that chemical depot and dispose of those poisons. The whole operation should not take more than eight Aphido hours. I suggest we set our watches for 18,000 *hours Maboza time. This should give us one and a half hours Aphido time.'* The field commander observed the Elders manipulating their watches on their legs.

Tommy and Balooza marched back to the barracks to say goodby to their friend, the Golden Dew. 'Moooooooooooooooooooooo,' she wept until Tommy's heart was nearly broken.

Goodbye, O gentle Golden Dew, pray for our safe return. Take care—
Suddenly, Balooza broke into a spirited yet mournful song.

We have moved pebbles, we shall move Aphido
beware, for we'll be marching thru
no more jaws of her fast creations
peonies with their sickening glew—Eww

take your chocolate mo / tel / s   O you're through eww
yeah, you call those Venusflytraps, your children?
feed them ugliness, not us Ohh   ewwwwwww
poison honey, everything's poison honey
ewwwwwww

hip hip—hail Tommy—hip hip—

—III—

Outside the central anthill millions of soldiers assembled from the other colonies to the beating of drums: do de do de do de do do de do do de do dee dee—The air was crisp and cold as Aphido's thumbs. The sky made Tommy quake, for he had once been as tall as that blue far above him. Commander Tommy was contemplating his diminishing state when Balooza approached with tears in his eyes.

'Commander Tommy, Sir, we've been betrayed for a load of sugar. The traitor has been beheaded and buried in an unmarked air-hole. We're finished! ruined! disaster! Our plans are known by Dirty Thumbs. She knows the *exact* hour of the attack. Our allies will destroy us if we change our plans —too late—do you hear them?'

Tommy leaned in the direction of the chanting. The merry breezes carried the busy tune: KILL KILL KILL KILL KILL KILL KILL KILL KILL KILL KILL KILL KILL KILL KILL KILL KILL KILL KILL KILL KILL KILL KILL KILL KILL KILL.

And now Commander Tommy of *Operation Lightning* cleared his throat. (Only the grasshoppers, hogsnails, elephant bugs, and mercenary moths revving their soft engines penetrated the dusty stillness.)

All aerial headextensions were TUNED *in.*

'Soldiers of the Carpenter division,' exhorted the youngster. 'Soldiers of the Bulldog Rippers—' A tidal wave of growls pursued by the contagious chant: TOMMY TOMMY TOMMY TOMMY TOMMY TOMMY TOMMY TOMMY TOMMY TOMMY TOMMY. 'Soldiers of the Harvest division—soldiers of the Maboza brigade—'

Tommy waved his fingers for silence. Deliberately neglecting to mention the betrayal, he outlined his grand stratagem. The soldiers picked up fresh leaves to be used as shields, and stones as missiles. Moments away from the battle hour, a scout on an elephant beetle approached. He confirmed Balooza's intelligence report; but from the scout's own lips, the news seemed more ominous. Dirty Thumbs had put out her shiny motel-like ant-traps: these laden with sweet toxic delights that even Tommy found hard to resist.

Dirty Thumbs prepared her spray guns with silver dust. Her garden hoses were poised. Millions of brave soldiers would be crushed by cascading water. The only bit of good news to lighten the thick gloom was that Mr. Arachnede, the postman, who was to have manned the water taps for an undisclosed fee, fled the yard when informed of the sheer numbers of the invading forces. Glad to fight another day, he mused. Besides, there was the matter of being taken alive—uglies—munchers—and for the sake of a notorious greenthumb who had a fetish for crazed drooling snapdragons, sticky peonies, voracious pesty little Venusflytraps with their infinite mindless appetites for the black and red beef steak of pure ant. And then there were the meat-eating lunacies, the cultivations of Aphido's feverish mind.

Best to continue delivering the mail, especially those pastel postcards from sunny climes.

Commander Tommy, feeling like an enormous electrical generator on full Killowatt power, turbines singing, urged his comrades: KILL KILL KILL KILL KILL KILL KILL KILL KILL KILL KILL KILL KILL KILL KILL KILL KILL KILL KILL KILL KILL KILL.

All around him he could hear drums (do de do de do de do do—) and the cries of the wounded. Ambulance and medical orderlies swarmed over to sort out the living from the dearly departed. Tommy observed wounded grasshoppers braying in pain; legs torn apart by a honey trap, the ground spotted with green blood (Tommy couldn't tell grasshopper's blood apart from the ants'). A heavy Bulldog was trapped under the carcass of a fat grasshopper: the little trooper was squealing for *stretcher-bearers.*

Now Tommy proceeded ahead with one passion, *revenge!*

Hordes of tough Bulldoggers, Carpenters, and the few stragglers of Harvesters (a pitiful number) met the silver dust as Tommy would later put it, with *gut courage.* It didn't save them from spontaneous cremation. Millions more disintegrated before his eyes. Balooza caught up with his superior: *It'll soon pass, Commander Tommy,* he panted, as the silver menace evaporated. Then, an even more terrifying sight greeted them: Dirty Thumbs, grinning and bubbling, aimed her deadly water hose at the advancing armies.

'Back, you dogged fools!' she screamed. Walls and walls of cold water struck home. Tommy heard the blood-curdling cries of Bulldoggers (who were more water resistant) fall on Aphido, growling.

She tried to wash them off as they abundantly blanketed her petit, conch-shaped ears, her tulip mouth, dilated daisy eyes and other anatomically sensitive regions. Biting here and there—in their infinitesimal bodies: sanguinary rhythms from a dark ancestry—'Devils—devils—' she shrieked.

—IV—

TOMMY'S WAR ODE
miniscule moments motoring to war
in the heat of battle motoring to war o
miniscule soldiers   minutiae spirritus
o woe   o gore   minutes away midnight soldiers
fissures of moonlight   laughing
moonlight soldiers motor
        spiritus diminutiae   away with your barbeque gases
dissolvents & glue   eww   meat munching
maniacal flowers
        blood slavering jaws   ewwwww   I HATE FLOWERS
                                                    ewwww
throats with spikey teeth white as snowdrops
coming up in bloom ewww
ewwwwwwwwwww   lunch   o   ewwwwwwwwwww
& then there's your wild
                        motels
            chocolate paradise O
        mouth watering
                free bloody
                    LUNCHES
                FREE
                    ewwwwwwww

                        I HATE FLOWERS
                        I HATE FLOWERS
                        I HATE FLOWERS
                        (O there's blood on those petals)

The Maboza sabotage unit tumbled into the dank basement. Tommy gleefully watched as the commandos emptied batches of chemicals; laughing to see torrents of sizzling liquid spill down the drains.

'Enough, my good fellows,' he cried. 'Let's get back to Dirty Thumbs.' They followed him to where Aphido lay bleeding on the ground. A few straggling medics kneeled beside her. Balooza hovered with his final injection.

'You're not so tough now, are you, Dirty Thumbs?' shouted Balooza, licking his antish white lips. Tommy moved to block him. He wanted one last word with her.

'Dirty Thumbs, I'm Commander Tommy. Do you have any last requests before you are put away?'

'Tommy, Tommy, it's *really* you, and now you're a *big shot*. Oh Tommy, I beg of you, I ask your forgiveness for all the wicked deeds I have perpetrated on your little friends. I did it to save my cabbages, Venus Fly-traps, Sanpdragons, and my precious Peonies. Brave soldiers, you have won. Take my garden, my house, they're yours. But let me live,' she sobbed.

Moved by her plea Tommy decided to put her case across to his comrades.

'My fellows-in-arms. Future generations will remember the great battle of Aphido Wall. I now ask you to perform an even greater act of bravery. Let Dirty Thumbs live! We shall give her four life sentences to be served in each colony: in the nurseries, to feed those poor orphans. Yes, my brave fellows, *four life sentences—*'

A few roars of protest, but the majority found the punishment appropriate and applauded the wisdom of their leader. He turned to Dirty Thumbs. 'Do you agree with your punishment?'

She gasped at the sentence, yet seemed resigned to her fate. 'Yes, yes, anything but those awful stings.'

Tommy stared at her: *I must miniaturize her through my mental powers.* Her twisted genius bent his brain waves. The ants weighed the two contestants in the field. Dirty Thumbs had to blink when Tommy came right up to her bleeding nose: 'Tommy, great snowpeas, you stop that!'

Tommy stared into her huge, swollen eyes which still resisted his powers. 'Oh dear, what's become of you, child?'

Commander Tommy's concentration was broken. He turned to

Balooza and requested the ultimate psychic conductor: the entire ants' energy field to overcome Aphido's resistance. Balooza barked his orders. Immediately the soldiers linked feeler to feeler. Tommy smiled. He had the power to bend her will.

She was shrinking by degrees. Her final piercing cry made his ears reverberate. Half the size of a fully grown ant, she offered little resistance to the rugged navvies who were dumping her into a straw cage. Balooza assured Tommy that she would be taught a useful trade. 'She'll make a superior mother for the colonies.'

The price of victory was dear. Tommy paled at the sight of a soldier who had been struck by horrid laughing gas: the poor creature was chuckling himself to death, and not even the news of his wife's demise could control that madness. The victim combusted from laughter.

Could such a monster as Dirty Thumbs be reformed?

Tommy called a meeting on the disposition of the spoils under the great tent where he declared Dirty Thumbs' garden, and her house *occupied territory*, subject to military law. Her kitchen was to be used as a skin graft lab for those who suffered the caustic sprays. There would be an *Arms and Legs Transplant Unit* for those who could not generate a missing limb. The livingroom was considered for a blood plasma clinic. A casualty list of those missing, maimed and killed in action would have to be drawn up. What was important was the settlement of spoils among the colonies: dividing up the brown sugar, sharing kitchen, bathroom, cellar and livingroom facilities. Tommy realized that a war was imminent if that issue wasn't resolved. He ordered Balooza to summon the Elders of the other colonies.

After days of haggling, an agreement was drawn up leaving one chore left: Aphido Dirty Thumbs. She was summoned to stand trial, but the Elders, finding victory sweeter even than brown sugar, forgave their captive. In time she became an endearing grandmother to millions of offspring, even receiving the *Super Mom Award* and a substantial increase in salary amounting to a more generous portion of golden dew.

Tommy was given a seat on the Council, the youngest member, his new title: *Marshalissimo of the Realm.* It meant that he was next in line to be Dean of the College of Elders.

The Golden Dew gave Tommy a wet kiss when she heard about his promotion, and the faithful multitude erected a huge monument to Marshalissimo Tommy: a great black stone mushroom. Everybody met in the field outside the main anthill to commemorate the fallen at Aphido's Wall. To signify their grief, the black ants wore red, and the red ants wore black. They chanted Tommy's name for hours until he delivered a powerful speech about his humble beginnings —

EPILOGUE
out there in the lesser worlds
peeping atoms are ants.   it is quiet out there
munch up the leaves my children   secret sentinels
grow in the darkness under the earth
your earth & mine   an ant is an orphan
o an ant is an orphan   you & I
a residue   erupting bodies   flow flow
burst into MUSHROOMS
out there the soil is damp
semi-colons breathe
you & I   now invisible
we are in the eyes   in compound pools
up in the sky   O see you in the sky
out there among the salt
there is a cow out there   afraid

Tommy Fry

Joe Rosenblatt, poet-painter, was born in Toronto in 1933. He has published more than a dozen books of poetry and fiction, with his own illustrations, including Escape From the Glue Factory, *a memoir about growing up Jewish in Protestant Toronto.* Top Soil, *his selected poems, won the Governor General's Award. Since 1980 he has lived in Qualicum Beach on Vancouver Island.*

A Story with Sex, Skyscrapers, and Standard Yiddish

NORMAN RAVVIN

The temptation was terrible. Norman Flax sat at his desk overlooking Seventh Avenue. The night behind the window turned the glass into a mirror in which he saw himself, along with Lola who stood naked behind him, holding in each hand a newly peeled lichee nut, two wet ivory balls like tantalizing pearls in her palms. A Flaxian simile if ever there was one! But Flax did not want to write about the lichee nuts. Lola called them professional aids. She said they were the most sensual objects in the entire city, and she had peeled each one carefully, using her big square front teeth, then licking them clean, to help him get in the mood to work on the sex scene he'd been starting and failing to write all week. Lola insisted that Flax—who worked by day as a Yiddish typewriter salesman—would never sell his fiction and become a famous writer if he could not write about sex.

But Flax wanted to write about skyscrapers and clouds. He'd gotten an idea from a recent accident in which the Empire State Building was hit by a private plane. One of the secretaries interviewed in the aftermath said that clouds wafted into the offices on the eightieth floor. Little wisps floated in through open windows, hovered by a vice-president as he tried to gather his flying papers, then went out the door looking for more interesting company. But the skyscraper and cloud story was not to be. Not tonight.

Lola stood close behind Flax, who rested his hands on the keys of his typewriter—a Smith Corona English model. He felt her hips against his back. Her breasts rested on his shoulders. Then each of her palms passed before his face and offered him the moist lichee nuts. He bent to take one out of her hand with his lips. The other she dropped as he kissed her palm, her wrist, the underside of her arm. He turned on his stool to face her and Lola began working his pants and underwear off so he could step out of them. She brought him up hard and sat, straddling his lap, raising and lowering herself. He felt himself disappear into their lovemaking. In his last thoughts he wondered what her hands were doing behind his back: were they resting on the desk so she could better lift and lower herself, or were they tapping out the words of their sex, the keys of his machine sticking to each slick finger?

—2—

Flax was flush. It was only the middle of the month, but the coming weeks were paid for, along with the next month and the one after that. He'd already made his season's sales quota, having struck gold at the big Hollywood-style synagogue at the top of Central Park. A thief had gone through their offices, taking all kinds of things that would be useless to anyone who wasn't running a synagogue: letterhead blessed by the-one-above, prayer books dedicated to philanthropic members, prayer shawls, and even the long plush blue-tasselled cushions that lined the benches before the ark. Of course, the thief had taken the typewriters—English and Yiddish models alike. Flax had read about the theft in the newspaper and got directly into a cab, which took him uptown. He managed to sell eleven machines: five standard Yiddish models and six English, which he arranged to be sent by a wholesaler he relied on in a pinch.

So Flax had time for his writing work. A panorama of days and weeks opened up before him. Most of the world was at war, but Flax was at his leisure. Lola had finished the story he'd begun about skyscrapers and clouds. She'd sat down at the typewriter one afternoon, read what he'd left half-finished in a pile on the desk, and promptly completed it. When she suggested he send the story out under his own name, Flax felt insulted. It was as if she were patronizing him, suggesting that without her he was hopeless. He refused to claim something that was really hers, so the story lay in the bottom drawer of his desk. He thought of it as a distant relative, prematurely buried.

Flax sat down to work and found, propped on the keys of his typewriter, a business card. The card read:

SAM FAIRWEATHER
CURATOR'S AIDE
SPECIALIZING IN LEGENDS
OF THE CANADIAN NORTHWEST COAST

He supposed this was another of Lola's professional aids, but what it had to do with sex Flax could not guess. He turned the card over. On the back Lola had printed:

43rd Street Automat. 11:30

The message was cryptic. Had she made the appointment for him or for herself? Flax didn't care. He had work to do. He had an idea for a story that was to be called "The Organ Grinder's Parrot Draws Lucky Tickets". The bird was something he remembered his father telling him about, a real spectacle back in the Russian town where his father was born. The man who owned the bird arrived whenever the circus was nearby. He was some kind of hanger-on, but no one knew what the organ grinder and his bird had to do with the other circus performers. He brought the bird to town along with a wooden box full of tickets, and stood in the market, yelling, "My parrot draws lucky tickets," tempting the townspeople to wager that the bird would reach into the box with his beak and pull out a ticket entitling one of the locals to a wonderful prize: a barrelful of Turkish tobacco, a set of spoons engraved with the image of Emperor Franz Joseph II, dinner for two at the Royal Hotel in Minsk.

Norman Flax sat at his desk, his chin in his palm, watching the rain roll down his window. He tried to decide where to begin. With the bird? Or the circus more broadly? Or the prizes? Minsk?

Just then, the front door slammed and Flax heard Lola come in. Her shoes were noisy in the front hall. He began to type, to signal that he was working and should not be disturbed. The letters gathering on the page looked like a crossword puzzle filled in by a child. As he rolled the sheet out of the machine, he looked up and saw himself reflected in the darkened window beyond his desk—not himself sitting, but another Norman Flax standing in the centre of the room, wearing his fedora and ancient rain coat, both of these a little darker than usual because they were completely soaked. He started, but as he looked more carefully at the reflection in the glass he realized he was not having an out-of-body experience; there was no spirit playing games with him. It was Lola who stood behind him, dressed in his clothes, her hair tucked into the collar of the coat.

He watched as her reflection came toward him, growing larger in the darkened window, her heels loud on the wood floor. She reached over his shoulder to remove his glasses, setting them down on the desk, and then took his hand. Everything was blurry before his unaided eyes as the figure dressed as himself directed him to the bed, pushed him softly so that he lay down, and slowly undressed him, the wet sleeves and lapels of his coat brushing his face and chest. He smelled the years of rain and city in the fabric. His rain. His city. Then the figure wearing his clothes got on top of him and began to undress, so that Lola's body appeared from under his unbuttoned shirt, and her hips slipped from a pair of his wool pants. He shut his eyes as the counterfeit of himself—so much more tantalizing and elegant half-undressed than he would ever look—began to make love to him. The last thing he glimpsed was fleeting, there and gone, a form conjured by the movement of Lola's hand and the flap of a lapel. As she rose and fell he thought he spied the parrot his father had known in Russia disappearing into a dark fold of skin and cloth. He listened, hoping to hear the number it drew, but there was no sound in the room except the noises their bodies made and the rain.

—3—

Norman Flax sat at his desk, clipping his nails. Paring his nails. Doing them—whatever it was he was up to, it wasn't writing. Lola had gone out before he woke. She had taken his hat and coat. It appeared she'd put on a pair of his shoes and the shirt he'd worn the previous day. Since the rain had blown through, there was no reason to get dressed up, but Flax didn't concern himself with this. He drank his morning coffee and read the paper. Milt Schmidt of the Boston Bruins had broken his thumb, while in Poland it looked like the end of the world was coming. On his desk, beside the typewriter, Flax found a sheaf of paper, tightly rolled and fastened by a black shoelace taken from one of his shoes. Flattening the papers on his desk, he read a letter addressed to him accepting a story entitled "Sex, Skyscrapers, and Standard Yiddish". Paper-clipped to it was the version Lola had completed, with a few suggestions for minor revisions. The acceptance letter was from a prestigious New York magazine that had rejected everything he'd ever sent them without even a cursory thank you. It was bizarre to see such compliments addressed to him. The story was a "gem", a "treasure". He had "plumbed certain depths of sexuality" that no other writer of his time could touch. Would he like to drop by the office of the editor and discuss arrangements for him to contribute on a weekly basis?

At first Flax didn't know what to do. He held the papers in his hands and circled the room in his stocking feet. He thought of his name in print, week after week. And cocktail parties. Didn't writers go to cocktail parties? But . . . but . . . no. It wouldn't do. He wrote the magazine to say he had changed his mind about his submission. Would the editor please forget he'd ever sent it?

With this out of the way, Flax got down to work. He had another story in mind with a rather complicated plot that brought together three newspaper articles he'd collected from the *Times*. These had to do with a photographer, a ruined national library, and a man on death row. Flax thought things could develop like this: among the losses brought about by the bombing of the National Library of N was the country's record of its own history. No one had ever written a thing about N, neither abroad nor in N itself. No foreigners were allowed within its borders. Cameras had been barred from private use, so, except for government photographers, no citizens had any pictures of the country. Because the ruler of N had been suspicious of modern technology—which he viewed as spy equipment in the employ of the major powers—he had banned all film and sound recording. The National Library alone had permission to own this technology, and its staff had kept meticulous records over the years using all the modern media. They had preserved these with utmost care, letting the public see exhibitions of photographs and films of themselves as part of seasonal national festivals. These festivals had proven to be extremely popular. But with the Library destroyed and the next festival quickly nearing, for the first time the festival-goers were faced with the prospect of there being no pictures, no recordings of local voices available for the celebration. This worried the leader of N. None of his advisors had any ideas on how to solve this predicament, except for one, whose name was Bruno. Bruno said he had once seen a security file concerning a state archivist who used government cameras to make photographs, for which he had kept the plates. Squirrelling them away, this man had created one of the most magnificent private collections of images in the world, and for a time his cramped apartment had become a den of underworld committees and countercultural sub-movements. A haven for dissidents who visited him to view his plates and revel in the sheer pleasure of looking. But the photographer had been arrested and was awaiting execution on death row.

As Flax was deciding what would become of the hapless photographer and the festivalless land of N, he looked out his window at the fall street. A crowd often lined up before the Canadian consulate, which rented its offices on the main floor of the building directly across from his. He saw the usual gathering of oldtimers and youths, Bohemians and renegades, who spent their mornings hoping they'd be given an entry visa. They stood for hours in the rain or sun or traffic smog, depending on their luck, waiting to offer their most polite face to the Canadian who manned the visa desk. There was one Canadian. One desk. Hundreds of visa seekers on the block.

Sometimes Flax scanned the crowd for familiar faces: which of his frustrated friends had given up on their lives and decided to go north? But today he didn't have to look long to see a familiar head—the hair a dark mirror in which Flax saw the shimmer of a chrome blue sky. Lola, halfway along in line, chatted with a tall man in an Elmer Fudd hat. As Flax watched, the man did up and then undid his earflaps. Lola wore Flax's raincoat and held his hat in one hand, but he would have needed his glasses to see whether the shoes she had on were also his. Lola looked up and saw Flax in his pyjamas, standing at the glass beside his typewriter. She seemed to squint as she waved. It was September and the city had softened a bit. Even the skyscrapers looked pretty in the low light. Maybe, Flax thought, the Canadian visa man would tell Lola *No*.

—4—

It was early October when Lola vanished. Flax went out less and less. He stopped writing altogether. His ideas would not gel but floated, like the cloud had through the shaken offices of the Empire State Building. He had his *Times* delivered, and he paid a kid who lived down the hall to buy him cold cuts at a nearby delicatessen.

Lola had left all her things behind. Her shoes. Her hair brush. A box of tampons and half a carton of cigarettes. He'd received no word at all from her. As far as he could tell she'd gone north. Flax didn't know much about Canada, but he assumed that wherever Lola had gone the hallways smelled of snow. He knew about those cold fronts they had up there. But beyond that, Flax had heard stories that were so third- and fourth-hand he assumed they were mythic. In Canada, he'd been told, you could flush a toilet from here to doomsday and you wouldn't use all the water they had in their rivers and lakes.

Unfolding his *New York Times*, Flax wondered if there was anyone like him up there. Was there a Norman Flax wandering around in Montreal, profiting from typewriter deficits? Was there a street in Toronto where the sounds at night included the *clappa-clappa-clap* of a Flaxian tale being typed out to an audience of none, the words stepping across the page, each one a proverbial bullet in the heart? Certainly there was no Norman Flax in Calgary, Alberta. He'd heard about Calgary from a friend of a friend who'd gone there for the funeral of a great-aunt. The old lady had left the man a few hundred bucks and he felt obliged to appear at the interment, though he resented blowing twenty-five dollars on a bus ticket just to make a good show in exchange for two-hundred. In wartime Calgary, you had a lot of beef-powered men planting gardens in the sand out front of their kit-built wood frame houses. You had a few newly minted millionaire farmers who'd struck oil in their wheat fields and were spending their fortunes as fast as they could. You had a lot of ladies going for tea at the Palliser Hotel's Rimrock Lounge, where the mural at the back of the room portrayed a big Indian massacre on the anonymous prairie.

Thinking of the mural, Flax remembered the calling card Lola had left with the vague scribbling on the back. He'd kept it—in a tea cup full of postage stamps and eraser ends, which sat on his desk—but he'd never bothered to ask what it meant. Could Sam Fairweather have put her onto Canada? It was conceivable. When Lola hit on something that pleased her, she just went ahead and did it. That was one of the things Flax liked most about her.

Since he had no other pressing duties, Flax began eating his lunch at the 43rd Street Automat. He arrived around eleven, ordering enough food to warrant the endless cups of coffee the waitress poured. After a few weeks of overeating and very little sleep, his patience paid off. At exactly 11:30 a man entered the Automat. Rather than take a table he stood and stared at the machinery as it dispensed sandwiches, steaming soup, and cream-topped wedges of angelfood cake.

Flax felt certain he'd found his man. The stranger wore a fringed buckskin coat and had hair far below his shoulders. Flax went and stood beside him.

"Can't decide?" Flax asked.

"Decide?" The man had an interesting accent—his face was muscular and weather-drawn, and this word came out of him as if it were monumental, chiselled in stone. At least that's how it sounded to Flax.

"I often can't decide myself, " Flax said. "It's usually between the pastrami and the scrambled eggs." He pointed at these two alternatives.

The man turned to face the machinery. "I'm not deciding. All the food here is terrible. I like the way the machines present their offerings." This, he explained, reminded him of a fairy tale he'd heard as a child.

Flax asked where the man liked the food. Without looking away from the automat machinery, the man named a dairy delicatessen below Washington Square.

"It's funny we don't see each other there then," Flax said. The delicatessen was one of his favourites. He offered to buy lunch, and as they walked down Fifth Avenue, Flax asked his companion where he was from. The visitor explained that he had only been in Manhattan for a few months. He was a Kwakiutl Indian from the Northwest Coast of Canada. An anthropologist had hired him as an informant, and he spent his days in the basements of New York museums and art galleries, explaining to curators what their collections contained.

Flax and the man arrived at the delicatessen and sat down to eat. A waiter with huge sweat stains under his arms took their order. The Kwakiutl man ordered three blintzes and an egg cream. When the egg cream came he beheld it—he truly beheld it, his shoulders back, hands on his knees—then he finished the drink in one long swallow.

Flax was too excited to eat. He enjoyed the man's company, but he was giddy with expectation and hope, and this caused him to lose his cool. He asked the man a question that he would otherwise have worked into their conversation more casually.

"You wouldn't happen to know someone up there named Lola?"

Flax's companion cut into a blintz. "Up where? Who?"

"In Canada. Lola."

"Lola. In Canada."

"Yes. She's about this high. She has dark hair. You two share a slight resemblance."

The waiter came and filled their water glasses. The ceiling fan thudded through the stale air above them. The Kwakiutl man beheld Norman Flax as if he couldn't wait to get back to his room and write this all down.

—5—

Norman Flax considered the alternatives. "From New York to Montreal. From NewYork to Quebec via Springfield. From Boston to St. John by railway. From Portland to Vancouver." Somehow, he liked the sound of the last route, but how would he get to Portland? He had an old Baedeker for Canada that he'd borrowed from the Public Library. It was written for the optimistic traveller of 1921. All kinds of information in it could probably be dismissed as out-of-date, but Flax was never sure. For instance "Hotel prices have been affected by the Prohibition legislation which now prevails throughout the dominion except in the Province of Quebec." Hotel-keepers, the guide added, "are also warned against persons representing themselves as agents for Baedeker's Handbooks." Now there was an idea! Flax began to feel more upbeat about his plan. Canada had a lot of land but very few people. This made his quest seem reasonable.

As he lay on the bed, imagining how he would introduce himself as an agent for Baedeker's Handbooks, he drifted off and began to dream a dream of Canada. He was an agent for Baedeker, visiting a massive old hotel in a Canadian town full of land but hardly a soul. The desk clerk was appreciative, welcoming, anxious to impress. He promised Flax the hotel's finest room: the Prairie Suite.

On the way up in the elevator the clerk chatted in a casual way about the oil well spurting in his uncle's wheat field. Flax asked about volume, quality of the crude, transport details—things he knew about only when he dreamed. As they approached the door of the room the clerk had chosen, Flax heard a familiar sound—the *clapp-clapp-clapping* of a typewriter, along with the satisfying spring-and-clunk of paper being pulled sharply from the machine. Suddenly the clerk was gone and the room was open before him. It had three windows, twice Flax's height, which let in a pale northern light. Under-foot, instead of linoleum or wood or rug, was a luxurious growth of wild grass that grew wall to wall. In one corner a bison grazed, its brown liquid eyes surveying the room.

The typing seemed to come from behind a closed door in the room's far wall. Following the sound, Flax opened the door and saw Lola, who sat at a desk with her back to him. His coat and hat lay on the floor beside her. And on her feet beneath the desk were his shoes. As she looked over her shoulder, her long fingers rested for a moment on the keys of the type-writer, and Flax was suspended, invisible, nothing more than the shadow of a character in one of his shelved stories.

But Lola always knew what came next. Would it be a Flaxian sojourn on the plains? Or a breakneck mystery set among the skyscrapers of Van-couver Island? Possibly she was tapping out the words he never could write himself—the words of their sex.

"Come here," she said, as her fingers regained their momentum on the keyboard. "Come here and see what I've written."

Norman Ravvin is a writer, critic, editor, and teacher. His books include a collection of stories, Sex, Skyscrapers, and Standard Yid-dish, *a novel,* Café des Westens, *as well as a volume of essays,* A House of Words: Jewish Writing, Identity, and Memory. *Most recently, he published* Hidden Canada: An Intimate Travelogue, *which draws on his experiences living in Alberta, British Colum-bia, Ontario, New Brunswick, and Quebec.*

The Murder

TOM WAYMAN

My family was haunted by the murder, even in the New World. I can't remember when I first was told the tale, since I'm unable to recall a time I wasn't aware my great-grandparents and a great-aunt died at the hands of an assailant in Amlin. This was the shtetl in Byelorussia where my father's people came from, a little distance northeast up the Dvina from Vitebsk.

Perhaps I heard about the crime originally from my Aunt Zifra, my father's twin sister, or from my uncles on my father's side, or maybe from Reb Lucharsky. He was a melamed who came from Velizh, a town in the neighborhood of Amlin, and so he was classified as a landsman and welcomed as such in our house. "A terrible, terrible thing," was the invariable comment that followed yet another retelling of how my zayde's father and mother and younger sister perished one dark night. Every reference, however peripheral, to the tragedy provoked the identical phrase. And a mention of the crime could occur in a conversation about almost any topic aired around the table or the front room—the women with their sugar cubes and tea, the men occasionally also enjoying a *Lomir machn a schnaps.*

The customary response to even an allusion to the murder was identical to that uttered automatically at news of any significant setback experienced by a family member, by an inhabitant of our street, by a fellow employee, by individual or organizations involved with the socialist movement, or by Jews anywhere in the world. Such predictable, never-omitted verbal tags sprinkled the texture of conversation. Anyone who had died was perpetually rewarded with the honorific *alav ha-shalom*, as in "my former boss, that crook Meyer Ablowitz, *alav ha-shalom*," or in the case of a female, "You look just like your Aunt Bessie, *aleha ha-shalom*." Similarly, discussions of *potential* troubles were sprinkled with an incantatory word guaranteed to ward off the *tsouris'* realization: "In times like these, surely the landlord *cholilleh* won't raise the rent" or "If Moishe *cholilleh* became a melamed like Lucharsky . . ."

So the never-omitted pronouncement regarding *tsouris* that had actually occurred failed to emphasize for me as a child the awfulness of events described. On the contrary, the familiar phrase rendered homey any mention by an adult of a bank collapse, a fatal streetcar and train accident, European pogroms, the refusal of Eaton's department store downtown to hire Jews, factory closures, or the furriers' strike that could affect Uncle Avrom's livelihood. Whispers about our neighbors the Maloffs' divorce, or my mother's friend Mrs. Gronsky's abandonment by her husband, or the appearance of a truck and men with handcarts to repossess the Halperin's furniture a few doors down equally were transmuted. Adorned with the ritual tag, any threat to my world implied by such occurrences was softened into safety: the expected words created a small island of normality, a safe haven in the midst of a wild ocean of adult catastrophe.

Of course, growing up on Major Street off Harbord in Toronto provided a lot of scope for the awarding of the appellation, "terrible, terrible thing". This was the Depression, but in its first years we didn't call it that. Shortage of jobs, shortage of money were routine to our neighborhood and our family before and after October 1929. If life was a little worse this year, every newspaper insisted that better days were just around the corner. *Nu*, isn't that why we *takkeh* were in America? All right, all right: Canada.

So even the murder was sanitized for me for a long time, the accounts of it mixed in with news equally remote from my world of public school, Hebrew cheder, evening card games with my relatives, Shabbes solemnity, snowball fights against the kids who lived a couple of streets over on Borden, playing marbles in the Spring mud, or watching men unload coal down a chute through our basement window or the ice deliveryman bearing on his shoulder huge tongs that gripped a sawdust-streaked block for our refrigerator. "That Mussolini fellow is a real *gozlin*, like whoever murdered our grandfather, *alav ha-shalom*," my Aunt Zifra might sigh, looking up from reading a Jewish-language newspaper that Reb Lucharsky had brought to the house the day before. At 10 years old, I could already make out many sentences in this paper, *The Advance*. "He and that Hitler are such *paskudnyaks*," agreed her husband Uncle Leo, seated beside my father on our sagging chesterfield. "How is it men like that can even exist?" And my father would duly chime in, as required, "It's a terrible thing."

Curiously, I don't remember my father often referring to the tragedy. But Aunt Zifra and her other brothers—my Uncle Chaim and Uncle Lemuel—more than made up for my father's reticence on the subject. Nor do I recollect my zayde mentioning the loss of his parents, but then my memories of my zayde are dim. I recall being taken on visits to a dank-smelling front parlor, where through a door a radio in the kitchen was deafeningly loud. My father was a little abrupt with me during and after these excursions, not like his usual easy-going self. We sat facing a beard-ed old man in a stained black suit-coat and skullcap, peering nearsight-edly at me occasionally. But he never asked me about my victory in the Grade Four spelling bee at school or whether I ever had been taken by ferry to the beach on the Toronto Islands or if I delivered papers or had some other after-school job—the way most guests or people we visited would. He and my father conversed in low tones, with long periods of silence. If I was referred to at all, it was as my father's *Kaddish*. "Your *Kaddish* would like tea?" Zayde might mumble.

He was an infrequent visitor to our home. When he was settled in the best chair, he appeared bewildered amidst the comings and goings of his sons and their wives (except for Uncle Chaim, who was single), his daughter Aunt Zifra and her husband, and a proliferating host of grand-children. At Pesach once during the reading of the Haggadah he sudden-ly shouted, "When do we eat?" Everyone at the Seder was shocked, but I was secretly delighted: this was a thought I had each year, yet I wouldn't have dared speak it. My father, who was in the early stages of reciting the Ten Plagues, faltered, until Zifra came to his rescue by suggesting an abrupt abridgment of the list and of the balance of the service.

Eventually came murmurs of doctors, examinations, tuberculosis, and Zayde's complete absence from the family circle. Then there were trips by streetcar to where he was institutionalized—which meant for my brother and me a Sunday picnic on the park-like grounds with my mother while my father went inside the grim-looking structure. I remember, too, the sad excitement of sitting shivah with my family, towels over the hall and bathroom mirrors, and receiving an apparently ceaseless stream of visitors paying condolences and bringing us food: hard-boiled eggs and odd-tasting ganef, kreplach, latkes, borsht and even a roasted chicken. My cousins and my friends from up and down the street in their Shabbes clothes, more subdued and well-behaved than usual. I remember, too, each year thereafter the Yorzeit candle my father tended, set on a white cloth placed on the chest that served as a low table in our front room.

So I never heard from my zayde a first-hand, almost-eyewitness, account of his parents' death. But the Velizhir rebbie, Lucharsky, and even some relatives from my mother's side such as my Aunt Tillie and Uncle Avrom, could be relied on to keep the memory of the event before us.

My relatives were killed with a hammer. As the story goes, my great-grandfather used to keep his money under the mattress in his hut. One day, he happened to notice the paper rubles had become moldy. He took the bills out, washed them off as best he could, and spread them on a table to dry. Someone passing by on the street must have glanced in through the window and seen the money.

That night, someone broke into the house. Because the doors and windows were locked, they came in through the thatch of the roof. My great-grandfather probably was awakened by the intruder searching for the rubles. In any case, the burglar grabbed my great-grandfather's hammer which had been left on a bench he was repairing, and after a struggle my great-grandfather was struck a mortal blow to the head. Perhaps his wife was already awake and terrified, or awoke now. In any case she, too, was killed the same way. Their youngest child, six years of age, who slept by the stove in the room, was found dead beside my great-grandmother, behind whom perhaps she was cowering in the face of this nightmare of adults grappling and shoving in the dark, shouts and curses, hammer blows, blood. My zayde and his two brothers slept in a loft above the main room. When at last they crept out to view the scene of horror, the murderer was gone.

Though the crime was investigated, the identity of the culprit was never determined. A regiment had been stationed in the area at the time, and suspicion fell on the soldiers. But nothing was proved. The boys ultimately were sent to live with a relative who had emigrated to Bracebridge, Ontario, in the Muskoka district north of Toronto.

Their upbringing in Bracebridge was not a happy one: their foster-father—an uncle on their mother's side—scraped an existence as a peddler going from farm to farm. The boys left home at the earliest opportunity. This is why we had relatives in Cleveland we seldom saw, although they did show up for Zayde's funeral. The New York branch of the family was closer to us, with plenty of letters and occasional visits back and forth. My earliest memory is sitting on my mother's lap on a bench at the Brooklyn Zoo, staring up at an impossibly-tall giraffe. I remember the wooden buttons on her gray-and-white striped dress.

Indeed, my father and mother first met in New York. My father had gone down to stay with his Uncle Hymie for a week, and was taken to a Jewish play. At intermission in the lobby, he happened to strike up a conversation with a young woman who turned out also to be from Toronto, temporarily living with relatives in the Bronx while she looked for work. Six months and a good deal of letter writing and train travel later, they were married.

The home my parents eventually created on Major Street was close to the garment district along Spadina Avenue. My grandfather had worked most of his life in the needle trades, and my father for many years ran a cutting machine for Tip Top Tailors—a large enterprise that boasted a chain of retail outlets as well as factories. I believe it was my father's happy disposition and relaxed charm that made our house the customary gathering place for most of his siblings and their spouses and children, not to mention my mother's sister Aunt Tillie and her husband Uncle Avrom. And not to forget the numerous friends of my parents, or the Velizhir rebbie, Lucharsky. I realized as an adult that the latter was the family *nuchshlepper,* the hanger-on who won't let go, a sort of permanent version of the needy person one is obliged as an act of charity and fellowship to invite home for Shabbes, to be *on oyrech auf Shabbes* for the household. In Reb Lucharsky's case, his role as he saw it extended to the rest of the days of the week, too.

Yet it was to my father's house that Reb Lucharsky came, not to that of any other family member to whom he could put the same claim as landsman. People gravitated to my father. Sometimes this was to my mother's despair, in her attempts to feed and entertain on very little money a veritable horde crammed into what I became aware in later life was a tiny parlor. Among my mother's papers after she died was a legal document giving the dimensions of the house: it measured eleven feet wide. Naturally, the place was vast to me as a child. In any case, the agreeable talk and tea and blintzes and sour cream or equally delectable treats that were usually available at my father's and mother's home acted as a magnet to their relatives and friends.

I believe, however, my father's cheerful outlook was the biggest draw. Despite his guests' frequent insistence on detailing the latest examples of the world's *tsouris*, my father—while truly sympathetic—never lapsed into gloom. He got enormous pleasure from the life he had built and that formed around him. His feet might drag up the front stoop at the end of a long day on the job. Yet he had an ear-to-ear grin when he saw us assembled in the hall to offer him a welcome home. He would be still beaming half an hour later as he greeted the guests at that evening's meal and pronounced the appropriate *broche* before we dug into our fish and a *tsimmes* of carrots, onions, prunes and potatoes.

His spirit stood him in good stead at work, too. The summer before my zaydę died my father was laid off due to shortage of work. When the news reached Major Street a great *tummel* of anguish, worry, advice, admonitions, and appeals to the Creator broke out among those who customarily frequented our household. But my father, seemingly unfazed by both losing his job and being the cause of such uproar at home, simply strolled a block over to talk to a friend, one of his *chaverim* from the Arbeiter Ring. This man, often a guest with his wife at my parents', had recently been promoted to a foreman's position at Salutin's, another Spadina Avenue clothing manufacturer. My father started there the next Monday, although on shortened hours. Three weeks later his former supervisor at Tip Top Tailors, Mr. Applebaum, was sitting drinking tea with my mother when my father returned from work. After the preliminaries were out of the way, Mr. Applebaum grandly announced, "Yaakov, I'm authorized to give you your old job back. We still don't have much work, but I'll *takkeh* find enough to keep you busy. The place is all long faces and endless *kvetching* and *krechtzing* without you around." My mother glanced over at my father expectantly. He only nodded. You could tell he was pleased, but then he perpetually looked delighted to be home among us.

His unfailing good nature extended to family grievances, too. One enduring complaint among my mother's *mishpocheh* was that their grand-mother Fruma, *aleha ha-shalom*, had for a time owned property near Bay and Dundas Streets but had foolishly sold it off for a song. Fruma was in fact the business head in her marriage. While her husband was in Mon-treal attempting to earn passage for her and the children to come to Cana-da, back in Poland she established a thriving trade in goose fat, selling into Warsaw. Her husband's ineptness at money matters was legendary, so Fruma was the one who amassed the necessary funds to permit her and the children to travel to Quebec. Family legend had it that she thought long and hard about whether she wanted to resume her marriage to such a *nebbech*. Fruma was offered grudging respect by her descendants for her overall financial abilities: when the family moved to Toronto, from oper-ating a tiny store off Brunswick near Bloor she ended the landlady of three houses. When her name was invoked, however, she was routinely casti-gated for having missed the opportunity of a lifetime to hang onto a valu-able piece of downtown real estate.

Even my Uncle Chaim, my father's oldest brother, would weigh in when Fruma's inexplicable failure to cash in on Toronto's future was dis-sected. Ordinarily he had little to say on any subject, yet his participation in a ritual denunciation that properly belonged to my mother's side matched Aunt Tillie's and Uncle Avrom's willingness to contribute to yet another reconsideration of the murder of my relatives in Amlin. And just as my father rarely joined in talk about that subject, so he abstained from pillorying the short-sightedness of his grandmother-in-law. "Don't we all do the best we can?" he would inquire. "*Nu*, who would like more of Raizel's excellent knishes?" Though my mother also appeared uncom-fortable when Fruma's sole failing was focussed on, there definitely were moments when my father's eternal level-headedness and even tempera-ment exasperated her.

Stressful domestic emergencies like a flooded toilet, a bird that had become trapped in the house, or news that her younger sister Rivke in Hamilton was engaged to a *shaygets* were never crises to him: he declined to engage in dramatizing a problem, but instead aimed at effecting a solu-tion. My mother found this attitude of his maddening. But she seemed grateful when my father refused to be drawn into one more speculation of the current value of Fruma's former property.

My Uncle Chaim differed from my father in more than a willingness to reflect on Fruma's unforgivable business error. In physical appearance the brothers scarcely resembled each other. My father was slight in build, with a mildly stooped posture, thin arms and tapered fingers. Uncle Chaim was squat and stocky, as though his body had thickened from his years at heavy manual labor. He had quit school as soon as he could and worked for CN Rail in the Toronto yards unloading freight. Then he was in and out of jobs, employed intermittently as a construction laborer and in a small foundry out Queen Street West. His fingers were swollen-looking and square-ended and even his face appeared a rough-hewn version of my father's.

Uncle Chaim, too, had far less connection to the Jewish community than my parents. I knew from occasions when I had met his friends on the street, as my uncle was taking me for pop or on a shopping errand for my mother, that he lived and worked mainly in a non-Jewish environment. If we encountered workmates of his, their repartee with my uncle suggested they regarded him as an equal. Yet their nickname for him was "The Schnoz". Even as a child I found this reference to a prominent feature of my uncle's face disparaging. My uncle didn't seem to mind. When we stopped to chat with these men, his talk was equally aggressive, peppered with words he later always cautioned me not to repeat in front of my mother. From the conversations he had with his pals in my presence I understood that he spent considerable time in a pub they frequented along College Street, and also that on sunny days when they were unemployed they often met at certain park benches at the Christie Pits. I was impressed by my uncle's ability to move with ease in a non-Jewish world. Although there were Gentile children in my school, I had very little to do with them.

Uncle Chaim's bachelorhood my mother took as a personal challenge. She would suggest he might like to meet various unmarried female friends of hers, or friends of friends, but my uncle waved off such ideas with one massive hand. "It's *takkeh* your duty as a Jew to marry and have children," my mother insisted. "Ahhch," my uncle dismissed the notion. Once she even offered to contact a *shadchen* on his behalf, to see if a match couldn't be found for him via a more organized approach. That idea, too, was speedily rejected. My uncle lived in a boardinghouse a few blocks over, but I remember a period of several weeks one winter when he moved out to live elsewhere. Though my father retained his habitual equanimity, I deduced from urgent whispers my mother directed at him—in which Chaim's name was hissed—that my uncle had somehow become a transgressor. During those months he never ate supper with us, he came by once on a Sunday for tea, accompanied by a woman I'd never met previously. My father tried to enliven the gathering by telling jokes, but the episode was strained on all sides. I couldn't remember such a lengthy stretch when Uncle Chaim had so little interaction with our family. One supper he was back at his accustomed place at the table, and life went on as before, except my mother was noticeably cold toward him for several additional weeks.

Also unlike my father, Uncle Chaim was not religious. He did not go to shul, and despite being the eldest son, he absolutely refused to preside at Pesach. Thus this role devolved to my father. Following one Shabbes meal, my uncle and I happened to be sitting side-by-side on the couch. In addition to drinking a glass of wine with supper, he had since downed two or three schnaps. And when he had arrived at the house late in the day, he had made a point of informing my mother he had come from the pub, not shul. He had been laid off again that afternoon, but he said he had a few ideas where he might search for work on Monday. His breath, when he suddenly leaned toward me on the couch, was redolent of alcohol. "Moishe, if I find after I die that there *is* a God, I'm going to punch him right in the face for the shitty mess he's made of this world." I was thrilled and terrified to hear an adult utter such monumental blasphemy.

My uncle's threat was pronounced on a hot, humid July evening. Later that night, as I lay sweating atop the sheets on my bed, one of Toronto's summer thunderstorms drifted noisily across the city northward from Lake Ontario. Wide awake, I nervously counted the space between each flash and the accompanying overwhelming roll of unearthly sound. The storm drew nearer and louder, then passed overhead. I wondered if Uncle Chaim, a few blocks away, was about to suffer divine retribution for his audacious statement. But nothing happened.

Except for this lapse, my uncle kept his antipathy to religion to himself, other than also steadfastly refusing to attend shul or partake in any of the prayers when he was at our house for a holiday feast. And my uncle displayed a tolerance for Reb Lucharsky, greeting the bearded melamed as dispassionately as he acknowledged any of the rest of us he encountered at my parents'. Uncle Chaim might have had little use for religion, but he obviously had travelled through strange worlds in Toronto inhabited by strange people. I had the impression he had learned not to judge too quickly or overtly the good and evil in those he met. In this regard he possessed a variation of the laissez-faire attitude of my father, although without my father's innate happiness. Uncle Chaim recognized the Velizhir rebbie as a fellow-satellite in orbit around my parents' hearth, and treated him accordingly.

My father's other brother, Lemuel, had his own family and thus was less frequently seen at our home. My mother often remarked that Lemuel had married into his wife's family, rather then she having married into ours. In a manner of speaking, Uncle Chaim occupied the place in our lives that might have been filled by both paternal uncles. I once heard him offer money to my mother to help defray the cost of his many meals at her table. She indignantly refused, saying *here* he was *mishpocheh* and no boarder.

Thus Uncle Chaim was present the evening a new dimension to our relatives' murder was revealed. I could tell something was amiss as I opened the front door about five p.m. one April day after cheder. I had run into Reb Lucharsky at the corner. He was not my melamed; he conducted his own after-school cheder in a neighborhood further east, almost to Ossington Avenue. But as he habitually did, he was making a beeline to my parents' house when instruction was over, the same as me.

As Reb Lucharsky and I entered the small vestibule, I heard a voice wailing horribly in the kitchen. I froze, my body tense. What disaster could have happened to provoke such anguish? In the midst of hanging up our coats, I looked over at Reb Lucharsky. He seemed as disturbed as I was. After a few seconds I recognized the voice as my Aunt Zifra's. I had listened to such grief from her only once before, when my zayde died. My mother spoke: she sounded nearly as upset. Had something happened to Uncle Leo? My father? My brother?

Reb Lucharsky tended to defer to me a bit once we were under my parents' roof, although on the street he was capable of grilling me regarding what I had or hadn't learned in a rival cheder. I realized now he was waiting for me to act first, to lead us both from the comparative safety of the hall toward a closer proximity to such sorrow.

I gathered my courage and stepped into the kitchen. Both women glanced up with stricken faces as I, shadowed by the melamed, approached the table where they sat. My aunt's cries ceased, and she wiped tears from her face with a handkerchief. My mother embraced me tightly.

Reb Lucharsky hung back, hands clasped near his chest, his fingers pulling at and wringing each other. "What's wrong? Something is wrong?" he blurted.

"Tea, Reb Lucharsky?" my mother sighed, climbing to her feet. "We've had some terrible news."

I noticed a torn-open envelope and some papers and a photograph resting on the tablecloth.

"Thank you, I would like tea," Reb Lucharsky said, his agitated hand gestures slowing a little. "I hope nothing *cholilleh* has happened to. . . ." His voice trailed off.

My mother busied herself at the stove. "No, but the news is upsetting. From Russia," she added, bringing the teapot over to the table.

The melamed moved forward and sat down. "And the news is . . . ?" He helped himself to sugar cubes.

"From the past. But I think we'll wait until Yaakov gets home. He'll know what best to do."

A strained silence fell, broken only by Reb Lucharsky slurping his tea. I heard the door from the street open. My mother and my aunt raised their heads expectantly. Then as one they rose, and hurried toward the vestibule. I heard my father's cheerful words, and then a hubbub of feminine cries and exclamations.

My father entered the kitchen with an arm around the waists of both my mother and my aunt. Fresh tears were evident on my aunt's cheeks. My father exchanged greetings with the Velizhir rebbie and tousled my hair. Once he was seated opposite my aunt, my mother brought him tea.

My father looked around at us. "From the beginning," he said.

My aunt took a breath. Her lips moved, but then as if her earlier expression of strong emotion had stripped her voice of power she whispered, "He's come back."

"Who has come back?" my father asked.

"The . . . the *murderer*." My aunt's speech regained force in the midst of uttering the phrase.

"Who?"

"The one who killed our zayde and bubbeh and poor Aunt Chana."

"Aha. How do you know this?"

My aunt pushed the pile of papers on the table toward my father. "Look, read."

My father spent several minutes examining the handwritten letter. I edged over to stand beside him as he studied the pages. I could see that the photograph on the table had been taken in a cemetery, with a particular tombstone front and centre. I picked up the picture and began to try to make out the Hebrew inscriptions on the grave marker. My father finished with the letter and gently took the photo from me. He put his hand on my shoulder as he stared intently at the image.

He lowered it to the table and leaned back in his chair. "Why do you say the murderer has returned?"

"Isn't it obvious?" shrilled Aunt Zifra.

"No, not to me," my father said.

"He's taken his hammer again and bashed away at the inscription that says our grandparents and little Chana were murdered."

"Anybody can deface a cemetery."

"But read, read what the relatives say. No other tombstone was touched. It has to be the murderer, come back after so many years. Perhaps he has been locked up in jail for some other terrible act. Now he's angry that his crime has been remembered and is determined to seek revenge." Her face was twisted.

"How could it be the murderer who did it, Zifra?" my father said. "Our zayde died forty years ago."

"A person *epis*—" Aunt Zifra gulped air "—does not live forty years? What if he *cholilleh* tracks us down? What if he *cholilleh* does to us here what he did to the stone there?"

"Zifra, that's not going to happen."

"Why not? A crime like that: to kill a harmless couple and their little child? Such a person would be capable of—"

"Why should anyone want to murder us? Some *meshuggener* took offense at the inscription, perhaps. That's all. Or maybe it was an accident."

"*Oy!* An accident!"

"Kids, kids looking for something to do. Perhaps they happened upon this marker and struck it."

My mother stood up. "Or a *shaygets*?"

"He would not be able to read the inscription," my father observed. My mother withdrew toward the stove and began to bustle about with preparations for dinner.

"Only the inscription was damaged?" Reb Lucharsky broke in.

"Just the word 'murdered'," my father said. He slid the photo in the melamed's direction.

Reb Lucharsky raised the photo close to his eyes, then lowered it. He stroked his beard. "I think . . . I think this is perhaps the work of a dybbuk."

"Dybbuk!" Aunt Zifra shrieked.

My father turned toward him. "Lucharsky . . . ," he cautioned.

"If the murderer is maybe dead, his evil spirit has inhabited another poor soul. Under the control of the dybbuk—"

"*Feh!*" my father said decisively. "Save such tales for children. This is the Twentieth Century."

"What does evil know of time?" my aunt asked.

"A dybbuk was driven out of a woman in Velizh when I was a boy," Reb Lucharsky insisted. "Less than twenty years ago. Maybe in this case—"

"No more, Lucharsky."

Reb Lucharsky, subsiding, gestured toward the letter. "*Nu*, what do the relatives say?"

"When they wrote, whoever committed this act was unknown," my father replied. "By now the mischief-maker has probably been caught. They ask for money, of course, to help repair the stone."

"Mischief this is not, Yaakov," my aunt said. A *gozlin* is loose in the world. He attacks our family's heart once more."

"We only know what we know," my father declared. "Let's not make two problems where there is one. I think—"

At the sound of the outer door opening, Zifra was on her feet. "Leo? Leo? Is that you?"

Her husband"s voice called from the vestibule. "I came quick as I could." Uncle Leo strode into the room, trailed by Uncle Chaim. "I got home and read your note," Uncle Leo said, crossing toward his wife. "Are you alright, Zifra-*léb*?" He embraced my aunt, who began again to sob.

"Sit down, Chaim," my father invited while my aunt was being comforted. "Tea?"

"I met Leo on the streetcar," Chaim said. "He told me something bad happened from Russia?"

Once Uncle Leo persuaded my aunt to resume her chair, the recent event in Amlin was revealed to the newcomers. Uncle Leo rejected Reb Lucharsky's idea of an infernal origin of the desecration of the monument, but sided with his wife that the blows delivered to the stone were the work of the murderer somehow manifest again in the village. His concern was how to advise the relatives to properly deal with the outrage.

My father attempted to nudge the conversation toward the more practical matter of sending money for the repair or replacement of the stone. "I'll telephone Lemuel tomorrow. His shop is doing well, he says. He should be able to spare some money sooner than Chaim or I."

Aunt Zifra had calmed down now enough to assist my mother in readying the ingredients for a *tsimmis*. My mother, flustered that the crisis had delayed her cooking, was desperately singeing the skin of a chicken with a candle to eliminate the remnants of quills. "We'll be eating very late," she apologized to the group around the table. "Moishe, find your brother and tell him." No one took much notice of her announcement, and I stayed where I was.

Ideas about the cause, significance and appropriate reaction to the assault on the tombstone swirled about the room. As meal preparation duties permitted, my aunt and my mother contributed their opinions. Only Uncle Chaim did not participate. My father swivelled to face him. "If Lemuel sends money immediately, you and I can repay him our share when we can."

Uncle Chaim lowered his teacup. His large hands lay on the tablecloth, one on either side of the cup and saucer, blunt fingers curled slightly inwards. His fingernails were long, and, as ever when he was employed, black under the tips.

"It wasn't the murderer who damaged that stone," he said.

No one spoke for a second. Then Leo burst out: "Who else would it be?"

"What makes you so sure?" Zifra added over top of her husband's exclamation.

"I know who the murderer is," my uncle continued.

"Do you mean—?" All the adults talked at once. "You can't." "How is it possible that you—?" "Did our *tateh* tell you something he didn't us?" "Chaim, how could you imagine such a—?"

My uncle wasn't through.

"I have *takkeh* seen him."

"*Gottenyu!*" "Where?" "How can you possibly recognize—?" "You can't know—" "*Where* have you seen him?"

"He is here. In Toronto," Uncle Chaim finished.

"Sha, sha," my father tried to quiet the uproar that followed my uncle's words. "This *tummel* isn't getting us anywhere." The excited voices of the others eventually faded to mutters, and my father began a quietly persistent questioning of his brother.

"You've seen the murderer, here in Toronto?"

"Yes."

"How, after forty years, can this be?"

"I'm not free to tell you."

"You can't tell us? What do you mean?"

"I'm not at liberty to explain. But he is here. It could not be him who damaged—."

"How can you know the murderer?" Reb Lucharsky interrupted. "You weren't born when your relatives were killed."

"I know who he is. I've seen him here. That is all I can say."

"I don't believe you," Zifra declared.

Uncle Chaim shrugged.

"I don't understand," my mother ventured. "Chaim, why are you so sure you've seen the guilty one?"

"He's just talking," Leo pronounced. "Unless one of his *goyisher* friends—"

"This has nothing to do with my friends."

"Chaim, then how—?" my father began, but he was interrupted by his sister. Wave upon wave of doubt, of rejection of his declarations, surged toward my uncle. But he was a rock buffeted by the combers of a gale. The dispute raged all through supper, once my mother at last disengaged from the controversy long enough to finish organizing the meal and my brother was found. Everyone quieted momentarily for my father's recitation of the *broche*. Then the argument flared again. I say "argument", but no one was able to pry a single additional explanation or particle of information from my uncle. I say "all through supper," but the response to my uncle's statements has never lessened.

Henceforward, whenever the murder was spoken of, whether my uncle was in the room or not, the ensuing discussion soon considered his stubborn refusal to account for his convictions about the murderer's identity and presence in Canada. Each possible interpretation concerning these mysteries was either rejected by Chaim or disallowed by some reasonable objection suggested by another family member. Did my great-grandfather and his brothers commit the deed? Unthinkable. Also, the boys were too young, and too pious. As well, they could have stolen the money any day when their parents were absent from the house rather than attempt the crime in the middle of the night when everyone was home.

Was Chaim simply bidding for attention, striving to regain his rightful place as head of the family, being the eldest? Unlikely: at gatherings Chaim shunned the spotlight, and he usually preferred to spend time with his Gentile friends than with his relatives. Or did a missing piece of the story suddenly occur to Chaim, a vital clue to the tragedy that everybody else had overlooked? He firmly denied it.

For my own peace of mind, I finally developed a sequence of events that might make sense of Chaim's assertions. What if my zayde had in fact witnessed the killings in Amlin? Then, decades later, he encounters the perpetrator. Completely traumatized by the chance sighting, Zayde informs only Chaim—possibly because Chaim functioned in the *goyish* world of which the person was part. Zayde swears my uncle to secrecy: maybe due to fear of vengeance if the man is identified, or an unwillingness to risk notice by, and hence trouble with, the authorities by alerting them. After Zayde's death, Chaim starts to betray that vow just once, at my parents' house.

I never tested my scenario by seeking to verify it with Chaim. I was afraid he would scoff, and I would be left again solely with questions. Also, I lacked total confidence in my reason for Zayde acquainting Chaim with his discovery. Chaim rarely visited the old man, and even as a boy seemed to have virtually no rapport with his father. Why would his father entrust such momentous knowledge to this one of his three children?

Chaim must have been aware of the effect his words would have. Yet in all the years afterwards, he doggedly repeated only that he knew who the murderer was and had seen him in the streets of Toronto. On any elaboration of these claims, my uncle, *alav ha-shalom*, remained as silent as the grave.

Tom Wayman's *stories have appeared in* The Hudson Review, Ontario Review, Windsor Review, The Fiddlehead, *and* Descant. *He edited an anthology of contemporary love poems,* The Dominion of Love. *His own recent collection of poems is* The Colours of the Forest. *He lives in the Selkirk Mountains of southeastern British Columbia.*

Hair

E LAINE K ALMAN N AVES

O nce, when we still lived in Budapest, before the Revolution, I
asked Shoshanna how a baby gets inside her mother's tummy.
Shoshanna was leaning over the kitchen table which had been
covered with a crisp white sheet. She was tugging paper-thin dough closer and closer towards her. A small tear formed in the parchment-like
piece near the edge of the table. Shoshanna jerked her head back abruptly in annoyance. There was a smudge of flour on her cheek, ruddy from
the heat of the oven or perhaps from emotion.

"Don't ask me about this," she said. "When you're old enough, I will
tell you all you need to know about this."

The next day it rained, so Shoshanna sang me her rainy-day song. The
song was from a musical version of *Cinderella* in which she had starred
when she was twelve. It started out, "*Oh, cream cakes are just so delicious.*"

A line in this song made tears trickle down my face each time
Shoshanna sang it in her heart-rending soprano. The little girl in the song
mourns the cream cakes she can't have because she has no *Anyu* and *Apu*
to buy them for her. What a very terrible thing it must be, to have no
Mummy and Daddy to get you a cream puff when you so long for one.

Shoshanna was an orphan and so was Gusti, if you thought about it
carefully, though they were not *child* orphans and Gusti was quite ancient
to be thought of like that because soon he would be fifty. They had met
in an orphanage. He had been forty-two and Shoshanna twenty-seven.
Perhaps they didn't consider themselves actual orphans, only as having
been orphaned.

How they had met was like this. Shoshanna told me about it after she had finished the rainy-day song and had begun to comb my hair for the third time that morning. Right after the liberation, she and her sister Lilli had come back from the camps together, to the small Hungarian town where they had been born. But it was so terrible in their house which had been stripped of all its furniture with the sole exception of their sister Ilushka's piano with Ilushka's portrait above it, that they had left this town forever. They took the painting with them, and travelled all the way to Budapest.

Shoshanna was able to get a job in an orphanage since she had been a teacher before the war. Lilli left the country and, after a time, ended up far away in Canada.

One morning when Shoshanna was pouring kerosene on the heads of the orphans to get rid of the lice, Gusti came looking for her. He had a message for her from her brother-in-law who lived in the country in the very same village where Gusti was an important man.

"Your brother-in-law has learned that you are here in Budapest working in an orphanage," Gusti had said to Shoshanna as he watched her emptying a keg of kerosene onto the head of a small boy. "How can he sleep nights knowing his brother's widow has to work among strangers when he and his wife have a roof they can share with you?"

And so, after a little while, arrangements were made and Shoshanna left the orphanage with Gusti and they travelled by truck to the village where her brother-in-law and Gusti lived, and it was not long before Shoshanna and Gusti had fallen in love. And that, Shoshanna concluded briskly, putting away the brush and comb, was all I needed to know about how I got into her tummy.

When the nurses laid me in a bassinet by Shoshanna's bedside right after I was born, she couldn't take her eyes off me. She had them leave the lights fully blazing though it was midnight, so she could feast her eyes on me. She wasn't disturbing anyone else, it was a private room in a private clinic—it was before everything was nationalized. Gusti still had money.

In the morning he brought her tea roses. *Roses* in November. The card read in his beautiful script, "Few flowers, much love." Then he slipped the heavy ring with her initials on it on her ring finger, where a wedding ring once used to be. He kissed her finger, then her mouth. He lifted me from the bassinet and started to cry. "To think," he said, "to think I could have a child again."

Shoshanna and Gusti kept a diary of my every ingestion. They laid me on the scales before and after each nursing, subtracted the difference, and entered it in a ledger. "2.80 kilos at birth," wrote Gusti neatly in pencil; 2.70 kilos ten days later when they took me home. Net weight at the end of the month: 2.91 kilos. On this day Shoshanna inscribed in her slapdash scrawl, "1/4 grated apple + 5 mocha spoonsful lightly sugared orange juice once a day."

Blanka *néni*, my paediatrician, paid us our first house call. Shoshanna unbound me for her from the *polya* on the dining-room table and removed my tiny undershirt and diaper.

"Her legs are bowed," Shoshanna said.

"Nonsense," retorted Blanka *néni*, "all babies have bow legs. It's the way the fetus folds itself up in the womb. Actually," Blanka *néni* took her eyes off me and fixed them on Shoshanna suggestively, "actually she has the shapeliest thighs I've ever seen on a baby girl."

"I'm not talking about her thighs," argued Shoshanna who never ceded a point easily, "but her calves. They are so, too, bowed, Blanka *néni*."

They stood over me, these two women, discussing my baby legs. Shoshanna had the most beautiful legs in the world: long and firm calves, patrician ankles. Gusti called them the legs of a gazelle. In Auschwitz where Blanka *néni* and Shoshanna had first met, Shoshanna had taken first prize in a beauty contest. It wasn't a formal contest, just something the girls had invented to pass the time. There they were, herded together in a cavernous hall with their bald heads and not a stitch of clothing among about a hundred of them. It was not so long after they first arrived, so they still had shapes. And they awarded each other "prizes" for best shoulders, best breasts, best buttocks. Shoshanna took the prize for best legs. Blanka *néni* and her special friend Vera, another doctor, had been the judges.

Blanka *néni* is stout and lumpish. She wears mannish suits of tweed worsted. Her chin-length hair seems shellacked in place; she wears it pushed back behind fleshy, large-lobed ears. Though she is as Jewish as Shoshanna and Lilli, the Canadian aunt whom I don't know, in the camps Blanka *néni* had power and privileges on account of being a doctor. Nothing clear cut, of course. To exercise them she had had to take risks.

Once, in the dinner line, Lilli didn't take the bowl of soup that should have fallen her due. The soup had nothing in it, not even the carrot chunk that ought to have floated in its scummy broth. Lilli held back her hand and reached instead for the bowl next in line. A guard plucked her out of the queue and beat her raw.

"Raw," Shoshanna says, "her buttocks were raw."

Shoshanna dragged Lilli off to show her buttocks to Blanka *néni*. Blanka *néni* applied salve to them wordlessly. But afterwards it was whispered that Blanka *néni* had let loose a torrent of invective at the camp commandant. *The camp commandant himself.* And would you believe, the commandant sent for the guard, chewed him out in front of Blanka *néni* and transferred him to another detail?

But it could just as easily have gone the other way, Shoshanna says. Blanka *néni* had been lucky. She had risked her life over Lilli's buttocks.

Shoshanna looks up from her sewing. She is embroidering a smocked dress that Lilli has sent me from Montreal. "Blanka *néni* loved women, you know, but she was just a plain good friend to me and Lilli," she says. "That's why she is your doctor now."

Blanka *néni* carries a doctor bag of dark leather fastened with a metal clasp. The tools of invasion originate in this bag. Shoshanna dips stubby, round-tipped suppositories in vaseline before inserting them in me with infinite care. The enema bag of rust-coloured rubber has a long tube and a black nozzle that Shoshanna also dips in vaseline. Warm water courses in my insides, fills me, fills me to bursting, as the nozzle is slowly withdrawn. Gusti rushes me in his arms to the toilet down the hall.

Shoshanna bends over me, untying the rags around which my hair is tautly wound. "I hope I can disguise the bald spot," she murmurs as she combs out my hair. In the mirror, my reflection is so fetching I can barely recognize myself. Fluffy curls frame my chubby face, but Shoshanna is still not satisfied. She heats a curling iron on the stove till it's red hot. She wets the ends of my hair slightly so they sizzle at the iron's touch.

Shoshanna parts my hair at the centre and ties silk ribbons on either side of the part. She dresses me in the white smocked dress that Lilli has sent from Montreal, takes out brand-new knee socks, and laces up my freshly polished two-tone boots.

At the studio, the photographer asks Shoshanna to remove my dress and undershirt. He is a young man who makes funny faces at me and when I don't laugh takes a feather duster and touches it to my bare shoulder. That photograph will depict me with an adorable dimple, my tongue between my teeth, head screwed coquettishly around my shoulder. In the other photograph that Shoshanna sends to Lilli I'm wearing the white dress hoisted high to show my panties. My legs are crossed and a large picture book rests on my knees. I gaze at the page, serious and absorbed.

"The photographer posed her so as to disguise the extent to which her legs are bowed," Shoshanna writes to Lilli. Her letters catalogue my many illnesses, in respites between which Shoshanna drags me to orthopaedic specialists who, though they find no fault with the shape of my legs, have diagnosed flat feet for which the treatment is customized arch supports. I sit with my feet in wet clay, ribbons of gauze wound up to my knees. Plaster moulds are taken, exercises prescribed. All this and more Shoshanna writes to Lilli who, when she finally meets me in person, will clutch me to her heart, smother me with kisses, then hold me at arm's length, her face wreathed in joyous smiles. "Ilushka, my precious," Lilli will say, "You're not a cripple after all!"

I lie on the sofa for my afternoon nap, right thumb in mouth, a bunch of soft hair with which I caress my upper lip twirled around my index finger. My left hand slides surreptitiously down the back of the sofa and surfaces with more precious treasure—a secreted hairball which I transfer to my right fist. The rough canvas back of the sofa is upholstered with many additional tufts of hair.

Shoshanna threatens to have my hair shaved if I don't stop pulling it out by the handful.

I glower and say nothing. I'm not conscious of the acquisition of new hair balls. When the booty behind the sofa loses it delicious softness, I somehow obtain a fresh supply. It never hurts. Never.

Above my head the sheep are grazing beneath the benevolent eye of the mustachioed shepherd holding his staff in the landscape on the wall. On the opposite wall, a portrait of Mancki *néni*, Gusti's first wife, holding Évike, her baby, on her lap. I close my eyes and twirl the hair ball beneath my nose.

When I wake up, I go downstairs to play, first asking Shoshanna to lift me up so I can reach the mezuzah on the front doorpost, as Gusti has shown me to. Shoshanna obliges but without enthusiasm.

Downstairs, my friends are sweaty and hoarse from running around.

I tag along as they head for church, a favourite hangout for catching your breath. The boys in the group doff their caps in the vaulted doorway. Following their example I shuck off my kerchief. I dab droplets of holy water from the font onto my forehead like the others and inhale the sweetish scent of mystery compounded of old wood and incense and must. In the chapel I cross myself and kneel. I feast my eyes on the play of sun on the stained glass. The blood-flecked statues and straining, sinewy Christ both repel and fascinate me.

Back upstairs Shoshanna confronts me at the front door. "I watched you from the window, missy. Since when does one kiss the mezuzah and then head for church?"

"I can't believe it," Shoshanna says, as she prepares supper and tempts me with sugared romato slices. "I can't believe that the namesake of my sister Ilushka would go into church after kissing the mezuzah."

"Your Aunt Ilushka was a remarkable woman," she continues, slicing off small pieces of *kolbász* and placing them almost out of my reach to whet my appetite. She smiles to herself as I reach for a piece, thinking I don't notice her ploy.

Aunt Ilushka's portrait hangs out in the hall where we eat our meals when Gusti is away on business. Shoshanna continues her monologue below Ilushka's portrait during supper. "Of all my sisters, Ilushka was the most beautiful. I had a reputation for being a beauty, too, but I didn't even come close to her. Her hair was gold and her eyes green as a cat's. The artist really hasn't caught the refinement of her features, nor the flawless quality of her skin."

The original Ilushka was statuesque and large boned. Shoshanna says she was always dieting to keep her svelte figure. She lived largely on apples. Little green apples overflowed her bureau drawers and sewing baskets when she shared a room with Shoshanna and Lilli. In the old days.

Shoshanna tells me how religious the original Ilushka was, how, after her marriage, the Rabbi sent yeshiva students to her house to eat, a privilege reserved only for the most pious families in town. I slurp my cocoa noisily and punch holes in my bread with my finger till Shoshanna notices and gets mad at me for playing with food.

When I come down with whooping cough, the city lies under a thick pile of snow. Blanka *néni* nonetheless upholds the view that fresh air is the only treatment for whooping cough. So, despite the bitter January cold, Shoshanna and I act like summer day-trippers. We climb Gellért Hill all the way to the peak. We go to the Zoo. We visit Margit Island.

On the island we follow the most exposed paths along the shoreline, for Blanka *néni* has decreed that wind in particular is beneficial for whooping cough. When I cough, the cold air enters my lungs with the sure thrust of a blade. Shoshanna stops at a small promontory, and tries to distract me from a bout of wheezing by pointing to a spot in the distance, a bay in the slate-coloured Danube. She says the orphanage used to be located there, the orphanage where she first met Gusti.

Absently she says, "If my parents had lived, I would have waited."

"Waited for what?" I gasp.

"Waited longer to see if Márton would come back."

"Who's Márton?"

"No-one. . . . I just wouldn't have taken up in such haste with your father. If my parents had lived."

"Why not?"

Shoshanna doesn't answer, doesn't tell me then of that other man, the one whose widow she thought she was when she fell in love with my father. No, she says nothing of that husband who came back from a Russian prison a few months after I was born. It won't be until I'm in my teens, as the two of us fold laundry in a suburban Canadian bedroom, a sheet pulled taut between us, that she'll hiss, it now seems to me out of the blue, "*You* decided for me. The fact I got pregnant with you! That's why I didn't go back to Márton, though he still wanted me. Because you were Gusti's child, not his."

I rack my brains now trying to remember what prompted this outburst of hers. I heard it then as a piercing accusation. Still, it may have been a lament.

But way back, way way back, when we stood together on Margit Island, she didn't tell me about how I came to be born, but about how the orphans gave her her name. My mother's real name is Anna, but since that day on the island I have always thought of her as Shoshanna. That's what the orphans called her. The orphans whose hair was thick with lice. The orphans who sobbed in the night and whom she comforted. They thought the name Shoshanna suited her because of her dark hair and her dream of going to Palestine. Shoshanna was a fitting name for a pioneer.

That's what she would have become if she hadn't met Gusti. She'd have gone to build a new country with her orphans.

I often dream these days of that scene on the island, of the weak sun glinting on the wave-puckered river, of the howling of the wind. Shoshanna's shoulders slump a bit, but her black hair under a jaunty red beret billows defiantly behind her. Snatches of her words swirl around me as, dressed in my woolly coat and pompommed hat, I struggle for breath. We stand together hand in hand, my mother and I. Once more I feel my fingers in their fuzzy mittens stretch to enclose her larger hand and squeeze it tight.

Elaine Kalman Naves *won a Canadian literary award for "Hair" in 1998. She lives in Montreal and writes a book column for* The Gazette. *She is currently at work on a sequel to* Journey to Vaja, *which was awarded the Elie Wiesel Prize for Holocaust Literature in 1998.*

Chestnusts for Kafka

IRENA EISLER

> No one came back
> The dead
> The living remained there
> The sky was full of them when they were leaving

Jiří Kolář, "Without Return"

It rained as if someone's life depended on it and Emma thought of going back to California. The water-logged sky pushed down on her, and she felt flattened against the slippery Prague pavement of her youth. Rain pounded the blue-and-white mosaics of the sidewalk and lashed the cobblestones. She tried to remember why the paving stones were called 'cats' heads', but nothing came except the loud gusts of November wind and more water.

The black shiny street was lined with cemeteries on both sides—Christians to the right, Jews to the left. Sandwiched between the massive bulk of a new, hideous hotel where she was staying and a narrow ledge leading to the underground, Emma stared down the broad, desolate street and prayed for Eva to come. Who cared today was All Souls Day? The dead wouldn't mind if the sisters came another day, when it was dry; the dead wouldn't even know. But Eva insisted and Emma, as always, felt guilty. After all, it was Eva who looked after the graves; after everyone, living or dead, that Emma had left behind.

The rain intensified, and Emma's umbrella swung dangerously from side to side, her feet soaked through already. The hotel façade, sinuous and out of character with the drab surroundings of the street, oozed the colour of fresh pork and Emma recalled the garish foyer with leatherette seats and strobe lighting. The rooms—many overlooking a busy bus station and, beyond it, the new Jewish Cemetery—were comfortable and, in a sharp contrast to the foyer, boringly neutral. As Emma pondered the contradiction, she saw Eva emerging from the underground exit with a large bottle of seltzer in one hand and a sheaf of rainbow-coloured straw flowers in the other. "How small she looks," Emma thought as she peeled her back away from the wall and, making large circles with her umbrella, signaled her presence. Eva's round face lit up and she strode across the giant puddles with legs so short, she was practically floating.

"Eva, don't," Emma yelled, "I am coming around," but the wind sent up a large gulp of rain to drown out her words and Eva barreled up the short flight of stairs that separated them, swinging her water bottle like a baton. Their difference in height made them avoid collision and the umbrellas fit snugly inside each other as they touched with freezing hands.

"Sorry I am late, Emmi," Eva said cheerfully, "everyone was buying flowers today." Emma's eyes fastened on the large bottle in Eva's hands.

"You did not think there was enough water around?" she asked mournfully, surveying her shoes that now resembled two dark sponges.

"It's just for cleaning up the graves, Emmi, you remember how polluted Prague is at this time of year." Living in the unrelieved clinical sunshine of a San Diego day, Emma has almost forgotten the thin film of soot that would coat everything in Prague as soon as it became cold enough to use the old coal stoves again. Still, she nodded.

"Where to?" asked Emma rhetorically and Eva pointed back over her shoulder. They started down the street whose name recalled medieval vineyards, all gone for centuries. Eva, who always compensated for being short, charged forward, bottle and flowers swinging erratically this way and that, her ample chest like a shield carried through the whiplash of rain, eyes fixated on the hidden grill of a gate in the distance. Emma, who was a full head taller, followed without haste.

Barely visible in the foggy perspective, the Christian cemetery began as a burial ground during a plague epidemic. Now it stretched in a vast fan of petrified shields like a miniature city. They were surrounded by obelisks and triangles, globes and stelae, toy houses under tiny copper roofs, granite pyramids, and the high sheen of polished stone everywhere. Emma remembered Dr. Craig, an English professor from New Zealand whom she had accompanied here years ago, and his unfeigned shock at the profusion of *real* marble in a place inhabited only by the dead.

"What a gigantic waste of money," he kept repeating, calculating aloud the cost of each marble slab, then hastily adding all the magnificent ornaments.

Those poor, stingy New Zealanders, Emma thought at the time, buried under some little patch of grass, ogled by sheep.

"Remember Dr. Craig, Eva," she asked, but Eva wouldn't have known old Craigie, it was crazy to think so.

Either way, Eva didn't hear. She was half-way up the central alley, focussed on counting off the side roads, nearing the turning point. All around them, dahlias, chrysanthemums, and bunches of straw flowers such as Eva carried, decorated the ornate tombstones. Small candles flickered in a few sheltered places, the rest all but extinguished by the pounding rain. "This way, Emmi," called Eva in a sing-song voice. Emma retraced her steps and turned left. The family tomb stood shining darkly, the marble rectangle as impenetrable as ever. A twisted metal stump hung pointlessly where once there was a magnificent turn-of-the century bronze lantern.

"What on earth happened to the lantern, Eva?" Emma asked anxiously.

"You know, Emmi, they steal them now."

"Who steals them?" said Emma uncomprehendingly.

"Kids do, for the antique dealers. It's a big business, I think."

Emma's eyes circled the little grove. Huge raindrops like unshed tears overlooked other signs of teenage vandalism. The pair of marble *putti* from the tombstone opposite was gone, and so were the twin copper lights from the ornate sarcophagus in the centre. There seemed to be something missing from every grave, although Emma couldn't tell for sure. Still, thought Emma bitterly, somewhere down the Danube or up the Rhine, curvaceous forms of the Secession lantern that once stood guard over her paternal ancestors probably shone upon a whole new generation of garden dwarfs.

Eva's voice was soothing as she tried to make light of the matter, promising a new "antique" lamp for Emma's next visit. She pulled an old flannel shirt out of her battered briefcase, and began cleaning around the grave, pulling out weeds and arranging straw flowers in their place. Emma, feeling deficient as always, tried to help, collecting small fallen twigs and raking wet leaves with gloved hands. The marble glistened and turned a mirror on their quiet ministrations. Slowly, it stopped raining.

They stood in silence pondering the names engraved onto the black marble: their paternal uncles, and below them their grand-uncles and aunts, big on longevity, some prematurely gray, all handsome with their tanned round faces and their trademark sea blue eyes. Emma and Eva looked like none of them. Here they all were, in an orderly line-up, smug in their stately coffins, seen to their final resting place by their good-natured country cousins, always rooted in the same earth, always so securely *present*.

Emma felt a sharp pang in her side. It felt so lopsided, Emma and Eva's dual heritage, the Christmas-and-Hanukkah routine, the idea of being a *Mischling*. Still, they were made of two parts, two sets of genetic codes and wasn't it absurd that their ancestors on either side faced one another across a busy highway?

They started walking back towards the main gates, surveying the string of small floral tributes squatting damply down the main alley. Emma felt chilled and began lobbying for a cup of coffee.

"What about Café Kinsky?" she ventured.

Eva laughed.

"Emmi, everything doesn't have to go back to the Kinsky, you know. Besides, that old café is long gone. Don't you remember? It's a travel agency now."

Emma didn't remember. A travel agency? Well, you could have called it that. And what a trip it was all those years ago. Under the circumstances, not the worst. With everybody else already gone east to the camps, with just her and Eva left to fend for themselves, Emma fresh out of high school, both of them newly homeless, German officers in the grand old apartment on the embankment, why, it was just a walk in the park, literally.

"Isn't there a café inside the hotel where you are staying?" asked the practical Eva, eyeing the middle distance. "If you like your coffee bordello style, there is one on the ground floor," responded Emma, surveying the undulating porcine walls of the Mozart Hotel.

"Well then, that should remind you of Pension Kinsky during the War," said Eva and propelled herself forward through the now stilled puddles.

On reflection, they both started laughing. Fifty years after the fact, the memory of seeking a temporary refuge in Nana's favourite place rang clear as a bell. The War turned what they had known as a genteel, slightly shabby *pension* that their grandmother used as a home away from home into a polychrome marvel of fake leather, and the pretty owner called Frau Ola into an unrecognizable fat shrew draped in green silk.

"No," she had no rooms, "really."

Eva insisted. She couldn't say they had nowhere to go, she couldn't even remind Frau Ola whose grandaughters they were. Eva knew her German was good and she switched to it easily, hoping to make Ola more responsive. Strangely enough, Frau Ola had changed her mind.

"You are sure you want to stay *here?*" she said quizically, and then, with a shrug of her shoulders handed over a large key to a room in the attic. They thought nothing of her sudden change of mind, nothing of the looks she gave them and how she seemed to size them up. They were exhausted, they were hungry and nothing really mattered except to get to bed. Feeling victorious, they took turns in the bathroom, washed their hair, rubbed themselves with soap. They were in their nightgowns and ready to fall asleep when the knock came on the door. It had taken a tub of hot water to melt all caution away and Eva marched confidently to the door, only to stare petrified at two German officers swinging a bottle of *Sekt* between them.

"*Guten Abend, Fräulein,*" said the taller officer.

"*Guten Abend, meine Herren,*" whispered Emma.

As if on cue, Emma started throwing up.

"*Entschuldigung, bitte, aber meine Schwester ist sehr krank.*"

And I am next, she thought prophetically.

What angel looked after them, they didn't know, but the sight of two retching girls in gray flannel nightgowns was enough of a deterrent: the officers looked annoyed, but they turned around and left. So, that very night, did Emma and Eva.

For years after the War, Eva avoided the Kinsky street like a plague, convinced that Frau Ola, by then possibly morphed into Comrade Ola, would recognize her. Thank God Nana didn't get to find out that her favourite quiet *pension* found a second calling as an army brothel in which they narrowly escaped harm. What mattered is that they, her granddaughters, had lived to tell the tale.

Much later, Eva wrote a novel, the story of their ultimate hiding place in a Bavarian mountain convent, a tale of two Jewish girls with fake papers and strange, quickly memorized prayers. They had lived under the watchful eyes of thin tubercular nuns, who must have known but didn't ask, who fed them wild mushrooms by the bushel and made them kneel on the freezing blue tiles, bottling blessed water from the Eagle's Nest Mineral Spring. Eva and Emma were the only ones who never asked for a leave, *never*, and even if they had, where would they have gone? Not until the Americans came and took them back to Prague in the back of an army truck did the word 'return' cross their lips. *Return* was a forbidden word and it made your ribs hurt, like unrequited love.

As the sisters reached the posh entrance of the Mozart Hotel, a flock of businessmen emerged with much backslapping from under the awning and headed for the underground. A large part of the café inside was roped off for a party of the American Express, so they sat down to the side on the slippery red banquette and Eva ordered two capuccinos.

"Globalization," Emma said wearily, "it's the pits."

She saw the danger everywhere, grafted onto the signs of Bohemia Bagel, Smichov Sushi, Bohnice Beach! There was no beach in Bohnice, just an insane asylum, but it gave the district an exotic flair just the same. She was a stranger in her home town, flown in for a conference she dreaded, and spending a little time with her big sister.

"How is the conference going?" Eva asked with interest.

"Oh, the conference," Emma replied with a sigh. "A bunch of academics discussing the meaning of exile. Exile and the body. Exile from the inner self. Creative exile. Exile and kitsch. Sex in exile."

Maybe they could call it sexile? Multiple exiles. Botched exiles. She was sick of it. How many big mouths were scanning the word in every direction, coming up with nothing but platitudes. Exile had no meaning other than its outcome. Coming out of exile was like coming up for air, and what if the air was putrid on the other side? What if exile was worse than death, its own finality uncertain, its duration suspended endlessly down the dark chimney of memory?

"What about your work, Eva, it sounds a lot more exciting," she said to get away from her usual thoughts. "Where are you at with Kafka?"

"Almost finished," said Eva shyly, but her eyes lit up at the thought of the translation of Kafka's letters nearing the end, the words now ebbing and flowing with the original text, everything preserved, yet born anew. Even though she was the one who always made it happen, it felt like a small miracle every single time, a feeling stretching back to her first inchoate efforts, but now possessed of a grown-up, confident voice that counted many dozens of books as half her own. She loved being a translator, and the joy she derived from her work now shone boldly in her face.

"So, what about the other half of the family?" said Eva as if on cue.

Emma looked out the window at the shingled, decorated wall of the Jewish cemetery and tried to argue that All Souls was a Catholic feast and couldn't they wait until things were dry to troop through yet another muddy burial field?

"All Souls means *everyone*, Emmi," responded Eva firmly, convinced of the irrefutable logic of her view. With a shrug, Emma paid for the capuccinos and picked up her umbrella from the floor. It had created a little tree design of condensation and it felt as if she was leaving a small art work behind. Crossing the street, they dodged a large bus with *Barcelona* posted across the windshield. Emma wished she was on it.

As they trotted up to the main gate fronting the sanctuary, a half-forgotten smell of roasted chestnuts permeated the wet air, bringing back memories of another kind of soggy-as-felt day much like the one they were just getting through. Emma looked down to the side gate and saw a makeshift stand being assembled by a young boy wearing a baseball cap.

"Maybe later," she thought, "maybe later."

The first thing they saw as they entered was a crude wooden sign, in English, *"To Kafka, 21-14-21."* It struck Emma as funny, the numbers vaguely reminiscent of a Miss America pageant (a very young, very thin Miss America). Beyond it, there was a large, rough granite boulder with Hebrew lettering and another cryptic inscription —. *"Remember the days of old, consider the years of many generations: ask thy father and he will shew thee; thy elders, and they will tell thee."* The Song of Moses.

The cemetery, framed by tall chestnut trees covered with ivy looked mysterious. Large rhododendron bushes marked the road leading to the back wall, interspersed with a long string of names etched into the sculpted stone: *Moritz Finger, Solomon Katz, Louise Jeiteles geb. Straschitz, Mathilde Klein, Baruch Guttmann, Ignaz Fuchs, Alphons Borges, Sigmund Rosenbaum, Ludwig Roubitzek, Alfred Taussig* . . . The back wall itself sheltered large family crypts in which first names no longer seemed to matter: *Ascher, Adler, Perutz, Pick* and *Popper* reigned supreme here, all draped in fantastic garlands of dripping ivy. Six pairs of raised stone hands suggested that the *Kohanim* had their own private club at the end of the alley.

"Look, Emmi, what a beautiful tombstone," said Eva quietly, pointing out a slab of rough granite on which an elegant relief of a tree was crowned with an imprint of an army helmet.

"*Otto Freund*," read Emma from the inscription below, "killed on the Russian battlefield, April 1915." Who was Otto Freund, she wondered, how old was he when he fell in Russia, and which battlefield was it?

"It really is exquisite," she agreed with her sister, turning her head back for another glimpse of the tree relief.

The rain started falling again. Emma's shoes were shot for good, but it began to matter less. She thought of Otto Freund, imagining who he might have been to deserve a tombstone of such uncommon beauty. She saw the helmet lie in the unplowed fields of the Russian lowlands, moved it around in her mind a few times and finally let it drop. She stored the image for some future use and hurried to catch up with Eva who was now way ahead of her. This part of the cemetery looked even more like an enchanted forest, the twisted coils of ivy covering the trees, the graves and the narrow paths between them.

At last, the large stone arch of the family tomb came into view, two doric columns supporting a marble pediment the colour of a wet charcoal. *Leopold B.*, owner of a printing press and his wife, *Hermione B.* plus all the other B.'s whose names rippled down the central slab between the two fluted columns: all of them with the same terse postscript—"*perished in exile, Lodz, 1943.*" There were no other dates.

Small wonder Emma hated the conference. *Exile* had been another forbidden word. Eva was already kneeling down, the end of the tattered shirt scrubbing the soiled stone of remembrance, the worn briefcase open to reveal the last bunch of straw flowers inside it.

"Let's just put a few pebbles here, Eva," said Emma gently, "there should be no flowers on a Jewish grave."

"Emmi, I saved these especially," countered Eva fiercely, "what does it matter, really?"

"It is not a Jewish custom," said Emma, feeling the thumping pedantry in her every word.

"So what, we are *Mischlings*, we don't have to do it by the book," pleaded Eva, as if she ever needed permission of her younger sister to do something she really wanted.

"Fine," said Emma tersely, "you put flowers, I put pebbles."

This solution made Eva happy and she poured the last of the seltzer on the tombstone, wiping off the remaining traces of dirt. She arranged the small straw bouquet in the middle and Emma walked off a ways, looking for pebbles. They were scarce in the soft muddy ground, but in the end she found the requisite number and laid them in a straight line, like a secret arrow, next to the column on the right.

Eva caught Emma's pensive, hangdog look and smiled up at her.

"It always feels so unreal, doesn't it," she said, "all of them gone."

Emma did not say anything but she kept thinking about the meaning of words. The word *exile* for instance, the great forbidden word. It wasn't just that her family died so horribly, and so anonymously. It was that they died in exile, away from home, expelled from the comfort and the company of their own, given no burial. Their grave was no grave, it was a *cenotaph*, a place with no bodies in it, with nothing to conjure, but the last train full of shadows going out into the void. There were no elders and no one to ask about "the days of old."

"Yes, it feels very strange," she finally answered, nodding her head. It was hard to grieve if no one was there. Slowly, they turned back towards the main gate.

"Let's stop at Kafka's grave before we go, Emmi," Eva said. Emma thought "Why not on a day like today? Not even the biggest fan is going to come."

This was hard to believe. Tours came to Kafka's grave like to a holy grail, trooping all around it with a vengeance. The grave was almost by the wall that separated the cemetery from the street and all week she had been noticing the crowd surrounding it. The tombstone was unusual, a large stone crystal embossed with the name of his parents, his own, and the names of his three sisters who died in the Holocaust. It stood, smothered in pebbles placed there by the writer's admirers, by those who only knew him by name, and even by some who thought he was somebody else. The earth in every direction was smooth and pebble-free and a neat line of small balls of crumpled paper slowly disintegrated on the rim.

Unexpectedly, Emma felt a great urge to put a pebble on his grave, a pebble among hundreds of others, a small token of remembrance. After all, *he* really *was* buried there. A search all around the site produced absolutely nothing, except more shoe damage. Everything was gone, pillaged, snatched away from them.

"Not everything!" Emma thought suddenly, catching another whiff of burning chestnuts on the other side of the iron grill.

While Eva looked on uncomprehendingly, Emma approached the boy in the baseball cap standing on the street outside the gate, and handed him a ten-crown piece across the metal bars. As she grabbed the small paper cone in return, her palm began burning slightly. She quickly turned the triangular bag upside down and arranged six roasted chestnuts end to end with the long row of pebbles. Looking back towards the darkened alley she tried to say *kaddish* as best as she could.

"Putting roasted chestnuts on graves is not a Jewish custom," said Eva later, and with much affection.

"So what, we are *Mischlings*," responded Emma with a smile, "we don't have to do it by the book."

Irena Eisler is the literary pseudonym of Irena Murray, linguist, architectural historian and chief curator of rare books and special collection at McGill University. Born in Prague, she came to Canada in 1968. Her first fiction appeared in Czech, in a collection from Toronto's '68 Publishers. She is currently working on a novella.

August

CLAIRE ROTHMAN

The summer I turned fourteen was particularly wet and grey. I stayed at home after school closed, staring at the world through rain-streaked windows, working my way through piles of romance magazines. My mother couldn't pass the livingroom without making some comment. She said I won the sweepstakes for laziness. Lists of chores hung on the refrigerator door in her neat hand. She had high hopes. But it was all I could do to rouse myself from the couch and wander down the hall to my room for nail lacquer, or to replenish the magazine supply. I had no energy for anything.

I was the eldest of five girls. My sisters still went to day camp. I had outgrown this but was too young to get a summer job. There was nothing to do but lounge. My mother called it an "in between" age. I wasn't like my sisters any longer, but I wasn't an adult either. She reminded me of that often enough. I had to be inside the house by nine-thirty every night. There was nowhere in particular I wanted to go, but it was humiliating all the same. My sisters got to play outside till dusk, which in the month of June fell just about that hour. If I came in late I lost my allowance just like them. It robbed me of my dignity.

Montreal had turned into a ghost town. My friends had left for cottages or overnight camps where they practiced riding and tennis. I wished I could leave home like them, but with five children in the family it was out of the question. I felt martyred for my baby sisters and moped all the more at life's injustice. Some days I roused myself and walked over to the park. There were tennis courts there and the attendant, a boy named

Arthur, was older than me and very good looking. He'd been elected King during carnival week at my school. I used to wait for someone to lob a ball over the fence and run to retrieve it. Sometimes Arthur even nodded in my direction, and struck up a conversation. But the courts were flooded every second day and closed down most of the time. Arthur hid out in the men's room or else gave up and went home. In the end, the park proved as lifeless and dull as anywhere else. I was forced back to the livingroom, to my magazines and daydreams.

After six weeks of this, my mother finally lost her cool. She kept up a stream of activity, not even breaking pace on the hottest days. Watching her depleted me. She aired blankets on the back verandah, washed the walls and floors, did laundry, cooking, packed four bag lunches every morning for my siblings. The sight of me stretched out on her couch, the floor littered with paper, a bowl of popcorn at my elbow, set her off. It was as if a horsefly got her. She literally went red with rage. One night at the end of July she telephoned her parents. They lived in Toronto, but were vacationing on a muddy lake somewhere in southern Ontario.

My mother had spent summers there as a child. It was called Bram-lea and she always spoke of it as if it were special, a place of real beauty. I'd seen it once on one of my father's summer vacations. We'd all driven down, an endless trip during which my sisters vomited one after the other, each spurring on the next, all over the back seat. I remember trying not to breathe for three hundred miles. It was the last long voyage by automobile my father ever took with us.

When we arrived we were desperate for water. We spilled out of the car, stripping off shorts and shirts as we went, littering the path down to the dock. We'd already fished the bathing suits out of our suitcases and changed in the car's back seat (coyly, beneath beach towels). Being the eldest with the longest legs, I was the first one at the dock. I peered in and set the tone for the whole visit by refusing to climb down the ladder. Weeds covered the lake bottom like a carpet. They waved, slick, hairlike, rippling the water's surface. At night we spread sleeping bags on the livingroom floor because there weren't enough beds. My grandmother, who for some reason went by the nickname Petes (her real name was Gloria), told us not to whisper or we'd wake up the mice.

My mother wanted me to go back there. I'd stay the month of August, she said. It'd do me good.

I arrived at the bus depot at Bramlea just as the sun was sinking. It had been hazy and uncertain all afternoon and with darkness coming the sky fumed a strange greyish yellow. Rain had followed me, my grandfather was later to observe, across the border and all the way from Montreal. That summer, I began calling my grandfather by his real name, Harry. Before, I used to call him Grampa Harold, but when I got off the bus that night I felt pretty grown up. I'd travelled over three hundred miles on my own, and I figured I had a right. All the way to Toronto I'd sat with a woman who'd just gone through a divorce. She told me the details. How she'd raised kids. How he was a drinker. How he had his little affairs, and gradually the marriage eroded. "We were like ships passing in the night. I barely knew him at the end." When she said goodbye to me at the Toronto station she got all sentimental. She didn't know anything about me (she'd done all the talking), but she said I was smart, and "mature beyond your years."

So when I got off the bus I called out, "Hi, Harry." I said it simply, looking him in the eye as if it were the most natural thing in the world. It's amazing what you can get away with when you look people in the eye. I was trying on a hat. He could have knocked it off my head, sent it flying, told me it wasn't my place, but he just laughed and hugged me as if I'd been using it for years.

Harry loved to work. He'd grown up on a farm where everyone was expected to pull his weight. If he was ever caught idling he once told me, his father or an older brother would take a leather thong down from the wall and remind him of all the chores that needed doing. You'd have thought he'd grow up hating work, but he was just the opposite. He abhorred idleness. There was a hammock on his lawn strung between a birch tree and the porch, but neither he nor Petes used it. It was there for show. A functionless emblem of summer. Harry couldn't sit, let alone lie, in one place for more than a few minutes. Like my mother he dreamt up an endless series of tasks and set about doing them in a resolute way. Unlike her, he was always cheerful about it. It was the thing he liked most and he was impatient when darkness fell and he was forced to rest.

The night I arrived, rain came down harder over Bramlea than it had all summer. I was in my jeans sipping cocoa (the real kind, made with honey and milk) when Petes disappeared. It was still light outside, barely nine o'clock, and I figured she'd gone to get a book or something. A few minutes later she came out of the bedroom in a ratty mustard-coloured bathrobe. She had flannel on underneath, I could see the collar, and her face was slathered with white cream. She kissed me lightly and said she was retiring. She pecked Harry's cheek as well. He slept in a different room. I'd known this from when I visited them in Toronto, but I'd never thought much about it. Now it made me wonder. Poor old Harry, banished to a separate room, and what was more, Petes didn't look all that appealing after dark. In Montreal my parents shared a bed. They were private about sex, and frankly I still don't know when they did it (I have no recollections of ever walking in on them), but at least the bed was there. A symbol brimming with adult mystery. I went to sleep wondering about Petes and Harry. Trying to picture them young.

I awoke to smells of frying bacon and toast. Rain was pummelling the roof. I dozed while Harry and Petes got agitated, wondering whether to knock and wake me or let me eat my breakfast cold. Finally I got up and Petes sat with me, watching me crumble dried-out pork into small bits and dissolve them on my tongue. Harry stuck his head in from the porch as I was finishing. The rain had stopped, he said. It was time to fix the road.

I was still in my pyjamas. By the time I changed into shorts and a T-shirt he was half way up the road that linked his cottage to the highway. This road was dirt, about a kilometre in length, and rose in periodic, gentle hills. My grandfather was wearing stained work pants. He carried an old bucket full of sand and two spades. I fell into step beside him and he explained what we would do with the pleasure of someone proposing a set of tennis, a boatride on the lake.

"This sand will do the trick. The rain really cut up the road's surface."

Harry didn't own the road. It was a public access and other cottagers and farmers used it. But Harry didn't think in terms of who owned what. It needed to be done and he had the time. It wasn't hard work, he said, and in the long run, life would be better for everyone. It struck me as pretty left wing. Harry had voted conservative every election since the First World War. In theory, he was all for the free market. In practice, however, he was something between a socialist and a saint. He was always weighing things with an eye to the common good. I admired Harry's zeal but at the same time I found it peculiar. It was just about as foreign to my fourteen-year-old lounging state as anything could be. I spent the morning squatting at his side, searching for holes and filling them with loose sand and gravel.

Several days after I arrived, my grandfather asked if I wanted to go driving. He would take me to one of the nearby farms. He knew the woman who ran it and she never refused a visitor. He was trying to think up activities. He must have realized that potholes wouldn't keep me going indefinitely and he didn't understand that my favourite way to pass the time was doing nothing. I'd already greased the chains on the hammock.

The farm was owned by a woman called Gwen, who was the county sheriff. When Harry told me this I pictured a stetson and six shooters, but it really meant she sat on committee meetings and made decisions about zoning and the parcelling of property. We turned down the dust road to her farm just as the sun was getting hot. Harry stopped the car near the front porch, got out and stood awkwardly for several seconds. He was very careful about decorum. I think it embarrassed him to call on a woman who was no relation.

He and Gwendolyn had known each other for years. She knew everyone in the area, cottagers included, and made a big point of stopping to say hello and catching up on news when she met people in town or on the road. Harry liked her friendliness. He understood it because of his own farming roots. Petes, who was a city woman, born and bred in Windsor, couldn't stand it. "That woman?" she would say whenever Gwen's name came up. "She's got her finger in everyone's pie."

Gwen appeared on the front doorstep wiping her hands on her jeans. She was a squat woman with silver white hair cropped like an overturned bowl. She looked about as old as Harry but was dressed more like me.

"Harry, you took us by surprise. We were just finishing the breakfast dishes."

I was wondering about the "we" when a thin, childlike person stepped onto the porch. She would have been beautiful except she had a harelip which skewed her face to one side. She didn't say a word, just stared over Gwen's shoulder at us.

Harry got flustered then, said he should have phoned first but he thought they'd be in the garden by now, or working with the bees. Gwen laughed and said they'd slept in. The girl faded back inside the house without saying anything, but Gwen hardly seemed to notice. She came down the stairs for a mid-morning chat.

"Sun for a change," she said looking about her at the yard steeped in light. "The Almanac promises August will be dry." She grinned, taking me in with her violet eyes. Her colours were startling; white hair, eyes dark as huckleberry, skin flushed brown with sun. She knew all about me before I opened my mouth: when I'd arrived, my age, the part of Montreal I came from, the fact I played drums with the band at school.

"Lee plays mandolin. Bluegrass mostly. We've got a set of bongo drums around here somewhere but neither of us knows how to make them sound good. You should come over some night and jam."

Since when did a woman as old as my grandparents use the word "jam?" She seemed old and young in the same moment. She was wearing jeans and a wine T-shirt. Her breasts hung pendulously underneath. I could see the eraser ends of nipples poking at the cotton. She didn't even have a brassiere on. She looked like someone from my school, yet she was talking credibly with Harry about the state of the roads. He smiled, nodded, thoroughly enchanted. Gwen straddled generations. She was a chameleon, charming whomever happened along.

She spent the morning giving us a tour. At one time she'd owned cows but now the barn was empty except for a sweet-tempered goat called Beulah. She'd sold off most of her pastureland. It was too much work, she said, for the small return. Now all that was left was a vegetable garden and her apiary. The garden was immense, straining at the sides of a mesh wire fence. It could barely be contained. Tomato plants drooped with the weight of pale orange fruit. Someone had placed them beautifully. They were spaced so that each was washed in sunlight.

From far off the garden looked like a quilt. Swatches of colour stopped and started in abrupt lines. Things were arranged as much for the eye as anything else. It was like a collage of origami papers. Gourds and pumpkins grew in one corner. A flame of nasturtiums carpeted the ground beside them. Gossamer fronds of asparagus waved delicately, airy as debutantes. I recognized vegetables when I could find them beneath the leaves and vines, but I was hopeless at naming plants. Gwen raised her eyebrows and said I needed educating.

She told me Lee was mistress of the garden. She'd arrived two years ago from the city knowing as little as I did about the land, but with a book on organic farming strapped to her rucksack. She stopped in the county to look for work. In the two years she'd been with Gwen she'd revolutionized things. They no longer used chemicals; Lee started a compost heap and used only natural pesticides. She planted things Gwen would never have tried: eggplant, herbs, new strains of squash. She also knew how to cook them. Gwen gave Lee free rein in the garden because she was hopeless with bees. She'd tried to train her. That had been the original idea, to get steady help for the apiary, but it hadn't worked out. Every time Lee went near a hive she got stung. At night she dreamt bees were eating her alive. I was secretly glad to hear Lee was fallible. I'd been more than a little awed by Gwen's heaping praise.

By her own account, Gwen was just the opposite of Lee. She'd worked with bees since she was five years old and had never once been stung. It was all in the mind, she said. If a person got scared, the bees sensed it. As long as you were calm and slow they'd let you do anything. She led us through a field in back of the house. At the far end was a row of huts. We stopped several yards away.

"And how are you with bees?" she asked.

One or two flew over to see what we were doing. My underarms turned to water. Sweat rushed down my sides in tepid rivers. I was wearing a pink sweater that day and I'd spritzed on cologne in the bathroom after breakfast. The bees hung suspended in the air around me, considering.

"They seem to like you," Gwen said when neither Harry nor I spoke. "If I were you I'd get rid of the sweater though. They hate getting caught in wool."

I ripped off the sweater and dropped it on the grass. My arms were bare in a light T-shirt. I felt vaguely like an offering, nubile sacrifice, as we stood in the heat of the noon sun.

The visit was the first of many that summer. Gwen gave me an old bicycle, rusted, without fenders or gears, so I could come and see her on my own. She understood, without a word exchanged between us, that I needed time away from Petes and Harry. My grandparents thought I'd struck up a friendship with Lee, but nothing could be further from the truth. On my first visit alone to the farm, Lee came out onto the porch where Gwen and I were drinking lemonade. She sat on a deck chair and began peeling paint flakes off the armrest.

I watched her hands, which were long and delicately boned. On the left, the nails were clipped short, but on the right she'd let them grow. Dirt was encrusted just below the point where the nail turned white and grew away from the fingertip. Later Gwen told me that Lee liked to keep the nails of one hand long to pluck her mandolin. They looked bad because of all the gardening she did, but they made beautiful sounds.

That day Lee said very little. She listened and seemed to be making up her mind about me. Gwen all but ignored her. Lee's face was narrow, draped on either side by limp black hair. She wore no make-up and her smile, which flashed at rare intervals and faded almost immediately, was marred by surgical scars. It was hard to pin an age on her. At thirteen I was better developed than she was, more fleshy. She was all limbs and bones, skinny as a child. She'd been to university and dropped out, so I guessed she was somewhere in her mid-twenties.

Gwen was talking about bees. She said keeping them was an art; a zen, if you will. At the time I didn't know what zen meant, but I nodded anyways. I kind of got the idea just from her tone. Bees were her passion; caring for them shaped her life. She told a story about collecting honey in a heat wave. It was so hot the sweat dripped in her eyes and slowed the work. Finally, in frustration, she stripped off her shorts and top. A neighbouring farmer, come to visit at dusk, found her at the huts, stark naked except for the boots on her feet.

I laughed at this. I could see her standing in the field, caught out with nowhere to duck and hide. I wasn't used to this kind of talk, to someone sharing past mortifications. In my family, embarrassments were seldom articulated. Adults shrouded themselves in respectable silence.

"She's exaggerating," Lee said. She hadn't said a word until then and I'd forgotten she was there. "She got her T-shirt on before the guy saw anything. She always embellishes."

Gwen was grinning with the recollection. She didn't seem to mind the way Lee tried to shrink the story. I was fuming. I couldn't stand Lee judging everything. She looked like she'd swallowed a quarry of stones and was having problems digesting.

We finished the lemonade and Gwen rose to carry the glasses inside. I followed her and just as she opened the kitchen door, I tripped. I was passing Lee's chair. Her legs were stretched out in front of her, blocking my way and as I stepped over them she jerked them up against one of my shins, hooking my foot and sending me sprawling.

"You okay?" she said neutrally.

I was already on my feet to face her. "Yeah. I guess I'll live."

Gwen hadn't seen. I could hear her running water in the kitchen.

Over the next weeks Gwen initiated me into the world of bees.

I avoided Lee whenever I could. She worked in her garden and I had to be home most days before supper, so our paths didn't cross all that often. About bees I learned many things. I never wore perfume again and I also dressed more simply. Gwen lent me gloves and a net for my head when we visited the hives. She herself only wore gloves. She worked without smoke, most of the time in sleeveless shirts. Her face and arms were exposed and she kept up a constant monologue as bees hovered about her face.

"Bees are so just," she said one day, laughing at the thought. "Everyone has her job. Everyone gets food and shelter. It's probably because they're run by females."

I didn't say much. I was still very nervous and only listened with half an ear. Bees landed on my sleeves, crawled up my pant legs, and it was all I could do to keep from yelling and thrashing out. I prayed fear wouldn't change my smell. Gwen told me how acute the smell sense of a bee was. When Lee came to the hives, for instance, they'd head straight for her, stingers taut and quivering.

One day she spoke unprompted about Lee.

"Her life's been rough. The world is kind only to unblemished packages. You're one of the lucky ones and you can thank the stars for that."

I didn't feel like thanking stars, nor did I forgive Lee. Who cared about her life? I hadn't done her any harm; I stewed with the injustice. It pleased me that the bees scared her off. It meant Gwen and I could have some peace.

Gwen showed me how to lift the tops off hives and how to fix the damaged ones. She explained bee roles in detail.

The queen laid every egg in the hive. All the workers were her daughters. "Imagine the efficiency," Gwen said. "One bee creating an entire world from her womb."

The mating practices dumbfounded me. Ordinarily, Gwen told me, the queen leaves the hive only once for what is called the "nuptial flight." The drones pursue her and four or five eventually catch her. They copulate mid-air, flying beneath her on their backs, and when she's had enough, she kills them. They drop like bombs, lifeless eunuchs spinning through the sky. She is a brutal lover, ripping off the testicles as trophy. Gwen always checked for bee gut hanging from the returning queen.

I loved to listen to Gwen's stories. She made the bees larger than life. A world overflowing with ritual and a violent kind of logic. One day we talked of coronations. One of her hives had lost a queen and she was trying to introduce a new one in larva form.

"It's not certain they'll accept her. They might starve or sting her to death. We'll know in a day or two."

Most often the hive produced its own queen and Gwen didn't have to do it artificially. On rare occasions a new queen was born before the old one died. Then things got hot. Either the old one killed the young one, or else she left. There was never room for two. Gwen said that if I ever saw a swarm travelling in the air, that would be the reason. A sign of *coup d'état*. One queen had forced the other out.

At night on the cot in my grandparents' cottage, I thought about bees. They invaded my dreams. I never was entirely easy with them. At first they terrorized me, crawling on me, smothering me with their whining bodies, but with time I relaxed a little. I was able to appreciate their beauty (their coats were sleek velvet, the gold shimmering like sequins), but my dreams never lost the sharp edge of threat. Once, I had a vision of a gorgeous queen, so huge she had to fold back her wings to fit in my small bedroom. She hung from the ceiling telling me stories. But her gut began to leak, rust-coloured liquid dripped onto my bed. I didn't want to touch it. I knew with the strange intuition of dreams that it was trouble.

It seemed I never spent time with Petes and Harry. The hammock lay abandoned on the lawn, I was too busy with the bees. In contrast to Gwen, my own grandmother seemed faded and pale. It was hard to believe they were the same age. Gwen was self-reliant. She drove a beat-up Ford wagon and delivered honey and vegetables to town herself. The farmers respected her. She could talk with anyone. Petes had to be chauffered by Harry. She only left the house a couple of times a week to replenish her cupboards. She wrote out lists in a girlish script and planned all our suppers in advance. That's how her days were spent so far as I knew, dreaming up menus and worrying that Harry or I would be late to eat.

I didn't know it but I'd half fallen in love with Gwen. I mimicked her smile, the peculiar way she had of rocking on the balls of her feet when she was listening to someone. I began to lisp and swallow the ends of sentences just like she did.

Petes was the first to notice it. We were at dinner, our plates littered with white cobs of corn. Harry and I always competed to see who could eat more. Usually he won with four cobs, but he paid for it. I'd hear him in the bathroom after Petes and I had gone to bed, wrestling with indigestion. That night, he told a long tale about his father's farm. It would have been interesting except he kept bringing in all kinds of bit players, names I'd never heard of. He traced an elaborate tree of family, sisters who married local pastors, brothers long-dead, entire branches of cousins, each with names and dates of birth and death assiduously recorded. He kept notes on family history. One day, he said, he'd pass them onto me. I rolled my eyes. Corpses of flies lay trapped inside the light on the ceiling. Harry didn't see. He never looked at people when he talked. When my eyes rolled down, however, Petes was staring straight at me.

"I suppose I should clear the dishes," I said. Harry's story had stopped.

"You're doing something with your s's," Petes chimed. She rarely spoke at meals and even more rarely this directly. "It reminds me of someone." It was so out of character, even Harry was staring at her. "I've got it," she said, excited. "It's Gwen. She's picked up that lisp, exactly like Gwen's."

I could have kicked her. She'd seen it before I noticed it myself.

Three weeks into August, the fields were dry as tinder. The haying had been good, but the farmers were beginning to worry. Everything was yellow, parched. The lake had shrivelled like an old balloon. Rocks lay exposed, their moss skins peeling in the sun. It was marvellous for me. There'd been no rain since the night I arrived from Montreal. I used the bicycle every day and spent most of my time out of doors with the bees.

Summer was ending. The hints were everywhere. The close, damp days of July were long gone and night fell early now, bringing a cold that reached its way under layers of clothing. In less than a week I'd be back in the city. School would start again. A first small wave of nostalgia hit me. What would it be like waking up without the bees?

One morning in my last week at the cottage we were sitting at the breakfast table when the phone rang. It was a party line and Harry always let it ring a few times to make sure it was for us. Two shorts and a long was our code. He picked up the receiver and yelled. Yelling was part of the ritual of the thing; Harry didn't trust that it would work or that a familiar voice would actually make it through the wires. Petes was even worse. She wouldn't touch it. She was convinced the other cottagers listened in on our conversations.

"Who?" Harry shouted. He was squinting as if it might be a crank call. Then his face relaxed. "Oh, Gwen. Didn't sound like you."

I couldn't keep still. I reached for a serviette and sent a glass of juice hurtling across the table. Petes mopped it up, but a plate of toast lay ruined and I'd soaked her table cloth. After interminable minutes Harry hung up, checking the receiver twice to see that the call was over and everything was under control.

"Gwen's off after some runaway bees. She thought you'd like to know."

That was all I needed. I jumped from my chair and began pulling on my tennis shoes. I didn't even stop to lace them. I kissed Petes and Harry and two minutes later I was pedalling furiously along the shoulder of the highway to Gwen's farm.

A queen forced from the nest. It was late in the season for a swarm to be spotted. Frost would soon set in. I pictured Gwen waving a butterfly net. I had no idea how we'd save them.

She was loading things into the back of the Ford when I arrived. I was sweating hard and my hair was tangled from the wind. "You're a sight," she said in her unhurried, lisping way. "Go on into the house and wash up while I finish packing."

It was nine o'clock or so, earlier than I usually arrived and the stillness around Gwen's farm was absolute. The only sounds were the lazy vocals of cicadas in the fields. Lee wasn't in her garden yet. Beulah the goat was nowhere to be seen, probably still sleeping in the barn. I slipped into the kitchen and suddenly a voice came from upstairs.

It was haunting. Unadorned, simple as a boy's. I'd never heard Lee sing. We could barely sit in the same room together, let alone think of making music. I thought of her as thoroughly hateful, an ugly creature. Yet here was this voice, the sweetness trapped inside her. I didn't turn on the faucet. I just stood and listened, and that's how Gwen found me when she came in from outside. "Oh," she said, her face going all soft as if someone had struck her. "She's really something, isn't she."

We drove west to the far edge of the county. A man out there had seen the swarm and phoned Gwen because he knew she kept bees. The law said that anyone who captured a swarm on the wing could claim title, Gwen explained as we sped past fields of splintered cornstalks.

They were just where he said they'd be, on a tree in the back of a dilapidated farmhouse. The tree was small and from far off the bees looked like a cluster of grapes dangling from an upper branch. The reality of our task hit me then. Gwen and I would have to capture this crawling, whining mass of life, move it into the Ford and drive with it for at least a half hour over rough dirt roads. I don't know what I'd been imagining. I guess I never expected we'd find them.

Gwen took a large sheet out of the car and spread it under the tree. She could have been preparing a picnic except for the angry buzzing at her head. The bees tolerated her, sending low warnings as she worked. She took pruning shears and deftly, in a single motion, snapped the branch about a foot above the swarm. It dropped heavily onto the centre of the sheet.

The bees spun in crazy orbit. Like planets with displaced magnetic fields. Gwen and I were statues. Neither of us moved; our breath slowed to the minimum. We didn't dare look at each other until finally the bees began to quiet and regroup about the queen on the severed branch.

Gwen passed me the shears. Then delicately, as if she were tucking in a sleeping child, she lifted a corner of the bedsheet and laid it over her prize. We did this with each corner, tiptoeing around the perimeter of the sheet, until the bees were folded safely away. There was still a hissing noise but it was muffled and the white surface gave the illusion that the bees had vanished.

On the drive back to the farm, Gwen turned to me. Bees hummed from the back seat. Six or seven had crawled out and hung suspended in the air inside the car. They crashed their small bodies against the windshield, unable to make sense of this transparent wall.

"You were marvellous," Gwen said. "Nothing fazes you." I grinned with a lopsided grin that wasn't quite my own, lapping up the praise. "I wish I could keep you here. Between us we'd get that apiary cooking."

I'd never been so happy. Visions of me living in the big old house somersaulted in my mind. I dropped Lee from the picture. She was the one dark spot, of course. Maybe Gwen would invite me back to work next summer and by that time Lee would have moved on. We drove slowly. Gwen turned on the radio and the rasping voice of Bob Dylan filled the car. I'd first heard of Dylan only two years before. I remember some kid playing *Lay Lady Lay* in class in sixth grade. There was plenty of static. Gwen said the bees wouldn't mind. It was probably opera to them.

When we pulled into the yard, Lee came running from the garden. She was smiling but she stopped several yards off when she saw I was there. Gwen yelled to stay away and told briefly about the swarm. She patted my arm and said I'd been a star. Lee turned without saying anything, without any congratulations or any soft word, and walked off, sullen, inscrutable, back to her work.

I didn't see Gwen for three days after that. It had rained steadily and I'd been helping Harry close up the cottage. I couldn't take the bicycle out and the walk was too long. I'd phoned once to let her know I was alive, but she and Lee must have been out. There was no answer.

The evening before I left for Montreal, I pedalled over to her place. The house was dark and empty-looking but the Ford was there, a sign that she was in. I ran up the steps, calling her name. The door to the kitchen was unlatched. No one locked their doors here. Gwen said it was rude. What if visitors came by and you weren't in? At least then they could leave a note on your table or fix themselves a juice. Through the screen I saw dishes and some papers on the counter, as if someone had eaten and not bothered to clean up. I called again.

It was past eight and the sky was turning a watery brown. Maybe she was off in the fields with Lee or perhaps she'd gone to check her bees. I decided she couldn't be far and that the best idea was to wait on the porch. I sat on one of the peeling chairs, tugging the sleeves of my sweater down over my hands. The night was clear and a crescent moon, amber-coloured and spongey like comb honey, hung low in the sky.

The air had that fresh quality that comes after rain. I could smell gum on the trees and the green of the fields was deep, saturated now that water had touched the land. The soil would be teeming with insect life. I sat hugging my knees, feeling cold crawl up the surface of my skin. And then

I heard Gwen. There were no words, just sounds, low, repetitive, breaking the still night.

I was rooted to the chair. It was a slow dawning. Gwen and Lee. A truth I'd known somehow, but never dared to look at. I closed my eyes but the sounds kept on, insistent, pushing through.

After a while I got up to go. I must have made noise because someone raised a window directly above me and light streamed onto the porch.

"Who's there?" Lee's voice, timid in the night.

I sidestepped the shaft of light and ran. I didn't speak. Didn't care if I was seen. The bicycle was leaning against Gwen's car exactly where I'd left it, but I ran on, straight to the highway. The only sound was my feet on gravel; even the crickets had stopped their song. And all the way home that August night the moon's grin followed me, glinting above the tree branches, ageless, vaguely mocking.

Claire Rothman has worked as a lawyer, a columnist for The Gazette, *and as a teacher. Her story collections are* Salad Days *and* Black Tulips.

The Black Valises

ROMA GELBLUM-BROSS

I first noticed Robert Engel on the platform of the old Kiev Station. Mother, Father and I were waiting for a train to take us into Russia and away from the German front. What caught my attention were his valises.

The station was densely crowded with refugees, who carried their belongings in knapsacks, bundles and old valises bursting open at the seams. Only Robert Engel had large new valises. They were black and shiny, had gold coloured locks and were braced with wide bands of metal. Robert Engel himself looked small and insignificant next to his valises; he was very skinny, had red, thinning hair and a thin, pale nose that supported a pair of gold-rimmed glasses.

He was standing not far from us on the platform. When the train finally rolled into the station and people crowded the entrance pushing and screaming, Father helped Engel up the steep metal steps.

But after we had boarded the train we lost sight of him. He was pushed to the left of the long dim carriage. We were pushed to the right. We settled quickly on one of the still-vacant benches. Even before Father had taken off his coat I fell asleep on his shoulder.

When I woke up early in the morning the train was moving slowly and heavily. It was emitting gasping, forced sounds which were interrupted from time to time by the long wailing cry of the whistle. The bolts underneath the carriage squeaked shrilly with every turn and the wagon shook and rattled. Chilly misty air shrouded the windows. Shadows of telegraph poles were moving hastily on the panes, and frost clung in uneven patches to the greenish-gray metal of the window frame. The leg of someone seated on the roof of the wagon dangled in front of our window.

When my eyes got used to the semi-darkness I saw human shapes that crouched, sat or lay on benches, on the floor, and on the luggage racks. They all looked as if they had just given up a night-long struggle with sleeplessness and had frozen into twisted positions, their hands clutching their belongings. Children were crying in their sleep. Enamelled night-pots attached to the bundles gave off a smell of urine that mingled with the smoke of handmade cigarettes, the sweat of dozens of unwashed bodies and the odour of rotting food. My parents' heads were moving silently back and forth, like the heads of marionettes forgotten by their puppeteer. It was stuffy, cold and deadly quiet.

The silence was interrupted by the metallic squeak of an opening door. When the door closed again I saw a man in a khaki uniform with Russian emblems, standing in the entrance. He squinted, then looked around in astonishment. With the tip of his boot he nudged one of the bodies blocking the passage.

"Move a little, batyushka, allow a fellow to perform his duty, ah?" He said loudly. He spoke Russian and the tone of his voice was deep, warm and melodious. Eyes opened and some faces lit up with smiles.

"Some aromatic stuff in this wagon, comrades," he went on. "How about opening a window or two. Mother Russia has plenty of fresh air, if nothing else. So go ahead and enjoy it."

He stretched a leg over a body that was curled up between two crowded seats and pushed one of the windows outward. Fresh cold air burst into the wagon, bringing with it minute particles of ice that melted on faces and beards. People shrank back, pulled on the edges of shawls and coats. Mother woke up with a shiver and wrapped me in her blanket. The official reached the middle of the carriage and planted his legs firmly on the two sides of the aisle.

"Mother Russia welcomes you with frosty breath, comrades. Enjoy it. It is better, I assure you, than the warm breath of the German dogs on your backs, ah?" He was smiling a wide smile under a thick, Stalin-style moustache. His eyes were dark and slightly slanted at the corners. His face, wrinkled and weather-beaten, was dark too, and robustly handsome. He nodded at the tired and dirty faces around him.

"Some trip for you, poor Jewish devils. And you have not seen the end of it yet. Wait till you get to Siberia . . . Nobody's told you yet how lucky you are. Nobody's told you, so I will. And what I have to tell you is that your all coming to a land of happiness."

He looked around to examine the impression his words were making. But some people did not understand Russian, and some were too tired to pay attention. Nevertheless he went on, unmindful.

"Yes, comrades, you may not believe it, but we are happy here. This is because our needs are small, unlike you, capitalists. We are happy when we have a piece of bread to eat, when there is a tiny bit of vodka to cheer us up. And you are going to be happy with us!"

An old man who was sitting on the bench behind ours, his face swathed in bandages, murmured, "Let the devil take their happiness. Couldn't he wait with his propaganda till after breakfast? It's hard to take on an empty stomach."

A voice from the rack shushed him and a man on our left said to him in Polish, "Be quiet, old fool! The commandant is offering you happiness and you complain. It's better to be named a 'comrade' than a 'corpse,' so smile nicely at the commandant and keep your bandaged mouth shut."

The official stood there for awhile, nodding his head, then he turned and proceeded towards the other end of the carriage. I followed him with my eyes and I saw him proceeding slowly, then stopping at the end of the carriage and eyeing something intently. I climbed up on the bench to see what it was he was staring at and saw that it was Robert Engel. He was squeezed into the back corner of the carriage sitting on top of his valises. The valises took the place of two people and their gleaming surfaces contrasted with the shabby surroundings and with Engel's stained jacket.

The official placed himself solidly in front of Engel. Engel did not move. He was totally absorbed in a small book he was holding to the dim light. His head was moving up and down rhythmically, as if he were trying to memorize the lines.

All the eyes turned, curious, towards them. Engel went on reading, oblivious to all, and the official just stood there patiently, cocking his head once to the left, then to the right, as if he were looking at a strange bird that just perched on a branch of a tree. His patience ended after a while, for he cried loudly, "Wake up, comrade, wake up and talk to us!"

Engel lifted his head abruptly, like a man rudely awakened from a pleasant dream. His yellow eyes blinked behind the gold frames, then filled with fear.

"Yes commandant, what is it you wish from me?"

Instead of an answer the official produced out if his breastpocket a crumpled scrap of paper, a pouch of tobacco and a box of matches. He leaned against the frame of the door, rolled a cigarette, then lit a match by striking it against the sole of his boot. He then blew a cloud of smoke into Engel's face.

"Learned Comrade," he said mockingly. "A fine place comrade found for his studies. I modestly presume the best in the country. I am sorry the light we provide here is inadequate, the heat insufficient and the stench just a tiny hit overpowering."

Engel opened his eyes wide, uncomprehending. He did not answer, only squinted and cupped his ear. The official drew near him and looked at him fiercely.

"I see the learned comrade is carrying his burial caskets with him, ah?" He examined the shining locks on the valises, then pulled on the metal band. "How long you have been dragging those with you across Russia is one thing I wish to know. And the second is how you managed to get on the train, ah?" Thousands of men lie under bare skies all over the land, people travel on roofs of wagons, we are all crowded here like spider's eggs in a pouch and comrade is riding on top of fancy black valises like a bloody aristocrat. I hope comrade has gold and diamonds inside. Anyhow, whatever it is I wish not to see it anymore. Next stop, out you go with the valises, or out go the valises and you stay with your small volume!"

I was afraid for Engel and watched the two intently. But Engel seemed to be regaining his composure. He straightened his back and put his hand on his breast-pocket.

"But . . . but . . . comrade commandant . . . it . . . it is . . . very important . . . ominously so . . ." he stumbled in broken Russian. "Here . . . the certificate . . . you may read yourself."

He fished out of his pocket a folded sheet of paper and handed it to the Russian. The official unfolded it and glanced at the bottom of the page.

"A round stamp . . . it bears a round stamp!" someone said. A round stamp was a sacred testimony to the fact that someone in the complicated hierarchy of Russian bureaucracy had dealt with the problem and issued a document.

The official seemed surprised, but he folded the paper and made a motion of resignation with his hand.

"There are some things in this life I shall never understand," he said, "and this is one of them."

Before moving on he knocked on the side of the valises. The muted sound testified that they were solidly packed.

The train moved on relentlessly, day and night stopping once in a while at small stations in the middle of nowhere. After a few days the wide expanses of whiteness had disappeared and we entered mountainous arid terrain. Sunshine started penetrating in thin slanted beams into the wagon. It seemed to melt some of the weariness and the fear. There were deep caves in the barren mountains gaping dark and mysterious, swirling water and strangely dressed people riding small agile horses. People seemed to unfold, become willing to share. Arms stretched from one compartment to another offering cigarettes, bundles were untwisted to dig out dried fruits and candies. It was still cold, but dry. We were crossing the boundaries of Europe and entering Asia.

Groups of people took turns by the window to admire the changing and beautiful landscape. I stood glued to the window too. It was like entering a story land.

At night the train rattled on narrow tracks. The darkness around was so complete that I thought there were only the few of us, the train and the stars left in the world. People around sighed and grunted and whispered, cigarettes glowed in the darkness and the *machorka* tobacco gave a strong aroma, like that of burning dry leaves.

Mother had a candle with her. From a lump of clay she had dug from a little hill at one of the stations she had formed a candleholder with a curved handle. She put the candleholder on top of a valise, protecting the feeble, shaky flames with the palms of her hands. Cupped around the candle her hands were red and almost transparent.

A few people moved closer to us. The light of the candle made the wrinkles on their faces look deeper and their eyes darker. Looking into the flame Mother said, "We are entering a magnificent land."

The eyes turned curiously towards her. I slipped off my father's knees to be nearer. Mother then said we were in Uzbeckistan. The people opened their eyes even wider. They had never heard of this land. She then told them it was an ancient, fertile and beautiful country, of mild climate and protected from harsh winds and enemies by high mountains. It was a part of Russia now, but hundreds of years ago, it was the proudest of lands, a centre of the Empire of the Mamluks, who came from the east and conquered those territories like a hurricane. She told them about the wild Gingis Han and the wise Tamerlane who ruled amidst unbelievable splendours.

The man with the bandaged face, who used to be a butcher's helper in the small Jewish town from which he escaped scratched his ear thoughtfully.

"And where do you know all this from, Mrs. Solomonovna? How does one know things like this?"

"I read about it, Mr. Kugelman."

"And you believe what you read?"

"Just as much as I believe what I hear, and sometimes more."

Mr. Kugelman smiled. "I can see that when asked, you can answer, Mrs. Solomonovna. But if you ask *me*, don't believe in any reading. What is reading good for? It is like the wind passing over a field of wheat. You can't eat it, you can't drink it, you can't sleep with it or use it for a blanket at night. But take, for example, a nice side of rib . . ."

Mother sighed, though I could see that the thought of a nice side of rib was not unpleasant to her. "It would take too long to explain, Mr. Kugelman. You are certainly right about some things. And yet, Mr. Kugelman, if it weren't for the wind, could the clouds accumulate and cause rain to fall?"

Mr. Kugelman scratched his ear again. "You are a difficult person to argue with, Mrs. Solomonovna."

"This is because I read a lot, Mr. Kugelman."

"But anyway, you do not convince me."

Other voices came from the darkened part of the carriage.

"Reading is empty words on paper to confuse your mind when your stomach is empty."

"No child was ever born from reading."

"Our Rabbi read all his life. So the Germans dragged him away from the reading stand. We did not read. We hid in the forest."

I looked at Mother. She seemed lost. I was sorry for her. It seemed strange to me; here she was telling them beautiful stories and they all turned against her. But I could also see that what they said was true. You really could not eat stories. The Rabbi did not run to the forest. As for the children, my mother did have one though she read.

Then a voice came from the other end of the carriage.

"And yet," the voice said, "all of you listened intently, with your eyes and ears wide open. It was so quiet around. It looked as if you forgot everything else."

It was such a loud and clear voice, that at first I did not identify it as belonging to Robert Engel. I was grateful to him.

Mother seemed grateful too, for she smiled and the thin wrinkles disappeared from her forehead. The others did not react. Then she blew the candle out.

Other than that one strong reaction, Engel seemed oblivious to all. Whenever I looked in his direction, more to see the valises than to see him, he was perched on top of them, like a strange bird, almost immobile in his hawklike position, his head bent above his small volume. People were making bets about the contents of his suitcases. Mr. Kugelman said it was tobacco. The skinny man who slept on top of the luggage rack said it was furs. Others were divided between meat, conserves and beans. But soon they lost interest in him. Only the Russian official still bothered to tease him and cause a thin smile to linger on Engel's lips for a while.

Engel was not very talkative, but after a while we did learn a few things about him. He told Mother that he came from a Polish town close to the German border. He told Father that he had been a lonely bachelor all his life. It looked as if everything he had was locked in those fancy valises. He often examined them with fondness, and, one could say, a certain degree of respect. He spread a blanket on them at night and then slept curled up on top. He had no food with him and was living on whatever the authorities rationed, which was not much. As they said in Russia—too much to die on and not enough to live on. A kind hand sometimes offered him tea leaves or a few dried tomatoes, and he accepted hastily and with some embarrassment. At the stations where we disembarked to trade cigarettes and tobacco for food, he stayed inside, guarding his black treasures.

"Learned Comrade," the official teased him, "take care not to stay too long on top of these valises. Your behind may stick to the lid and then you may have some trouble opening them. And then what . . . ?"

Engel usually shied away from the adults in the company. Only two other children and I were allowed to share his seat on top of the valises, close to the ceiling. He was fond of children. Sometimes, when he tired of looking into his small book, when his eyes were red and swollen under the gold-rimmed glasses, he told us stories. It was he who first told me the story of Aladdin and his lamp. When he described the lamp which was made of brass, his eyes wandered to the shiny locks on his valises.

Then, one day he said something strange, something I wished I could believe. He said there were many lamps like Aladdin's around, but people did not know where to look for them. "I hope," he said to us, "I hope you find yours one day."

Once, when I thought he was in a better mood than usual, I pulled on his sleeve to divert his attention from his small volume and then, slowly and hesitantly, I asked him what it was that was hidden in his valises. I did not believe for a moment, I said, that those were furs or conserves, the way others did. So what was it? I asked. Were those princess's garments entrusted to his care or perhaps some secrets of a powerful king? Was he, Engel, an important person in disguise?

He smiled slyly and his eyes narrowed under his gold-rimmed glasses. "So you want to know everything, eh? So curiosity is eating at your head like a green worm?"

I lowered my eyes innocently and started fingering the button of his jacket. "I just want to know, Uncle Engel. Just in case you do not mind telling me. I'll keep it a secret, I promise."

He observed me for a while, as if trying to decide what to do next, then threw a quick glance around and bent his head towards me. "Could you not guess till now?" he whispered, "It's the complete pre-war production of Aladdin's lamps. I am salvaging them from Hitler."

I looked at him with disbelief, but he only smiled slyly again, then went on reading in his little book, which had minute letters, very thin pages and a nice leather cover.

One day we arrived at a train station in a city, the name of which was Samarkand. The station was large and had a few lines of tracks and some solid whitewashed buildings. We were told to disembark for de-lousing, showers and rest. We crawled out of the wagons, stretching our limbs, basking in the luxury of fresh air. Our scanty belongings were to go with us to the disinfection centre. Rumours spread that typhoid and cholera were rampant in the area. Lice were the chief transmittors of these diseases and we all knew that we were infested. Engel was the last to emerge, his thin frame almost bent under the weight of the valises.

People were now emerging from the other wagons and the platform was soon noisy and crowded. Somebody coughed into the loudspeakers. The sound reverberated across the platform, silencing everybody. Then a voice announced a list of people who were to report to the station's commanding officer immediately. Robert Engel was one of the first. He was standing not far from us, and I noticed his desperate confused expression. Others were already on their way, running towards the large building, in the centre of the complex. He seemed to be weighing something in his mind. He tried to lift the valises, then approached a man on his left. The man shrugged his shoulders, as if reluctant to take it upon himself, and agreed to keep an eye on them.

Engel joined the others, turning to look back every few steps. He seemed desperately torn between the need to obey and the will to return. But like all of us he knew that one did not disobey the authorities for any reason in the world and, casting one last glance backwards, he entered the building.

Shortly afterwards, the loudspeakers directed us to the exit, where trucks were standing ready to transport us to the disinfection centre. The man assigned to watch the valises tried to lift them, but they were too heavy and he proceeded without them. The line of people divided, leaving them behind.

We saw Engel later that afternoon in the disinfection centre. With swollen eyes, his hands moving wildly, he was running from person to person.

"Have you seen my valises?" he cried. "Have you seen my valises!" Nobody had seen them after leaving the station. He returned to the platform, then came back, dishevelled, tearful, desperate. He held his head between his hands.

"They stole my valises!" he cried. "They stole my valises!"

He ran back and forth, asking questions, still hopeful, then collapsed on the floor. He sat there crouched and broken. People were passing by, nodding, moving on. Mr. Kugelman approached him and laid a hand on his shoulder.

"Calm down, Mr. Engel, calm down. Myself and other people lost families and homes and they are not that desperate. What was it that you kept in those valises?"

Robert Engel lifted his face and, slowly, as if every syllable was causing him pain, uttered, "My books, all my books." The old man retreated smiling cynically.

Someone started laughing loudly, then someone else joined in. Word passed around and after a while there was a crowd of people standing laughing, unfeeling. Engel stared at them blankly, unseeing, unhearing, engulfed by despair.

"My books," he repeated, "my research, my life's work, all gone."

Nobody seemed to understand. I too stared at him in astonishment and fear. But the intensity of his anguish touched me in a strange way. I wanted to run to him, to put my arms around him, to tell him not to cry, that perhaps he would find his valises. But I was too shy and I remained in the distance, just staring at him, like the others.

The train continued on its way, but we decided to remain in that city. It was a beautiful city and it was the ancient capital of the conqueror Tamerlane.

Engel stayed too, hoping to locate his valises. He posted notices everywhere, promised rewards and gratitude.

He found work as a water carrier and I met him often on my way to school. He had to balance two metal buckets suspended from a long wooden pole that rested on his shoulders. He carried the water from the public cistern, next to the train station, and people jokingly said that he hoped to empty the cistern to find out if the valises were at its bottom.

"Not much of a difference," he remarked to me once. "I used to quench people's thirst for knowledge, now I quench their thirst for water. One can't live without either."

I was one of the few who would still listen to his oft-repeated story. The grownups had their own problems and Engel's loss seemed to them to be trivial and unimportant. I too could not understand the depth of his despair. People were dying in the streets, husbands and fathers were going to war—maybe never to return—and he was still mourning his books. People said he was an 'old *nudnick*'—a bore—and though I liked Engel, deep within myself I was starting to agree with them.

But one day I saw things differently. At the school for refugee children, the ones who did best in their studies were given a special privilege: they could borrow a Polish book from the principal's office and take it home for a few days. There were only five or six books in the principal's glass case and he handed them out with reverence and many words of admonition. I received *The Fairy Tales* of Oscar Wilde—a beautiful old book, illustrated with dreamy prictures in tones of gold, light blue and purple. I read while walking and eating, and also stealthily at night, under the blanket or the dim light of the kerosene lamp. I cried with the Happy Prince and the swallow, laughed at the unfriendly miller; the mermaid and the selfish giant followed me wherever I went. For a few days I lived in an enchanted world.

One evening I went down to the square, where I played with the neighbourhood children, to show the book to my friend Samenchyk. I lay the book on the step, next to where we were sitting and I forgot it there. I remembered it only after I returned home. I immediately ran back to the square. But the book was not there. I spent a tormented, sleepless night. In my nightmares I saw my parents stooping above me with angry and disappointed faces. I saw the principal's finger, long and accusing, pointing in the direction of the empty space in the glass case. I thought with sorrow that I should never again be given the privilege of taking home any of the other books he held there. I knew the children were going to nickname me 'the book loser' and that the nickname would stay with me forever.

But even more painful was the realization that I would never know what happened to the mermaid, or to the characters in the other, unread stories. I had a feeling of being left suspended in a void and I cried over their fates and mine.

The next day, my eyes still red and swollen, I ran after the water carrier. "Uncle Engel, stop, stop!" I wanted to tell him about the book, to ask whether he knew the end, whether he had read the other stories. I was gasping and puffing when I reached him. He paused and looked at me surprised.

"What is it, my child?" His gold frames sparkled in the sun.

"Uncle Engel, I . . . lost a book. Oscar Wilde. Do you know the stories?"

I wanted to tell more, but something held me back. Perbaps it was the memory of the scene in the disinfection centre.

He stooped above me. "You did? Oscar Wilde, you say? No. I do not know his stories. Never read them. But don't be sad." He patted my head softly. "You know, when the war ends and you come back to Poland, the stores are going to be loaded with books. All you'll have to do is walk up to the lady at the counter, and she will bring them to you. There are going to be libraries too, with miles and miles of books, on many bright floors. In the corner, just next to the window, you'll find Oscar Wilde's stories . . . with beautiful colourful pictures . . . you'll see."

It sounded impossible, but nice. Then he said quietly, sadly, "As for me, it's all lost."

"No, it's not, Uncle Engel, it's not!" I cried. "Remember Aladdin's lamp!"

Then I ran away, embarrassed by my audacity. When I looked back he was still standing there, shading his eyes with his hands, the dark surface of water in the buckets sparkling and shimmering.

Roma Gelblum-Bross was born in Poland and has lived in Israel and Montreal. Her work has appeared in The Fiddlehead, *in* Souvenirs: New English Fiction from Quebec, *as well as in her collection* To Samarkand and Back.

Fuller Brush

KENNETH SHERMAN

It was not work I would have chosen, but at sixteen you can't be choosy. My mother couldn't stand the thought of me hanging about the house in hot weather and introduced me to the district manager for Fuller Brush, an Englishman by the name of Nigel MacMillan. He had bryl-creemed auburn hair, a pigeon chest, and a moustache like General Montgomery's. He had all the seriousness of a general too; he planned campaigns, kept sheets on which he ticked off those homes his salesmen had invaded, those which had resisted. When I told him I'd never sold any-thing before he stared solemnly at me and said, "You'll do fine boy, just fine. You've got a Jewish head on your shoulders, haven't you?"

The glossy brochures he handed me advertised different waxes, aerosol sprays, mops, brooms, silver polishing agents. And brushes: some to brush your hair, others to remove the lint from your jacket. In all of the photos people smiled; their furniture gleamed and shone as much as the glossy paper.

Nigel said it was best to dress up a bit to do the selling so I traded my faded denim shorts and T-shirt for grey flannel pants, a white short-sleeved dress shirt, and a blue paisley tie. He gave me a lesson on how to sell, explaining that the trick was not to let the ladies close the door on you. "Once you're in," he explained, "you just talk." To gain entrance it was best to hold out some small free gift: a comb, a key-chain.

"Know what our top salesman uses to get in?" Nigel asked.

"No," I answered.

"A bloomin' nail-file. Know why?"

"No."

"Use your brains, boy." He tapped his pale forehead with his index finger.

I stared back at him blankly. He looked into me a though he'd totally miscalculated my potential.

"Because, you can slip a nail-file between the door and the frame," he explained. "The missus closes the door on you, but there's the nail-file sticking through. She can't resist. She opens the door and you," he paused a dramatic second, "walk in."

He glared at me triumphantly. People tend to look down on salesmen but in fact they are serious scientists. Every home they enter, each person they attempt to sell is an experiment. And they learn from their mistakes. They take notes, attend seminars, study statistics, and share tactics. One I met at our monthly conference showed me a notebook filled with hundreds of jokes he had collected. "Tell a good joke and they love you right away." Another wore an authentic white cowboy hat. "Who can forget *me?*" he asked.

I kept my catalogue and samples in my wide, caramel leather school briefcase. During the school year it was filled with thick textbooks that weighed down my right shoulder. My father owned a clothes store and was an expert on physiognomy. "You're right shoulder is becoming considerably lower than your left," he said in a concerned voice. Now the heavy books were replaced by cans of pine-scented aerosol, white tubes of hand lotion that smelled of lilac, black brushes, and pink combs.

To make the idea of the job more interesting, I indulged in all kinds of fantasies. I imagined bored young housewives inviting me in for more than just a sale. I imagined homemakers oohing and aahing over the sweet, flower-scented products and envisaged copying out mammoth orders. Dangling from my lightened briefcase, on Nigel's insistence, was a sample of the Johnny-Blue Toilet bowl Cleaner and Deodorizer, a new product I was to flog. In the area of hygiene, Fuller Brush was way ahead of its time. Johnny-Blue turned the water in your bowl the colour of the Pacific Ocean; it helped keep the white enamel on American Standard from discolouring; it promised to keep your bathroom smelling like a park. It was guaranteed for no less than twenty-five messianic flushes.

I trudged in the heat of early July along the bleached pavements. I must have been inauspicious. Even the dogs took no notice of me; as I passed, they dozed with their paws criss-crossed over their snouts. But to my disappointment, there were no housewives in negligees, no looks of sexual hunger. Most of the women seemed frazzled, or suspicious.

"Always demonstrate." Nigel had instructed. "Show 'em your wares."

At one house a woman in candyfloss-coloured curlers stretched out her hand. I squeezed out some moisturizing lotion but it was far too much and she had to smear it up her arms and elbows to massage it all in. Embarrassed, both she and I turned the same colour as her curlers. In another house, attempting to show off the scent of some deodorizer, I failed to check the alignment of the hole from the nozzle and sprayed myself in the eye. Fortunately, there were a few steady customers, like the well to do Mrs. Silverman. I never once saw her. I would ring the bell and be admitted into the bright vestibule by her housekeeper. After it was announced that the Fuller Brush Man had arrived, I would hear a voice from an upstairs room call out "Yes, we've been expecting you." The maid would run upstairs. I'd hear muffled voices. Then the maid would trot down the long winding staircase and dictate the order in the slow and serious voice of a foreign ambassador.

After the first three weeks my prospects did not look promising. Aside from the rare Mrs. Silverman or some young homemaker who took pity and ordered a single tube of cream (small size) the entire enterprise would have been condemned as useless. Perhaps the fault was mine. I was a shy, withdrawn teenager, deeply interested in literature. When the summer had started, I noted my mother's dark face peering through the kitchen window as I lay on the backyard lounge chair reading Camus' *L'Etranger* under a bright late-June sky. Most likely I did not have the right character for a sales job. I felt silly doing it and my potential customers probably sensed it. I wanted to be a writer but I did not know what to write about. And although I felt I had been forced into taking the Fuller Brush job, part of me felt I ought to be out selling. I felt an obligation to the suburbs. Wasn't this reality? After all, it wasn't by reading *L' Etranger* or *Nausea* that these houses with their en suite bathrooms, convertibles, and double driveways had been built.

Not only was I a recluse with my books but also a dreamer. As a child I was always storming some fortified machine gun nest, riding alone into a sunset after saving a pretty woman, or taking on the mob. My favourite television show had been *The Untouchables* and I used to walk around, tight-lipped, imagining myself as tough as Eliot Ness. Now, with mature and serious books, I still engaged in such fantasies. I was a Hemingway hero, a guerrilla bomb expert during the Spanish civil war, or a sullen ex-soccer star making love, dispassionately, to women in my apartment overlooking the Mediterranean Sea.

Two streets away from ours, in a modest bungalow, lived the famous Maxie Green—a real live gangster. He had made the front page of our city newspaper more than once. I had never seen the man but passed his house with a mixture of trepidation and reverence. Here, in our dull and mundane suburb, was a man who lived on the edge. Gambling, sleazy taverns, rumoured Mafia associations. Twice I had done Maxie Green's street without knocking on his white painted door. Was he married? Did he live with other gangsters? What use would a mobster have for aerosol bathroom spray or wood protector?

Boredom must have inspired me to try his house that day. From the outside it was unremarkable. Nothing differentiated it from the others on the street. I noted the large diagonal crack in the cement as I climbed the steps of his porch and knocked hesitantly at the door.

In a moment, Maxie Green's bear-like figure appeared. A tuft of black chest hair sprouted from his V-neck shirt. I took in his dark, hairless head, his thick lips, and the legendary ruined eye—a pale particle of blue swimming in a white mollusc. I tried not to stare at the eye but it was impossible. The story behind it had made front-page news. It had something to do with an unpaid debt. Strong arms had arrived at Maxie's tavern after closing time; they tied him to a chair and beat him and his bouncer senseless. The newspapers had printed a photo of Maxie Green's face, rivulets of blood branching down from the injured eye.

I held out the brochure half expecting him to slam the door or worse, but instead he took it from me and flipped through its pages with a slow and studied concern. "You're selling?" he asked in a soft voice that took me by surprise.

"Yes. Fuller Brush."

He was flipping through the pages. He seemed to take a great interest in the brochure and yet I had the sense he was not taking it in. It was as if he were reading something in a foreign language.

"Who's there, Max?" a female voice enquired from the interior of the house.

Before he could answer, a middle-aged woman with carrot-coloured hair appeared. She was beaming. "How wonderful!" she exclaimed, snatching the brochure out of Maxie's hands.

"Yes," she said excitedly, flipping through the pages "I can use this . . . and this . . ."

As she spoke, I noticed Maxie Green retreating slowly into the interior of the house. I assumed that this woman was his wife. She pointed at various items in the brochure and I wrote. I could hardly contain my excitement. I was taking an order worth an entire month's work, maybe more. I couldn't believe my good luck, though there was a voice in me that asked, "Why would a mobster's wife need all of this?" Who knows? A few rare people seemed to have a fetish for the stuff. And though the Green house did not appear luxurious, Maxie probably had tons of dough stashed away. It would have been unwise for him to display his wealth in a fancy house or racy car for the income tax people to see.

The fact that I did not make another sale for the next three days did not trouble me. I endured the heat, the desolate sound of tires picking up tar and gravel in the freshly filled potholes, the blank windows of the homes whose residents were off in cottage country. I had filled my quota, and more. I told my parents about the huge Green sale and decided to take a holiday from selling though a voice inside me cautioned against taking a break.

The guy who delivered for Fuller Brush wore a white T-shirt with the sleeves cut off and sunglasses with lenses that were little mirrors. He had a tattoo on his tanned shoulder—a cherry red heart with a dagger stuck through it.

"Quite an order," he said.

I could see my bulbous face with a ridiculous smile reflected in his sunglasses.

He unloaded the cartons onto a wagon the company lends you so that you can move the goods from your garage to the customers' houses. It was made of blond wood and had the initials FB in blue on its sides. I'd never needed the wagon before. In the past, what I sold I could carry in a shopping bag. So this was an event. That morning I walked along Glen Eden Avenue, proudly pulling my cart filled with cans of floor wax and furniture polish, sprays, lotions, a lone mop and an entire case of Johnny-Blue. I had a few stops to make before I delivered to Maxie Green's house. It would have made sense to go there first—my load would have been lightened; but I wanted to impress my other customers by letting them have a look at this huge order.

At the first house I went to the woman seemed to have forgotten that she had ordered anything. When she couldn't find her purse, she asked me if I would please return later and collect the two dollars and fifty cents. At the next house, a woman in black shorts and stained cotton blouse handed me five dollars. She took her deodorizers and quickly closed the door without saying a single word.

Maxie Green's house looked desperately quiet. All the drapes and blinds were closed and it seemed as if the inhabitants were away on vacation. I knocked on the door and Maxie opened it; he showed no sign that he recognized me.

"Is your wife in?" I asked

"I have no wife," he said in a matter of fact tone.

"But I spoke to a woman here two weeks ago," I said

"Two weeks ago? Oh, that must have been my sister."

His good eye panned over my loaded cart. I looked into his face but saw no guile there. He truly did not remember me from the week before. I thought that perhaps the beating he took had destroyed more than his eye.

"She ordered all that?" he asked.

"Yes," I said.

"She would," Maxie shook his head. "She's a loon. A real loon."

"Well, is she in?" I asked in a faltering voice I knew that she wasn't but I felt obliged to ask anyway.

"In?" He chuckled softly. It was not malicious "In San Francisco. She lives in the States."

He took in my confused look.

"She was just visiting," he explained. "A loony tune," he said, "A real kidder."

"What am I going to do with all of this?" I asked, my voice rising in protest.

Maxie stared blankly at the ridiculous wagon and the cans of floor polish piled in neat columns. He shrugged as if I had asked him a metaphysical question about God, or about the origin of the universe.

He mused for a moment. Then he said, "I'll tell you, kid—once, when I ran a little operation down on Spadina . . ." And then he stopped. Just like that. As if knowing that the telling of it would not have changed my predicament. "Jeez," he said a moment later, shrugging in disbelief. "A real kidder."

He gently closed the door.

They have a very good system, Fuller Brush. Nothing's on consignment. You buy the stuff directly from them and sell it to the customer. That way if someone reneges, you're stuck, not them. That's why they are big. And you are small.

All my hopes for making a short, quick killing vanished with Maxie's shrug. I was steaming with the injustice of it. What was I to do with four hundred dollars worth of merchandise?

"Full'er shit," is what I said to Nigel MacMillan when I opened our garage door to show him the mountain of wax I'd been stuck with.

His Montgomery moustache twitched.

"A minor setback. It happens to us all once in awhile. But I'm sure in the next few weeks you'll be able to sell the stuff . . ." He couldn't get his moustache to stop twitching.

It was a good thing my parents both came from large families For the next three years my aunts and uncles received free samples of Fuller Brush products. My Father took the fancy mop and broom downtown for Wild Bill, the half-wit who hung around my father's shop and cleaned the floor. Guests complimented us on our blue toilet water. Didn't they notice that when they urinated, it turned the sickly, off-green colour of Lake Ontario?

I returned to school. I had proven to be a complete failure as a salesman but had managed to read some books and still harboured dreams of travelling and becoming a writer. One warm September day I passed Maxie Green's house and saw him in the front garden. In all the years we'd lived in the neighbourhood, I'd never once seen him outside. But there he was, puttering in his garden, his back stooped, his frayed suspenders beige and benign. No, he wasn't the sort Eliot Ness was going to bother about. Then again, Ness himself had probably lived in a similar house in some suburb. Things were smaller and more banal than I had ever imagined. Maybe they were like this everywhere. I experienced a sinking feeling and shifted my heavy briefcase to my left hand so that I wouldn't become too disfigured, and walked on.

Kenneth Sherman is the author of several volumes of poetry, the most recent of which is The Well: New and Selected Poems. He has also published a collection of essays, Void and Voice. He lives in Toronto.

About the Editor

EDITOR NORMAN RAVVIN is a writer of fiction, criticism and journalism. His books include *Hidden Canada, Café des Westens, Sex, Skyscrapers, and Standard Yiddish,* and *A House of Words: Jewish Writing, Identity, and Memory.* He has also edited the short story collection *Great Stories of the Sea.* His short fiction and nonfiction have appeared in Canadian magazines as well as on the CBC. He has taught literature and creative writing at the University of Toronto and the University of New Brunswick. Presently, he is the chair of Canadian Jewish Studies at Concordia University in Montreal.